THE THERAPIST

THE THERAPIST

A NOVEL

Sandylee Maccoby

SILVER BIRCH PRESS

LOS ANGELES, CALIFORNIA

ISBN-13: 978-0615519371

ISBN-10: 0615519377

Contact: silverbirchpress@yahoo.com

www.silverbirchpress.com

"…in analysis the transference provides the strongest resistance to the cure…"

"The erotic transference …betrays itself unequivocally as resistance to the cure…"

SIGMUND FREUD

"…is the goal of psychotherapy to discover the authentic self? Or is it to become fully individuated? To create an identity?"

NORMAN BROWN

PART I

ONE

The moonless December night in Cambridge was bitter. Hugging her mink coat close to her body, she hurried down the dimly lit street, silent at this late hour.

From her house just three doors away, she'd seen his light on. She knew his nightly routine well. For days, hiding in the shadows of the leafless trees, shivering from the cold, she'd been watching him. He never lowered the shades and was always at his desk, recording his brilliant insights. Tonight he was scrutinizing the yellow pad he used for note taking during the therapeutic hour. What had he written about her? She wanted to know.

At their therapy session he hadn't even said goodbye but her skin still burned where his fingers touched her.

Her moment was now; she would go to him. He wanted her as much as she wanted him; of that she was sure. They belonged together.

Ice glistened beneath her feet in the lamplight. She held firm to the stair railing so as not to fall and when she reached the landing, she touched the bell. Its loud shrill ring startled her.

"Ms. Giuliani!" He was standing before her in the open door, the light behind him, his eyes wide.

"I must see you," she whispered.

"My God, it's one o'clock in the morning!"

"Can I come in?"

"Of course." He closed the door behind her. "Can I take your coat?"

One by one she undid the buttons, all the while searching his face, then slowly opened her coat. He gasped at the sight of her nakedness.

"Erika! What do you think you're doing?"

"I couldn't help myself."

"But this is crazy! You're my patient! There are rules!"

"I know," she said softly, dropping her coat to the floor, "but do we have to follow the rules?" A small smile crossed her lips as she slipped into his arms.

TWO

Erika's husband's death was officially explained as drowning due to a fatal cramp that rendered him helpless during a morning swim in the Mediterranean. Their first baby was due in five months and Frank had proposed a couple of weeks to soak up the sun, swim, eat in gourmet restaurants, and make love. A second honeymoon, he said, a last chance to relax before the happy event, and Erika agreed.

On hearing the news of his drowning back at the hotel, she collapsed and was taken by ambulance to a local hospital. The doctors were unable to save the fetus and the pain endured not only in her body but her soul as well. The French doctors urged her not to cry. She was young and healthy; there would be other babies.

Frank's death and the loss of their unborn child came only two years after their marriage and a year after a plane crash that killed her parents. Once again she was thrown into shock and weighed down by grief. Was there a hex on the people she loved? Was she somehow cursed?

Her father had been especially fond of Frank, boasting to his friends how his handsome, well-spoken son-in-law, a recent graduate of Harvard Business School, was in line to be president of his family's hotel chain.

Erika's enduring depression could not be relieved by drugs. Racked by dreams of her parents plunging earthward in flames, and Frank holding up the bloody fetus of their unborn son, Erika believed she was going mad.

Exhausted, she avoided friends and slept fitfully until noon. One day, she adopted a small dog and his joyful presence comforted her. Her gloom eased.

Ever since childhood, she had loved animals and rescued baby squirrels fallen from their tree nests or birds with broken wings discovered in her father's gardens. When her goldfish died of old age, she gave them elaborate funerals and her father was moved by her sorrow. "They're in heaven now, Princess," he would say gently, "so here's a handkerchief to wipe away those tears."

Her little dog was a warm and happy presence awakening her when the sun came up by licking her face. He demanded his breakfast and a short walk through Harvard Square so she no longer slept until noon.

One foggy, wet afternoon, her dog slipped out of his collar to chase a squirrel across the street and was instantly killed, run over by a car. Devastated, Erika was thrown back into her depression. Another violent death. The hex would not let go of her.

Late at night, suffering from insomnia, she took to thumbing through old college textbooks from the dusty shelves above her bed. She came across *The Forgotten Language* by Erich Fromm, the famous psychoanalyst. In a literature course her sophomore year at Smith, his works had so inspired her that she wanted to become a therapist. When she told her father, he laughed derisively. "Treat crazy people? You've got to be nuts! A big waste of time and talent, Princess. Take a business course instead!"

Her father understood quite well how she hated anything to do with business and that she would defy him by continuing to study literature and psychology. When she went to Paris her junior year, she immersed herself in French literature, philosophy, and the latest theories in psychology.

Now, in her crisis, she couldn't get Erich Fromm out of her mind. Why was Frank reappearing in her dreams holding the bloody fetus and calling out her name? If only she could talk to Fromm about her nightmares and what they were trying to tell her! Did she have any negative thoughts about Frank or the baby? Of course not. She had wished for their baby with all her heart and soul and her love for Frank was true and good.

Fromm had a theory that the conscious mind often repressed negative observations from waking life which later emerged unfiltered in dreams. But he wasn't there to help her understand. He had died years before.

Her college notations in the margins of *The Divine Comedy* reminded her how little she had empathized with Dante's suffering when she was young and full of hope. Now, a long time later, her perspective had altered. Like him, she was living a deep unhappiness and had lost her way. He was rescued by the wise poet, Virgil, and she prayed there might be a Virgil somewhere out there for her.

Her doctor urged her to seek professional help. "Go see Dr. John Starr."

"Who's he?"

"He's a Harvard man, a professor of psychology, an analyst and TV star all rolled into one. He's got a fine reputation. People are raving about his creativity research. Maybe he'll discover *your* creative talents! Watch for him on TV. He's always getting interviewed and you'll be impressed."

When she saw him for the first time on TV, Dr. Starr seemed oddly familiar. Had she met him somewhere before? Perhaps in another life? A handsome man with a lean face and boyish grin, he looked directly into the camera and spoke with the authority of a Harvard professor. She noticed his tie matched his bright blue eyes.

Barbara Ryan, a middle aged no-nonsense interviewer on Roundtable WGBH TV, frequently interrupted him with questions about his creativity research. " And you're saying that you don't get into your patients' psychopathology? Their childhood traumas?"

"Naturally, we can't ignore a patient's pain and suffering, Barbara," he said patiently, "but my research suggests that therapists who focus only on the dark stuff are not helping anyone. They're just stirring dirt and their patients get worse. Unless we affirm the positive, no one gets any better and they often hang onto the therapist for a lifetime."

"But isn't psychotherapy supposed to deal with neuroses from childhood?"

"Sure, but we like to think real healing takes place when the patient discovers his creativity. Everybody is creative. It's the spark that fires up humankind," he exclaimed, his eyes flashing.

"That's lovely. 'The spark that fires up humankind'," Barbara Ryan repeated with feeling. "Tell me, how do you discover your creativity?"

"It's not easy. You have to reject the group mindset and people are afraid to do that. Just look around you. Everybody's following everybody else."

"So what should we do?"

"Find support systems that encourage you to take your own path in life. Look at Einstein and Picasso. They were geniuses, of course, but they would never have been so creative without their support systems."

"What do you mean by 'support systems'?"

"Wives, husbands, friends. In Einstein's case, his wife. She devoted her life to him. In Picasso's, it was wives and mistresses and rich intellectuals like Gertrude Stein. With my patients, I myself provide them with the support system they need so they are free to discover their creativity gene."

Erika shivered with excitement. He was impressive in so many ways: handsome, brilliant, creative. She was in love with him already.

He would be her Virgil and lead her out of the abyss, chase away her demons and be her support system. Together they would discover her creativity gene and he would be by her side forever.

THREE

When she met Dr. Starr, Erika was overwhelmed by his charm and air of self-assurance. Taller and younger than she expected, he welcomed her warmly and she knew at once she could trust him.

"You must be Ms. Giuliani," he said, his ice blue eyes blazing as he took in her grace and luminous beauty.

"Yes." Her voice trembled and she could feel the racing of her heart.

"Please come with me." Smiling, he guided her into his office where she quickly handed him the notes she had scribbled down in the middle of the night.

"I wrote up the dream that's upset me so much. It never goes away." The words tumbled out in a rush.

"Ms. Giuliani," he said, handing back her notes. "Tell me the dream yourself, that's better than my reading it. We're meeting today to see if I can help you so if you'd like to start with analyzing your dream, we can go ahead." Offering her a chair, he settled down in a twin chair across from her and studied her intently.

Ever since Erika was a little girl, people always stared at her and her mother told her it was because she was beautiful. Born with perfect features, dark blond hair, a creamy complexion and hazel eyes fringed with heavy, dark lashes, she discovered early in life that if she smiled, she could get whatever she wanted. But "beauty is as beauty does," her mother never ceased to remind her, because true beauty meant being modest and kind.

Dr. Starr's stare was different; he seemed to be looking into her very soul.

"Take your time telling me the dream," he said gently.

She tried to keep her voice steady. There's Frank, standing in the doorway, calling out to her, the bloody fetus in his arms. The dream ends abruptly and she awakens in a sweat. He is not there. He cannot be there because he is dead. Frank and her baby are dead.

"Was your husband unhappy?" said Dr. Starr.

"Oh, no! This trip was to be our special time together before the birth of our child."

"What was his work?"

"He was a vice president of a hotel chain."

"I see."

"It all happened so fast. He was there one minute, and the next..." Her voice broke.

"Yes?"

That fateful day, so sunny and bright with promise. The sea was the same transparent blue as the sky so the horizon line was invisible. Waving cheerfully to Frank from the hotel balcony, she couldn't have imagined he'd never come back alive. Two hours later, his body was discovered floating beyond the buoys in the glittering waters of the Bay of Nice.

"How did he die?"

"He drowned from a severe cramp. I still can't believe it. Right after that, I lost our baby, a little boy. Such pain. In my body and in my heart." Her eyes stung with tears.

"I'm so sorry, Ms. Giuliani."

"It's been three years now and the crying never ends."

"You wake up in a sweat, you say?"

"Yes."

"Frightened?"

"I can't stop trembling."

"This voice you hear, Frank's voice."

"His voice, exactly."

"It's not his, Ms. Giuliani, it's yours."

"Mine?" Her eyes widened in shock. "What are you saying?"

"It's *your* dream, isn't it? Frank is dead and you are running from life. Why?"

"Because I'm trapped in an abyss and there's no way out! I'm jinxed!" Angry tears welled up in her eyes. "All these deaths? My parents, then Frank and the baby? Just like that, happening out of nowhere?"

"I understand." His voice was deep and comforting. "But jinxed? You actually believe you're jinxed?"

"Am I crazy to think that?"

"Well, I'm a scientist," said Dr. Starr, leaning back in his chair, "so I'm wary of superstitions because they exert a debilitating power on the psyche. However, I have to tell you it's a bit egocentric to say you're 'jinxed.' After all, you are still here. It's the others who are gone."

She thought for a time. "Yes, you're right, it's egocentric to say I'm jinxed when I'm still alive. But with this darkness all around me I might as well be dead!"

"We must change that, Ms. Giuliani. A Russian psychic once told me that the only way to get rid of bad luck was by reinventing oneself," he said with the hint of a smile.

"Reinventing oneself? Oh, I'd like that; I'm miserable the way I am now. Can you help me reinvent myself?" Suddenly elated, she wondered if the process would be like the little green snake in her mother's summer garden who was able to shed its dried-up skin and slide away, shiny and new.

"Psychoanalysis can play a part by getting back to childhood issues and resolving them," he said. "I would be your support system so that a new you could emerge."

"A new me?"

"Yes, a creative you."

She searched his face. " I've never been a creative person. How would you make it happen?"

"We would make it happen together. Therein lies the key. I'd be there for you every step of the way. Of course you'd have to take the therapy seriously."

"Naturally. Psychology makes sense to me. When I was in college, I read all of Erich Fromm's books. I believe in his theories. Are you a follower of Fromm?"

"In some ways, yes. A great man and a great thinker."

"His books inspired me to study psychology. I had dreams of becoming a psychologist so I could help people."

"Be a therapist?"

She nodded. "I suppose that sounds absurd to you, I'm such a mess, now."

"It's not in the least absurd. Tell me, why didn't you become a therapist?"

"My father was opposed and I always tried to please my father because he could make my life miserable if I crossed him in any way. He told me to take a business course instead so rebel that I was, I went to study literature and philosophy in Paris. Actually, he was very supportive with that turn of events." She laughed softly. "He greatly admired French culture."

A long silence ensued.

"Do you have a job?" Dr. Starr said at last.

"No, after I married Frank I never worked again."

"What was your job before?"

"Tutoring French here in Cambridge to junior high school kids." A feeling of loss swept over her and she suddenly choked up. "I was happy then."

"Tutoring?"

"Living in France when I was a student."

It wasn't all studying. She remembered how one time she rode down the Champs Elysees on the back of a motorcycle in the middle of the night with a handsome boy she hardly knew. He was wild and crazy but what a trip, going sixty miles an hour and she wasn't even scared! It was magical. When he gunned up the motor, they flew through the air without touching the ground, all the way up an empty Champs Elysees to the Arc de Triomphe where they landed on the grave of the Unknown Soldier. It was the most exciting experience of her life. It didn't get any better than that.

Dr. Starr was talking and she hadn't even heard him.

"I'm sorry, what did you say?" she said in a rush.

"That there's nothing like an immersion experience when you're young, getting into the culture, mastering the language."

"And switching off my American identity."

"You did that?"

"Because I always wanted to be someone else."

"You felt freer, more creative, playing a part?"

"How did you guess?"

"I knew, that's all."

Now he was leaning forward in his chair. His blue eyes searched her face and she was reminded of the sea on a bright summer's day.

"Have you family, Ms. Giuliani?"

"I live alone."

"Do you ever feel lonely?"

"Often." She was stirred by his empathy, the rapt attention he paid to everything she said.

"Ms. Giuliani, I will help you."

He had said the words she wanted to hear and she sighed with relief. If only she could be with this man for the rest of her life! If only!

"We will work together to bring you to full emotional health."

"'Full emotional health'?" A miracle, what else? She had been sick for so long.

"It's never easy to deal with tragic events or to throw off the shackles of a lifetime. But you must be totally open about what you are thinking and experiencing," he intoned.

"I'd be discovering a hidden self I didn't know was there, wouldn't I?"

"Yes."

"The real me?"

"Yes, the real you." He smiled gently. "Are you worried what I might find out about the real you?"

"No, of course not," she said, but he was right. His opinion of her mattered more than anything.

"You have to understand I'm not in the business of judging," he said. "I'm merely your guide in your journey to self discovery. Like Virgil in Dante's *Divine Comedy*, I'll be the voice of reason."

"How did you know?" she burst out.

"Know what, Ms. Giuliani?"

"That I've been reading *The Divine Comedy*!"

"I didn't know. Why are you reading it?"

"I told you, because I'm lost."

"And you're looking for a way out of the abyss."

"Exactly," she said in a trembling voice, the tears streaming down her face.

"Here, take this." He handed her a box of tissues from the table beside him. "You're crying and that's a good thing. Only by fully experiencing our pain can we feel the joy of life and liberate our innate creativity."

He was wrong; she was crying from joy not pain, because she had found her Virgil.

"Your complete recovery will be when you become fully creative, Ms. Giuliani. It's a sad fact, but most people just don't know that's possible, they don't even aspire to it." Dr. Starr sighed heavily. "All around us are potential artists, singers, writers, you name it, who will never develop their talents. How impoverished poetry would be without Donne, or Milton or Keats, wouldn't you agree?"

She smiled. "The very best of the great poets. And are you aware that all three poets are named 'John', like you?"

He laughed. "Indeed."

"Were you ever inspired by them?"

"Absolutely." His eyes flashed. "In my undergraduate days at Harvard I wrote a couple of poems that were accepted by the *Advocate* and I guess I aspired to be another John Donne. Now I simply write articles about my research for *The Atlantic Monthly* and psychology journals. Pretty dull stuff, I'm afraid."

"What is your research, exactly?"

"The cognitive processes of children that lead to creativity and how conforming to the group mindset represses that creativity."

"As a Harvard professor I suppose you give courses in creativity," Erika observed.

"I am not presently a professor at Harvard, Ms. Giuliani, but I've been offering courses on creativity at the Summer School and the Harvard Extension Program for a number of years," he said dryly. "My patients and my research come first."

"I greatly admire your priorities," she said with feeling. "You're saving so many unhappy people."

"That's nice of you to say," said Dr. Starr, "but let's keep to the subject here and that subject is you. We'll start your sessions right away."

Rising from his chair, he searched her face, then smiled and showed her out the door.

FOUR

Dr. Starr's administrative assistant, Marsha, handled all his appointments, bills and speaking engagements at places like Boston College, Emerson College, Boston University, churches and synagogues. She also edited his work. "It's the best part of my job," she told Erika. He tells me I'm obsessive in the best sense." She giggled. "Ever see Dr. Starr on TV? Take a look over on that table by the window. You'll find his latest article in *The Atlantic Monthly.*"

Her cheerful demeanor annoyed Erika; she was not ready to talk to happy people.

After their first meeting, Erika's therapy took place in a small, intimate room just beyond his office with prints of Frida Kahlo's self-portraits on the walls.

Today the weather had turned warm so she threw off her white Italian cashmere sweater and settled back in a large, leather chair. She was wearing a black and white wrap-around Diane Von Furstenberg dress that showed off her curves; fitness trainers told her that for thirty-eight, her body was as perfectly toned as a twenty-year-old. Would Dr. Starr notice?

He seemed more distant than that first day and asked questions about her family.

"Your mother grew up in Hingham? You mean the small town outside of Boston?"

"Yes, and she left at seventeen after winning a scholarship at the New England Conservatory."

"She was a musician?"

"A very talented pianist. But at twenty, she met my father in a cocktail lounge where she played jazz piano to make extra money and they married."

"What happened to her musical career?"

"That was the end of it."

"Any regrets on her part?" Dr. Starr asked.

"I don't think so. She was an old fashioned kind of wife; family came first, and she enjoyed accompanying my father when he sang Italian arias. He had a fine tenor voice and if he'd trained it he might have sung opera."

"Too bad to waste all that talent, don't you think?"

"Yes, but of course, I couldn't follow in their footsteps."

"And why was that?"

"I'm tone deaf, you see. Ironic, isn't it, with a great pianist and talented singer for parents? Sometimes my mother tried to teach me the piano, but she'd get so frustrated she'd slam the sheet music down on my head. I guess you could say she wasn't the best teacher for a child," Erika laughed softly.

"Pretty scary times those piano lessons?"

"Very scary, and about that time, I started having spells."

"'Spells'?" Dr. Starr's voice registered concern and she was relieved. He didn't think her crazy.

"That's what we called them."

Dr. Starr asked if there were any discomfort associated with these episodes. She described sharp, needle-like pains running through her body. Though lasting only a few seconds, those childhood spells seemed to go on forever. When she was eight years old, her parents consulted a famous Harvard neurologist who concluded there was nothing wrong with her, that she was making it all up because she was a rebellious, difficult child.

"Ms. Giuliani, it seems likely that your attacks are emotionally triggered."

"That's what my father always said."

"Well, he might have been right. Sometimes unconsciously we react in radical ways to defend ourselves."

Her emotions brought on these attacks? How could that be true?

"I've always wanted to be normal, like everyone else."

22

"'Everyone else' and 'normal' are not part of my vocabulary," said Dr. Starr. "Each one of us is unique."

"Yes, I've always felt I'm different, somehow."

"You are right about that."

For a time, neither spoke.

Breaking the silence, she blurted out that her parents died in a plane crash a year after she married Frank. "It was a terrible shock. I was pretty much of a wreck for a long time but Frank was always there for me. Oh, god, I can't stand remembering!" She grabbed her handkerchief and furiously wiped her wet cheeks. She couldn't help the tears. Everything seemed all mixed up together. Regrets, anger, sorrow.

"Not wanting to remember is to be expected," said Dr. Starr. You've got a lot of trauma to deal with. Tell me, how did the crash happen?"

"It was Uncle Robert's fault."

"Uncle Robert? Who's he?"

"My father's younger brother. He was at the controls of his plane and there had been warnings about stormy weather over Tuckerman's Ravine. He paid no attention and the little plane went down."

"Where were your parents going?"

"To a meeting up in New York State."

"What happened to your uncle?"

"His back was broken; he'll never walk again."

"I'm sorry." After a long pause, he said, "Tell me about your father."

A second generation Italian American, her father was an admirer of Puccini and Verdi and learned their most famous arias by heart. He ran the family construction business with the passion of an operatic conductor.

Money and making it in society were his obsessions.

Dr. Starr wanted to know more about her father's role in the construction business.

"I'd say he had a creative vision of exactly what he wanted to do to make money. He would finance hotel reconstruction, buy up harbor property and old buildings in South Boston and rebuild them on the cheap. He would sell them at a huge profit and realize his dream. It worked. He was very ambitious and ruthless. Maybe that's what it takes to make a lot of money." She paused. "To get the contracts, he paid off people," she said quickly.

"Oh?"

"That's how it's done around here, you know. Payoffs. Big time. When newspaper people or muckrakers questioned him about that aspect of the business, he blew them out of the water with his charm."

"His charm?"

"That's right, and they forgot what they wanted to ask him."

Growing up, she'd watched him do his dance. Sometimes it was a quick turnaround from pugnacious to conciliatory with a word or a smile and in a micro second, the skeptics were disarmed. Sometimes he changed the subject to talk about his vision of rebuilding the slums of Boston.

"Charm is a special talent," observed Dr. Starr. "It can be very useful."

But that talent didn't help her father much with upper crust Boston society while she was growing up. At least not until he became very rich. Then the socialites overlooked how he'd made his money and who he was. After all, didn't the upper class Rhode Island Browns make their fortune on rum and slaves before they founded a university?

Her father was asked to serve on important boards because he could be counted on to make generous contributions but was rarely included at small, private dinners.

"Can you tell me more about your Uncle Robert?"

"No, I can't really get into that right now," she said softly. Dr. Starr was opening up wounds that had never fully healed and she wasn't prepared.

"I understand. We'll come back to your uncle at a later time."

FIVE

Sitting in the large, leather chair, Erika wiggled out of her shoes, threw off her sweater, and crossed her legs under her. She was wearing a blue satin shirt and matching skirt and when she stretched out her arms, she caught Dr. Starr watching her. Ready to talk about her parents, she was overtaken by a sudden chill and pulled her sweater back on.

Erika's mother, whom she closely resembled, allowed little intimacy with her daughter during her growing-up years. Erika tried to penetrate that aloofness but never fully succeeded.

Her mother was known not only for her blond beauty and musical ability, but also for being smart. Although Boston Society ignored her because of her small-town roots, she inspired fervent loyalty among her friends and eventually became president of the Theosophical Society and a champion bridgeplayer at her club. Though Erika admired her mother, it was her father she turned to for warmth and affection. Before she went to sleep, he read her fairy tales that told of murderous kings and queens, beautiful princesses in distress and heroic knights in silver armor who came to their rescue. "Fairy tales can teach you about real life," he told her. "Bad people pay up in the end. Like the Greek myths, it's all about avenging wrongs. It's a lesson I learned as a boy. Get back at them. You hear me, Princess? Are you listening?"

"Yes, Daddy." But her thoughts were far away with knights in silver armor rescuing princesses in distress.

As she grew up, her father and mother controlled nearly every aspect of her life. They closely watched her academic progress, allowed her out on weekends only with groups of boys and girls they approved of, and forbade dates alone with boys. "There are gold diggers out there, princess, and we have to protect you from lowlife like that," her father said. "When you're older, you'll thank us for it."

Saturday mornings, they took her shopping and afterwards stopped for an ice cream sundae in downtown Boston where so much hot fudge was poured over the ice cream it overflowed onto the saucer below. Erika cherished those times with her parents.

If it hadn't been for her father's violent mood swings that grew worse with age, he would have been the ideal father, but his tirades came loud and furious if Erika dared to challenge him. Later, she could never figure out what she'd said to upset him and she suffered from feelings of guilt and shame.

Her mother blamed Erika for his fits of temper. "You're setting him off, dear. Why are you crying? You've no right to cry. Don't you know that your father's tightly wired? It's his 'Italian temper', the devil within him he can't contain. Please stop making him crazy, Erika. When I'm alone with him, I'm very careful not to be confrontational."

When Erika was fourteen, her mother discovered from medical experts that her father's mood swings had nothing to do with his "Italian temper" but were caused by a chemical imbalance in his brain. The doctors made it quite clear that if he refused to take lithium on a regular basis, he would end up in a mental institution. At his wife's insistence, he reluctantly agreed to follow the doctor's orders.

Dr. Starr wanted details. Were there any warning signals that her father was about to explode?

Yes, there was that moment when the sparkle went out of his eyes like a light bulb being switched off. She was never prepared for what was coming next. The heavy smack with the back of his large hand could land anywhere on her body. Then the pain would become excruciating and her skin would turn black and blue. He never touched her face, however, so no one except her mother and her nanny knew of the abuse.

"Were there others in the house?"

"The cook, the maids, the chauffeur, but they weren't ever upstairs when my father got mad at me."

"As a child, you grew up with so many servants?"

"Yes, there were a lot of them."

Now he would see her as a spoiled rich girl and she was angry with herself for mentioning the servants.

SIX

Considering how hard he had worked to get accepted by the Boston elite, her father took a special pleasure in informing Erika just how out of touch these people were with the real world, including the nouveau riche like himself. A self-made man, he resented the old guard's tenacious hold on status. These people didn't count anymore he asserted, and he mocked the way rich Bostonian men still went around pretending to be poor by wearing frayed collars and sweaters with holes at the elbows and their women, frumpy dresses and sensible shoes. Hypocrites, every one of them! They had plenty of money, belonged to the best clubs and their kids attended the most expensive private schools. Their daughters became debutantes, were given elaborate balls, and later on, were members of the Junior League and the Vincent Club.

Her poor father! An Italian American in the construction trade? Possible connections to the Mafia? He didn't belong and never would. It didn't matter how much he railed against Boston society because the cards were stacked against him. Her mother made little effort to develop relationships with Boston socialites whom she found snobbish and boring. Her passion was theosophy and winning at bridge.

Erika's father wouldn't give up, however, and he convinced her mother that Erika must attend only the most exclusive schools if she was to make the list for the Eliot Hall dances because every girl who was invited to those dances became a debutante later on.

It was a lost cause. Her parents couldn't get past Miss Souther.

A self-appointed doyenne of that dying Boston society, she ran the Eliot Hall dances with an iron fist even into her dotage. Nobody got invited until she had carefully scrutinized the family pedigree and decided who was eligible for her affairs. The Giuliani girl? Absurd! The family wasn't even listed in the Boston Social Register! She'd been told the mother was from a small town somewhere outside of Boston who once worked in a cocktail lounge as a piano player when she was young. Quite unacceptable, of course. And the father made it impossible to even consider including the girl in her dance evenings. An Italian American with dubious connections? Good heavens! So what if he had money! It wasn't all that much anyway and he clearly didn't belong in society and neither did his daughter. The family wasn't suitable; it was as simple as that.

Erika was not totally surprised to be excluded, but it made her angry and sad to see her closest friends attend the dances without her. Furious, her father hired a professional ballroom dancer to come to the house and teach his daughter. After two years of private classes, she excelled at every dance, old and new.

Erika never had any interest in being a debutante; it seemed absurdly snobbish and dated. Perhaps long ago when girls were overly protected it was a way for the WASP establishment to find rich, social husbands for their daughters. The girls could dress up in beautiful white gowns and be presented at a glittering ball. When she told her parents the whole thing was absurd in this day and age, they accused her of being brainwashed by the liberal media. Her radical views caused them both such intense unhappiness that Erika pitied them.

"Being an outsider, Ms. Giuliani, can be painful as it was in your parents' case, but it can also make a young person more critical of conformity as it did with you. And that is a good thing," said Dr. Starr.

"Yes, it helped me see Boston society for what is was."

"Tell me, did you ever attend any musical events when you were a girl?"

"Oh, yes. As members of the Benefactors Circle, my parents always took me to the opera openings."

"Who are your favorite composers?"

"Verdi and Puccini, like my father."

"Why?"

"Operas like Traviata, Aida, and Madame Butterfly are about betrayal and an all-consuming passion that's punished in the end."

"Because?"

"The lovers are too happy."

Those openings with her parents were inevitably marred by people in the orchestra below their box who stared up at her and she wanted to run away and hide. Why did her father insist on having a box so exposed to the prying eyes of strangers?

"Most likely, your father wanted to show off his lovely daughter," said Dr. Starr.

"And my beautiful mother, too. He was so proud of her."

"Yes, of course. But Erika, you are like a flower, of a rare and exquisite variety. There is a poem by Lord Byron, 'She Walks in Beauty'. Are you familiar with it?"

"Yes."

"Indeed?"

"When I was seventeen, my English teacher actually compared me to the subject of that poem!" she cried out.

"As I have done today," he said with a triumphant smile.

SEVEN

Leaning back in the chair, she could feel the burning eyes of Frida Kahlo's self-portrait boring into her, prying out her most hidden thoughts.

George Healy, her high school English teacher, was now back in her conscious memory, stirring up emotions long suppressed. She had loved him with all her girlish heart. Of course, she had kept her feelings hidden, but whenever she was close to him, she could hear the rapid beating of her heart.

A star hockey player when he was at Boston College, George was in his early twenties and the most popular teacher in the school. Even-featured, with dark hair and grey eyes, he introduced his students to the great figures of English literature and on warm spring days, held his classes outdoors beneath the flowering cherry trees lining the lush playing fields. They studied the poets of the nineteenth century and zeroed in on Walt Whitman who celebrated himself, men and women, death, the cosmos and love. Naturally, he emerged as everybody's favorite.

At dinnertime, Erika found herself talking about her teacher. "Mr. Healy's only a few years older than the rest of us so we call him George among ourselves. He's cool and he knows so much about the great American poets. We're studying Walt Whitman now and it's incredibly inspiring!" Flushed with happiness, she sang the young man's praises and missed the warning signals of her father's mounting anger.

Her schoolgirl infatuation excited her mother. That's what it's like when you're only seventeen, she thought. At that age, I was in love with all the handsome, older boys but I never let on. Oh, how I wish I were back then! My darling little girl! Love this wonderful young man in secret. He must never know.

Her father was thinking that maybe he'd been too protective shielding his daughter from all those unsavory types who were attracted to her money. Her childish enthusiasm was pathetic; he'd have to go on the attack and reduce George Healy to rubble. It upset him that Erika couldn't see the guy was a phony.

She didn't know how to tell the real from the fake. Was it George Healy's youthful charm that had swept her off her feet? It was easy to trick girls like Erika. He'd done it himself as a young man. And why was the guy teaching Walt Whitman? Whitman was no poet! His verses didn't even rhyme! The man was a reprobate, a male nurse, a crazy person who wandered around the country. He was America's original hippie for God's sake!

Her father slammed his clenched fists on the table. "I'm going to make it my business to get rid of this incompetent teacher! I'm taking action right away!"

"How can you do such a thing!" cried Erika's mother, her face suddenly white and drawn. "Please don't, Emilio."

"Stay out of this, woman! You're just like your daughter."

Erika jumped up from the table in a storm of tears. Her father's words were like bullets in her heart. She was accustomed to his cutting her friends down, belittling them without mercy, but in George Healy's case, he'd gone too far. He was punishing her for loving a penniless young man.

"Did anything actually ever happen between you and Mr. Healy?" Dr. Starr was asking.

"Oh, no," she murmured.

But it wasn't true. When George found her weeping behind the library stacks, he took her in his arms to comfort her.

"What's the matter?" he asked her. "Tell me. Why are you crying?"

"It's not important, really, it isn't," she answered between sobs. She would rather die than tell George Healy what her father planned to do.

"You're quite sure that nothing at all happened between you?" Dr. Starr was saying.

"Well, not exactly," she said, wondering if he had guessed the truth. "He kissed me."

"Kissed you?"

"Yes."

"A friendly kiss?"

"No, a lover's kiss. On the lips."

Dr. Starr cleared his throat.

"Anything else happen?"

"He held me very tight."

"I don't understand. Am I missing something? You don't think this behavior had sexual overtones?"

"Not really."

"No? Tell me what you mean by 'a lover's kiss'." His intense questioning was propelling them forward.

"I don't really know," she said hesitantly. "I guess he shouldn't have kissed me, but I didn't care."

And why should she? She would never forget his warm lips melting into hers, his powerful arms encircling her.

She stared directly at Dr. Starr and he gave her a gentle smile.

"So your father had the idea that Mr. Healy was after your money?"

His question startled her. "I don't want to talk about money," she said flatly.

"I understand. In my experience, Ms. Giuliani, money is more difficult to talk about than sex. There is a natural resistance, tied up with power."

"Well, my father was into money and power. So what do you want me to say? That my father was a monster?"

It would have been true, but she couldn't say it. After all, she was his little princess and he was only trying to protect her.

Her eyes filled with angry tears. Her father got his revenge by telling the school to get rid of George Healy or he wouldn't back up his promise to donate millions for a new gym. The school complied at once; the young teacher's contract was not renewed.

Erika refused to return to the school and in her heart a strange numbness lingered. She entered Winsor in the fall, an elite school for girls.

"Were there other men?"

Sighing deeply, she stretched her arms over her head, lazily, like a cat.

"Other men?"

"Before Frank. Surely you must have had many opportunities to meet eligible men."

"Yes, but it wasn't until I met Frank that I was ready to commit. The men I thought I wanted disappointed me."

"In what way?"

"I don't know; they just didn't live up to my expectations, I guess."

EIGHT

"Ms. Giuliani," Dr. Starr said, "I have a question which is related to your feelings of victimization and self-worth. Did your father ever discuss who would take over his business after he retired?"

"His business?"

"Yes. Did he want to keep it in the family?"

"What do you think? His fortune was his baby; he'd built it up from scratch and he expected to live to be a hundred."

"So who is CEO now?"

"My Uncle Robert."

"Your father's brother? The man who crashed the plane?"

"Yes, and he's riddled with feelings of guilt, as you can imagine. He's suffering not only from his paralysis, but a severe depression The crash and my parents' deaths were his fault. He deliberately ignored the weather report, all those warnings about bad weather."

"Sounds like very poor judgment on his part."

"Yes, I'm afraid so. But he's managing the company very well and I don't know how he does it. It's amazing."

A shriveled-up figure in a wheelchair, Uncle Robert was so severely handicapped from the plane crash that Erika felt he would be confined to the life of an invalid, never be able to run anything, least of all the family business. But at her parents' funeral, she saw him play the part of the dignified CEO reaching out to all who gathered there to pay their respects and communicating easily with Boston's power brokers and the business community.

Along with her husband, Frank, his calm and caring presence gave her the strength to get through that fateful day without breaking down.

"Do you believe in 'love at first sight', Dr. Starr?" She was changing the subject and her boldness surprised her. How could she have asked him something so personal?

He cleared his throat. "Why does it matter to you what I think about 'love at first sight'?"

"I value what you think about everything. You're my Virgil, guiding and protecting me."

"I am not your Virgil. I am simply your therapist and you're projecting the infantile experience of a protective parent onto me."

"No, that's not true."

What was he trying to tell her? That he was not her Virgil? That he was a "protective parent"? No, no, he was trivializing their relationship with his psychological jargon; he had no right. She would not let him off.

"This phenomenon occurs in all therapy, Ms. Giuliani. Freud calls it 'the transference'."

"What I feel for you is quite different from that," she asserted quietly. "Anyway, what do you think about 'love at first sight'?"

"It's entirely irrational, often a narcissistic illusion and usually of short duration," he replied curtly. "It's like what happens in therapy. These are transferential feelings towards the therapist, masquerading as love."

"You mean that 'love at first sight' is 'transferential'?"

"Almost always."

"But there *are* exceptions."

"It's rare."

Freud had come up with the idea of the transference when his patients began falling in love with him. So he set them straight, showing them it was merely an illusion, and that he was very different from the person in their childhood who had cared for them or they had revered. Transferring or projecting feelings about a parent from early childhood onto the analyst was common in psychotherapy and analyzing the transference was now standard practice in psychoanalysis.

John Starr would not allow any further discussion of the transference issue with Erika. He had told her quite enough. In recent weeks, he could see that she liked him, in fact, more than liked him, and their relationship could get hot. Maybe he should be looking into the transference but it was early in the analysis and perhaps it wasn't merely transference: she simply liked and respected him. Anyway, it was something where he would take a wait-and-see attitude and if it became irrational, he'd begin to analyze it. At least, that is what he told himself.

Erika wasn't sure what Dr. Starr meant by "transferential", but she knew in her heart that her feelings for him could not be defined by a long word made up by Freud. Just one small word could describe what she felt for him and that was "love'. She loved him. He was the Virgil she had been searching for all her life, the miracle worker who would help her reinvent herself.

NINE

"Can we talk about Uncle Robert?" she asked Dr. Starr at their next meeting.

"If you like."

"I've told you he's wheelchair-bound and depressed. And he's racked with guilt because he knows my mother and father didn't have to die in the plane accident. It was his fault that he took them up when the weather was so bad." She paused. "He's not the same person he was before the accident." Her voice trembled.

"How do you mean?"

"He was once a happy man who made everyone else happy, too. But now…" She looked away, her face drawn. "If he was your patient, he could be happy again."

"Only if he wanted to change."

"Oh, but he would, I know he would! You're his only hope. Won't you please see him? Please?"

"I have a very heavy patient load right now," he said guardedly.

"You'd like him, I know you would," Erika continued, tossing a lock of luxuriant hair back over her shoulders. "He's a good man. Besides the family business, he raises millions of dollars annually for a Haitian orphanage."

"'Millions of dollars'?"

"That's right."

"A very talented fundraiser, I would say."

"It's because he cares so much about homeless kids and orphans."

"Quite unlike his older brother."

"My father was caring in his own way!" she cried.

"How so?"

"He was always trying to protect me."

"Protect you? The man abused you!"

"I know, he had a nasty temper and he beat me when I was a little girl. It was very, very wrong."

"And now we're having to deal with your repressed anger and resistance to seeing your father as he really was."

"It's hard to face the reality of my father because he loved me and was always worrying about me."

"Did your mother worry about you?"

"No."

"What did your father worry about?"

"Fortune hunters duping me."

"Fortune hunters?"

"He told me that after he died I would come into a large inheritance."

"Oh?"

"Yes, and when both he and my mother were killed, I inherited two thirds of his fortune and my uncle the rest."

"So you and your uncle are rich?"

"You might say that." Erika took a deep breath. "Please, won't you help him? Please?"

Dr. Starr did not reply at once and Erika worried she had gone too far in asking a favor from such a busy and famous man.

"Perhaps I can squeeze him in," Dr. Starr said finally.

"Oh, I'm so glad! Thank you, thank you!"

Dr. Starr said nothing and she supposed he was thinking about Uncle Robert's unhappy life in a wheelchair.

"Tell me, Ms. Giuliani, how much are you actually worth?"

Momentarily confused by the question, she was unable to reply.

"Can you tell me how much you're worth?" he persisted.

"How much?"

"Yes, how much money do you have?"

He was leaning forward, searching her face.

"Maybe two hundred million or so," she said quickly.

She thought she heard him take a sharp breath, though it might have been a gust of wind passing through the open window. An eerie silence settled over the room.

"That's a lot of money," he said at last, leaning back in his chair.

"Yes, and if you're rich like me and people know, they treat you differently."

"You think so?"

"I know so."

Suddenly hot, she removed her cashmere sweater. Dr. Starr rose from his chair and walked slowly to his desk and drank from a glass of water. Then he approached her chair and stood silently before her, his arms folded, his blue eyes flashing. He seemed to fill the entire room and she felt a kind of rapture.

"Are you warm?"

"A little. Maybe you could open the window." She watched him as he stepped to the window and edged it slightly open. A cold gust of air filled the room.

"Still warm?"

"Yes." She gripped the arms of her chair.

"Let's get back to your father for a moment," he said, walking slowly towards her. "Since childhood, you've been carrying around a lot of repressed guilt and anger towards him. Heavy baggage, I'd say. But he's dead and buried now so it's time to throw off all that guilt and anger."

"And what will happen then?"

"You'll be free to love and be loved."

"Oh, I want that more than anything."

He was moving away, back to his chair. Her eyes filled with bitter tears.

"You must come to terms with the truth," he said.

"The truth? What 'truth'?"

"That your father was an abusive force in your life."

"And you will help me," she murmured, burying her wet face in her hands. Her whole body cried out for his touch.

"We will do this together."

"You and I," she said softly.

"That's right," said Dr. Starr rising to his feet. He glanced at his watch. "I believe our time is up for today." And reaching for her hand, he gently guided her towards the door.

John. John. John Starr. Staring at herself in the long mirror of her room, she observed how her nipples grew dark and hard when she repeated his name. She imagined herself on the sofa in his office, drawing him down to where she lay, sliding into his arms, his long, slim fingers caressing her skin, his lips searching hers.

Opening the bedroom closet, she hunted for her ankle-length mink coat, hidden away behind boxes of discarded shoes. A gift from her father, she hadn't worn it since his death, but now she pulled it out and wrapped herself inside of it, luxuriating in the sensation of the satin lining against her bare skin.

Running her hands up and down the glistening fur, she strode back and forth in front of the mirror, swinging the coat like a model on the runway. Would he be angry and send her away? No, he would ask her in. He wanted her as much as she wanted him.

Her high black suede boots stood by the door and she drew them on with trembling hands. Returning to the mirror, she opened her mink and stood very still, marveling at the smooth whiteness of her body clad only in the black boots.

Yes, she would go to him now!

PART II
ONE

The crickets are chanting and the sweet smell of narcissus wafts through the spring darkness. His horse, black in the moonlight, is champing at the grasses by the lakeshore, and he kneels by the still water, gazing at his reflection. His face is strangely familiar and he racks his brain trying to remember. No name comes to mind. He leans closer to the water's edge for a more careful scrutiny of this image when a woman's hand rises up from the water, holding out a crown encrusted with precious jewels. He reaches for it, feels himself falling, and wakes up.

This dream repeats itself endlessly and John has analyzed it so many times he feels drained. That hand has to be his mother's, the water, clearly, the womb. The crown must be meant for him; she often called him her "little Prince."

Now he would be king and Erika his queen. This time the crown would not slip through his fingers.

But why this dream, over and over? Is his mother holding him back from fully embracing Erika and his good fortune?

Only Maria Di Brioni, the guru of creativity, his mentor and analyst of long ago, would have the answer.

After being officially escorted out of the country eight years before, he was back in Mexico, staring out the window of her study at the sharp mountain peaks now bathed in the amber light of late afternoon. He could just make out the ancient Aztec pyramid nestled high up in the rocks where he and Maria had once climbed together. Now, in the starkness of her study with its white washed walls and colorful bark paintings from the Indians of Guerrero, he sat facing her in one of her straight-backed colonial chairs from the city of Puebla.

"It has been so very long a time," said Dr. Di Brioni. "I have thought so often of you, John, those years here in Mexico with me for the psychoanalytic training and your psychoanalysis. The hard work you did on the statistics for my book, and all the time you were carrying a full patient load."

"The statistics were critical to the success of your book."

"Yes, yes, and I am very grateful to you. And recently I have been hearing from colleagues of your fine reputation as a therapist and researcher at the Institute for Creativity Studies in Cambridge. Perhaps you will end up with the chair at Harvard sooner than you think." She smiled archly. "I know that is what you have wanted for so long a time. How you make this happen is the question, is it not so?"

"I guess you could say that," he said stiffly, annoyed how she always went right to the heart of the matter.

"How quickly the time it passes," she continued smoothly, "and today I see you again here in Mexico and it makes me so very happy. You are a man of courage to return. So terrible a business it was."

"Awful," he said with a bitter smile.

"The goons. I cannot forget how they snatched you right off the street and forcibly deported you from this country! Such an outrage, and all because you were defending the use of peyote here in the villages. We know it to be a traditional practice and relatively harmless. And now we have the real drug problem here with murderous gangs and corruption. This country is now in crisis."

"Yes," John agreed, "and the United States fuels that crisis with its insatiable thirst for all the drugs Mexico can smuggle into our country."

Di Brioni shook her head sadly. "So let us talk of better things. How is Catherine? And your boy?"

"Catherine's very well, I think."

"You think? You do not know?"

"Actually, we are now…"

Di Brioni did not wait for the answer. "I often think of her, and how shocked she was by this terrible business of so long ago."

"Yes."

"And pregnant with your child, and driving all alone those thousands of miles through the very dangerous parts of Mexico to California! But you were there waiting for her and everything turned out okay, no? Your little boy is well?"

"Roger's a terrific kid."

"That is wonderful." She smiled briefly. "I must tell you that these days I have good friends high up in the government and they have promised me you will always be welcome in this country and your safety is assured. You will never be kidnapped again!"

Now he understood why he was immediately given permission by the Mexican government to visit for a few days. Friends in high places. It always worked.

He hadn't wanted to talk about his ignominious departure from Mexico. It made him sad and angry and he quickly changed the subject.

"Maria, I have some good news," he said in a rush.

"Oh? And what is that?"

"I'm in love with a beautiful, brilliant woman. Her name is Erika."

Erika, his most precious possession, an exquisite work of art, like Botticelli's Venus Rising from the Sea with her shimmering dark blond hair cascading over her shoulders. She was a living painting belonging to him alone. With her tantalizing smile, her lovely, softly rounded body, she set him on fire, but he wasn't about to tell Di Brioni.

"I know that you were always very fond of Catherine," he added, "but our relationship went sour once we were back in the

States. Cambridge was never her favorite place—she resented having to leave Mexico and couldn't handle the intellectual snobbery of the Harvard community. She became quite destructive, actually."

"'Destructive'?" Her air of disbelief caught him by surprise. He had forgotten how easily Catherine manipulated people with her flattery and desire to please.

"She was always mocking my success, belittling my work."

"That is a pity. Out of character, it seems to me. I see her always as so empathic. She related well with the people here."

"Yes, but her view of Mexico was excessively romantic, she ignored the negatives."

"That is perhaps so."

"In Cambridge, I encouraged her to write short stories and she lost some of her anger. When we first met, writing was one of her interests."

"I did not know that."

"She's done very well. Her work has appeared in a number of small journals and she's known by a lot of people."

"That is so very good," intoned Dr. Di Brioni, "so perhaps you are a little bit jealous, no? Do I not remember you bragged you were a great poet in your Harvard days?"

"Bragged? Maria, I was just a young man trying hard to impress the great Dr. Di Brioni," laughed John.

Di Brioni was on the attack, he could see that, so he would not get defensive. But to suggest he was envious of Catherine's pathetic scribblings was a low blow. Hell, her work wasn't even close to his league!

"A year and a half ago, we divorced," he continued. "She's much happier now, teaching up at Bennington College. I see my son during vacations; we have great times together."

"I am sure you are an excellent father." Dr. Di Brioni's black eyes bored into his. "Tell me about this woman, Erika."

"She's extraordinary, a modest and cultivated person and we plan to marry."

"Marry? It is so very serious?"

"Yes, this woman has everything I want and she appreciates the importance of what I'm doing."

Di Brioni smiled but said nothing.

John took a deep breath but his heart was suddenly turning over in his chest. A momentary sensation of dizziness swept over him. It must be the altitude (they were at over 6,000 feet in Tepoztlan) though he couldn't recall ever feeling this way before. He clung to the arms of his chair for support.

"However," he continued, making an effort to breathe slowly, "while I should feel elated at having finally discovered the love of my life, I am strangely depressed."

He related his dream that mercilessly pursued him, casting a shadow over his newfound happiness.

Dr. Di Brioni's expression gave him no clue as to what she might be thinking and her large black eyes remained fixed on his face. Since he had last seen her, she had markedly aged. He had heard that the fatal heart attack of her second husband, the noted art collector Clyde Milestone, had come as a great blow to her and all who knew him. In his mid-sixties, he was universally admired and had appeared in robust health.

Dressed in a loose Indian hand-woven blouse of primary colors, and a long, shapeless dark skirt, Di Brioni seemed smaller and thinner than he recalled and her gray hair was pulled severely back in a bun. Her handcrafted thick brown leather sandals completed the unisex image so popular with older women professionals, particularly anthropologists and social workers.

"John, John, dear boy," she said in her warm, soothing voice, "In this dream you tell me, it is trying to warn you of danger to come."

"Danger? Whatever do you mean?" he said angrily.

"I cannot analyze the dream without knowing more, so we will come back to it later. Right now I want to talk about the detachment that is so much a part of your character. Remember Catherine's fever of one hundred and three? Do you not recall how you pretended she was not so very sick?"

He tried to recall his wife's illness but his mind went blank. Why was she harking back to that? He'd long since put it out of his mind.

"Remember? You were visiting Acapulco and Catherine became ill with the paratyphoid, so very sick, but you insisted she was okay and not to worry about her dangerous fever. It is your way of denying the reality, no? Detaching yourself from what you don't want to see and pretending everything is good, no?"

So she was on to that once again. It had always seemed obvious to him that a little denial and detachment from painful realities was helpful when things got tough. He liked to think that the British Empire out in India could never have survived if its soldiers, standing at attention for hours in full dress uniform, had allowed themselves to be fully aware of the one-hundred-and-ten-degree heat of an Indian summer.

"Sometimes it's necessary," he said flatly.

"And so you make up stories. It is your gift to charm people so that they believe those stories are true."

Indeed, charm was his greatest weapon, the boyish grin, the subtle compliment, the self-deprecating joke that disarmed critics and won admirers.

"This gift, you know, it can be a curse because it blinds us all to the truth and in the end, we cannot fully trust you," Di Brioni said.

John watched glumly as she sprang up from her chair with an alacrity that belied her age and hurried across the room towards the kitchen.

"Come, come, I will tell Juana to make us a nice hot soup. There is nothing better for the depression than a warm soup. Mother's milk must never be cold," she giggled. "My boy, this negative energy you bring now to me, this depression, we will analyze it over our meal. Also, we will look more deeply into this dream that disturbs you."

She led the way to a massive circular table of carved oak covered with colorful hand-embroidered mats from the local market and with trembling hands, she lit the thick white candles at the center of the table.

"I believe a round table encourages communication more than the rectangular or square shape, do you not agree?" she asked, her black eyes narrowing.

"Absolutely." He had never thought of it before but it seemed right.

"And you will sit close by me so that we can talk."

For a few moments, they sat silently sipping *sopa de tortillas con aguacates* while the room darkened around them as the sun sank behind the mountains and the air grew cool.

"How does this woman, Erika, support herself?" she casually asked.

"She is independently wealthy," John said, dipping his spoon into the last remnants of soup.

"How do you mean this?"

"Just what I said. She has money."

"Much?"

"Yes."

"How much?"

"A lot." The tortillas in the soup suddenly stuck in his throat and he coughed loudly.

"You do not wish to tell me?"

"Several hundred million, maybe," he said, coughing again, several times.

"You know this to be true?"

"I do." John reached for his glass of red wine and gulped it down. His throat burned. "So what are you getting at?"

"The money. It is so very important to discuss. That is a great deal of money you speak of. How did you meet such a woman?"

"I met her in a book club in Cambridge." A little distortion of the truth was worth the trouble of avoiding the issue of transference. If she knew Erika was a patient, god knows where that would lead. She'd never be able to accept the fact that Erika and he were different from ordinary people and the arbitrary rules of behavior between patient and therapist did not apply to them.

"She lives just up the street from me in a small house like mine," John said brightly.

"By herself?"

"Yes."

"Was she married?"

"Briefly, years ago. Her husband died."

"That is sad. But her money. So much it is! So very dangerous!"

"Why do you say that? Whatever do you mean?"

Her statement was absurd. Money made all the difference. Not having enough kept him miserable all his life and for years, he had been forced to play the frugal intellectual. Catherine's constant demands for more child support, the relentless fundraising at the institute, left him emotionally drained. Erika's money was like a miracle. With her, he could live out his dreams. She would give him everything he had ever wanted.

"This is a very rich woman and you were once such a poor boy, it is not a good thing for you, John. How does it make you feel?"

"Relieved, actually. Erika's been very generous and Catherine's finally stopped harassing me. Everything in my life will be easier now."

Dr. Di Brioni remained unmoved. "You are not afraid?"

"Of what?"

"That this woman is buying you?"

"Buying me? What would she be buying? A simple scholar? A psychoanalyst of limited means? You don't understand. She's not that way at all. She's not materialistic, she's very loving."

"You think this? If you think this you are a fool. Do you not know about the very rich?"

"Of course I do! After all, I was in school with those people." As a poor student among the rich, he had assumed their identity. How could he not know them?

"Thanks to your grandfather's help, if I remember correctly, no?"

"True enough."

"You were always the poor little boy out in the street, staring in the window of the big house to watch the rich children opening their presents on Christmas day, and you wanted to be there with them, be one of them. Is this not true?" Her eyes burned like black coals, and he wriggled uncomfortably in his chair. "But you can never be one of them, no matter how much you try," continued Dr. Di Brioni, without waiting for him to speak. "They are not the same as you and me. Because they were raised with all the money in the world, they think themselves superior. They may pretend otherwise but we know better, is this not true?"

"Not all of them are like that, certainly not Erika. She loves me and needs me."

"'Love', what does this word mean?" she scoffed. "We could take some time now to talk about that. And the word 'need'. So she 'needs' you now, but later? Will it be the same? The very rich play nasty games."

"Games? What kinds of games?" He grimaced.

"Nasty, cruel games when they tire of you and throw you away. And who is to say that she and her uncle will not play such games with you?"

Her voice dropped away and he suddenly remembered rumors of Di Brioni's ugly divorce a number of years before. Her first husband, the wealthy industrialist, had left her for a younger woman. Obviously, this explained her bitterness and concern with the issue of money.

"Erika doesn't play games. She's fine and generous and lovely. We're committed, absolutely, and we'll always be together," he said with certainty.

"You have the stars in your eyes," Maria Di Brioni said sternly. "You are blinded by the promise of the good life with this woman so you are in danger of losing your authentic self. Up until now your work on creativity has been impressive but I am afraid for the future."

"Don't be afraid, Maria. Marrying her will actually help me with my creativity research. She wants to support the Institute because she believes in what I do."

"And she will also perhaps contribute the money to Harvard for a professorship, yes?" Di Brioni gave him a sly look.

Taken aback that she had guessed his plan, he shifted uneasily in his chair. There was something of the witch about Maria Di Brioni with her penetrating black eyes and her uncanny ability to ferret out his secrets.

Yes, he was still waiting for that professorship in the psychology department after all these years. Goddamn fools. Too stupid to recognize talent when it was right in front of them. His creativity work was now hailed across the entire country so what was the issue? Anywhere else a professorship would have been easy to get. But he wouldn't give up hope. Someday, they'd come around with an offer. Harvard was his alma mater and his rightful home and Erika could help make it happen.

He would ignore Di Brioni's remark.

"You must understand that money means nothing to Erika," he said easily. "She actually pretends to be poor."

Dr. Di Brioni laughed loudly. "But nobody believes her, of course."

"It doesn't matter, don't you see? Have faith in me. I can handle this."

"Because you are resisting looking at the obvious, we must think again about your dream. You are trying to gain the crown from the mother figure using it as bait to trap you. Who do you think is this mother figure?"

"Erika?"

"Good. You're getting there."

"But the so called 'bait' to trap me? Are you talking about her money?"

"What else can it be since she is so very rich? The dream is a warning, it is trying to tell you something so very important. You must listen to yourself."

"But I *am* listening to myself!"

"No, I do not think so. In the dream you are afraid of losing the crown or the great career you might have had."

"I can't agree with your interpretation. Maria, I can't fail! I've got everything going for me right now!"

"I do not feel happy with this, no, I do not feel happy at all. Your dream, it is very clear but you cannot see because you are in denial." She gave him a piercing look. "We will discuss it again to-morrow."

Abruptly, Dr. Di Brioni stood up and John pulled on his Zegna cashmere sweater, a gift from Erika before he left. It was time to return to his hotel; fatigue had settled back in every muscle of his body.

TWO

He was her little prince, hers alone, and no one else's. A reader of gothic tales and historical novels, his mother was a southern belle who grew up on a large estate in Mississippi with four older brothers. Her father, a widower, expected his daughter to follow in her mother's footsteps. She, too, would graduate summa cum laude from Sweet Briar College.

It never happened. At seventeen, she eloped with a handsome, fast-talking Yankee boy with no money and seven months later, John, their only child, was born at Georgetown Hospital in Washington the day after his father left to fight in Vietnam. They would never see him again.

Their life was one of impoverished gentility. Work was out of the question; in those days, a woman of her class remained at home. There was never enough money; the small, monthly allowance they received from his grandfather was barely enough to provide for the bare amenities.

"But we need to be grateful for every little penny my daddy sends us," his mother said. "I ruined my life running off with your father and my daddy will never forgive me. We'll never see a single penny of my rightful inheritance!"

After reading John Updike's' novels, his mother decided her son must one day go to Harvard. Like John Updike who also had little money, he would be empowered by gaining entry into that elite, rarified world.

"You're going to Harvard when you grow up," she told him. "If life had been different, I would have lived in the North and married a Harvard man. You hear me, Johnny baby? You hear your mother talking? Look at me, boy!"

"I'm looking at you, Mom."

"You'll be going to Harvard! Did you hear me say the word, 'Harvard'?"

"Yes, Mom. What's 'Harvard'?

"It's a place, a university where you learn things. And you're going there someday. We'll make it happen, you and I. Maybe you don't understand what I'm saying now, but you will in time."

His favorite authors were J.R.R. Tolkien, Mark Twain and Sir Walter Scott. He could quote entire pages from Dickens and Thackeray, and his mother bought him high-school chemistry sets and grown-up artist materials.

"He's got the brain of a young adult in the body of a nine-year-old," his teacher said admiringly, "and he's also very talented at drawing."

"Yes, my boy's a natural artist as well as a brilliant student."

"And he's got good social skills too, gets along well with the other kids. He's a charmer, that one. How proud you must be to have such a wonderful son!"

All during his childhood, John believed that his father died a hero in the Vietnam War. That's what his mother told him, but when he turned twelve, he learned it wasn't true.

"You're old enough to know the truth, Johnny boy," his mother said. "You will have to swear never to tell another living soul what I am about to tell you. Promise? Cross your heart and hope to die?"

"Sure, Mom," he replied, crossing his heart. "Cross my heart and hope to die I'll never tell a living soul I swear!"

The truth was that his father was alive and well in California, living with his Vietnamese wife whom he'd met during the war. He wasn't dead at all and he wasn't a hero.

Johnny was filled with an aching sadness. His father was alive somewhere and he felt an overwhelming longing to see him.

He'd call him "Daddy" like all his friends called their father. Daddy would take him to football games and baseball games, wrestle with him, throw balls around. But it wasn't going to happen and he felt a tiny kernel of hurt harden in his heart, out of reach even from himself.

He could try to run away and look for his father but his mother would stop him. She was all-powerful in his life and he did as she wished. But why had she had lied to him? It made him very angry and one day he asked her why she had made up such a story.

"I was trying to shield you from the truth about your daddy so you wouldn't end up like me. My heart was broken right after you were born when he deserted us."

"If your heart was broken how can it keep on beating?"

"Oh, I don't really mean that, darling," she laughed. "It's beating just fine."

"But you said it was broken!"

"Well, it's all healed now. And that's because of you, sweets, you're my healer."

"Why did you say my daddy was dead when he's alive?"

"I shouldn't have. I was a naughty girl to tell you that."

"Can't my daddy come and live with us?"

"He's got a wife, son."

"He could bring her along, couldn't he? Wouldn't that be okay, Mom?"

"We can't have them here, son. They aren't nice people, your daddy and that Vietnamese woman. Has he ever come around here to see his precious little boy?"

"Nope."

"You see? He's forgotten all about us."

"Why?"

"Because he's selfish and thoughtless and he's got another wife who wants him all to herself. But it doesn't matter, baby, because I'm here. It's just you and me and we don't need anybody else, do we, Johnny?"

"No," he said, though he wasn't so certain anymore.

"Remember, I'm the only one in this whole wide world who loves you."

"Sure thing, Mom."

"And nobody you'll ever meet in your entire life will love you as much as I do. Don't ever forget what I'm telling you, baby."

"No, Mom, I won't."

"And remember you can't trust anyone else but me. Are you listening?"

"Yes, Ma'am."

"Thank you, dear. You're such a little gentleman."

"Yes, Ma'am." He blushed with pride and they both burst out laughing.

"If something ever happens to me, darling, I'll be there in spirit watching over you, no matter where you are."

"But what can happen to you, Mom?"

"Oh, nothing. Don't pay any attention to silly old me. You know perfectly well I'll always be right here with you."

Now and then, his mother dressed up in her best clothes and went to meet friends from St. Albans Church for lunch at the Jockey Club. She enjoyed regaling them with stories of what it was like to grow up a southern belle in Vicksburg, Mississippi with four handsome older brothers. The fact that she eloped with a scoundrel who abandoned his young wife and son inspired sympathy among her women friends. Several women tried introducing his mother to eligible men but nothing ever came of it. Her son was the center of her universe.

THREE

Riding the bus to Wilson High was a drag, and John vowed that someday he would own a car. Maybe if he got lucky, he'd get a Jaguar.

On winter mornings when it was pitch dark and cold, he'd give himself an extra few minutes in his warm bed before getting dressed. Then he'd hurry downstairs, heat up the coffee and take a cup up to his mother. He didn't wait for her to drink it all because his body would automatically tense up at the exact time he had to leave for school so as not to be late. After giving her a hug, he'd run down the stairs and head for the bus. He never ate breakfast so he was ravenous long before the lunch bell rang.

At the top of his class academically, studio art was his favorite class with its slow, easy pace. There he could daydream and imagine becoming a modern Gauguin running off to a distant island in the Pacific to paint naked brown women. It was a titillating thought.

"I know you love your painting class, Johnny boy," his mother said, "and you're very talented. Maybe someday you'll make lots of money so you're free to become an artist. It's a shame to waste all that talent but life is cruel; you can count the number of successful artists on your fingers. I'm always pushing Harvard because you'll get an academic education there, meet the right people, make good connections and never be poor again!"

The high school Spring Fling was coming up and his mother wanted to know what girl he was taking to the prom.

"You're getting so many calls, Johnny. You're so popular."

"Yeah."

"Are you taking that girl, Sally?"

"Sally?"

"You know, the one with all the money."

"You mean Sally Johnson?"

"That one. A little bit dumb, though, don't you think?"

"I'm going with Doreen, Mom."

"Doreen? Oh, but darling, she's so ordinary and I worry you'll never meet anyone around here who's up to your level. You're a catch, Johnny boy, a real catch."

"Mom, it's just a stupid dance!"

"I know, but next year when you turn sixteen, I'm going to send you to a private school where you'll meet the right kind of people. Nobody in our family ever attended public school, you know."

"Mom, we don't have the money for private school! You've told me so yourself. We're...? How do you say it?"

"Impoverished gentry."

"Yeah, that's it. We're 'impoverished gentry'."

"That's right, and all our clothes come from a thrift shop. But despite that, didn't I always buy you the best toys in town when you were little? Didn't everybody want to come play with you because you had the most beautiful toys?"

"I guess so, but I never got to go to their house."

"No, we weren't invited."

"Why not?"

"Because we were poor and you didn't go to the right school. You went to a public school. All those people were terrible snobs and social climbers. It's all about having money, lots of money! It's so common. Why when I was a girl in Vicksburg the subject of money never came up. It was considered poor breeding, like talking about religion or politics."

"Can't you get more money out of Grand Daddy?" he asked his mother one day. "Maybe he can send us enough for private school!"

"You know that Grand Daddy still won't speak to me or see me, even now. He sends us those itty bitty checks that barely keep us going and I break down and cry every single day when I think about how it used to be when I was the apple of his eye."

"Don't be mad, Mom."

"It's a fact, son. But Johnny, baby, I'm not giving up. This time instead of me, you're going to write your Grand Daddy and tell him he has to help us out a lot more. You're his only grandson – my brothers all had little girls – and I swear, you're the spitting image of him. He's going to want to meet you! You're going to get what you deserve and you'll be doing me proud. Someday you're going to live in a beautiful big house and have the finest life in all of this world, I just know you will."

That night, he sat down and wrote his grandfather for the first time.

Dear Grand Daddy,

I am John Starr, your only grandson, and I want to thank you for the help you have given me and my mother all these years. I have never met you, but my mother tells me that I look exactly like you. I would like to meet you someday.

At this time, we have a big problem. My mother tells me that no one in our family has ever attended public school except me, and now that I am in high school, she wants me to go to Andover, a private boarding school for a couple of years but we can't afford the tuition. Can you help us?

Sincerely, your grandson,

John Starr

Some weeks later, his grandfather sent him a check for twenty thousand dollars and a short note in which he agreed that no grandson of his should be denied a good education in a private institution and that henceforth, he would pay his tuition bills and room and board if he maintained an A average. His expectation was that John should attend Harvard University after graduating from Andover. However, he cautioned that all communication between them would be limited to letters since meeting together was not a possibility. If he wanted to know the reason, his mother could tell him.

FOUR

Coming from a public school unknown to most of his new classmates, John received a less than friendly welcome at Andover and he missed his old friends, especially Doreen, who was always warm and cheerful, firing him up with her sexy body,

Small, with long tawny hair, brown eyes and a toothy smile, Doreen's family came from farm country in West Virginia. She wore tight skirts, chewed bubble gum, and followed him around school. After a while, they went out together on a regular basis, engaging in heavy necking in the back row of movie theaters, but she began to get on his nerves. She liked making small talk and had no interest in books. His mother begged him to drop her. One evening he told Doreen it was over between them and was surprised at how easy it was to get rid of her. She cried a little, then dried her eyes, saying she understood; they came from two different worlds.

Doreen was friendly to him right up to his last day at the school. Kissing him chastely, she told him how much she would miss him after he left, how he'd probably forget all about her. He promised they would still see each other during vacations because going to another school didn't mean they'd lose touch. But in his heart he knew she was right, he would put her out of his mind, and once he settled in at Andover he made no effort to see her or any of his old friends from his high school again.

It didn't take him long to become the ideal Andover boy. He learned how to fit into that bastion of privilege by copying the more popular students, their dry wit, their easy conversation and their elegant accents. His good looks and natural charm inspired admiration among both boys and girls and by the end of his junior year, he was made captain of the swimming team and president of his class.

On her thirty-fifth birthday, his mother succumbed to a virulent strain of pneumonia three days before his spring vacation visit. He grieved for months. He had loved her, they'd been together in good times and bad and he felt as if she'd been stolen away from him by an alien force, leaving him abandoned in an uncaring world. Her expectations had always been that he claim his rightful place in society and succeed where she had failed. He vowed never to let her down; money and fame would one day be his.

Alone in the privacy of his room at school, he wept. Mornings, his eyes were red and swollen but he grimly soldiered on. He found himself mourning his mother's loss at odd moments like when he walked across the campus on late December afternoons with the sun setting and the pink and gold light shimmering on the new-fallen snow; or when Miss Davis, the motherly librarian, smiled at him in a special way, reminding him of his mother.

The funeral service was a private and somber affair. Only John and his mother's youngest brother from Mississippi were in attendance. His grandfather sent money for cremation and his daughter was buried in an old cemetery in Maryland, surrounded by empty fields that had recently been purchased for a shopping mall. The old man wrote of his great sadness at his daughter's passing and promised substantial financial support if his grandson was accepted at Harvard.

Despite years of neglect, her house in Georgetown was sold at a modest profit and with the money, Riggs Bank set up a small trust fund for John. According to her wishes, it was only to be used in cases of dire emergencies.

A month later, John's swimming coach, Bob, assured him he was in line for an athletic scholarship.

"Where do you want to go to college? I'll make that scholarship happen. You're a super candidate, kiddo."

"Harvard, Sir. It's where I've wanted to go ever since I was a boy."

"You've got what it takes and they have a good swimming program, not the tops, but competitive," Bob said, giving John a friendly pat on the back. The kid was one cool customer.

FIVE

John's undergraduate years were dedicated to winning swim meets for Harvard and maintaining a high grade point average to keep his scholarship. He rarely slept more than five hours a night and feeling increasingly pressured, enrolled in a studio art course on Saturdays at the Boston Museum School. Painting and drawing revived his spirits and nourished his soul.

Lack of money was becoming more oppressive. Especially galling was that despite his popularity, membership in a Harvard club was not an option, not even the Hasty Pudding, a kind of minimum club for preppies. His finances were well below those of the average member and nice restaurants, concerts, the good things in life, were out of reach. He feigned indifference to material things but he never bought cheap or ugly clothes; his fine Brooks Brothers suits came from Filene's Basement, the popular discount store.

Hanging out with the elegant, affluent crowd was what he liked to do and he rarely refused invitations to parties at country houses, but he felt a certain bitterness at his friends' disregard for his difficult circumstances. He was careful never to join them at expensive restaurants or take a date out on the town.

Handsome, impeccably dressed and witty in that effortless way he had acquired at boarding school, he found himself on the select list of debutante parties despite his reduced circumstances. An extra man was always a high priority at these events so invitations flowed in and he accepted most of them. It cost him only the price of a tuxedo and he could see for himself how the Boston upper class lived. Girls he had known at Andover invited him to both their debutante dinner parties and the dances that followed, a special honor since a number of socially prominent boys were not included at the dinners. It always made him chuckle when he recalled Alice Roosevelt Longsworth's much quoted comment from long ago about her cousin, Franklin Delano Roosevelt: "He was the sort of boy you invite to the dance but not to the dinner beforehand." No one could ever say that about him.

John was increasingly aware of his power over women. He noticed how the debutantes with their cheerful, open faces, bubbled with a special excitement when he gave them his full attention.

In truth, he had little interest in them, they weren't beautiful or sexy and their aimless chatter bored him, but it washed over him like a cool shower on a summer's day. What pleased him most was dining in yet another stately home with high ceilings and faded oriental rugs that bespoke refinement and old money. Someday he, too, would be giving dinners like these, serving food on porcelain plates, filling the dining room with bowls of brilliant flowers, adorning the tables with towering candelabra that glowed with masses of candles, and a retinue of servants at his beck and call. If he played his hand right, all this could be his.

After the dinners, everyone met at the Copley Plaza Hotel where most of the debutante balls were held, and when he drew a girl out onto the dance floor to the throbbing rhythms of the latest hit song, he felt rich and free like everyone around him.

To reward his academic success, his grandfather treated him to a European tour in the summer of his freshman year and he was sure that somewhere out there on the Other Side, his mother was smiling.

"The old man came through," he said to himself. "It's amazing. It's not enough money, of course, but it'll have to do."

Wherever he traveled that summer in Europe, his charm and good looks attracted women, but his relationships were short-lived; he became easily distracted. Lingering in cafes, bars, museums and hotel lobbies, he hoped to run into the perfect girl, brainy, beautiful and rich, but it never happened.

Sophomore year, he was elected to the *Advocate*, the literary magazine, and for the first time at Harvard, he felt at home. His ambition to be a star burned like a small, hot flame and he was labeled a "creative intellectual" because he wrote on serious themes. He relished challenging the widely popular views of retired researchers like B. F. Skinner in his famous book, *Walden Two*. Comparing it to Thoreau's *Walden*, he maintained that Thoreau had the more authentic view of human nature because he emphasized the striving for freedom, not merely behavioral conditioning.

Aged and frail, Skinner responded to John's article with an angry letter to the editor challenging John's conclusion. Hadn't he proven in his studies that the absence of punishment and the use of positive reinforcement was all that was needed to help human nature flower? What could this arrogant young man be thinking when he debunked a legitimate scientist like himself?

Stung by Skinner's negative reaction and determined to get him on his side, John invited the old man to tea and though Skinner refused to retract his assertions, John charmed him by comparing his work to other versions of utopia and got him talking about his early interest in the theater.

In another article, John wrote about the persistence of the glass ceiling that kept women out of important leadership positions. A national female leader in the United States fit no American prototype while a country like England could boast a history of powerful queens such as Elizabeth I, Queen Victoria and the imperious Prime Minister Margaret Thatcher. Early America's only role models were Betsy Ross who sewed the flag and the author of *Uncle Tom's Cabin*, Harriet Beecher Stowe.

John's favorite professor was the silver-haired, debonair Pierre Fouquet, a French professor of psychology with an M.D. from the Sorbonne in Paris and a Ph.D. from M.I.T. in neuropsychology. He lived in a large, handsome house on Brattle Street and his wife was Livia Cabot, a Boston socialite. John imagined that someday he, too, would find an adoring rich woman, live in a grand house, and stand on the same podium as Fouquet – dazzling the students.

Fouquet's meticulously researched work on the brain and emotional behavior was published in prestigious peer-reviewed journals around the globe, and being an especially gifted teacher, he was able to make complex ideas comprehensible to both students and faculty. But his was a balancing act. The Harvard psychology department was divided into those who sought a rigorous quantitative approach to their subject and others who favored a more interpretive, nuanced one. Fouquet cleverly covered both approaches by offering not only courses on the brain but a hugely popular series of lectures on the interpretation of dreams in famous works of fiction. Besides Fouquet, the students themselves were encouraged to give their own interpretation of these dreams and for John, this was exciting and profoundly stimulating.

Senior year, John was elected to the Signet Society and could now be counted among the Harvard intellectual elite. A special friend at the club was his classmate, the amiable Arthur Watts. Witty and urbane, from a prominent Boston family, Arthur wore horn-rimmed glasses, torn preppy clothes, and smoked Players, a cigarette made in England. At six feet four inches tall, he was thin and gawky. At Groton School where he spent six unhappy years, he was forced to play soccer and vowed that in later life he would never run down a field again. Both he and John were set on the same career path; four more years at Harvard to earn their doctorate in psychology and then with any luck, professorships with tenure at Harvard. The promise of a brilliant future was never in doubt.

SIX

Elaine Locke entered John's life during his last year of graduate school. A native Californian, she had a round, soft face, lively brown eyes and tawny, shoulder-length hair. Small, with narrow hips, slim, shapely legs and full, pointed breasts, she exuded an aura of sexual availability despite her conservative, preppy clothes. Like him, she was enrolled in Professor Edwin Plunkett's Child Development course. The author of seven highly acclaimed books on human intelligence, Plunkett was widely admired for his expertise in statistical analysis and John intended to acquire some of his brilliant techniques for analyzing data.

From the very first day of class, Professor Plunkett appeared to direct all his observations to Elaine. Despite his middle-age spread and thinning hair, he was known as a womanizer; his present wife (there had been two before) had once been his graduate student. John wasn't sure that Elaine was aware of her effect on Plunkett and he considered warning her, but when he ran into the pair drinking beer together at a popular hangout in Harvard Square, he quickly dropped the idea.

When Professor Plunkett assigned John and Elaine a project together at the Michael Driscoll Elementary School in Brookline, she immediately initiated a friendly conversation with John. Something about her seemed familiar but he couldn't place it. Then it all came back. Doreen, his girlfriend in high school. The same toothy smile, the long, tawny hair, the sexy body.

"It'll be fun working with you," she said. "I'm impressed with your ability to come up with the big concepts. I'm different from you, John, and maybe it's a little weird, but statistics grab me; collecting controlled data can be a real turn-on." She smiled seductively.

"Not me. I believe in the chaos of creativity. We should make a good team," John said.

"Maybe that's why Plunkett put us together. We complement each other, don't you agree?"

"Yeah, you've got a point," John said, though he wasn't quite sure.

At the Driscoll School, they measured the self-confidence of children who succeeded well in the third and fourth grade. Did they ask pertinent questions of the teacher? How often did they speak out in class? Did they get along well with their classmates? What was their IQ, their parents' professions? Was there a distinct variation in teaching styles depending on the child's abilities?

Elaine's eagerness to learn the answers, her meticulous notes, her statistical expertise, impressed John as well as the teachers and administrators who asked to read her notes.

"You go about getting what you want," John observed. "I like that, Elaine. You've got faculty support and it looks like Plunkett's in your corner as well."

"He's taken an interest in me," she said quickly.

"That's pretty obvious," John said. For a second, John felt sorry for her and regretted bringing him up. Plunkett had all the power and this pretty little girl was such an innocent. Or was she? Maybe she wasn't as dumb as she seemed and in the end, she'd get something out of the relationship.

"It looks like you're headed for a fine career," he said.

"That's nice of you to say, John, though I'm a plodder. I don't have the grand vision like you."

"But you're getting support where it matters and you believe in yourself. Tell me, what does your father do?"

"He's the manager of a car dealership. He does very well and spends a lot of time checking the books. That's probably why I'm good at math. He's also a champion chess player, and got me playing early on, when I was six. He coached my sisters and me in soccer and tennis and I became captain of my tennis team in high school."

"A good father, I'd say. And your mother?"

"She's a real estate agent, one of those people who could convince you to buy the Empire State building." She laughed, then grew serious. "I like my parents. I guess that's not a very popular position these days."

"You're lucky," John said.

"I know. And you? What about your family?"

"My mother died when I was a junior in high school. I never knew my father."

"I'm sorry."

"You don't have to be. My mom and I were very close. No regrets there."

"That's good."

"Let's talk about you, Elaine. From what I've picked up, it looks like you'll go into the quantitative side of psychology. That's a popular field right now. You'll do well."

"You think so? You're very supportive." She blushed and John was charmed by her modesty.

"It's true," he insisted. "You're so good at numbers you'll probably chair some psychology department somewhere."

"What about right here?" she said brightly. "Maybe they'll want me back here someday."

"Here? You mean here at Harvard?" John was momentarily caught off guard. This young woman must be full of illusions. He gave a short laugh.

"You've got a lot going for you, Elaine, but landing something here would be almost impossible."

"Oh, I know, I know, they want the big fish, the stars. I'll have to play it right, make a name for myself some place far away, work up to the top in a small university."

He was impressed by her determination, her clarity of purpose. She gave him a sharp look. "And what about you?" she said.

"Oh, I'll hang around here, climbing the ladder, I guess." A wistful note crept into his voice. "You know, Harvard's a part of me now, it's like family."

She leaned closer to him. "And you'll reach the top, John, because you're talented and you have an original mind. You've got something else going for you, too."

"Like what?" His interest was momentarily sparked.

"Charm. That's an extra talent, you know." And in the brightness of her Doreen smile, John's heart filled with happiness.

As their study progressed, John had the feeling that if he gave Elaine any encouragement, she would sleep with him and it would be no more important to her than brushing her teeth or eating a good meal. Maybe that's what she was up to with Plunkett and the old man believed she was really hooked on him. Such a fool, that Plunkett, tricked by a sexy, graduate student who was making all the right moves, using him even more than he was using her.

In the final week of their project, John proposed a visit to the Rubin family because their two children, Artie and Rachel, both excellent students, scored highest in self-confidence for third and fourth grade.

"Their parents are doing something right and we need to know what it is. Maybe we'll get a free meal besides," John said with a twinkle in his eye.

"I like the idea of dinner," Elaine said, "but our presence might make the kids behave differently."

"Look, we've been watching them in the classroom, they see us there every day."

"Still, we'd be in their home with their parents. But I'm up for it. We've nothing to lose."

The Rubin apartment was small, but decorated in such a way that it seemed larger. Abstract paintings hung on the walls and the dining room was painted different shades of high-gloss white and gray. Their hosts immediately proposed dinner, and John noticed that a glass table with six white chairs was already set for dinner.

A stylish blond, Beth Rubin was dressed in black slacks, a white tailored blouse and black patent leather flats. Next to her burly husband Sam, dressed in chinos and a dark green cashmere sweater, she appeared delicate and petite.

"We'll eat right away," she announced. "The food's ready and the kids are hungry." As though on cue, the children ran into the dining room and took their seats at the table.

"Kids, say 'Hi' to Mr. Starr and Miss Locke," Sam said.

"Hi. We already saw you at school, today," Artie began.

"You write stuff down," Rachel interrupted with a frown.

"Good things," John cheerfully assured her.

Later, as dinner came to an end, Sam asked John and Elaine what they had learned from their study at the school.

"I'm one of those people who likes to get the lowdown," he said. A successful state's attorney for seven years, he was now working for George Abrams, a counsel to CEOs who had worked with Senator Kennedy.

"We're documenting the role of self confidence," John explained, "and how much it influences success in school. Your children are lucky; they've got lots of it."

"You hear that, kids?" Sam said, grabbing his son who was scurrying out of the room with his sister. "Look, you and Rachel are part of this conversation so don't run away. We want you here. We're talking about self confidence." Grinning sheepishly, the children returned to their seats.

Artie said, "What's the word? I've forgotten already."

"Self confidence, my boy. It's an important word so try to remember for next time."

"Daddy, it's a long word!"

"You think so?"

"Yep."

His father chuckled.

John glanced across the table. "Tell me, Mr. Rubin, how do you encourage your children's self confidence?"

"We're supportive and we let them challenge us."

"We encourage discussion, they can ask us questions," his wife added. "And we like to play twenty questions at the table. They learn a lot."

"Hey, kids, what was the name of Ted Kennedy's famous brother?" Mr. Rubin asked.

"Jack Kennedy!" both children shouted.

"And what was he?"

"President of the United States! He got shot and he died!"

"You children know your history. I'm impressed," Elaine smiled.

"It's easy," said Rachel, "'cause we saw the movie with Mommy and Daddy where President Kennedy gets shot."

"I *never* want to be president of the United States!" cried Artie. "It's too scary!"

"Yeah, it's too scary!" shouted Rachel.

"So what do you guys want to be someday? Artie, what do you say?" John said.

"You can be whatever you want, can't you, Artie?" their mother broke in. "You, too, Rachel. You'll both make that decision when the time comes. Right, kids?"

"Right, Mommy," Rachel said.

Later, driving back to Cambridge with Elaine, John analyzed the Rubin family dynamics.

"The children are allowed to confront their parents, ask questions. And they're put to the test in front of strangers at the dinner table and expected to supply answers. There was just one hitch, did you notice?"

"Artie never wants to be president," said Elaine. "The movie scared the children. They don't want to die."

"Smart kids. Anyway, who knows, maybe Artie will be president someday. You never know."

They laughed and Elaine snuggled close to him in the front seat of the car. John made no effort to draw away; she was smart and sexy and pretty. But he played dumb to the signals she was sending his way. He didn't want another man's woman and besides, though he enjoyed her company, she didn't attract him that much. She was too transparent; he liked a little mystery.

SEVEN

In later years when discussing his career at Harvard, John said that its defining moment came during his final semester of graduate studies when he met the famous psychologist, Dr. Maria Di Brioni.

She was the daughter of Francesca Di Brioni, a famous Italian analyst, whose writings on psychoanalytic theory attracted the attention of Carl Jung. Though most of Maria's training was provided by her mother, Maria was able to complete her studies at Carl Jung's institute in Zurich, thanks to his help.

Brought to Harvard from her institute in Mexico City by the School of Education during John's last term, Di Brioni was a star lecturer that spring. A svelte woman in her early sixties, with large, black eyes, a Roman nose, and smooth dark hair worn in a French twist, she spoke passionately of her creativity studies in Mexico, inspiring even the most cynical students to give her standing ovations. She had run clinical trials with troubled adolescents and unhappy housewives who under her guidance became successful writers and artists after a brief period of psychotherapy that included an emphasis on discovering their latent creativity. The idea of unlocking human creativity through therapy excited John; his psychology professors at Harvard had never raised such a possibility.

"You must listen to me!" Di Brioni cried out to the audience in her quaintly accented English. "The so-called experts worship the tests like multiple choice and IQ, but these tell you *nothing* about the creative personality! Nothing at all! Such absurdity, such nonsense! This is so very crazy!" Her best selling book, *We Are All Artists,* translated into eighteen languages, and her interviews with *Time* and *Newsweek,* repeated her charge that predicting creativity through mechanistic, statistical correlations was deeply flawed. Human beings are able to defy all manner of predictions.

John had recently seen an exhibition of bamboo brush paintings from Taiwan at a gallery on Beacon Hill and the idea of delving into the creativity of traditional Chinese art intrigued him. The sign at the entrance of the gallery read: "The bamboo symbolizes uprightness and responsibility, endurance and truth. Bamboo bends to the wind, but it never breaks."

Before studying the paintings, John carefully read the comments of the 14th century critic, Li K'an, pasted above the art works. "Joint after joint, leaf after leaf, first concentrating on the brush manner, training without getting tired, possessing the bamboo completely in the mind, knowing the rules and principles of painting, becoming so faultless as to transcend the rules."

A very different approach to creativity from the West, John thought. Asian art wasn't about "doing your own thing", becoming famous and making money. It was about diligence, strict obedience, immersion, and in the end, spontaneity and freedom.

"That Taiwan exhibition was amazing," John later told Arthur Watts. "I've decided to take a course in Chinese brush painting at the Museum School. Non-credit, of course."

"That's ink on rice paper?"

"Right, though you're over simplifying it a bit. How about joining me?"

"I could never do that stuff. Anyway, even though you're talented in art, what makes you think *you* can?"

"Why not? If the Chinese can do it, why can't I?"

"*You*? But you're not Chinese!"

John did not expect to actually meet the great Di Brioni in his art class when he signed up for a class in Chinese brush painting. But there she was beside him, and he was impressed by her dogged efforts to elicit answers to her questions from their Chinese teacher, a wrinkled, non-communicative master of brush painting. What exactly were his techniques for maneuvering the brush across the rice paper so effortlessly? How did he achieve his exquisite "bone" strokes?

His response was always the same; "In China, student for twenty years. Then, assistant to master for thirty years. Then artist."

After several weeks of class, no one was any nearer maneuvering the brush across the rice paper in the Chinese manner and it was obvious their teacher was not about to reveal his secrets. John and Maria Di Brioni agreed that the techniques of the ancient masters were forever hidden in the flick of his brush.

"John," Di Brioni said one day after class. "Come to my evening discussions on creativity with my graduate students. We meet at Quincy House because it is there I am living during the spring term."

"I would like that very much, Dr. Di Brioni."

"Call me 'Maria'. These evening discussions are always a nice occasion for a little Chianti and good Italian cheese," she said with a wink and a smile.

At her meetings, students and younger faculty members stretched out on frayed oriental rugs scattered over the scuffed wooden floor to sip a glass of wine and consider Dr. Di Brioni's insights. She liked to shock them with her views on monotheism.

"Monotheism narrows creative potential," she told them. "When we had the pagan gods there was no separation of the feminine and the masculine. Jung's archetypes show us how they are still buried deep in our psyche and the creative person liberates and integrates them in art and everyday life.

"Take our Christian saints because that, too, is so very interesting. Pagan gods in disguise – that is what they are. If you are a woman and a Christian, it is good to be an Italian Catholic. Our Virgin Mary is a powerful figure. Motherhood is sacred in Italy."

Every night, John reviewed his notes before bed. Di Brioni's focus on archetypes excited his imagination.

The Good King, the Mother, the Hero or the Magician, were all archetypes to be retrieved from the unconscious mind. Among her clinical examples was the weary and sorrowful Abraham Lincoln who transformed himself into a great president during the Civil War by discovering the Hero archetype within him. Another example was a young girl on the verge of suicide due to her cruel and destructive mother. Minutes before plunging a knife into her heart, she had a vision of the loving Mother archetype that existed within herself and was calling her back to life.

"I do not know if Middle Eastern and Asian creativity include similar archetypes," Di Brioni said, "and when I took a Chinese painting class, I was unsuccessful in discovering the answer."

Di Brioni and John formed a close friendship that year and John was flattered that this brilliant, famous woman confided in him.

"It is so easy at Harvard to suffer from loneliness, John," she said one evening over dinner. "I have made few real friends though everyone treats me like I am a queen. It is so very intense, so competitive here, do you not agree?"

"Yeah, it's pretty much everybody for himself."

"Do you not feel that many of these people, the professors, the students, are they not alienated from their true selves? How can they be truly creative in such an environment?"

"A good question, Maria."

"And you?"

"Me? What about me?"

She was smiling warmly and he leaned across the table, ready for her to invite him down to Mexico.

"What plans you have, John? I think you must cut the umbilical cord to Mother Harvard and start your career in a less competitive environment."

"'A less competitive environment'? Like where?"

"Boston University, maybe, or should I say, 'B.U.'?

"Teach at B.U.?" He had clearly misread her. Her intent was to cast him as an outsider at Harvard like herself.

"Maybe you apply at B.U. for the position of assistant professor of psychology? You have no real mentor here I have observed and that is not such a good thing if you desire the tenure."

"B.U. isn't in the same league as Harvard, Maria," he said coldly. "Frankly, I can't imagine leaving here. I don't think you understand; this is where I belong."

"Do I hear the Harvard snobbery, John? Such a very silly remark! You could become the big fish in the little pond at B.U.! They would treat you like a prince!"

"Yeah, that's probably true." He reflected for a moment on this last point. "It's actually an interesting idea," he grudgingly admitted. "Things around here are pretty slow. Fouquet used to take an interest in me when I was an undergraduate but he's an old man now, he's off the radar. Plunkett's friendly, of course, but for some reason we don't connect."

"That is because he is a technocrat and you are not."

"Yeah, I guess I'm basically a humanist. I'll give him credit, though. He really taught me statistics."

"Yes, and that is a good thing; you will be a better researcher. When you are ready, you will come to my institute."

"Your institute?" He feigned surprise. She'd waited long enough to tell him, but he wouldn't refuse her. "I'd like that," he said simply.

"Good. I will need your expertise with the statistical analysis," Maria Di Brioni continued. "It is the trend, you know, and to have pages of statistics of what you learned from Professor Plunkett will be so very useful to my work. But it must be only after you have some experience away from Harvard. You will become psychologically healthier, more creative, and then I will train you in psychoanalysis. You will be analyzed by me."

"You do me a great honor, Maria."

He'd have to swallow his pride and apply to B.U.. Oh, well, what the hell, it would only be for a couple of years, at the most. Then on to Mexico and the work with Maria. He'd use the statistics he'd learned in Plunkett's course. But would Plunkett or any of his Harvard people ever read her books? Since she didn't push the numbers, they probably would ignore her work, but if they ever ran across her new book with his statistics, they'd sit up and take notice!

EIGHT

After earning his Harvard doctorate, John was accepted at Boston University as an assistant professor of psychology and his course became among the most popular in the psychology department. Students found him amusing, interesting, and supportive, but after two years, despite his success, his feeling of isolation returned to plague him. He was experiencing a growing uneasiness with what he saw as pockets of mediocrity in the faculty and student population at Boston University. He had been too eager to please Di Brioni; his true allegiance was to Harvard.

Arthur Watts reported to John that it looked like the numbers approach was beginning to dominate the Harvard psychology department, a depressing development.

"But at least you're in there," John said. "You can influence things."

"No, I can't, John. I'm only an assistant professor like you and that's the bottom of the barrel as we both know."

"Well, at least you're still at Harvard while I'm stuck across the river," John said bitterly.

"Hey, are you sorry you didn't stay on?"

"You can say that again! B.U. just isn't where I want to be. Outside of the East Coast, who's ever heard of the place? Sure, there are plenty of great professors and students, but there's no star quality. The right move would have been to hang in at Harvard after I got my doctorate like you did."

"And we could have had a ball in the process," Arthur laughed. Growing serious, he said, "You think we could have made a difference, John?"

"Why not?"

"Well, we've got all that new orthodoxy taking root at Harvard right now. It's a new religion and it's called science and technology. That's what Plunkett believes in like all the other big shots.

The humanists are being eased out, just look around you. Take Fouquet. He's now totally sidelined, and I figure it's only a matter of a few years before psychology gets dumped and some kind of radiology or magnetic imagery takes over the study of the mind."

"Arthur, you're over-reacting." Ever the optimist, John was not happy to hear his dismal assessment of Harvard's future.

Arthur stared despondently at the floor, his chin resting on his hand. Suddenly, his face lit up. "Hey, John, are you really serious about coming back into the department?"

"Absolutely."

"Well, I've got a proposal. You might not like it, though."

"Why not?"

"It's pretty radical."

"Radical?"

"Yeah. Look, why not take an extended leave of absence from B.U. and go on down to Mexico. Remember, Di Brioni promised you a job."

"That's right but I haven't followed up on it because I figured working with her is not going to help me out much these days. The guys here have her pegged as a lightweight, talking nonsense about oppressive patriarchy being at the root of lack of creativity."

"I know, but if we tell Plunkett you'll be using his methodology he's going to be turned on. You'll be working with the numbers, the statistics, all the crap he lives by. He'll see you're bringing rigor to this woman's work. Think of it, John! Rigor! That's the battle cry here! There's nothing that would turn him on more, other than fucking his graduate students!" At that last thought, they both broke into raucous laughter. "Besides, you can learn about the creativity stuff she does with the villagers and get some training at her psychoanalytic institute in Mexico City."

"Not a bad idea, actually."

"Best of all, Di Brioni's a real celebrity these days. More than when she was here. She's a big media favorite, and like most of

Harvard, Plunkett's into fame, the greatest aphrodisiac. Just the other day he was boasting that when she was a lecturer here, he escorted her to a Harvard dinner."

"Wow, am I impressed!"

"Fame rubs off, John."

"But there's a problem. How do I know Plunkett would bring me into the department when I get back?"

"It'll depend on how much good feedback we give him about you. If the stuff you do with her is impressive enough and what you write gets into the academic press, you could be up for a Harvard professorship."

"Not so easy to pull off, Arthur."

"I'll keep after him. He's always claiming to have an open mind, looking at all sides of the argument. Of course, he plays his cards close to the chest and being an obsessive-compulsive personality, it's hard for him to make decisions."

"If I go forward with this, you've got your work cut out," John said.

Arthur nodded in agreement. "For sure. And I couldn't expect much of a response for a while, but it's all about getting his attention, keeping the pressure up, talking about the great contributions you could make to the department."

"You would do that for me?"

"What do you think? You're a great talent and my friend. Once you're in we could create the right kind of balance in the department, break the hold of the numbers people, the brain geeks, bring back the grand concepts of psychology and psychoanalysis. The chances are slim, but what the hell?"

"I'm up and running," John said, flashing him a winning smile.

NINE

John applied for a fellowship at Maria Di Brioni's institute but to his disappointment, the institute could not provide funding and he wondered briefly what kind of place had no endowment. He would have to search elsewhere for the money.

Late one afternoon, Arthur told him about a party on Beacon Hill. "They say it's going to be mostly the Boston Opera crowd, as well as a few artists. We might meet some great girls for a change. How about it?"

It was at that party he met Catherine, a dancer in the ballet corps of the Boston Opera. Tall and graceful, she was dressed in a black velvet dress with a wide belt with a large silver buckle fastened around her slim waist. Set in a wide Irish face, her eyes were a striking green, and she wore her long, luxuriant auburn hair in a bun, high on her head. Like the ballerina she was, she stood ramrod straight. Her knowing smile intrigued John: it was as though she was privy to his most intimate secrets. She spoke with that slight drawl peculiar to privileged girls who attended prestigious private girls' schools like Winsor or Farmington and it was only later he learned that she could imitate any accent, assume any identity whenever she felt like it. She had, in fact, attended public schools all her life.

When John told her he had a doctorate from Harvard, she wanted to know what his thesis was about and laughed when he told her. "It sounds so complicated, with all those graphs and statistics. You must be a brain, like my uncle who's in the same field at B.U.."

"B.U.? But that's where I'm teaching, now. Who is your uncle?"

"James Digby, the chairman of the psychology department."

"James Digby? Incredible! He's the guy who interviewed me for the job!"

"Well, that's a coincidence," she smiled. "So my uncle hired you. He's a big-time professor, that's a fact, though he's old. Right now he's also chairman of some important committee at the National Institute of Mental Health. They give out research grants."

"Oh, really?" His interest quickened. "You said NIMH?" This was going to be one lucky night; this girl's uncle could make his career.

"That's right. I live with him and my aunt in Brookline because I'm poor and my mother couldn't cope with all of us kids. My father left us long ago so my aunt and uncle took me in. I was lucky, I guess. I haven't seen my mother or any of my six brothers and sisters for years and years. They don't like me, I guess. As you can see, I wasn't born with a silver spoon in my mouth like you Harvard people."

"What makes you think I'm rich?"

"Well, aren't you?" There was a wicked glint in her eye.

"No, I'm not. I'd like to be, of course. My grandfather was rich and supported me, but he died a couple of years ago and I've had to make it on my own ever since."

"Well, you're into the academic, I can see that, but not me. I'm a ballet dancer with the Boston Opera. I'm a storywriter, too, though I've never been published." She gave him a defiant look. "Someday I'll be famous; you'll see."

"Sure, sure." He smiled sympathetically. "So what do you write about?"

"The dance world. It's like anything else, lots of divas and autocratic types. It's not much of a life, you know, being a dancer. It's a total dedication, but because we're making art together, some of us get into relationships that aren't real. We find out later it's all fantasy." She looked at him with a special intensity. "I expect to tour with the New York City Ballet in a couple of years."

"Wow!" His interest was piqued; the girl had ambition and he wanted to know more about her.

"Who's your favorite author?" he asked suddenly.

"Krishnamurti. Ever heard of him?" she asked. John was startled by the question, and embarrassed to say he hadn't.

Swept up in the warmth and merriment of that crowded room on Beacon Hill, his heart swelled with a simple happiness he had not felt in a long time. The next day, he stopped in at a bookstore in Boston where he picked up a copy of Krishnamurti's *Education and the Significance of Life*. He was profoundly moved by its anti-materialistic message: the freedom to Be. Maybe he'd been wrong all these years, looking for a woman with money. Catherine was a pure soul, her richness came from deep within herself.

Shortly afterwards, he called her up for a date. Later, without her knowledge, he spent a number of evenings watching her perform with the Boston Opera Ballet. She had a rare grace, but she loomed taller on stage than all the others. Her statuesque beauty might have succeeded better on the Broadway stage but he did not plan to tell her.

John's bright personality and intellectual gifts impressed her uncle who wanted to be on a first name basis.

"No 'Professor Digby', John. I'm 'Jim' to my niece's friends."

"Fine, Jim. Sounds good to me."

After some months of dating Catherine, John sat down with her uncle one evening and announced he might leave the country to work with Maria Di Brioni. Jim Digby could not hide his disappointment.

"I guess I have to recognize you're young and full of energy and this is a great time in your life, but I'll miss you. I hope you'll consider coming back here to B.U. afterwards. I agree with you that Di Brioni's an interesting thinker and working with her might be an effective inoculation against the overly quantitative and reductionist psychology you've had to adapt to at Harvard," he said. "Her program at the Institute for Psychoanalysis in Mexico City is pretty well respected and you might be able to combine her methodology with Plunkett's while you're working on her field studies. You could make a real contribution."

"That's exactly what I had in mind," John said. "Naturally, I hope to go beyond Maria Di Brioni's interpretations."

"Good. I have to warn you, though, she's a controversial figure in academic circles and your promising future might be compromised by choosing that career path."

"It would only be for two years at the most," John said. "I'd like to come back to Boston, naturally." For a moment he was silent. "There's another matter I need to discuss with you, Jim."

"It's about Catherine, isn't it?"

"You guessed it. We want to marry."

"I suspected as much." He gave John a wide smile. "Congratulations! My wife and I will be delighted at the prospect of having you in the family."

"But I'm in a bit of a dilemma at the moment, Sir," John added quickly.

"Oh, what's the problem?"

"Well, for quite a while I've been looking into grants to cover my expenses in Mexico but so far I've had no luck."

"Well, I suppose I could help you find the funding, make a two-year research grant available for you." Jim gave him a kindly glance.

"Gee, thanks, Jim. I sure appreciate that," John said.

It was all working out as he had planned; his dreams were about to become reality.

Later, John met with Arthur Watts.

"I'm good!"

"What?"

"Digby's going to get me a grant to work with Maria Di Brioni."

"Hey, that's great!"

"And I'm going to marry his niece!"

"Catherine? You mean the beautiful dancer you met at that party on Beacon Hill?"

"The very same."

"You've been holding out on me, John, I had no idea, but I'll forgive you. Congrats."

"Thanks." He flashed a smile. "And Arthur, you won't forget, will you?"

"Forget what?"

"You know, getting something going for me around here."

Arthur smiled. "Look John, if I'm ever going to survive the crap that's going on, I need you on board."

"Thanks, Arthur. I'm counting on you."

"Good. And from what I remember of Di Brioni, you won't be bored down in Mexico."

"I'm expecting a creative experience," John said and they both laughed.

In August of that year, John and Catherine were married in a small Methodist church in Dedham. Arthur Watts was his best man. Catherine's uncle escorted her up the aisle and her aunt wept with pride to see her niece marrying a Harvard man. Jim Digby enjoyed taking credit for the match. "When Catherine learned I'd hired John to teach in the department, she decided he was worth pursuing!" he boasted to the happy crowd of well-wishers. "We're going to miss this fine young couple. Good luck in Mexico!"

Later, Catherine confessed to John she wouldn't be missing her uncle Jim at all.

"He thinks he's so great just because he's the chairman of the department at B.U.," she said. " But in fact, he's boring."

"Boring?"

"He's totally conventional, John, he's never left Boston, never lived anywhere else. He played his little power games to make himself chairman of the department. And who cares? What you're doing, darling, is radical, daring, different, and I can't wait to live in Mexico! You know what we're going to do in the land of *mañana?* We're going to make lots of babies!" She smiled her knowing smile. "And we'll have plenty of money now that you've wheedled a fat grant out of my uncle! I knew from the start you were a con artist!"

TEN

Once settled in Cuernavaca, Catherine and John not only studied the Spanish language intensively, but the culture and history of the country as well. Their social life in Mexico was a mix of rich, American expatriates who gave lavish parties and owned handsome villas staffed with servants, and Mexican artists and intellectuals who invited them to elegant, late night dinners in Mexico City.

During their first year, Catherine enrolled in ballet classes at the Bellas Artes but dropped out; the level was far below her professional standards. She took up modern dance, catching the eye of the German dancer, Alexander Von Swain, recently returned from a world tour with his Mexican partner, Carmen Blumenkron. Catherine's statuesque beauty and grace impressed him, and when he lifted her in the air, he was astonished. She was light as a feather, something Carmen was not.

John worked daily with Maria Di Brioni to learn her psychoanalytic techniques and she did not hesitate to give him explicit directives.

"You must discover and support your patients' creative potential," she said. "Do not under any circumstance stir up the shit."

"'Stir up the shit'?"

She laughed. "I mean the obsessive focus of American analysts on childhood trauma. It is so very destructive! Some attention to early trauma is very necessary, of course, but to return over and over to the shit? Patients only get worse. More depressed. Life has no hope. Do I make myself clear?" She searched John's face, her black eyes burning.

"I see what you mean."

"It is so very important. But you are smart and you will make a very good analyst." She smiled happily. "Tomorrow we will travel out to the more remote villages for our interviews with the indigenous groups. It is a lot I expect from you, John, in this cross-cultural creativity study. Your pages of statistics will impress so very greatly Professor Plunkett by their rigor."

Damn right, thought John. I'll show that bastard!

Until the fateful day when he met the anthropologist Jorge Amara, guru of exotic mind-enhancing drugs, life in Mexico had been an exciting adventure for both John and Catherine.

It all began innocently enough. Amara, recently back from southern Mexico where he had eaten hallucinatory mushrooms, showed up at a party in Cuernavaca and invited John to come along to a village near Amecameca, where the Indians chewed peyote and shared their strange and exotic visions.

"I've arranged it with the villagers. They've agreed to include us in their ceremony so that we can learn more about the creative process. It'll be great, you'll see," he told John.

This invitation was too tempting to turn down. John admired Jorge Amara; his lectures and writings described the creativity of the indigenous people and the ancient secrets of the Indians, like those of the Chinese, had much to teach the West.

It turned out to be a mind-bending event. Seated on a dirt floor in a circle with nearly ten Indian men of varying ages, John joined them in chewing peyote. Soon he was talking to God and God was answering back in clear and audible tones. Such an extraordinary experience convinced him that peyote should be the drug of choice for patients unable to get in touch with their creative energies. It would give them the ability to break down resistances, penetrate the ego and tap into their unconscious. He was filled with the excitement of discovery and intended to promote peyote as a breakthrough for psychotherapy.

But it was never to be. In a speech in Mexico City among the world's psychiatric elite, he appealed to those psychoanalysts who were interested in creativity to open their eyes to the wisdom of the impoverished villagers who had so generously shared their peyote with him. He urged them to experience for themselves its liberating potential and apply the drug routinely to their patients. Then he decried the oppressive government in Mexico that was run by people who were prejudiced against the noble Indian.

A day later in Mexico City, he was kidnapped by six burly men wearing dark blue suits and mirrored sunglasses. Hustling him into a large, black car, they drove at high speed to the airport where they placed him on a commercial plane headed for San Diego. He was declared officially *persona non grata* by the Mexican government and forbidden to ever return.

Shaken, angry, and chilled by the violence to his person and to his honor, left completely without funds, he sent a message to Catherine to wire him money immediately. The next few weeks were spent in a small, dingy motel room near the San Diego airport where he obsessed over his traumatic experience, his shattered dreams, and waited for Catherine to join him.

He finally was able to call Maria Di Brioni who had been alerted to the kidnapping. "It is terrible!" she cried. "Very primitive, dragging you off the street like this without giving you a chance to be heard! To take you away from your patients here, they are so traumatized by this! Such an abandonment! So bad, so unhealthy! They hate you, John, though of course it is not your fault. I explain to them so many times over because they are *furiosos*! I have much work to do, you see, with this terrible thing that has happened. And to interrupt our work together! It is madness! We were making such breakthroughs! And your poor Catherine, pregnant besides! She suffers, John. She suffers so greatly from this. Such a cruel country, this Mexico. Why am I here? This is the question I ask myself. But now is not the time to talk about me. It is you who needs help."

A long silence ensued and John thought the line must have been cut off but then he heard Maria lighting a match. She had recently taken up smoking again. Her voice was lower and less agitated when she spoke again.

"I am thinking now of a small institute for creativity studies located somewhere near Harvard Square, I believe. There is some good work being done there and it is funded by some very rich people in Boston. You must go to this place. They are searching for an acting director, someone like you who will carry forward our very important work in research and the practice of psychoanalysis. Immediately I will contact them. They know me so very well."

Several days later, he received an offer to be the director of the Institute for Creativity Studies. He was promised two post doc research assistants, an office where he could practice psychoanalysis, and an administrative assistant.

He was relieved and excited at once. Though in recent months he had heard nothing from Arthur about Harvard, he felt certain that Plunkett would read his most recent article published in *Psychology Today*. Beginning with an analysis of Leonardo da Vinci, he was able to connect Jungian theory of archetypes with the Freudian view of creative narcissism. Fame was just around the corner; he felt it in his bones.

When a weary Catherine, three months pregnant with Roger, finally arrived in California after her harrowing drive from Mexico, John greeted her with the happy news.

"We'll be going back to Cambridge, Catherine," he said exultantly, "back to our roots. I'll be practicing psychotherapy and running an institute that studies creativity as well."

She accepted the news without comment and that night, John insisted on making love despite her protests of exhaustion. He had been without a woman for too long; she was his wife, after all.

The next day, Catherine suffered from chills and fever and remained in bed for a week before she was able to speak to him about her journey.

ELEVEN

"It was a nightmare, John. I was alone, driving thousands of miles to the border, the car packed to the ceiling. The maps made no sense, my eyes glazed over."

"I'm sorry, Catherine. I understand what you went through."

"No, you don't! You have no idea how many times I was lost driving over the mountains, crisscrossing that terrible lunar landscape!"

Poor Catherine, he thought to himself, she had never learned to read a map and she was easily distracted. Alone in the car, listening to those sentimental Mexican love songs on the radio all day long most certainly clouded her judgment. Songs of longing and loss. Obviously, she couldn't focus on where she was going.

"There were vast stretches of empty country with marauding bandits lurking in the underbrush, John. I was scared, so scared."

"You're safe, now, darling." he said, taking her hand.

"And the heat! Northern Mexico is suffocating this time of year and the air is full of dust. My throat felt like sandpaper because I had to keep the windows open."

"I know."

"You should have put in an air conditioner, John. Why didn't you?"

"We didn't need one in Mexico City or Cuernavaca. It never gets that hot."

"It was so hard! I should have sold the car, taken a plane out of the country. I'm pregnant, John! You have no idea what I went through! My body ached so much, cramped up in that driver's seat. Our baby will probably be born with a crushed head!"

"Babies in the womb are surprisingly hardy, Catherine. Everything's going to be fine."

"How can you talk like that! Where is your compassion?"

"Forgive me, Catherine. I completely understand you've been through a difficult time."

"Yes, I have."

"But what's also bothering you, my darling, is that you're conflicted about the pregnancy. It's put an end to your illusions of having a part-time dance career."

"Illusions? But Alexander von Swain invited me to tour the country with his dance troupe!"

"He's a mediocre dancer, Catherine. His career has been over for a long time, now. The man must be sixty, at least. But I'm really sorry we had to leave Mexico at this point in our lives. As a mother, you'd have been put on a pedestal, worshiped like the Virgin Mary. Motherhood is venerated there."

"Not like here."

"Let's be positive, Catherine. The worst is over and we need to look ahead, now."

Catherine said nothing. He could feel her deep resentment.

"You were a fool to believe that the Mexican psychoanalytic elite would prescribe peyote to their patients!" she suddenly cried out. "How could you be so stupid? You put them in the same category as the poor, illiterate Indians! Those people have all been to the best schools, they live in fabulous houses with servants at their beck and call. Their choice of medication is obviously dictated by the American drug companies, you know that. They were insulted by the idea of using an Indian drug. You're the Ugly American, John! What did you think you were doing? You've destroyed our happiness!"

Showing no scars from his mother's unhappy journey up from Mexico, their son, Roger, was born healthy and hearty at the end of that year. But Catherine suffered from postpartum depression that never entirely left her. John allowed for no further discussion of their Mexican trauma because she would never appreciate his effort to enlighten the Mexican analysts about the creative potential in their country.

Settling down in a modest house in Cambridge near Shady Hill School, John established himself in just a few years not only as a well respected director of the Institute for Creativity Studies, but also as an outstanding researcher and psychoanalyst. Besides offering a course on creativity at Harvard Summer School, he became a popular guest on local radio talk shows and TV.

But the marriage began to unravel. Resentful of John's growing fame, his long working hours and his evening meetings with colleagues at the Institute, Catherine complained he was neglecting her.

"You're late every night and I'm sitting in the kitchen waiting for you! The dinner's cold and the baby's asleep! What kind of a family life is that?"

"Catherine," he said patiently, "I understand your frustration but I have to work very hard. It's expected of me, I'm the director of the Institute. Remember how it was when you were a professional dancer?"

"How can I forget?" she sighed. "Total exhaustion."

"Well, it's the same for me right now and I'm doing all this for you and Roger so try to help me."

"Come off it, you know it isn't just about me and the baby!" she burst out. "It's about *you*, John! You're obsessed with your career; you're after fame and money. Admit it!"

"Sure, I want fame and money. So what? Anything wrong with that? Look, we're rising up in the world, we can finally afford some luxuries."

"Like what?"

"Like our new antique chairs and etchings of Boston Harbor in the 1880's. They're worth a lot of money."

"John, *you* chose those!" she cried. "I had nothing to do with it! You are so ego-driven, you never even asked me if I wanted those things! I guess we can fault your mother because from what you've told me, she never stopped worshipping you."

"Leave my mother out of this," John said sharply. "And despite my being 'ego-driven' as you call it, I'm a faithful husband and you don't seem to care. Have you noticed that fidelity doesn't count for much around here, Catherine?"

She shook her head.

"Think about it. Do you ever hear my colleagues praising their wives' beauty and mothering skills the way I do?"

"No," she said, looking away. She was momentarily stymied. He was so clever, this husband of hers. He knew exactly what to say to soften her up, get her off track.

At parties, John was the center of attention while Catherine languished in his shadow. His creativity research was the focus of conversation and many of the Cambridge professors and tech executives who were present felt they knew him because they watched him regularly on TV. They were eager to get tips on how best to access their own creativity and because they were distinguished members of the Cambridge community, he willingly obliged.

John took note of his wife's resentment of his popularity and traced its root to her lack of self-esteem.

"Catherine, I'm going to be blunt here. It's pretty obvious you're miserable when I take center stage at parties. You become envious and that's not good. If you work on developing your self-esteem, you won't be envious anymore."

She glared at him. "I'm envious of you? You have to be joking. Besides, what's envy and self-esteem got to do with it, any-way? You know my opinion of those intellectual sycophants who pick your brain at parties. They're rude and snobbish and because I don't have a Ph.D., I don't even exist for them."

"Of course you exist for them. You're a beautiful woman."

"Not anymore. I'm fat and ugly."

"Maybe you've put on a few pounds, but you're still very pretty."

"Not pretty enough for you to want to make love to me," she countered.

"It doesn't have to be like that, darling, and you know it," John insisted. "There are two sides to this issue and we need to talk."

"Please, not now."

"Okay, then let's get back to your problem with envy."

"Do we have to? I have a headache."

"Forget the headache; this conversation is important." He moved closer to her. "You're envious of my success, Catherine," he said flatly.

She was suddenly filled with rage. How dare he! "You are so totally wrong!"

John said, "You're in denial if you don't recognize your problem with envy."

Who was he to lecture her about envy? Wasn't he envious of every single rich friend they had?

"It would be helpful, Catherine, if you could listen to me for a minute."

"Okay." It was easier to go along with him than to argue.

"Unlike any of the other seven deadly sins, envy elicits no satisfaction, even in its early stages," he intoned. "It's like a cancer, it bores deep into the soul and if you want to be free of it, you'll have to rediscover your creative potential." He paused expectantly.

"*My* creative potential? Oh, my god." She laughed derisively.

He plunged ahead. "Don't beat up on yourself. You wrote stories in high school, right?"

"Right."

"You can get back to writing. It's never too late." He spoke slowly and clearly as though she was a recalcitrant child.

Maybe he was on to something, she thought. Taking up writing again just might make her feel better. Later that week, she signed up for writing courses and set up a small area for her books and papers in the back of the kitchen. When Roger was in school, she attended class, and at home, she worked tirelessly on crafting essays and stories.

She became a popular member of a woman's literary salon with established female writers who mentored younger talent, and when two of her stories were accepted by an obscure literary journal, John was relieved. She'd be easier to live with, she wouldn't be so bitter and envious. Later in the year when she won the prestigious Fletcher Prize for a first-published short story, John was astonished. Her stories were amateurish, her writing style awkward. The judges were not interested in content or style; that was obvious. But what were they interested in? Who were these judges? Did Catherine know them?

As she became more successful, tensions grew worse between them and she decided that their love no longer existed, if it ever had. When rumors reached her that John was keeping company with other women, she felt finally free of him.

One day in Harvard Square, she ran into a member of her women's group, an English professor on sabbatical from Bennington College who was one of her staunchest supporters. An instructorship in creative writing was opening up at the college, she told her. Was Catherine interested? If so, she would like to recom-mend her for the job.

That night, she announced to John that she had decided to accept the offer.

"But you've had no teaching experience, no resume, Cather-ine," he said. "Face it, you're a fledgling writer. And teaching at Bennington means you'll be away most of the time. Have you thought about what will happen to our marriage?"

"I have." She gave him a stony look.

"Well?"

"We'll be leading separate lives, I guess," she said.

"Have you considered the effect on our son?"

"I have."

"Children want their parents together, Catherine."

"I'm aware of that, John," she said coldly. "You don't have to tell me."

"Let's not get defensive here, but I suspect that your Ben-nington mentor is one of those feminists who likes to break up marriages."

"You don't even know her, John; she's not like that."

"Well, good, but she probably thinks marriage inhibits a woman's creativity. Frankly, Catherine, you've never been more creative than you are right now."

"Well, I have something to tell you, John, because you're too dense to have figured it out for yourself. I'm creative *despite* be-ing in a bad marriage! And you're the big creativity guru so you should know how much more creative I could be once I'm free of you! Our relationship isn't working and I want a divorce!"

"A divorce? You want a divorce?" He was stunned. All these past months when he was helping to strengthen her self-esteem she had been planning to leave. How could he have missed the hostility he was hearing now? How blind he had been to the depths of her anger! That feminist gang she hung out with had certainly done their dirty work. They'd brainwashed her into thinking herself the victim of an egomaniacal husband. And now she was filing for divorce.

"What about Roger, Catherine? What about our boy? What's your plan for him?"

"I'll take him up to Bennington with me. He'll be fine because I'll be happy and creative. I'm not right for this place, you know that, John. I'm sorry, but that's the truth. And you can have Roger every vacation."

"I don't like the idea of being separated from him. It's going to be very difficult."

"I understand," Catherine said. "You're a great father."

"My role in his life is absolutely critical, you know how much I missed not having a father when I was growing up. I'll pay all his travel expenses because I want him with me holidays as well as summer vacations and long weekends."

"You can have him whenever you want," she said with an exasperated sigh.

He'd fight for his son but not for her, John was thinking. He wouldn't plead with her to stay because she wasn't worth fighting for. What did she bring to the marriage, anyway? A wonderful son, and that was it. He was shaken by the fact that she actually disliked him though her envy should have warned him. She did not wish him well and her dislike of his friends and her hostile attitude were wearing him down. For months, now, she no longer aroused his sexual interest and a number of attractive women were making themselves available to him already.

He wouldn't miss her; she'd become a noose around his neck and he looked forward to the divorce.

Let her go out into the world of small-time academia and discover for herself how they were just as full of crap as Cambridge intellectuals! He started laughing loudly, and Catherine's eyes grew wide. What was happening to her husband? She'd never seen him out of control like this! She asked him what was so funny but he couldn't stop laughing, and he waved her angrily away, escaping finally into his study.

After Catherine and Roger had departed, John moved into a small house on a back street near Harvard Square where he led a quiet, scholarly existence which came to a dramatic end when Erika burst in on him that late wintry night in December.

Her recklessness sent him reeling. An affair between analyst and patient? Marriage? If he accepted her offer, he was breaking the rules of professional ethics. He was committing a social crime.

It briefly occurred to him that this extraordinary happening might be the dynamic of transference in the analytic relationship, masquerading as love. Early on in the therapy he had pointed out this phenomenon to Erika, then did not explore it further because she might discover she was not in love with him after all. What if she had concluded that idealizing him had nothing to do with his own personal qualities and everything to do with someone from the past, most likely her father? Of course, it wouldn't be the crooked, abusive father she hated, but the caring, protective side of him she loved. Then once cured of her neurosis, she would have ended the therapy and been lost to him forever.

Her smoldering naked body suffused him with desire. For weeks now, he had been aware of the intense mutual attraction building up between them but he did not analyze it. He was falling in love himself. This exquisitely beautiful woman who so appreciated his work, the heiress to an enormous fortune, was intended by God for him alone and that night on his doorstep when she dropped her coat, she was daring him to break the rules.

They were different from ordinary people; rules did not apply to them. They were destined to be together and she had been the first to know it.

PART III
ONE

Bishop Andrew Cope, an admired figure throughout the Episcopal diocese of Massachusetts, agreed to marry John and Erika in the Emmanuel Church chapel, a graceful gothic construction reminiscent of Sainte Chapelle in Paris. A few doors down from the Ritz on Newbury Street, the church drew large crowds on Sunday mornings with Bach cantatas performed by students from the New England Conservatory of Music.

Recently their happy state of mind had been severely tested by a slew of vicious letters addressed to Erika from Catherine. In the spirit of sisterhood, she warned Erika that John was an egocentric monster and to always be on her guard. She recounted how despite her frequent bouts of depression, he had regularly forced sex on her without any concern for her delicate health.

John explained to Erika that these letters were delusional, caused by her envy and resentment of his newfound happiness.

His son, Roger, would not be able to attend the wedding. As the star player on his hockey team at his school in Vermont, the most important game of the season was scheduled that same day and he was expected to lead his team to victory. Immediately contacting Roger, John expressed his disappointment not to have him at the wedding, but emphasized the importance of standing by his team. Winning the hockey game came first, and when things settled down, he wanted his boy to visit for a long weekend. Roger agreed right away, he was eager to see his father.

Uncle Robert would be at the wedding. He had not yet met John and so far had refused any therapy with him but Erika was convinced that eventually he would agree to see him. Marsha, John's office manager, would also be coming to the wedding.

Up to the very day of the nuptials, Marsha couldn't believe Dr. Starr was actually going through with his plans to marry Erika Giuliani. She was gorgeous, of course, and very, very rich she'd heard, but there was something that concerned her in particular: the woman was, in fact, his patient, and wasn't this marriage against the ethics code of the American Psychological Association?

When she brought up this concern with Dr. Starr, he immediately discounted it.

"It's actually quite simple, Marsha. Erika Giuliani's treatment has not been in any real sense a deep analysis. We've mainly worked on confronting her troubled past as a way of releasing her innate creativity. It's been more coaching than therapy and in the process of our journey, we fell in love."

Maybe Dr. Starr believed as Erika's husband he could help her more because as lovers, they would know each other intimately. Marsha recalled being shocked to learn how many of the early famous German and Viennese analysts slept with their female patients. Some of them actually believed it helped these troubled women.

What she would wear to the wedding had become an issue because she had recently grown a bit heavier; nothing seemed to fit her. She finally chose her green velvet pants and a knee-length black velvet jacket that covered the extra pounds. Around her neck she wore a matching green silk scarf that showed a hint of cleavage and in the mirror at home, she'd been pleased with what she saw. Her makeup was light and subtle, just right for a late afternoon wedding and her sparkling green eye shadow set off her large brown eyes. The crimson lip liner emphasized the soft contours of her lips. So kissable, she thought, but so what? There was no man in sight.

As Marsha emerged from the warmth of the subway, she was greeted by a blast of cold air; New England weather was frigid through March, but in just a few minutes she'd be at the church, just a few doors down from the Ritz Carlton. It saddened her that this hotel was soon to be sold. She had often visited the tea salon upstairs, sipping her tea and enjoying the warm scones, never tiring of the view down the hall of the empty dining room that looked out on the Boston Commons. Not yet open for dinner, its tables were laid out with fresh white linen, sparkling place settings, and the trademark Ritz cobalt blue goblets. A slim crystal vase holding a single pink rose stood at the center of each table. An exquisite touch.

When she arrived at the church, guests were already climbing up the long set of steps to the chapel. Ushered into her pew several rows back from the nave of the church, she settled down to listen to the muted strains of a Bach prelude. A strikingly handsome man in a dark suit was being wheeled to the front pew and despite his pale face and grey hair, Marsha noted his resemblance to Erika. Was this the uncle who became CEO of the family company? She'd heard all about him from Erika, that he'd once been a photojournalist for National Geographic and that his career ended when he crashed his plane over Tuckerman's Ravine.

The organ was now opening up to full power with the stanzas of the wedding march and the guests rose as Erika walked down the aisle on the arm of Dr. Starr's friend, Arthur Watts. She wore a crown of miniature white roses in her dark blond hair, and her loosely cut cream-colored chiffon dress fell just below her knees. Her luminous beauty reminded Marsha of a Botticelli painting. When she approached Dr. Starr who was dressed in striped grey pants and a morning coat, he gently took her hand. Marsha sighed with satisfaction. Two beautiful people and so much in love!

Wearing heavy brocaded robes of crimson and white, the bishop invited the congregation to join him in prayer. Marsha hesitated to join in; as a secular Jew, she was uneasy with all religious ritual and only enjoyed celebrating her Jewish culture. Hadn't Freud pointed out that God was a father figure created by man?

A reception followed next door at the Ritz where there would be dining and dancing. When Marsha arrived, a smattering of guests was milling around awaiting the bridal pair. She sat down at an empty table while the band assembled across the room and began to play softly. A few couples danced. The man in the wheelchair appeared at the entrance of the room and after glancing around, turned and spoke to the young man pushing his chair. He was then wheeled across the floor to the table where Marsha sat alone.

"Do you mind if I join you?" he asked politely.

"Not at all, please do," Marsha said with a bright smile.

"Thanks, Matt, you can go now."

"When shall I be back for you, Sir?"

"I'll call you."

"Very good, Sir."

Matt walked quickly away and Marsha and the man in the wheelchair sat silently together, watching the dancing couples. He seemed not to notice her and she studied his elegant profile, so like a Roman emperor sculpted in marble. His features were finely chiseled, his gray hair closely cropped. Though his expression was somber, his choice of a bright red tie suggested a lighter side to his character. Marsha wished he would turn in her direction, he seemed so remote. From what Erika had told her, his life was solitary, his friendships few. She groped for words, then plunged ahead.

"My name is Marsha Romano," she said. "Are you Erika's uncle?"

Startled, he looked directly at her. "How did you know?" She could feel his dark eyes taking her in.

"I work for her husband." Her voice sounded like it belonged to someone else.

"Her husband? You mean Dr. Starr?" He frowned slightly. "Yes."

He said nothing, but continued to fix her with his intense gaze. He seemed to be searching for an answer to a question he did not want to ask.

"I don't know Dr. Starr." He paused, then leaned forward in his chair. "You know him well?"

"I guess you could say that. He's quite a brilliant man."

"You think him brilliant?"

"Oh, yes. And kind. He's been very good to me."

"Indeed. That's nice to hear. I wouldn't have guessed." Marsha was taken aback. How could he not know of Dr. Starr's reputation for kindness and goodness, his effort to help the emotionally disturbed realize their creative potential and peace of mind?

"You haven't told me your name," Marsha said. She was pushing the boundaries, initiating an intimacy he seemed not ready to give her.

"Robert Giuliani. Sorry." He held out his hand. His grip was surprisingly firm. "I'm not much out in society so sometimes I'm a bit awkward with people." For the first time, he smiled. Marsha was so moved that her eyes welled up with tears. She hoped he hadn't seen.

"Erika has mentioned you to me. I'm sure it means a lot to her that you're here," she said.

"Yes, we're very close. Lately, though, I haven't seen her much. I've been very busy with the family business."

"And Erika's been getting ready."

"Getting ready?"

"For the wedding!"

"Oh, yes, the wedding," he said absently. They sat without speaking for a time.

"May I ask you something?" he suddenly said, leaning closer.

"Yes?" She was somewhat unsettled; he was so direct.

"Do you think he's the right man for my niece? You work for him. What's your view?"

"Well, I don't know if I can answer that. I'm outside the loop, if that makes any sense."

"It does, and the question was unfair. Please forgive me." He turned away to look across the ballroom floor at the dancing couples. The bride and bridegroom had still not appeared. "You probably want to dance," he said quickly. "Don't hesitate because of me."

"Oh, no, really, I'm fine right here," Marsha said with a cheerful smile, and just then, a waiter came around and offered them champagne.

Erika and John had lingered at the church to thank the Bishop for a wedding ceremony that exceeded their expectations in its beauty and simplicity. Then they complimented the organist for his fine performance. When they finally arrived at the Ritz, the guests applauded and Erika whispered in John's ear. "I can't believe you belong to me! You're mine, all mine!"

"I'm yours forever and ever," John said thickly, nibbling the back of her neck and drawing her into a passionate embrace before the cheering crowd. Moments later, waving and smiling, they joined the others on the dance floor.

When Erika caught sight of Uncle Robert, she stopped dancing and pulled John over to meet him.

"Uncle Robert," Erika cried, her eyes sparkling, "I'm so happy you came!"

"Congratulations to you both," he said quietly.

"Delighted to meet you," John said, shaking his hand. "I've heard so much about you from Erika. It's great you were able to come today. You've met my assistant, Marsha Romano?"

"An unexpected pleasure," Robert said, his face lighting up.

Erika gave them both a brilliant smile. "I'm so glad you two met," she said, bending down to kiss Uncle Robert. "Thank you for coming, darling. It means so much to have you here." Moving away, her hand lightly touched Marsha's shoulder.

"Enjoy the evening," John called back to them as he led Erika to the center of the dance floor. She was radiant, the beautiful fairy princess with her handsome prince.

"I hope she'll be happy. She deserves it," Robert said, his eyes following them as they danced alone after the other dancers drifted away to watch them. "The perfect couple, wouldn't you say?" he observed without looking at Marsha, a thin smile on his lips.

TWO

Erika and John temporarily rented a large Tudor house with a lovely terrace on Carlton Street close to downtown Boston. Built in 1923 by a professor at Harvard Medical School, the property had a spectacular rose garden and stately elm trees. But John had his eye on a house that was up for sale at eight million. Located on nine acres in the more exclusive Chestnut Hill area near the Longwood Cricket Club, it reminded him of the great houses of his mother's society friends in Washington where as a little boy he was never invited to their children's birthday parties. Until he went to Andover, he was always seen as a public school boy who could not afford to attend a private school like Beauvoir or Potomac. As Di Brioni put it so aptly, he was "a poor little boy out in the street staring in the window of the big house to watch the rich children opening their presents on Christmas day."

Well, now everything had changed. Married to Erika, lack of money would never be an issue again and he could live in a grand house and enjoy what the rich took for granted. As a man of property he would take his rightful place in society as his mother had expected him to do. He would give his son, Roger, all the things he himself was denied and once the boy had a taste of his father's new-found wealth, he would never agree to return to Catherine's shabby little house in Vermont and its dark, claustrophobic disorder.

Unprepared for Erika's insistence on consulting her financial advisors before buying the Chestnut Hill property, John sharply questioned her motives.

"Why this unhealthy dependence on the so-called experts?"

"Is it unhealthy? Oh, I hope not, darling! I've just always assumed these people know a lot more than I do."

"Are they supposed to tell us whether or not to buy this particular property? That should be our own decision. Aren't we adults?"

"Well, I just thought we needed their expertise. Is that a problem?"

"Well, maybe you don't know I have a pretty good understanding of today's market forces," John said. "In fact, if I took over managing your money it would simplify everything." He waited for her response but she said nothing. "This property is an excellent investment, Erika," he said. He was quite serious and she looked surprised.

"John," she said firmly, "your expertise is in the field of creativity and psychology. Just think what would have happened to me if I hadn't come to you; I'd be at the bottom of the Charles River!"

"Listen to what I'm trying to tell you, Erika. There's a message to their madness. Your financial advisors *want* you dependent on them so you're afraid to make any decisions on your own." He spoke with convincing authority.

"You're probably right about that, but they've been spending all their professional lives managing money, John. They can't do what you do, darling; they won't make a difference in the world like you will, but they're experts in the world of finance so why not let them help us?"

It was obvious she wasn't about to change her mind so he dropped the matter. Later, eating supper out on the terrace in the pale evening light of early spring, he noticed for the first time the appearance of permanent control lines between her eyebrows, casting a shadow over the rare and perfect beauty of her face.

He would not give up; the house and grounds must be his and he brought up the subject at every opportunity, weakening Erika's resistance. There would be no interior decorators he told her. Their mutual on-going creative project would be deciding for themselves how to decorate the rooms.

When Erika finally saw the massive brick house at the end of the oak-lined driveway, she recognized it at once as the haunted house that was next door to the home of Emily Stuart, a childhood friend.

"Emily's Irish nanny loved to scare us," Erika said. "She told us a ghost lived here. We weren't allowed to climb over the wall because the ghost would grab us and take us away!"

Laughing, John swung his arm around Erika's shoulder and strode with her across the grounds. "You don't have to be frightened anymore, darling, because I am here to protect you from the ghost!" He hugged her briefly, then motioned towards the house. "Isn't it incredible?"

"The house?"

"What else?"

"I hate it!"

"You're joking, of course, because this house is so right for us, Erika."

"The house is ugly, John! Can't you see that?"

"Nonsense! Hey, what's going on with you?" He stared at her with concern. "I'm hearing a lot of anger from you."

"I don't want to buy the house, John. You're stressing me out."

"Why can't you open your eyes and see the beauty of this house?"

"Tell me what you like so much about it and maybe I'll see it through *your* eyes."

He directed her closer to the building. "First of all, it's a fascinating mix of ancient and traditional styles here. Roman and Greek, French, English."

"Well, maybe we can find a smaller house that has the same mix of styles. Remember, I grew up in a huge place like this so it's not exactly my dream house."

"I understand, but we can change the façade, add some windows and skylights. You'll love it, then."

114

"It's too big, John."

"Well, let's explore the size issue. It's too big? Have you forgotten you're reinventing yourself? All your feelings from childhood of being insignificant won't exist once you buy the house. "

"How can you say that?"

"Because you'll own this space, you'll learn to dominate it, too."

"'Dominate it'?"

"Absolutely."

"Of course we'll need a full staff," he added.

"'A full staff'?"

"There's no way you and I can take care of this place alone, Erika. Besides, there's also the baby issue."

"What?"

"The time will soon come when we'll need a nursery."

"A nursery? You're serious, John?"

"Do I have to repeat myself?"

Despite the chill of the day, Erika threw off her coat and flung her arms around his neck. "Oh, John, I love you!"

He was moved by her happiness. Maybe he would agree eventually to have a child though right now he was merely placating her. Gently, he pulled away. "Now let's try to stay focused on the house, my love. Take a look at the classical pillars and long French windows. Does this building remind you of anything?"

"No," she laughed, "just the ghost."

"Be serious, darling. What we are actually looking at is a perfect replica of a late nineteenth century home of the very rich."

"How can you tell?"

"Because I have studied the subject," he said dryly. "Architecture has always been an interest of mine. And I feel strongly that this kind of house and all the land around it will trigger our creativity juices."

"I like the sound of that!"

"See that slope over there? We'll get rid of the weeds and create a sea of crocuses in spring. Tulips and daffodils, too. Remember Wordsworth? 'A host of golden daffodils, fluttering and dancing in the breeze...' We'll have azaleas, lilacs, peonies, and lots more."

"And in the fall?"

"Chrysanthemums, of course, hundreds of them, golden brown, orange, bright yellow. And purple asters, different flowers that reflect the flux and flow of the seasons."

"And roses? Let's have roses!"

"Not in the fall and winter, naturally, but all the rest of the year they'll bloom. We'll build a small, walled garden to cultivate them for the house. You know, the blossoms are best when cut from the stems, their fragrance is sweeter and they last longer than outdoors."

"Is that true? What a shame the winter has to come!"

"Not entirely, because we'll plant holly bushes that will sprout red berries," John smiled. "A burst of crimson on the darkest day of the year!"

"You make it sound so romantic. Always the poet."

"It's about creating beauty, darling, and you and I can make it happen!" Sweeping her up in his arms, he kissed her until she was breathless. "Now shall we go inside the house?"

"Yes!" She would never refuse him anything when he kissed her like that.

The rooms (John counted thirty when he was shown the house for the first time) were generous in size, with ten-foot ceilings and elegantly carved moldings. The living room, with French doors facing the back gardens, extended the full length of the house. Nearly all the six bedrooms on the second floor had carved marble fireplaces in working order. Four smaller bedrooms on the top floor led to the servants' wing at the back of the house. All the bathrooms on the second floor had showers as well as sinks, bathtubs of the finest porcelain, and toilets set apart by a glass partition.

With its tall, wide bookcases, long French windows and a window seat upholstered in dark red velvet, the library was an invitation for quiet reading on rainy afternoons. John could imagine himself as a small boy curled up by the window, reading *Little Lord Fauntleroy*.

In the basement, he would design a study for himself with a sleek mahogany desk and chair set, filing cabinets, tables outfitted with the latest iMacs and HP printers. There would be an entertainment hall with a giant screen for movies and a bar with leather chairs and sofas. This modern Mecca would present a dramatic contrast to the classical decors upstairs.

"We'll need a cook, at least two maids, a houseman, maybe. Certainly, half a dozen gardeners. I'll supervise them but we'll want George."

"George Brewster?"

"Best landscape gardener in the country. He won those awards for the Cabot gardens in Dublin; you know all about that."

"Yes, he's very famous."

"I'll add a small gazebo and Japanese viewing pool to the garden so we can practice meditation."

"Fantastic! A spiritual retreat!"

John did not mention their social life, it was not the right moment, but he had big plans. No more chicken a la king and lamb stew in the scruffy homes of Cambridge's impoverished intelligentsia. They would give dinners for the city elite in the larger of the two dining rooms, organize weekend parties at the Brookline Country Club. And most important, he would invite the Harvard bigwigs to their events, get Arthur Watts to renew his campaign to bring him into the psychology department. He couldn't sit around anymore waiting for miracles to happen. He would have to be proactive and make them happen himself.

THREE

John returned often to visit the Chestnut Hill estate, sometimes with Erika but usually alone. He imagined himself waking in the early hours of a winter's morning to light the fire in the master bedroom. Erika, pale and dreamy, would reach out for him to make love to her again. Recently her sexual appetite had become nearly insatiable; she was ready for him at any time of day or night. He could never have imagined a woman whose erotic tension so closely matched his own. They were spending hours together in mutual ravishment.

One night as they lay sated from lovemaking, he said, "I want to make love to you in our own room, in our new house."

"That mausoleum?" Erika said, running her nails across his cheeks.

"Erika, you're scratching me!" Abruptly, he pushed her away.

"I'm sorry."

"You're still worried about the size of the house and the money, aren't you? You're scared. You've got a huge fortune but you won't let go and enjoy it."

"Who says I won't? I just might surprise you."

"Good, because there's another matter I need to discuss with you."

"What's that?" she said, burrowing her face in his shoulder.

"Have you ever thought what would happen if one of us dies?"

"Oh, John, why are you talking about death?" Sitting up, her eyes were bright with tears.

"Well, sometimes things happen and we have to be prepared, my darling. If I should die, everything I have will go to you and Roger. It's not much, I admit. Making a lot of money has never been a priority of mine, but what little there is will be for you and him."

"Roger should keep it all. I'd never take your money, John. I don't need it."

"No, of course you don't, but I want you to have it anyway. However, if something happened to you, would you leave your money to me?"

"Why are you asking these questions? Do you have some kind of a premonition?"

"No, of course not," John said smoothly, "but I'd like an answer to my question."

"What are you getting at?" Her voice was shaking; what did he want her to say?

"Things happen, tragic things. Remember Frank? We have to be prepared, Erika. What are your plans for me?"

"My money would be yours, naturally."

"You've never told me that before."

"You're my husband; I wouldn't have it any other way."

"Are you able to handle that? Leaving all your money to me?"

"How could you think anything else? John, you're being so morbid! We're still young, our whole future is in front of us! Why are you acting so strange? Why are you bringing this up now?"

"I'm not in your will, am I?" he said.

"I don't know, I haven't even thought about it!" If anything happened to him her whole world would collapse. He was life itself! But she realized suddenly she'd forgotten to change her will. She'd been selfish and blind.

"It'll be taken care of right away, you'll see," she said quickly. "I'll see to it that you get everything." Cuddling up close to him, she said, softly "Let's not talk about money any more, darling. I have something much more important to discuss."

"Like what?"

"Like creating something together, you and I."

"Yes, the house will be a showcase that stirs the imagination!"

"No, John, not the house. I'm talking about the baby!"

"The baby?"

"Yes, you promised we could start a family! Don't you remember? A little John Starr, that's what we'll make!" Rubbing her body up against him, she cried out, "Oh, John, don't say no! Make it happen now!"

His momentary arousal vanished in a surge of anger at himself. It was his fault; he shouldn't have given her any encouragement. Now she wouldn't stop pestering him about a kid. A baby would take over their lives; she'd focus entirely on the child as Catherine had done and like her, come to resent the importance of his work. But he needed to be careful; her trauma at losing the baby after Frank's death haunted her. He sighed deeply. She was always armed with that lethal weapon, her psychological fragility.

"Darling, we'll create a family when the time is ripe," he declared.

Turning away from him, Erika buried her face in the pillow. "Did you hear me, sweetheart?"

Slowly, she raised her head. "'When the time is ripe'? What's that supposed to mean?"

She was pushing him too hard. Closing his eyes, he fell back against the pillow and tried not to listen, but her voice was shrill and filled the air.

"If I buy this ugly house you want so much," she was saying angrily, "then we can start a family because we'll have plenty of room for the children, right? You said so yourself, John."

"Did I?" he mumbled.

"Yes, you did. So it's settled!"

Drawing the covers up over his ears, he feigned sleep, and bending down, Erika kissed him gently on the cheek and blew out the jasmine-scented candle on the bedside table. Then she settled happily down beside him. She had won.

FOUR

"Growing up you were running and hiding," John told Erika. "A beautiful girl who was lost."

"Until I met you, darling." Erika said, sitting down close to him on the living room sofa.

Smiling, he kissed her hand. "Darling, when you enter a room, all heads turn."

"I don't care about that," she said. "You're the only one I want looking at me."

"Because you know how much I love you and appreciate you. You're my very own work of art and I'm a very lucky guy." He pulled her into his arms and kissed her hungrily. "But we need to talk about your attitude towards money, darling, your inability to enjoy your fortune," he said, his expression growing serious.

"'Money dirties the mind and heart as well as the hands,'" she said, proud of being able to remember the exact quote.

"Who wrote that?"

"I don't recall but I think Mr. Healy, my teacher in high school, taught it to us."

John gave a short laugh. "Of course, only a child of privilege could talk down the value of money as you are doing. You've never experienced the kind of pain that comes with growing up poor so how can you understand that having money can be a precious gift? For me, it's an extraordinary stroke of luck that offers limitless opportunities for creativity so I'm not going to pretend I'm sorry you're rich."

Erika flushed. "Darling, I've been insensitive again." Setting down her glass of wine, she snuggled closer to him on the sofa.

"Money can save people who otherwise would never flower, Erika," John said, stretching out his long legs and staring up at the ceiling. "And if you like, we can figure out where some of your fortune might be directed so you feel better about having it. There are many worthy causes, though a little more funding for my institute would be most welcome, I can tell you. There's Harvard, too. Arthur Watts is working on getting me in there and if we play the game right, we'll need your help."

"Game?" she murmured.

"I'm talking about landing a professorship at Harvard. I've mentioned the idea to you a number of times."

"I don't recall you ever talking about it, darling."

"Because you weren't listening," he said sharply.

"I'm listening now. You're saying a contribution from me would get you a professorship in the psychology department?"

"It might help. If it's large enough, we could even include a proposal to develop a world-famous institute of creativity at Harvard. What do you think?"

"I like that: a creativity institute at Harvard. But do you really want something so academic, dealing with all those professors? You're a media star, John, and your research on creativity is known around the world. Harvard should be begging you to come! Anyway, why do we need to give money to them? Harvard's endowment is bigger than the treasuries of most countries!"

"Money talks."

"That's what my father used to say, and if it's something you really want, I guess I could help. I'm not totally sold on the idea, but…"

She sat very still and he kissed her again, this time with more passion.

"That was nice," she giggled, "Mr. John Starr, Dr. Starr, Dr. John Starr, Professor Starr, Mr. Professor of Creativity at Harvard! Wow!" Flinging her arms around his neck, she said, "You can have all the money you want! How's that?"

"Sounds good to me!" He sprang to his feet. "We have to do this thing right," he cautioned. "The contribution can't be too large or we'll look like we're buying them off. But not too small, either, and we'll have to include key members of the psychology department at our dinner parties. It's called 'greasing the wheel'."

"Yes, my father used that expression, too, and put it into practice very successfully. I wasn't aware that you and he thought along the same lines," she said archly.

"Erika, your father doesn't belong in this conversation. We're talking about strategy here. There are certain moves you have to make in life so dreams become reality."

"I know just what moves will make my dream comes true," Erika said softly.

"Like what?"

"Like making love to you, Professor Starr."

"Sure thing," John said, pulling her against him and kissing her long and hard.

"And when it's time for our little John Starr the Second to come into this world, you'll be happier than you've ever been in your whole life because he'll be exactly like you!"

"Oh, you think I'm such a narcissist that I need a little copy of myself?" He gave a hearty laugh and his blue eyes danced with merriment. "You're probably on to something, darling. Very insightful. You're getting smart, married to me," he chuckled. "Hey, we can't forget the house, that's part of the deal, you know." He embraced her again.

"I haven't forgotten," she murmured. "Hmm, nice," she said, her voice growing husky.

"And we've already discussed hiring a full staff." He kissed her neck and earlobes as she leaned back against the sofa cushions.

"Can I cope?" Their bodies were moving together.

"You're a brilliant, sexy woman and in our new house you'll discover your authentic self."

"And what will that authentic self look like?"

"The creative woman who happens to be John Starr's gorgeous wife!"

Over breakfast the next morning, John announced he was taking the Prendergast paintings out of storage for their new house.

"They'll be perfect in the living room, Erika. All that wall space. Your Uncle Robert will be happy that his wedding present will finally see the light of day."

"He'll never be happy, I'm afraid, but did you notice at the wedding how pleased he was to meet you?"

"You think so?" The man seemed opaque, difficult to read.

"Oh, yes, your secretary, Marsha, was there with him, remember? They were sitting at the same table so she surely would have told him wonderful things about you. If only I could convince him to see you in therapy!"

John smiled briefly and after glancing at the sports pages of the *Boston Globe*, settled back in his chair to enjoy his morning coffee.

"Darling," Erika said, reaching across the table to take his hand. "My heart is so full! Do you really love me as much as I love you?"

"Didn't I tell you all night long that I love and adore you?" John looked deep into her eyes. How radiant she was, his picture perfect bride. He had never been as happy. "We're soul mates, my love, and that's why we're together. Nothing can ever drive us apart. You should know that by now."

FIVE

Construction workers came and went in the merciless summer heat, pounding and hammering, blasting and tearing apart whole sections of the front façade of that dark and dreary mansion. An endless parade of architects, landscape architects, contractors, stonemasons and fabric experts met with John and Erika. Drawings, plans, sketches, photos, and swatches were scrutinized and discarded or sometimes retained for yet another look.

"The heat and dust of the construction are getting to me, John. And why do we have to have so much punishing noise? I'm getting fiendish headaches," Erika said when the August humidity reached ninety percent. "I'm going to lie down."

"The creative process is never neat or clean, my love. Sorry about that, but it's true. Works of art, new ideas, breakthroughs, all emerge from chaos."

"Well, we've got plenty of chaos around here!"

"Understand we're at the beginning of something great, so keep the faith because it will HAPPEN! You'll see!" His eyes blazed and he kissed her with a special intensity.

Months later in the fall when the ground was frozen and the trees stood dark and bare against a slate-gray sky, Erika and John huddled together in the frigid cold, staring at the new exterior of the house.

"The brooding, sinister look has gone!" cried Erika.

"Yes, with the long symmetrical façade and oak door, and the tall arched windows on the first floor, we were able to get the light and airy look you wanted. On the top floor, we've now got skylights in every room so it's totally different."

"A complete transformation!"

"If you listen to me, darling, things usually work out."

She hugged him tightly. "You're a miracle man, that's what you are. I couldn't have imagined such a difference in that house. You took a total wreck and made it beautiful. That's what you've done for *me*, John. I was a total wreck, too, and you put me back together." She tossed her mane of shimmering hair. "Living in such an architectural jewel makes me a little scared, though."

"Don't worry," John said, pulling her into his arms. " You'd be amazed how quickly you get used to the good life!"

Once settled in, John proposed giving a party at the end of November. The social season was heating up, a good time to open their house up to the Boston and Cambridge elite. Erika was resistant at first to the idea of entertaining people she didn't know.

"I'm not a people person like you."

"Erika, I've told you a thousand times you are a gorgeous, brilliant woman." His blue eyes sparked. "Look, we're joining the community of Boston's best and brightest; we can't live in a cocoon forever."

"I like our cocoon."

He laughed. "Sure, so do I, but there's a world out there we need to be in touch with because some of these people are important to me."

"How will I know who they are?"

"I'll tell you. When I was at Harvard, I used to go to a lot of debutante parties so I know quite a number of these people. Your challenge will be to put them at ease. That's the hurdle to overcome Erika, and it will happen."

"What will happen?"

"You won't be afraid anymore."

"You'll help me, won't you?"

"Of course I will! What do you think? We've got a full staff now so all you have to do is say a few words and stand there looking beautiful."

"I guess I can manage that," she laughed.

In the beginning, Erika was nervous meeting their guests and when famous singers from the Boston Opera came to perform, she was especially awkward. John advised her to ignore her feelings of discomfort and concentrate on the singers. It seemed to work and the more parties they gave, the less apprehensive she became.

Before turning in at night after a party, she asked John to analyze her performance.

"Tonight you were great, Erika, just great. You see? Entertaining is like being an actor in a play. We speak our lines and move the plot along. There's a beginning, middle, and end. Tonight you stepped out of your safety zone and took on your hostess role. You're a terrific actor, my love. But I noticed Ben Friend, the real estate developer, put you on the defensive. Remember, *you* are the star!"

"How about the staff? Did I give them the right orders?"

"Absolutely, but you're a little too hesitant giving orders. You can be nice and assertive at the same time, informal but not too familiar. I learned this in Mexico where we had an endless procession of cooks and maids. Being an American, Catherine was on a perpetual guilt trip about having servants so she treated them like old friends. A mistake."

"A mistake?"

"They were totally confused. One minute she'd be ordering them around, the next, giving them clothes right off her back. Naturally, they took advantage of her. It was hopeless."

"She gave them her clothes? 'Right off her back'?"

"That's right. But let's not talk about her; she's irrelevant."

"No, she's not! She was once your wife!"

"Darling, let's change the subject, we're talking in circles. You were wonderful tonight and I'm very proud of you."

"Making small talk with people I hardly know isn't easy but tonight the party was actually interesting. I never supposed entertaining could be creative but maybe it is."

"If we do it right it can be very creative. And we'll matter, Erika."

"John, you already matter. Everyone wants a piece of you. Don't you know that by now?"

"It's beginning to sink in. But it's not just me. It's you, too. We make a great team."

At one of their parties later in the month, Erika was so swept away by the festive atmosphere that she flung her bare arms around John's neck in front of the crowd and kissed him long and hard on the mouth. Gently, he pulled away from her, drawing her aside.

"That was a lovely kiss, my precious, but did you smudge my collar?"

"Smudge your collar?"

"With your lipstick."

She looked quickly at his collar. "No, not a trace!" Her voice fell to a whisper. "I know you're touchy about your clothes, John, because you never had nice things when you were poor. But you're rich now so who cares about a little lipstick on your collar? Anyway, it's *my* lipstick and it's there because I love you!" Her eyes were shining; she had never looked more stunning.

"Erika, go easy on the champagne," he said. And gently taking her glass, he guided her back into the crowd.

"Talk to people, darling. Pretend interest."

"That's what I'm doing. I just stand there looking cute and smile." She giggled and he laughed loudly.

"Whatever you're doing, it's working, darling, so keep it up." With a reassuring squeeze of his hand, he went off to greet more guests.

Richard Billingsly, Dean of Arts and Sciences at Harvard, was standing a mere few feet away with members of the Boston Opera. A commanding figure who favored bow ties and wide-striped Brooks Brothers shirts, he wore his thick gray hair in a youthful crew cut, and when he noticed Erika, he immediately joined her.

"A lovely party, Mrs. Starr, and a welcome escape from the trials of academia, I can tell you."

"Thanks. We're happy you could come. You must be ready for some relaxation this weekend. I admire how well you manage all those competing factions at Harvard."

"Never boring," he said cheerfully. "Always a challenge."

"John has spoken very highly of you," she murmured.

"Has he? That's nice. Good man, your husband."

"He'd be happy to hear you say that." She smiled.

"I like what he's doing."

"You mean his creativity research?"

"Yes. We need more people like him. The field's wide open."

"He's very dedicated."

She would take the plunge. "He'd like to be on the faculty, you know, a professor in the psychology department."

"Oh? He'd be right for it."

"You think so?"

"Absolutely. Of course, my job doesn't give me any say over who gets hired and who doesn't. It's pretty frustrating some-times."

"I suppose."

"Frankly, it's a real problem for me when I see talented people like your husband because I'd like to bring them on board." He sighed heavily. "By the way, I've noticed tonight that John Starr has great people skills; I've been watching how he works the room. I'm sure I'm not telling you anything you don't already know."

"He has a real talent for communicating with all kinds of people, old and young alike."

"Mrs. Starr, may I ask you a serious question?" The dean inched closer.

"Yes?"

"Would your husband ever consider being director of admissions? He could help us here at Harvard to identify the more creative kids, not just the bright ones. I'm aware that he might feel it's a bit of a comedown since he's such a big creativity guru," he chuckled softly.

"Director of admissions?" Erika exclaimed. "Is this some kind of joke? What makes you think John Starr would ever consider such an offer, Dean Billingsley?" His face fell and she added with intensity, "Creativity research and his patients are his whole life!"

"I don't doubt it," said the Dean quickly, stirred by this beautiful woman's fierce defense of her husband's work.

She took a step away from him. "But he'll be interested in hearing about your offer, I'm sure. I'll tell him." Forcing a bright smile, she hurried off to greet the new arrivals.

"I saw you talking to Dean Billingsley," John said after all the guests had left.

"You saw us? Where were you?"

"Just across the room. You seemed to be having a lively conversation. Anything I should know?"

"No, nothing that would interest you, darling," Erika said.

Their Christmas event was held despite a December blizzard. A gigantic tree sparkling with white lights and embellished with gold and red Venetian glass dolls, dominated the foyer. A brilliant jeweled star glittered atop the tree.

The house blazed with the warmth and cheer of the holiday season and members of the Boston Opera chorus sang a short program of Christmas music. Goblets of hot cider and plates of Belgian chocolates were passed around and no one left until well after midnight.

As Erika and John were preparing for bed, he said with a smile, "Tonight, somebody told me we've been chosen by *Boston Life* as the most sought after couple in Boston society. How does that strike you, darling?"

"Well, it's really your doing, John. You know perfectly well I'd still be hiding away somewhere, tormented and terrified if it hadn't been for you."

"Give yourself some credit, Erika. You are naturally a radiant hostess and I think you're finally allowing yourself to enjoy the good things that life has to offer."

"Yes, and you're the very best thing that life has to offer," Erika said, stepping into his open arms.

SIX

On bright days, Erika gave small, intimate luncheons in the winter garden where the sun shone through the long, arched windows, setting off a shimmering world of dark green leaves and brilliant flowers. For large, black-tie dinners, they used the formal dining room. Thirty guests could be seated at the sixteenth century hand-carved Spanish table that ran the length of the room. John's favorite setting was the Audubon pattern of Tiffany china with Waterford goblets and a handsome Alencon lace tablecloth over a fuchsia undercover. When the tapered candles burned, the room was bathed in a warm, pink glow.

Tilly and Ben, the most experienced of their staff, presided over the service. All the maids wore black satin uniforms with starched white aprons and lace caps, and Ben, dressed in tuxedo and spotless white gloves, was in charge of the waiters. He took great pride in his role of greeting the guests at the front door and announcing them in the foyer. Over six-feet-two, he was an imposing figure, standing as erect as a drill sergeant.

A Starr dinner often began with soup. A favorite menu was clear consommé of wild duck served with Meursault. Belon oysters, broiled in the shell and served with a puree beurre blanc followed the soup. Afterwards would come a broiled rack of lamb with mint sauce, oven browned potatoes, creamed petits pois with champignons and braised leeks accompanied by a Margaux wine. To "clean-se the palate," a tiny portion of raspberry sorbet would be served followed by a simple salad of Boston lettuce. John's recipe for vinaigrette dressing made with walnut oil, lemon juice, sugar, a touch of Worcestershire sauce, a bit of garlic, and balsamic vinegar was always a hit with the guests, but when asked to divulge his culinary secrets, he refused. "It's all about creativity," he smiled. "It's about experimenting until you get it right. Everybody here is capable of inventing a great salad dressing so just go do it!"

For dessert were crepes filled with brandied apricots topped with vanilla ice cream. A plate of fruit and ripe cheeses (crema danica, brie, chevre, or Roquefort) rounded out the meal. Malmsey, sauterne, or marsala wine usually accompanied dessert, and Remy Martin brandy was offered after dinner along with coffee.

Their dinner guest list often read like a Who's Who of the intellectual and artistic elite. Among their stars were Martin Feldstein, economist; Reverend Peter Gomes, popular rector at Memorial Church; Mark Strand, the famous poet; Robert Coles, psychiatrist and author; Helena Stern, artist; Theda Skocpol, political theorist; Mike Maccoby, guru of leadership and author of fifteen books; Robert Drew, curator of the Boston Museum; Jonathan Weil, the world's expert on Hopper; Diana Zentay, author of six best selling novels; Izette Folger, artist and doyenne of Boston Society; Anne Berglof, science writer for the *Financial Times*, and Richard Tixier, journalist from *Le Monde,* both Nieman Fellows at Harvard; Nora Hathaway, screenwriter and energy expert; Max Francis, justice of the Massachusetts Supreme Court; Roberto Brady, Mexican American muralist; Blair Weille, composer, and Rimal Kacem visiting professor of political theory from the Sorbonne. John always made sure to seat Erika near their guests from France so she could be heard speaking her impeccable French.

Arthur Watts was one of the few guests who was not famous. He expected to be, of course; he had recently been promoted to associate professor of psychology and was presently at work on a book about strategies for uncovering innate creativity. His efforts to get John into the department continued unabated and he was confident that it was only a matter of time before Edwin Plunkett came around. He urged John to include Professor Plunkett in all his black tie events. Wining and dining the head of the psychology department should certainly help his case. Pierre Fouquet was also a favored guest though John and Arthur were under no illusion he could influence the department decisions anymore. Still, he was an impressive and revered figure in the Harvard community and John was proud to seat him at his table.

According to Arthur, Plunkett remained distracted and ill tempered after the death of his wife and made little effort to curb the nasty bickering around him. The feminists' voices were growing increasingly strident as issues of diversity and gay power dominated faculty meetings. Arthur, who prided himself on his keen observational skills, took note of Plunkett's special fondness for Erika and suggested to John that the best strategy for getting Plunkett to hire him was to work through Erika.

"She could give a donation. A large one," John said.

"No, that would be a fatal error," Arthur countered. "They'd think you were buying your way into the department so you'd get nothing back for it. Believe me, I know what I'm talking about."

"I trust your instincts, Arthur. It was shortsighted of me to suggest such a thing. If she were to speak to Plunkett about supporting a world-class creativity institute at Harvard, she could tell him I should run it."

"There's a small problem, John; she's your wife! I'd say that could be a bit controversial, but she can make the case to Plunkett for giving you a professorship. I don't see anything wrong with a wife speaking up for her husband. Plunkett won't be able to resist."

"You think she's capable of that? Asking for favors is not one of her talents."

Arthur was a loyal friend, but in John's estimation, not always the greatest judge of people.

Stooped and precariously overweight, Edwin Plunkett never turned down invitations from the Starrs but he did not reveal the reason even to his closest friends. How could he tell them that

Erika had become his obsession, that he fantasized they were lovers? Her beauty overwhelmed him and when she was near, his unhappiness over the recent loss of his third wife, Emily, quickly vanished away.

Of course, Emily had been such a stalwart support! With her withering comments about his colleagues in his fractious department, she provided a soothing balm to his frazzled soul. Her vitriolic attacks on the noisy feminists around Cambridge were particularly gratifying. Louise Schwartz was one of their pet peeves. So absurdly popular at one time, this woman pretended to be a scientist! How could her psychobabble be taken seriously? She actually admitted she wrote "out of her soul." Out of her soul? And what was that supposed to mean? Her central point was women and men were "different". So this was new? Her so-called research had no rigor; she never bothered to explain the genesis of her "discoveries." She was right at home at the School of Ed. Both Edwin and Emily agreed that it was a good place for second-rate minds to acquire a Harvard connection.

Twenty years his junior, Emily's early death was unexpected. He was caught utterly unprepared. It had never occurred to him that the simple chore of walking their dogs in frigid weather would have overtaxed her heart. He had no idea that she even had a heart problem; she'd never mentioned it. Far more fit than he, she never tired of riding her bicycle through heavy traffic in Harvard Square or hiking in summer with her friends over steep and perilous trails in New Hampshire. In the days before the fatal event, he was startled to see her gripping the banister with both hands while ascending the stairs and pausing on the landing to catch her breath. But like so many worrisome moments in life, he chose to ignore those ominous signs. After all, he was the one who was constantly in and out of the doctor's office! Wasn't he being treated with just about every new medication on the market to treat the debilitating symptoms of old age? Emily was young and vigorous so her health problems appeared insignificant compared to his.

On these social occasions at the Starrs, Plunkett rarely bothered to talk to John, though he enjoyed observing him out of the corner of his eye. He couldn't help thinking that John was a very lucky fellow, landing such a gorgeous girl as Erika with all that money. The boy was smarter than he remembered but his good looks most likely played the major part in capturing such a princess. The subject of Starr's doctoral thesis was a blur in his mind. Extensive interviews with artists and school children, he vaguely recalled. There was a girl that year, a voluptuous girl who was in his course. Her name escaped him right now, something like Melanie or Eleanor. Which was it? Or was it Lainie? God, there had been so many girls he couldn't keep track. Not remembering all the graduate students he had slept with was a recent failing. Age related, no doubt. This particular girl possessed not only a great body but an unusual aptitude for statistical analysis. So why was this memory important? He waited patiently for the answer to click in. And then, out of nowhere, it came to him. Elaine, that was it. Elaine Locke. He had selected the girl for a project with Starr because the boy had difficulty defending his theories with enough hard data and she saved the day by coming up with impressive numerical figures to support their conclusions. She was a hot number, that one, and you'd never have guessed it looking at her. All preppy and proper. He wondered momentarily what had become of her.

Tonight, Starr could be heard down at the other end of the table discussing his creativity research. Plunkett couldn't catch every word, but he knew that Starr had gone off to Mexico to study with that head case, the creativity guru, Maria Di Brioni. Recently, he'd had an article published in *Psychoanalytic Dialogues* making a connection between Jung and Freud and their views of creativity. A "breakthrough," Arthur Watts told him, a "must read". So Plunkett forced himself to read the article through to the very end. Not his cup of tea, of course, and it was no "breakthrough," simply Ed School level stuff. But Starr did come up with some interesting insights on the subject of creativity and he was willing to give the man credit.

Anyway, he wasn't here to think about Starr. Erika was the one he came to see, the divine Erika. Why couldn't today's girls be like her? She was elegant and refined but she smoldered too, he could feel the heat. Of course he knew it wasn't directed at him, it was all meant for John Starr. But never mind. He would bask in her glow and dream they were making love.

His reveries were disrupted by H.G. Walters, professor emeritus of anatomy at Harvard Medical School, laughing so hard at his own jokes that tears streamed down his cheeks. "It feels wonderful, crying like this, the best therapy!" he shouted. Yes, tears provided a certain relief, Plunkett thought. He'd cried when Emily died and felt the better for it, but wasn't H. G. really talking about laughter? Everybody knew *that* was therapeutic. Or sitting close to a gorgeous, desirable woman like Erika.

Now H.G. was praising John Starr's latest article on creativity as "insightful" and calling for him to write a book. Then he heard Arthur chiming in at the other end of the table. "A great idea, John! A book! You've got to write it!" Clearly, Starr and Watts had been enjoying a homoerotic relationship ever since their undergraduate days, not homosexual (everybody always confused the term), merely a deep and lasting affection. His own warm friendship with Morty Connor at MIT was also homoerotic, a fact that led Dora, his first wife, to accuse him of homosexual proclivities. Later when she discovered he was bedding down his pretty graduate students, she called him a disgusting heterosexual predator.

Increasingly, Plunkett was losing patience with the gays. For one thing, they were always usurping definitions for themselves. Take the word "gay." Couldn't use it anymore to describe a fun party like this one. What was the world coming to? He kept his counsel, of course, he didn't want those invitations to stop coming. They provided the only happiness in his life right now.

SEVEN

Everything about Norman Katz was big; his head, his hands, his body, and his ego. He seldom suffered self-doubts, a quality Erika admired since she was feeling her own so often. At fifty, he was a famous painter and a popular studio art teacher for advanced students at the Boston Museum School. Besides painting, his passion was collecting works of art and he was known for the paintings and sculptures he brought back from his visits to Africa, and India. Occasionally he wrote for *Art News* about his adventures in discovering new artists.

He rarely gave private painting lessons, but as an admirer of John, he agreed to take on Erika after John showed him her early pen and ink drawings from college days. "She has talent," John said, "You can see it right here in the drawings, but she's kept that creative spark locked up inside her, and you can help her release it."

On first meeting Erika, Norman asked himself why he was teaching her to paint. She should be posing for him and he would make a magnificent portrait of this beautiful woman! But he had been hired by John to unleash her creativity spark and he didn't want to disappoint him. Reluctantly, he began the art lessons.

Patient at the start, Norman grew frustrated with Erika's slow progress. The still life he assembled was too difficult for her to copy. At one point, she tossed her brushes aside.

"I can't do it," she said flatly.

"Maybe not," Norman agreed. "You're a typical Sunday painter, Erika. Muddy colors."

"What colors should I use? Tell me!" She flushed with anger.

"I can't. You must discover the colors yourself."

"How? It's all a jumble!"

"Discovery comes only through observation and interest."

"You sound like John," she observed with annoyance. "He's always making statements like that. But I never will be an artist so why should I paint your still life? I could get my camera and the picture would turn out so much better! Or should I try an abstract version?"

"You mean an abstract version of the still life?"

"Well, then I won't have to copy and I can use whatever colors I want."

Norman sighed in disgust. " Sure, sure, but let me tell you something, Erika. Abstract art is a piece of cake – that's the dirty little secret. No rules at all. You can do stuff like pouring a can of red paint on a canvas and everyone who's hip will love you for it. Then comes all the intellectualized crap from critics who aren't even artists and write important-sounding reviews. It's a scam, honey. A real scam."

"But some abstract art can look great when you're decorating a room."

"Right. It's decorative all right. But these pieces are not works of art, Erika."

"You sound bitter, Norman. Is it because you're not as famous as some of the abstract artists?"

"No, fame has nothing to do with it. It's about painting from the heart, not just the head."

He moved away from her and she heard him drawing up a wooden chair on the other side of the room behind her. When she turned around to look at him, he was scanning the sports section of the Boston Globe. Norman was an enthusiastic Red Sox fan.

"I'll try this time to paint your still life but without any color," Erika said a few minutes later. "May I paint it black and white like an old movie?"

"No color?" He looked up from the newspaper and stared at her. "You're depressed, aren't you, Erika?"

"A little."

"You can confide in me." He folded the paper and came over to her.

"Well, I really don't understand why I'm depressed because I have therapy every day with John and I should be cured by now."

"Right. He's a world famous therapist so he *must* be helping you."

"I know he's making me better," she said. "He has to be making me better." Turning back to her painting, she said softly, "He's a great man, you know, and he's all I want in this world." Her eyes brimmed with tears and Norman quickly changed the subject.

"Erika, forget the colors. It's no big deal."

"I'd make a mess of it, I know I would."

"The creative process is a struggle for everyone, including me." He made a long face. "We all suffer, you're not the only one." Smiling, he suddenly said, "Hey, give me a brush. That thick one right in front of you." With the brush, he delicately picked up some paint from her palette.

"Hold onto my arm and feel how I move the brush. Can you see that behind the red apples there's a green shadow? Can you see it? It'll help you center your composition. Watch me. See that negative space there? See it?"

"No."

"But that's impossible! It's right there! Use your eyes!"

"Norman, it's not there!"

"Never mind, Erika, we'll look at it again on Monday and I'm sure you'll see what I'm talking about." He released her arm and laid down the brush.

"I need a cigarette break right now to relax a bit," he said. "I'll just have a smoke outdoors for a minute. Can't help myself. Think about what I've just told you. You can do it!"

He was wrong, thought Erika, but he was right about the creative process being a struggle; John had told her the same thing but she hadn't listened. Anyway, she'd lost any desire for painting lessons and John would have to step in and take her place.

The next lesson, Norman finished the painting for her and when John saw it, he said, "Erika, that's great!"

"That's what I say!" Norman winked at Erika but she looked the other way.

"I'd like to join your class, Norman. How about it?" John said.

"Take my place," Erika said quietly. "I can't go on."

"Might be a little hard for him, Erika," Norman broke in, "seeing as he hasn't done the introductory still life. Besides, I don't like the idea of your dropping out."

"John's the real artist, Norman, believe me."

"None of that self-deprecating talk, my love," John admonished her. "But if you've had enough, we won't push the lessons." He turned to Norman. "How about it? Can you give me a couple of classes?"

Indeed, when John began his first impressionistic landscape, he used the brightest mixtures on his palette and Norman was impressed. "The spontaneity of his brush strokes and the accuracy of the values tells me your husband is an natural artist. This is very remarkable."

"I know," Erika said. "I've seen some of the Chinese paintings he did at Harvard and they're wonderful."

"I sometimes fantasize about giving up psychology for art," John said, applying still more paint to his canvas. "If I'd taken 'the road less traveled by' to quote Robert Frost, I'd probably have ended up a painter. But my mother frightened me with tales of starving artists living in a cellar. Are you starving, Norman?"

"No, quite the opposite. My portrait business has done well."

"So my mother was wrong, bless her heart. You know, I loved my mother. Her life was never easy after my father left her. I miss her still, though she died a long time ago." His voice grew husky and Erika moved closer to him.

"Darling," she said softly.

A grown man still mourning the death of his mother, thought Norman, and he couldn't help wondering what kind of a woman would scare off her gifted son from becoming an artist. It would be like tearing the wings off a bird.

John was saying, "I have to admit though, there's nothing quite so liberating as taking brush in hand and letting it all flow!"

"That's the spirit!" Norman said.

The next day, Erika commissioned Norman to do a portrait of John standing at his easel.

"I'll paint him in the shorts he was wearing yesterday," Norman said. "He's got great legs so I'll use a large canvas. He'll look like a Greek god and I'll put his painting in my next show."

Erika laughed with happiness and it was decided to start the portrait in the spring and John was delighted to be included in Norman's exhibition.

Norman invited them to his opening at the Newberry Galleries. Erika decided to wear her long, clingy Yves Saint Laurent gown of red velvet and her Gucci red satin shoes with the spike heels John had chosen for her.

Sipping a glass of Beaune Racheo wine and wrapped in a towel, John walked into the bathroom where Erika was stepping out of the shower. "I'm not ready for Norman's show, are you?" he said, setting his glass on the dresser. "Shall I dry you?" Coming up behind Erika, he slowly dabbed the water off her body then dropped the wet towel on the marble floor. Together they stared at their reflection in the mirror. "Are these two lovers not perfect mates?" he said, his voice thick. "You, the Moon Goddess, floating in calm and radiant beauty? Me, the Sun God, burning with the fires of love?" He pulled her against him, covering her damp neck and shoulders with hungry kisses. "Come with me and be my love," he said and drew her gently into the bedroom, now illuminated in the glow of late afternoon.

Sinking down onto the white satin sheets, they entered into a world of caresses that drew spasms of pleasure from them both. Minutes later, reeling still, they were again ready for another round of lovemaking.

When they arrived later at Norman's show, Erika noticed that people were staring at them. Did they recognize John from Norman's likeness of him? Could they have guessed that John and she had risen, sated from their bed, only minutes before?

Strolling through the crowd, John pointed out Norman's portraits of some of Harvard's most prominent contributors. He seemed particularly intrigued by a small painting in the corner of the gallery of a famous poet presently teaching at Harvard. The man had been in and out of mental institutions and through the use of background shadows and the careful rendering of gesture and facial expression, Norman was able to suggest not only the writer's intellectual power but the depth of his melancholia as well. John thought that if he had painted the man, he would have used more color and rendered the subject less meticulously. Then the portrait would have truly come alive.

EIGHT

"All Mom's women friends feel real sorry for her, Dad," Roger told him during one of their weekly phone conversations.

"What does she tell them?"

"Like Erika's loaded and that's why you dumped Mom so you could marry Erika."

"That's a lie, Roger! Your mother got rid of *me!* Erika's money had nothing to do with it. I know that reality is hard for your mother to accept."

"Sure, Dad, sure. It's just that Mom says you're so rich now you could send us more child support."

Catherine was always complaining about child support. Why? Didn't she know she received way over the legal amount? Those feminists on the faculty must be egging her on, celebrating her victimhood.

According to Roger, his mother's creative writing course was hugely popular with the women. John couldn't help but chuckle that Catherine was now calling herself an academic. All during their marriage she had mocked him for being a nerd with no street smarts and now she was a nerd herself! Though her stories had won her a small fan club, John remained unconvinced of her ability. Recently she was focusing exclusively on female victimhood, which got the critics on her side, but in his view, her writing was opaque, repetitive, and rambling.

Periodically, he received a batch of letters from Catherine, and tonight he was sitting by the fire in his study rereading some of them. He couldn't help wondering if the girls there were still as sexually uninhibited as was their reputation back in the good old days when he was at Harvard. To his regret, he'd always been too busy to find out for himself.

He knew if Erika saw Catherine's letters she would want to read them so he was careful to file them away. Recently he had come upon her rummaging though his drawers and he was certain she was after the letters though she pretended to be looking for an old picture of herself at Smith College. Once he had shown her an old photo of a ravishingly lovely young Catherine standing in the doorway of their Cambridge home. Holding Roger in her arms, she was smiling at the camera.

"That's what I want, John, a baby."

"Yes, Erika, I know."

Noting the delicacy of Catherine's features and the hint of a mocking smile on her lips, Erika asked John if she was as pretty in real life. "Perhaps even more so," he replied. "She had a great body, perfect legs – showgirl legs – and liked to wear short skirts and high heels to show them off."

"Really?" Her voice was barely audible.

"Darling, there's no comparison. You are a great beauty. She was pretty, at best."

He couldn't explain why he repeatedly reviewed Catherine's scribblings – a streak of masochism, no doubt. They were full of bile, but her descriptions of their first encounters in Boston drew him irresistibly back into a past where everything seemed simpler and the future was bright with promise. Recently he was feeling a sadness he couldn't shake off. He would reread her most recent letter at the top of the pile.

Dear John,

I won't be writing you very often anymore. An occasional letter or phone call to talk about Roger, that's about it, because my life has finally become my own; I no longer stand in your shadow.

For so long I hoped you'd grow weary of your trophy wife and her obscene money and come back to me. But it never happened.

I don't know if you are aware that long ago in Mexico when you refused to recognize I was seriously ill with fever, something of the love I felt for you died. We had no medications in the house, no ice to bring the fever down. Remember? The electricity was out because of the storms. But by some miracle I survived, thanks to our cook, Josefina. She single handedly dragged me into a bathtub full of cold beer cans where the fever finally dropped below the danger point. A brilliant woman!

I will never forget that exhausting drive up from Mexico to California when I was alone and pregnant with Roger. You didn't care that I was physically and emotionally drained when I arrived. Your needs came first; you wanted a quick fuck. Afterwards, all you talked about was how you'd been picked to head the Institute for Creativity Studies in Cambridge because you were "ahead of your time".

After Roger was born, I saw I was merely the incubator from which he sprang fully formed into your arms. You cared about him because he was the male extension of yourself.

At parties you dominated the conversation with your talk about creativity while I sat in a corner ignored; I wasn't an academic, merely a wife and mother. Those needy, homely wives whose professor husbands never gave them a second look, sat at your feet, transfixed. I know you never took any of them to bed, you weren't in the least tempted, but adoring women have always made you feel important. And why not?

I had no desire to have an affair like so many of our friends who wrecked not only their families, but themselves as well. I believed in the sanctity of marriage. It was only in those last days together when you started running around with rich society women that I knew our marriage was over.

Let me admit something to you now: I was actually happy when you failed in your career trajectory! Does that shock you? All your kissing up to academics came to nothing; you never got into the Harvard psychology department, did you? You would have been better off spending time at home with Roger and me.

If it hadn't been for my fellow women writers, I would never have been serious about developing my gifts. I'll give you some credit here, though. You made me sign up for writing courses and helped get me back on track. But it

was the women who pushed me to attend professional workshops, start network-
ing and meeting editors. Remember, I was a nobody.

And just look at me now! Would you have ever expected I would be on
the faculty of Bennington College?

I love this place, John, and I'm constantly expanding my horizons. I
have become an active feminist and environmentalist. Lester Brown, World-
watch's founder, is my hero. I'm chairman of a committee that is writing tracts
about the degradation of our natural resources by the multinationals and I feel
really good about myself. At long last!

I haven't time to be bitter anymore, as you can see. I am my own per-
son and my emotional wounds have mended quite nicely, thank you.

Catherine.

He would burn this letter. An environmentalist? What could
she be thinking? All the time he knew her, she never even glanced
at a tree. He was the one who pointed out the flowers when she
passed by them, who redesigned the gardens and made sure the watering systems were up and running.

And this claim he ran after rich women? What about her
own behavior? When he desired her she refused him, turned away
from him and went to sleep. Her attitude towards his work was always negative. What did she expect? He sought out the company of
other women because they appreciated and admired him. It was
simply a happy coincidence that some had money.

He was not surprised she took pleasure in his setbacks. It
was so like her to bring up the Harvard thing. She always knew
where to aim her arrows.

Crumpling up the letter, he tossed it on the smoldering logs
in the fireplace where it quickly flared up and burned. Then slowly
and deliberately, he picked up all the bundles of letters he had been
saving and heaved them into the fire. For several minutes, the darkened room was bathed in a warm and brilliant light.

PART IV

ONE

At breakfast one cold day in early March, John brought up the subject of his son.

"I'm worried about Roger, Erika."

"Roger?"

"Yes. His mother's neglecting him and things aren't working for him in school. He's losing it."

"How do you mean?"

"Bad grades, drinking, drugs. He's acting out and clearly needs his father," John said, taking a sip of his coffee and leaning back in his chair.

"Catherine's a basically narcissistic woman who's too busy to pay attention to him. She's become a literary luminary these days and is too busy to deal with his needs." He stood up. "During our marriage, I offered her therapy but she laughed in my face."

"Laughed in your face?"

"Yes."

"And you're the greatest analyst in America!" Erika cried in disbelief.

"It was her way of hiding unresolved emotional conflicts." He gave a dismissive shrug. "But let's not get into Catherine's issues now. It's Roger I want to discuss." Pulling his chair beside her, he looked at Erika with grave concern. "You might not be able to handle what I'm going to propose."

"What is it, John?" A shadow crossed her face. "Tell me what you want."

"Roger needs to cut his incestuous ties with his mother and firm up the bond of father and son. I'd like to bring him here for the summer. How would you feel about that?"

"Feel about what?"

"Having my son here."

"He'd be here with us?"

He picked up the anxiety in her voice. "Is there a problem with that?"

"It's a worry, that's all."

"What kind of worry?"

"That something bad will happen." She gripped the arms of her chair.

"When Roger's here?"

"Yes.

"By 'bad,' what do you mean?"

"Things could go wrong. I mean, we're so happy now."

"What could go wrong?"

"He'll think I'm some kind of crazy person. I'm the patient you married, remember?" Angry tears welled up in her eyes.

"You're my wife whom I worship and adore." Moving his chair closer, he sat down and took her hands in his. They were cold and he gently massaged them.

"You're my whole life, you know," she murmured softly.

"Yes, my darling, I know. But it's going to be all right. You'll like my boy."

"He'll hate me, John. I took you away from his mother, didn't I?"

"You did no such thing. My marriage to Catherine was over long before the breakup. Roger understands the situation perfectly and he's very eager to meet you."

"But if he comes to live here with us, things will be different." A sensation of impending doom swept over her.

"How do you mean?"

"You work all day long. The only time we're together is when you come home. If there's somebody else around, it would change things."

She stood up from her chair and slipped into his lap, leaning her head against his shoulder.

"Erika, that 'somebody else' is my son. Think about it. My own flesh and blood!"

"But I'm going to have to share you with him!"

"Sharing is part of loving, we've gone over this before, darling. You're being overly possessive and that's not healthy. It's related to those dependency issues with your father which we need to address at a deeper level."

"John, not wanting to lose you, is that a 'dependency issue'? I love you so much!"

"Darling, I'm going to propose something." He pulled her closer. "Try to imagine us as two separate trees in a great wood, growing straight and tall together, our branches intertwined but each of us free standing, not blocking the other's light and air."

"I'm blocking your light and air?"

"You're resisting, Erika. What do you think I'm trying to tell you?"

"That I'm in the way."

"You are distorting."

"No, I'm not distorting!" Sliding off his lap, she brushed away her tears with the back of her hand and walked to the window. The sun was emerging from behind a dark cloud, framing its edges in luminous gold.

John stood up and walked over to her. "Listen, it's very simple. My son wants to visit us and he should be made welcome here. He needs me. I'm his father. Please understand. I love you, nothing can change that." Pulling her roughly into his arms, he kissed her damp cheeks.

"Oh, John." She was melting under his touch.

"I want you to try something."

"What's that?"

"Taking on the mother's role."

"The mother's role?" She abruptly drew back. "You've got to be kidding! Are you talking about Roger? John, he's a grown boy!"

"Not quite. He's only fifteen."

"May I remind you that you promised if I bought the house we'd start our own family, have a baby, a *real* baby? What happened to that?"

"Please, Erika, calm yourself. I also made it clear we'd have the baby when you were strong and healthy and you're not there, yet."

"Why do you always say I'm not there yet? I am. You know I am."

"Your dependency issues have to be resolved first," he said flatly.

He was backing out of the agreement they'd made but she would keep her calm. If she raised her voice even slightly, he stopped listening.

"You're always going to find something wrong with me, aren't you?"

"That's not necessarily true but for now, how about trying out the mother role with my son? You'll be empowered by the process, develop a whole new confidence and maybe at that point, we can seriously consider having our own child. You have to remember, though," he added, "fifteen's a tough age. You'll make mistakes, but I'll help you every step of the way."

"Really?"

"Absolutely."

It was clear to her now that to get what she wanted, she'd have to go through the motions, like winning over Roger. It shouldn't be hard. All fifteen-year-old boys were alike, she'd never had any trouble with them when she was tutoring French though sometimes they tried to grope her and she had to scold them.

"I'll see that he's happy here with us," Erika said with a bright smile. "I'll be a wonderful mother to Roger, you'll see."

John sighed with relief. "Thanks, darling," he said. "I knew you'd come around."

Later that day, they visited the local bookstore and purchased several books about adolescent boys by leading experts. They would study them together.

TWO

On a sultry late June afternoon, Roger showed up at the front door with a girl following closely behind. They were both carrying heavy backpacks and wearing cutoff shorts and dirty tee shirts. John greeted his son with a warm hug. Roger was a tall young man with a shaved head who bore little resemblance to his father.

"Dad, this is my girlfriend, Adriana," Roger said, pushing his companion forward.

"Yeah," mumbled the girl, glancing nervously around her. Small and pretty with round blue eyes and an upturned nose, her straight black hair reached down to her waist and her fingernails were painted black.

"I guess I forgot to tell you about Adriana," Roger said. He grimaced slightly. "Well, like, we've been planning this for a while now."

"Is that so?" John looked intently at his son. "Well, let me introduce you to Erika. Darling, where are you?"

"Right here," Erika laughed, hurrying to join him. "Come on in, kids! You both must be so exhausted after such a long trip."

Did John notice how friendly she was, how she made it a point to be there when they arrived? She'd show him how easily she could get Roger on her side. The girl, she wasn't so sure about.

After dropping their backpacks in the hall, Roger and Adriana followed Erika out to the sunroom. They stared in amazement at the lush gardens, emerald lawns, and shimmering swimming pool below in the distance.

"Wow! It's all yours?" Roger exclaimed, turning to Erika.

"Yes, it's all ours." Her soft voice thrilled him. This woman beside him who had stolen away his father was incredibly beautiful and so young! Barely older than himself, or so she seemed.

"The house is humongous!" broke in Adriana. "Ohmygod, like humongous, man!"

"What's that?" John asked, coming up behind them.

"Big, man, like massive. Hey, this place is *so* cool. You actually live here?"

"We live here with our staff," John said with a frown. Obviously, these two young people were seeing great wealth for the first time.

"Staff? Like cooks and maids and stuff like that?"

"Right, 'stuff like that.' Now let's go and put your things away. Roger, your room will be on the second floor. Adriana, you'll have the small room facing the back gardens on the third floor."

Later in the day, John called Roger and Adriana outside to join him in a game of croquet while Erika watched them from the terrace. The sun was warm and the smell of freshly mowed grass hung in the air.

"But we don't know how to play," Roger protested. "Baseball's my kind of game and hockey, too. Adriana isn't into sports, right?"

"Whatever," she shrugged.

"Well, we'll have to rectify the situation," said John cheerfully. "Watch me!" And he whacked a long, straight shot down the grass and through the wickets.

"Come! Let's see if you can beat me!" he shouted. After handing them each a mallet John waved up at Erika who smiled back.

Ohmygod, Roger was thinking as his shot went wide of the wicket. That woman is watching me make a fool of myself! Why did his father have to show him up like this? Roger wasn't used to losing but croquet was stupid and boring and he didn't want to learn how to play. It seemed a totally old-fashioned game for the rich and he guessed it must be a snob thing and that was why his father liked it.

John cut down on his patient load for July, put off his daily therapy meetings with Erika, and postponed most of their social engagements until after Roger and Adriana planned to leave. Spending time with his son was his main priority and since most of the staff took their vacation in July, there would be ample opportunities to bond and Erika agreed. Cooking meals together would be a priority and her task was to order the proper ingredients for meals.

"Learn by doing, that's the best way," John said. Over the sink, he hung up a poem meticulously embroidered in needlepoint and framed in natural oak. It had once belonged to his mother.

BREAKFAST, OH, BREAKFAST, THE MEAL OF MY HEART,
BRING PORRIDGE, BRING SAUSAGE, BRING FISH FOR A START.
BRING KIDNEYS AND MUSHROOMS AND PARTRIDGES' LEGS,
B.U.T LET THE FOUNDATION BE BACON AND EGGS!

John insisted on the very best ingredients for the evening meal and on one occasion ordered Erika to exchange an inferior brand of balsamic vinegar for the more expensive, quality kind.

Roger and Adriana rarely washed their clothes but having no wish to injure their self-esteem, John gave each of them a specific day of the week when they were to use the washing machine.

"We're responsible for ourselves here," he said. "With a little organization we can have this household running smoothly while the servants are on vacation."

THREE

John soon learned that Adriana lied. Earlier in the week at the Cricket Club where they played tennis, he had slipped and fallen on the grass court during his doubles match and he spied Adriana on the sidelines, doubled over with laughter.

"Did you think it very funny when I fell down, Adriana?" he asked her later. She assumed a blank look.

"You were laughing at me when I fell. I'm concerned."

"Oh, I wasn't laughing at *you!* It was somebody else on the next court."

"The next court was empty, Adriana. There was no one there."

"Are you trying to say I'm lying?"

"Aren't you?"

"I don't know what you're talking about!" She gave a toss of her long hair, newly dyed purple.

"I'm trying to understand why you laughed, Adriana. I'm asking you a simple question."

"But I didn't laugh," she said, a sulky look crossing her face.

"You've just contradicted yourself. I'm not going to pursue this conversation further," John said and walked away.

She clearly enjoyed provoking him. The girl was hostile and the only reason he tolerated her was that she was helping Roger cut his unhealthy ties to Catherine. Sooner or later Roger would meet someone else.

Erika had noticed that whenever John was openly affectionate with her, Roger looked upset. Did he resent her for supposedly luring his father away from his mother? Determined to set things right, she made a point of seeking out his company. It wasn't until she caught him staring hungrily at her breasts during their moments alone together that she realized he was an adolescent boy with raging hormones. Citing pressing social obligations and important fundraising luncheons that would take up her free time, she made herself scarce for the next few weeks.

Roger, who initially rebuffed Erika's efforts to be friendly, had decided it was cool to be "hanging out" with such a sexy step-mother but he couldn't figure out why from one day to the next, she turned to ice, shut off the heat, just like that. No more hot vibes coming his way. What had happened? All that talk about her "social obligations"; he didn't believe a fucking word. Probably out shop-ping with her friends. That's what his mother always did when she was mad about something. Anyway, he wasn't going to let the whole thing get him down, especially now that she was pretending to be friendly like his fucking homeroom teacher in his high school back home.

He'd once seen a movie about a woman with three different personalities. Scary stuff! Maybe Erika was like that and went from one personality to another. He decided that his father hadn't been able to cure her and that she was still insane.

"Hell, she's old as hell," he told a sleepy Adriana who was stretched out on the newly mowed lawn one hot afternoon. "She must be thirty, at the very least, though she sure fooled me into thinking she was young! Still, what a body! Jesus, is she ever *built!*"

"You are *so* gross!" Adriana screamed, jumping up. "Get lost!"

Roger didn't like it when his father leaned over and kissed Erika on the lips in front of everyone and whispered stuff in her ear. Who knows what he was saying and it actually made him feel nauseous. Of course, he could understand his father's behavior. Erika was a sex goddess, for sure, and his mother hadn't bothered to tell him. Maybe she didn't even know. He guessed his father must have fallen in love with Erika the very first day she showed up at his office and she was so sexy and crazy he didn't stand a chance.

Recently, a strange thing was happening, though. The more he watched her, the more she turned him off and made him wonder why he'd gotten all worked up in the first place. Now, whenever he was near her, he assumed an air of studied boredom.

But he couldn't help noticing when he joked around with his father she looked like she was going to cry.

Erika was one weird woman.

Erika was impressed with John's special ability to sense what was going on with troubled people. He was often able to pick up on her own emotional turmoil before she was aware of it herself. He saw Adriana as a disturbed girl and traced her hostility to unloving parents.

"John, you're a great psychologist; you zeroed in on this girl's unhappiness right away."

"It was perfectly obvious."

"So how can I help her? What should I do?"

"Well, clearly, she's envious of Roger's position in our family so we should try to bring her into the fold more, maybe arrange a trip together."

"A trip? Where?"

"Think about it. We'll discuss it at dinner."

Over dessert that night after consulting with John, Erika proposed a holiday in Nantucket.

"Oh, we've been there already with Mom," Roger said, stirring his soup. "It's a three-hour boat ride from Woods Hole."

"We'd fly, of course," Erika said. "Did you like Nantucket?"

"It's okay. Not much to do, though. The Vineyard's better."

"Why is that?" John asked.

"More action, more kids our own age."

"Lots of Kennedys," interrupted Adriana. "I know some of them."

"You know the Kennedys?" John was surprised.

"Yeah, they're friends with my dad."

"Friends of your father? And what does your father do, Adriana?" asked John.

"Stuff."

"What kind of stuff?"

"Lawyer stuff. Roger, pass me the bread."

"And your mother?" Erika asked gently.

"Oh, my mom lives in Argentina with her third husband and I don't see her much. They raise thoroughbred horses." Erika caught John's eye. A clear case of neglect as he had surmised, and clearly, the parents didn't lack for money.

"How interesting. Do you ever go down there?" Erika said.

"Nope, not yet, anyway. Maybe one of these days, who knows." Her face looked suddenly old.

For a time, no one spoke.

"Well, I'm certain we'll have a wonderful visit in Nantucket. It's such a beautiful island, and we can bicycle and swim," Erika smiled.

A trip with the children was the right thing to do, she could see that now.

"I'm always falling off bicycles," said Adriana, "and the water in Nantucket is really yucky. There's so much seaweed and it isn't even warm."

"Not warm?"

"We should go to Caneel Bay."

"Caneel Bay?" Erika was stunned. The girl was talking about a faraway resort for the very rich.

"What do you know about it?" said John.

"It's neat. I've been there with my dad."

"But it's the hurricane season, isn't it?" Erika said.

"Not until August or September. July's the best time, better than winter and cheaper."

"Cheaper?"

"Yeah, it's the off season."

"Let's go to Caneel Bay! A great idea!" John said, rising from his chair and going over to Erika. "How about it, darling?" He leaned over her and gave her a kiss.

"I'll make the reservations right away," Erika said quickly, forcing a smile.

FOUR

When Marsha answered the office phone, she was not expecting to hear Robert Giuliani's voice on the line. He was calling for an appointment with Dr. Starr.

"Erika convinced me it might be a good idea," he said.

"So when would you like to come in?" She tried to keep her voice calm, but her heart was beating wildly. He gave her some possible dates.

"I can fit you in three weeks from this Tuesday at four o'clock. Will that suit you?"

"Sounds fine. What floor?"

"Second floor, suite 24."

"Is there an elevator?"

"Right in the lobby, you can't miss it."

"Thanks. See you then." He quickly hung up.

With a brisk sweep of the pen, Marsha entered his name in the appointment ledger. Then rising from her chair, she walked over to the window. No one was in the waiting room, she had it all to herself. The day was fine, bright and warm with a clear view of the Charles River. The water was a ribbon of sparkling silver blue, the color of the sky. A single scull skimmed along its mirror-like surface, disappearing under the footbridge, trailed by a thin dark line where the oars had disturbed the water.

In the months since the wedding, Marsha had often revisited her conversation with the man in the wheelchair. He had made her feel fully alive with his edgy humor, the hint of suffering that marked his pale, handsome face and his radiant smile. She did not expect to see him again, they lived in different worlds, but being together with him that day remained a bright spot in her life as she tried to cope with her mother's illness.

Once alert and quick, her mother was now dull and slow, beset with the confusion and anxiety that comes with Alzheimer's.

On the doctor's recommendation, Marsha placed her in the Jewish Home of Brookline where her mother continued to decline.

Marsha remembered his aide from the wedding. Minutes before the ceremony he had wheeled Robert Giuliani to the front pew of Emmanuel chapel where he could see the nuptials take place. He appeared again later with Robert Giuliani at the Ritz ballroom. Now he stood behind the wheelchair, dutifully awaiting his orders. They had arrived at the office fifteen minutes early.

"You can go, now, Matt," said Robert Giuliani. "I'll call you."

"Very good, Sir." Nodding politely to Marsha who emerged from her tiny cubicle, he quietly slipped out of the waiting room. His movements were surprisingly lithe for so large a man. A high school football star, perhaps, once upon a time.

"I know I'm a little early, it's a habit of mine," Robert said. "Learned it when I used to take photos for the National Geographic and wanted to get out fast from some of those hell holes I was trapped in." He managed a boyish smile.

"Can I get you a cup of coffee? It's freshly brewed in my little cubbyhole over there." She nodded in the direction of her cubicle.

"Hey, thanks." He seemed pleasantly surprised. "Yes, I'd like that very much. A touch of milk and a spoonful of sugar if you've got any."

It didn't take Marsha long to bring out his coffee with milk and sugar, and her own, black, with saccharine. She had chosen special cups from Chiapas, and he commented on their beauty.

"Lovely. Where are they from?"

"Chiapas. That's in the south of Mexico."

"Yes, I know. I once visited San Cristobal."

"How interesting. So few Americans ever go there," Marsha said. Drawing up a chair, she sat down next to him.

"You were working there?" His gaze was so intense that Marsha felt the blood rush to her face.

"Yes, I was teaching literacy to the Chamula Indians." Her mouth went dry.

"Must have been a great experience," he said. "Pretty poor down there, though."

"I never got used to it, the poverty I mean. But the people are amazingly resilient no matter how desperate their situation."

"That seems to be true everywhere. I know Haiti pretty well, and it's a miserable place with shocking poverty but the people there seem to get more happiness out of a single day than most of us in a lifetime." His expression suddenly darkened. "At least, it used to be like that. Right now, Haiti is in crisis and nothing seems to help."

Marsha nodded and they sat quietly together, sipping their coffee. Minutes later, John Starr abruptly threw open his door.

"Robert, good to see you. It looks like you're enjoying Marsha's special brew. Best coffee around." Beaming, he strode over to Robert and shook his hand. Marsha was impressed with his warmth, his visible concern for the man in the wheelchair. Never had she been so proud of Dr. Starr as at that moment.

"Yes, the coffee's very good. Thanks a lot," Robert said, giving her a brief smile. Handing her his empty cup, he looked up at Dr. Starr.

"Are we ready? Need any help?" Dr. Starr asked him.

"I can manage," Robert said grimly, wheeling himself briskly towards the office door. His face had lost its brightness and his eyes had turned cold.

Jason Marcus was Marsha's tenant and he had noticed she wasn't herself, hadn't been for a while now. A fellow Brandeis alumnus, he had moved into her apartment shortly after she placed an ad in the alumni magazine. A room to rent, well situated, close to

Harvard Square, just where he wanted to be. Shady Hill, the prestigious elementary school where he was working as a third-grade teacher, was just down the road. Marsha was friendly and cheerful and for a couple of months she made it a point of eating dinner with him almost every night in her small kitchen.

Early on, Jason praised her collection of Mexican artifacts and colorful pottery that brightened up the dark rooms throughout the apartment. Her connection with Mexico was spending a couple of years after college teaching literacy to Indians in the mountains. When she mentioned a romance with a Chamula native, she got all choked up and Jason pretended not to notice. It seems the guy got sick with TB and eventually died. Jason found it strange that an educated Jewish girl would fall in love with an illiterate Indian with TB.

When Marsha's father died, the mother, whose small, dark room he currently inhabited, ordered her daughter back home to live with her. That didn't sit very well with Jason. How could she have a life if the old woman was hanging around watching her every move? Marsha finally packed her off to an old folks home and that was a good thing but why did she visit her mother every single day?

With his head of curly dark hair, his even-featured face and his well-muscled body, Jason considered himself a real catch. Once a girl told him that he had Bambi eyes, large and dark with pools of light.

He thought Marsha was pretty when she smiled. He figured she was somewhere in her early forties but he never asked her the actual year she graduated from Brandeis and he was too lazy to look it up in the alumni directory. Too bad she was a little plump, but her feet and hands were surprisingly slim and delicate which seemed to him a bit odd. Being overweight carried a serious health risk and Marsha never bothered to exercise. A physical fitness buff himself, his body was toned to perfection and he even challenged his buddies to punch him in the stomach. He enjoyed seeing the shock in their eyes when their fists connected with a cement wall and they cried out in pain.

Recently, Marsha had been acting like she barely knew him after they'd spent a couple of friendly evenings together discussing important philosophical questions like the meaning of life and the existence of God. He remembered draping his arm around her shoulders when they were sitting together on the living room sofa because he was enjoying himself so much, just talking to her, and his gesture was an expression of camaraderie, nothing more. If she thought he'd be interested in her, hell, she was living in a fantasy world. A guy like *him*? Running after *her*? It was pathetic!

Tonight, Marsha was sitting in the kitchen, staring at the floor. Was she about to cry? He hated women who cried because he didn't know what to do. He'd try the sympathy approach, though. Maybe it would work this one time.

"Marsha, something wrong?" He made his voice warm and caressing.

"I'm sorry, I hoped you wouldn't notice. Yes, I'm actually pretty miserable," she said softly.

"What's up?" He didn't really want to get into her problems but right now he didn't have a choice.

"It's a hopeless situation," Marsha said.

"How do you mean?"

"I can't really talk about it. Let's just say that it's affecting everything I do."

"You've been bitten by the love bug! I recognize the symptoms!" So that's what was wrong with her! How could he have missed it? He prided himself on being very quick to figure out what was going on.

"You're very perceptive. Anyway, I'm caught up in something I can't handle. There's no future in it, I'm afraid."

"Marsha, take it from me. Forget the relationship, don't hang around."

"But..."

"Spare yourself the hassle. You'll feel better in the end."

"You're so wise for such a young person. Thanks for the advice." She gave him a sweet smile and headed to her room. Yes, when he put on the charm and acted caring, he could make just about any woman feel a whole lot better.

FIVE

John was right. Their trip to Caneel Bay was making a big difference in the way Adriana and Roger related to Erika. After only a day of snorkeling and scuba diving in the limpid, sparkling waters of the island, they were distinctly friendlier. On John's advice, Erika purchased special equipment for them because he said ownership for adolescents was an important ingredient of the learning curve and they were touchingly grateful.

One afternoon at a fancy shop in St. John, John tried on a thirty-five-hundred-dollar white Armani suit that made him look so handsome Erika bought it for him without blinking an eye. Then John turned around and spent four thousand dollars on her by buying the Dior cocktail dress on display in the shop window. "It's got Erika written all over it," he said. "It's you, darling!" That night they wore their new clothes to dinner and John winked at her as they walked to their table because a few guests at the hotel mistook them for movie stars.

Every day, despite the tropical climate, tea was served in the hotel lobby at four in the afternoon. After a day of swimming, Roger and Adriana were ravenous, grabbing up handfuls of chocolate chip cookies fresh from the oven.

Erika made a special point of always asking them what they had seen.

"The fish are all gold and orange and blue," Adriana said.

"Wonderful, wonderful."

"That big blue fish nearly took a chunk out of my neck!" Roger laughed one day, pointing to his jugular vein.

"Yeah, and I was chased by a school of barracudas!" cried Adriana. She was adding something new, grand and exciting, just to see if she could get a reaction out of Erika who immediately looked concerned.

"Hey, you two," John smiled. "Trying to frighten us?" The girl blushed and looked away. Roger grinned sheepishly, glancing sideways at Erika.

Several attractive women were settling down at the far side of the lobby for tea and one of them smiled flirtatiously at John.

"She's pretty, isn't she?" Erika said.

"Not really, not in your league, anyway." He kissed her, and Roger made a face.

Besides afternoon tea, the hotel offered other agreeable touches. At night, the maid placed one pink hibiscus blossom on top of each pillow and underneath, two tiny Belgian chocolates wrapped in gold paper. The next morning, with the soft tropical air drifting through the wooden slats and the rays of sunlight stroking their face, they awoke from their nocturnal embrace and rolled over to bite into their soft Belgian chocolates, luxuriating in their rich, succulent taste.

One afternoon, John suggested that Erika join him for a swim.

"You've been avoiding the water. What's going on?"

"I'm still frightened of swimming in the sea, John. I don't know why. Maybe it's because of Frank."

"Frank? But we've gone over all that."

"I can't help thinking about him, sometimes, John."

"You're back to playing the victim." He looked at her sternly, then smiled. "You and I are going swimming together today, sweetheart. I'll be right beside you in the water and we'll head out towards the reef."

She wasn't sure she could swim that far, but John kept insisting. Hesitantly, she followed him into the water and they started out together. He swam next to her very slowly, maintaining the fluid rhythm of the star swimmer. The day was sunny, the sky an electric blue, and John was right beside her. Settling back in the waves, she felt a oneness with sea and sky. Life was good. Earlier in the day he had complimented her mothering skills. "The kids are responding to your initiatives, so hang in there. I knew they'd come around, it was just a matter of time before they appreciated your special qualities." Darling John, he always looked on the bright side.

As the water gently cradled her, she glanced back from where they had come and could barely make out the shoreline. How could they have swum so far? Where was John? He'd gone on ahead, of course, and who could blame him? Being a champion swimmer, he hadn't wanted to wait for her. But why hadn't he told her? There was a growing weakness in her arms and she felt oddly sleepy. Closing her eyes she decided to let the waves carry her back to shore. But then she remembered Frank and panic gripped her. The undercurrent was pulling her out to sea. She was sinking. Would she drown like Frank?

"John! John! Where are you?" Flailing about, gulping saltwater, she coughed and screamed. "I'm drowning, John! Save me! Save me!"

A powerful arm suddenly hooked around her waist and John was yelling in her ear. "What are you trying to do?" As she struggled to breathe, he steered her smoothly through the waves, finally releasing her just short of the water's edge.

"You disappeared," she said later that afternoon in their room. "I lost you out there, John."

"I was right beside you."

"No you weren't, you went on ahead. Why?"

John was standing by the window, looking out at the sea. His back was to her so she couldn't see his face.

"Erika, I only left you for a second. I was always near you." He sounded far away.

"So why didn't I see you?"

"You were having a panic attack."

"Yes, that must be the reason I didn't see you were close by. It all happened so fast, John! That's the way it must have been for poor Frank except nobody was there to save him. You were there for me, though, weren't you?"

"Of course, my love. I took all the necessary measures," John said, closing the slats of the blinds to block out the crimson rays of the setting sun.

SIX

John was after her to read Wolfgang Edel's *Studies of Creativity and Genius* so every day she settled down on the beach in the shade of a large, pink umbrella set up by the hotel staff to try to decipher Edel's book. His language was opaque with none of the clarity of Erich Fromm or Sigmund Freud. A mammoth tome of historical, philosophical and psychological insights into creativity, his book emphasized how the spirit of play unleashed the power of invention. For geniuses like Shakespeare or Tolstoy, this creativity was at its most exalted.

John was creative in ways she was not. He was childlike in the clarity of his vision, gifted with a deep faith in his own destiny. Did she need to believe more fully in herself to tap into her creative force? When Edel wrote about risk taking, shedding restrictive boundaries, she judged herself too frightened ever to become fully free. Had her father's early abuse destroyed her confidence forever?

Since her panic attack swimming with John, she focused mainly on the book and if she swam at all, she stayed in shallow water.

One afternoon, she grew tired of reading Edel so she took a walk and ended up on a path that ran along a ledge above the sea where the spray from the turbulent waters below rose hundreds of feet in the air. It was an exhilarating sight but the tropical sun burned hot and she began to feel lightheaded. Turning back towards the hotel, she left the path to stroll through luminous sun-drenched glades of tall yellow grasses and pink hibiscus. A strange moaning from behind a clump of palm trees startled her. She smiled to herself: probably male cats fighting over a female in heat.

Curious, she peeped through the underbrush and saw a man on the ground resting on his elbows. Naked from the waist down, his head was thrown back, his eyes closed. A woman, fully clothed, was kneeling over him, her head buried between his thighs. Erika gave a sharp cry and the couple sprang apart, their eyes wide, like deer caught in the headlights of a car. It was Adriana and Roger.

Turning quickly away, her head spinning, Erika ran blindly through the tall, yellow grasses.

"Erika!" Roger shouted after her. "Nothing happened! I swear! Nothing at all!"

Liar, liar! Did he think she was some kind of fool? The image of those two was burned into her brain and she doubted she could ever forget what she saw. How could she have been so stupid not to know what they were up to? John probably knew all about it; nothing escaped him, but why hadn't he told her?

Once again in the cool of her room, she fell on the bed and flinging off her sandals, wondered if she'd been hallucinating. The sun had drilled down on her and she felt dizzy. Maybe nothing had happened at all. John liked to point out that certain things she believed to be true were actually illusions. Was what she'd seen an illusion? Was her mind playing tricks on her? Reaching down to the floor, she picked up her sandals and scrutinized them carefully. They were covered with sand and her arms were scratched from the tall grasses. So she hadn't been dreaming. It was true.

When he arrived later, Erika was still lying on the bed.

"Are you alright?" he asked. "You skipped tea. I didn't see the kids, either. Were you with them?"

"No," she said.

"So what's going on? Something's happened. Tell me."

"No, it's nothing, really." She made an effort to keep her voice steady and calm.

"Okay, we'll talk later," he said. He bent over to kiss her but she turned her head away. "You're upset," he said.

"No, I'm not."

"Come on, out with it."

"I really don't want to talk right now."

"Why not?"

"Can't it wait?"

"Tell me what's bothering you." He kissed her neck.

"It's just that by mistake I ran into Roger and Adriana in the bushes." She sat up and looked at him.

"In the bushes? What were they doing in the bushes?"

"They were having oral sex. And so young! Adriana's only fifteen so what can they be thinking of?"

John laughed abruptly and strode briskly over to the window. The sea was calm, shimmering brilliantly in the sunlight.

"Oral sex, you say?" He did not turn around to look at her.

"I didn't want to tell you, John."

"So what's the big deal? That's not really having sex, you know."

"No?"

"These days the kids don't consider that kind of activity to be sex, Erika."

"Then what is it?"

"It's an intimate way of communicating, that's all."

"Did you know all along they were having oral sex?"

"No, but it doesn't surprise me."

"So what should we do?"

"What do you mean 'what should we do'?" He sounded annoyed. "We should not do anything, that's what! I'll have a word with Roger, however." Spinning around, he stared at her. "Did they see you?"

"I'm afraid so."

"Did they say anything?" His eyes sparked ice blue.

"Just that nothing happened."

"Did you speak to them?"

"I can't remember."

"Not remember? Oh, Erika." He turned again to look out the window.

"What's the matter?"

"You have shamed them by finding them out."

"It was by accident. I never meant to…"

"You've made them feel they're bad people and that's not a good thing. Not a good thing at all!"

"What are you talking about?"

"Let me explain." He moved away from the window, his expression glum. "We've been working on their self-esteem, right? It's all about bonding and now it looks like you've undermined our whole effort!"

"Undermined what?"

"You're hyperventilating, Erika. Calm yourself. Remember, you sometimes imagine things in the past that didn't really happen."

"You're accusing me of making this up?"

"Try to breathe slowly and deeply."

She struggled to do as he asked.

"That's good, you're relaxing. Now, what you think you saw may not have been entirely accurate," he said smoothly. "My advice is to let it go." He took her hands.

"'Let it go'?"

"Erika, you've humiliated them and I doubt they're very happy right now. We've been working on building trust, that's the most important component of our relationship with Roger. We agreed on that, remember? Now you've made them feel ashamed. You need to understand that when someone is shamed, he loses his self-esteem. We've talked about this before, darling. Surely you can understand since your father used shaming as a tool when you were a child."

"Of course." She was getting angry. What right did he have to bring up her father right now? How could he say she was making things up?

"We've got two adolescents here and it's obvious that Adriana is the sexual aggressor," John continued evenly.

"Why do you say that? Maybe Roger ordered her to do all that stuff."

"So you're taking Adriana's side in this? That's a mistake because Roger's going to dump the girl first chance he gets."

"Dump her? What do you mean?" His casual tone shocked her.

"He's getting tired of her but I told him to hang in there. After all, she's serving a purpose and we mustn't forget that. She's cutting the umbilical cord with his mother and initiating him into manhood."

"That poor girl," Erika said. "She'll be dumped in the trash?"

"You're getting hostile, Erika."

"No, I'm not hostile, John, I'm angry. Here's a fifteen year old girl who's being used and doesn't know it and it looks to me like she's not getting much back for her services."

"Services?"

"Servicing your son!"

"You're jumping to conclusions! What makes you think Roger doesn't take care of *her* needs? That girl is very demanding from what I've seen."

"So we're just going to ignore the whole thing?"

"It's the best way," John said. "How many times do I have to tell you it's a common activity among young people today?"

"How do you know?"

"Have you forgotten, Erika, that I have other patients beside yourself? Some of them tell me things. So that's how I know, okay? Now, let's go to dinner. It's time to get ready."

John liked nice clothes and the dining room rules for the evening meal called for jacket and tie. Removing his chinos, he carefully hung them up in the closet and selected a pair of freshly pressed white linen pants, a navy blue sports jacket with three brass buttons, a blue-striped, hand-ironed cotton shirt and a yellow Hermes tie. Looking at himself in the mirror, he smiled with satisfaction.

"Hurry up darling, we'll be late for dinner if you don't get ready." John started towards the door. "I need a drink. See you in the bar. And let's see a smile on that beautiful face. We wouldn't want the kids to know you're upset."

"I don't feel like smiling."

"Darling, come to me." His voice was a command and she found herself obeying him. Opening his arms wide, he pulled her close. "Who loves you? Who is trying to free you from your fears and traumas? Now, no more pouting. Get dressed and meet me in the bar for a drink before dinner. Shall we say in ten minutes? I'll be waiting for you."

After kissing her on the lips, he went out the door and she walked slowly into the bathroom. A long, cool shower was what she needed and she wasn't going to meet him in the bar. She'd let him wait for her and later he'd tell her she'd spoiled his evening but she didn't care. It served him right.

At dinner, she noticed Roger and Adriana barely touched their food. John talked cheerfully about next day's plans for scuba diving but no one seemed to be listening to him.

"I gotta go home, Dad," Roger blurted out just as the dessert arrived. John took a bite of the kiwi pie, chewing slowly.

"Home?"

"Yeah. I've got stuff to do and Mom expects me."

"Are you saying you're ready to leave Caneel Bay and return to your mother?"

"Yeah, like that's what I'm saying."

"Adriana?"

"I'm okay here, but you know, he's right, I guess. I mean, like, we're ready to chill out. Roger feels pretty strongly about going back." She stared down at the table and Erika noticed her eyes were red from weeping.

Poor girl, Erika thought, and he doesn't even love her. He's just using her.

"We're very disappointed you want to leave so soon but you must promise us you'll come to Boston for Thanksgiving. John and I will be expecting you," Erika said, looking tenderly at Adriana.

"You mean that?" said Adriana in a shaky voice.

"Absolutely," Erika said, turning to John. "Isn't that true, darling?"

"Of course!" He flashed a brilliant smile.

"I guess I'll have dessert," said Roger. "How about sharing a kiwi pie with me, Adriana?"

"Sounds good."

"So that's settled then," John said. "You'll come for Thanksgiving!" Satisfied, he reached across the table to take Erika's hand. "And Roger, I'd like to have a word with you after dinner. Just the two of us."

"Sure thing, Dad, no problem."

Father and son settled down in their beach chairs and looked up at the sky. The stars were twinkling and the moon was big and bright.

"I guess you heard what happened today," Roger said. "Sorry about that. It was pretty embarrassing."

"Well, what's done is done. Erika doesn't hold it against you. It's quite normal behavior these days."

"Glad you see it that way."

"Can you tell me what you know about sexual relations? You and I have never had a discussion on the subject and I always assumed your mother took care of it early on."

"No, Dad. She never had to talk to me about it. You see, at school we get sex ed starting in the fifth grade, except it's called 'human development'." He chuckled.

"Tell me about it."

His son's candor left him reeling. He explained to his father that by eighth grade, he and his friends were regularly practicing oral sex, an activity not considered sexual relations by his human development teachers or any of the girls and boys he hung out with. Later on in high school, he availed himself of the free condoms offered in the boys' bathrooms and wore them dutifully during sexual intercourse, but he preferred oral sex. It was less of a hassle and the girl could do all the work because he had to admit he was one lazy guy in *that* department! Oral sex was safer, too. His teachers had given him scary warnings about what could happen fucking without a condom. Yuck! Totally gross diseases like syphilis and AIDS and worse still, a *baby*! An unwanted pregnancy must be the most horrible thing that could *ever* happen to a human being! A total disaster! He and Adriana would never make *that mistake*; they were definitely staying with the oral sex thing, even though sometimes, Adriana demanded he take care of *her* needs. Pretty gross, but that's the way it was.

Recalling his own awkward groping at Roger's age, John could not help feeling envious. What took him years to learn, his son already knew; his knowledge and sophistication astounded him.

He felt suddenly old. He had to smile at Erika's resistance to the notion that today's young people looked on oral sex as not being sexual relations. Like him, she was part of the older generation.

SEVEN

Arthur Watts had some excellent news for John on his return from Caneel Bay and was waiting for him in the club lounge of the St. Botolph Club. He was wearing an old grey Harris tweed jacket, baggy blue corduroy pants and a blue button-down shirt frayed at the collar. He'd remembered to put on his Jerry Garcia tie with large yellow and green swirl. John ordered a martini with Absolut vodka, very dry. That was the way he liked it, with a round, shell-white onion on a toothpick resting at the bottom of the glass.

John definitely planned to join the club. He wasn't going to miss out not being among so many distinguished scholars and prestigious members of the Boston elite. So far, however, no one had come forward to put him up for membership but he was sure he could count on Arthur when the time was ripe.

"So, what's new?" John asked, settling back in his favorite leather chair.

"You won't believe this, but there's going to be a newly endowed chair in the psychology department that will be entirely for creativity studies. How about that, John?"

"Finally." His voice trembled with emotion; he'd been waiting so long.

"And it's called the Francis Lee Walker Creativity Chair," continued Arthur. "It seems like this guy Walker dropped out of Harvard in the late fifties and went on to make a fortune selling tranquilizers. The gift is his way of giving something back to Harvard. And here's where the guru in the creativity field comes in." He brightened up. "That's you, John."

"Sure thing." John took a large swig of his drink.

"Don't get too carried away, though," Arthur warned. "We have a small problem."

"Like what?" His throat went dry. Had his elation been premature?

"Well, Plunkett's all excited over the latest research that promotes the brain as some kind of computer and that worries me."

"Hey, why should that worry you?" John laughed. "Our guy's always been seduced by the fancy numbers."

"Yeah, but maybe he'll choose someone like himself for the Chair. You know, a numbers nut."

Arthur had a point. Perhaps the whole idea was doomed to failure. No, he must stay the course and not allow himself to be affected by Arthur's negative take on it. His moment had arrived. He would get the Chair. "Come on, let's anticipate the positive here, Arthur. How about talking strategy?"

"Sure, sure, but you need to know that Plunkett's been reading Sternberg."

"Sternberg? Whatever for?"

"Well, he's got the theories and the numbers to go with them and that's a turn-on for Plunkett. He also likes the fact that he can use him to put down Howard Gardner."

"In what way?"

"He's always said that Howard Gardner presents no hard evidence to back up his case studies of different types of creative intelligence. Now he can cite Sternberg's quantitative results as being real science."

"That's just plain nonsense. We all know we can build on Gardner's theories of creativity and we can't do a damned thing with Sternberg."

"That's right, and people like Sternberg have even sunk to the point of measuring preschoolers' IQs! It's pathetic! The numbers game is now center stage in school policy across the country!"

"Uncreative academics; that's what they are."

"You know, John," said Arthur, draining his drink. "Sometimes I feel like taking off."

"You mean, leaving?" John jumped forward in his chair.

"Right."

"But you can't! I need you there; you're my advocate! Look, if I get the Chair, you'll finally have departmental support for your work on creative thinking."

"Maybe, though I'm not so optimistic these days. In a couple of years, human development courses and studies of different cultures may no longer exist here at Harvard. We'll be another MIT."

"Maybe yes, maybe no."

"Listen, John. Our foreign policy stinks because we haven't the faintest clue how other cultures function and nobody around here seems to think it's an issue."

"I know."

"Who's reading Aristotle or Thomas Aquinas? Nobody!"

"It's hard to believe."

"You can say that again. Right now I'm working on the relationship of creative thinking and its application to political and military strategy and no one besides me understands how our interpretive, psychobiographical model of understanding human behavior is essential for national security. I can tell you, it's damned isolating. But this should surprise you; CIA seems interested."

"I would think so. National security is their main concern, after all."

"And speaking of strategy, John, I've come up with an idea that just might work."

"In relation to what?"

"Getting you in the department, setting you up for the Chair and I'd stay at Harvard if it works."

"Tell me."

"You can give a lecture at Harvard in the spring on your creativity work. I'd make sure all the big shots in the psychology department are there, Plunkett in particular."

"A lecture? On my work?"

"Look, John, the Erika approach failed because Plunkett wanted more from her than just flirting. Now it's your turn. You've got to wake him up, give him new insights. When he hears everyone praising you to the sky, he'll want you for the Chair."

"You think so?"

Maybe the idea could work. It was worth taking that chance. "Arthur, you're a true friend," John said with feeling.

Arthur laughed. "The hour has struck, John. We're ready to make our move!"

EIGHT

In his regular therapy sessions with Erika, scheduled at home after dinner, John no longer took notes or offered hypnosis to recall repressed childhood memories. After a long day working with patients, he was bone tired, and listening to her soft voice endlessly describing scenes he now knew by heart induced in him a kind of twilight sleep. Her resistance confronting her dependency issues, her lack of autonomy, left him frustrated. When she occasionally halted her monologue, an alarm went off in his brain and he snapped back to attention, ready to respond. On the few occasions she agreed to analyze her dependency, he remained fully alert for the entire session, but for the most part, her therapy remained superficial and unproductive.

After talking with Arthur, John decided to curtail daily therapy. He was quite unprepared for the intensity of her reaction.

"Are you really so busy?"

"Darling, you know I need enough time to write a good lecture for Harvard. When it's over, we'll return to our usual schedule."

"And when will that be?"

"In the summer."

"But that's ages from now!"

"Not really. If you're productive, time goes by very quickly."

"But you've already cut me back to thirty minutes a day as it is! We don't even have enough time to discuss my aggressive reactive patterns or whatever you call them!"

Lately, Erika had been moody and short tempered and he'd labeled this behavior "aggressive reactive patterns."

"We'll get to their source and chase them down I promise you, but for now, my first priority is the Harvard lecture."

"What Harvard lecture?"

"You haven't been listening to me, darling. The Harvard psychology department has asked me to give a lecture on my creativity findings and we're trying to get the Chair, remember?"

"But nothing seems to be happening!"

"That's not exactly true. There's a lot of interest in what I do and if my talk goes well, I'll get the Chair."

"Yes, but..."

"But what? Look, this lecture is a big challenge for me so you need to be supportive. You're not thinking of me."

"Not thinking of you? But that's all I do!"

"You think of me like I'm some kind of possession. You forget I'm not only your husband and therapist, but a researcher and I'm on to something important. I've got big plans, Erika."

Pursing her lips, she said, " I understand, and I'm really happy for you that Harvard is finally recognizing your work."

"Thank you."

Her expression grew anxious. "Recently, though, you've seemed far away."

"What do you mean?"

"You're in some place I can't reach."

"Well, you're wrong, there, darling; I'm right here with you." He adjusted his tie. "I must go now, Erika. I'm late."

"Late?"

"I'm meeting Arthur at the St. Botolph Club."

"Didn't you see him the other day?" she asked impatiently. "By the way, John," she said in a small, hard voice, "I have to ask you something."

He felt suddenly drained. Outside, it was turning dark though it was still early in the afternoon. The rumble of thunder sounded in the distance and raindrops began to beat gently against the windowpanes.

"Do you like the car?"

"What car, Erika?"

"The Ferrari I just bought you."

"The Ferrari? What's the Ferrari got to do with this conversation?"

"Well, aren't you going out in it now?"

John strolled over to the window. He was glad it was raining; the weather had been dry and the plants needed water. His automatic watering system would have to be replaced; it was not working to capacity.

"Yes," he said wearily, "I'm very grateful you gave me such a wonderful car and I've made that point repeatedly. You want to put me on a guilt trip?"

"A guilt trip? Of course not, but you never thanked me, John. Never!"

"It's significant that you don't remember. Clearly we're dealing here with a control issue."

" A 'control issue'? What do you mean?"

"You're angry, Erika."

"Angry?"

"Yes, for two reasons; the first is having to shell out all that money to buy my car. That's your 'obsessive hoarding personality'. The second is that I can't be with you as much as you'd like. So let's picture again those two intertwined trees we've talked about, each with separate trunks, open to the sunlight and fresh air, never reaching too far into the other's space. Visualize this picture once more. What do you see?" His intensity bore into her.

"See?"

"We're imagining those two trees, Erika, free to grow on their own but intertwined. Let your imagination flow."

"Why do you constantly make me repeat this exercise? I don't want to think about being a tree! We're people, not trees!"

"But Erika, I keep pointing out to you that those two trees are you and I, remember? Think about it, you and I."

"Yeah, you and I, you and I…"

"Right, so imagine that we're two trees in a ..." Erika interrupted him with a burst of sarcastic laughter. "I'm talking about the car and you're talking about trees! That's what you do, John, you change the subject and make me feel crazy! But I'm on to your tricks!"

"'Tricks'? Hey, let's back off here for a minute, Erika. You're upsetting yourself over nothing. The car's magnificent, perfection itself. I love it, particularly the beige leather seats."

"Then why didn't you tell me?" Throwing herself into the deep armchair, she gave him a blank stare. "I don't understand you," she said coldly.

"Don't you remember how I expressed my appreciation at the time?"

"You never thanked me for the car. You're lying, John." In all their time together she had never accused him of that. Until now.

"Erika, you simply don't remember but it's not a sin to forget so don't get defensive."

"I didn't forget."

As he had learned to do in stressful situations, he made an effort to detach himself. The matter wasn't worth fighting over but Erika was determined to win at all cost. The expression on her face was grim and her lips were set in a thin line.

Rain was battering the windowpanes and heavy claps of thunder shook the house.

"We'll talk later," he said as he hurried towards the door. "I love you, Erika, don't forget that," he said, " and I'm sorry if I hurt you."

Once outside, he stood for a minute with his head thrown back so the pelting rain soaked his face. He felt immediately refreshed. The house had become oppressive; he had to get away.

Starting up the car, the purring motor soothed his nerves. She was a difficult case, no doubt about it, and for the first time, he questioned his ability to help her. He had believed that with his guidance she would discover her innate creativity but he was not sure any more she wanted to make the kind of effort that was necessary for such a discovery.

He was ready to hand her over to another therapist. She would resist, of course; he had long ago agreed to be her therapist, lover, and husband all rolled into one and their marriage was predicated on this arrangement.

He would have to present the idea of someone else as a temporary solution while he worked on his Harvard speech. Secretly, he hoped the therapist would agree to take over her analysis permanently. But who would that therapist be? Maybe it should be a woman who treated other women like Erika.

On his way to meet Arthur, he made a quick detour to visit the Picasso exhibition at the Boston Museum. Fortunately, he had remembered to bring his extra-large Brooks Brothers umbrella but he was chilled and his shoes were soaked. However, upon seeing Picasso's powerful works, his discomfort vanished. Nude Woman, a complex distortion of the female body, so revolutionary at the time Picasso painted it, warmed him to the very core. The man had a fresh, invigorating, childlike vision of the world. In this particular painting he was demonstrating how women wore different faces, like Erika.

NINE

"Wish you'd been with me at the Picasso show," John told Arthur once they had settled into their chairs in the bar and ordered a drink. The club was full of people tonight and John wondered if it was the heavy rains that drew in the members and their friends. Such a cozy spot, St. Botolph's; the perfect escape. He breathed a sigh of contentment.

"It would have been great, but you know how pressed I've been, going over my manuscript for the publishers," Arthur replied. In actual fact, he had never liked Picasso and considered him a trickster, a self-promoter who stole his ideas from African art so as to shock the bourgeoisie and titillate the critics and intellectuals; his early efforts to copy the impressionists had hardly rated him a second glance.

"Those later works," John remarked in reverential tones. "You immediately see their freshness, their power," and Arthur grudgingly conceded that the artist's Blue Period was both original and beautiful.

"Picasso had an extraordinary ability to see things in a new way, as children do," John continued.

"Children? Young children?"

"Aged twelve or younger."

"So young? How so?"

"In my clinical experience, adolescence muddies the senses but in Picasso's case, he retained that clarity of vision from childhood."

"He was a pretty devious character, though, and from what I've read, betrayed his friends and lovers," Arthur said. "Wouldn't you say that's relevant when you judge an artist?"

"Picasso was a precocious child; his moral conduct is irrelevant when you're considering genius. His level of creativity excludes him from being judged as we would ordinary men."

"You think so?"

"Absolutely," said John, "I'm quite prepared to argue that position if challenged."

"Good, because it might come up at your lecture," Arthur said, taking a small sip of his scotch and soda. "Be prepared for all kinds of questions. There are forces out there..." His tone was ominous.

"What do you mean by 'forces'?" John said impatiently, wondering if Arthur was displaying a bit of unnecessary paranoia.

"Well, it has to do with Elaine Locke. Remember her?"

"My God, haven't thought about her in years." Why on earth was Arthur talking about that woman?

"I think you did some kind of study with her in your last year of graduate school. She was very sexy as I recall." Arthur threw him a wink. "Anyway, it seems she's become some kind of expert on gender issues and their effect on different types of intelligence. The women love her."

"Elaine Locke? Yes, I remember she was really into the quantitative side of things, even back then when I knew her so I guess that explains why she's become so popular."

"Plunkett's being attacked by the feminists. They're calling him a misogynist."

"He's no misogynist, the guy loves women! My god, he couldn't keep his hands off the girls when we were students and Elaine was one of them, for sure," John chuckled.

Arthur gave a brief smile. "Standard behavior for professors at the time; they were all bedding down the women. That's over now because nobody wants a lawsuit and the faculty women are trying to dismantle the university structures of male domination. That's where Elaine comes in. I've heard if I decide to leave he'll replace me with her."

"What? He'll replace you with Elaine Locke? You've got to be kidding!"

John was recalling how in the first few years after she left Cambridge, Elaine had sent him postcards from small, unknown colleges in the southwest where she worked as an untenured research assistant. He never bothered to reply and she eventually dropped off his radar screen. That she was now so successful in the academic world came as a surprise and he wondered if it had to do more with her ability to flatter the big shots than with her quantitative skills. He occasionally ran across an article she had written with her colleagues and he remained unimpressed. The idea that Harvard would seriously consider her astounded him. What an awful thought that she might replace Arthur! She could never take his place, not in a hundred years!

"Arthur, bringing Elaine to Harvard is ridiculous! Besides, you can't leave! Who's going to be my advocate with Plunkett?"

"That's why your lecture is all important, John, and I know you can pull it off. I have total faith in you. If it's a winner, how can you lose?"

"And Plunkett will support me for the Creativity Chair?"

"Absolutely. Who else is there?"

"You're right, there isn't anybody else."

TEN

On a Saturday morning, several weeks before Roger's Thanksgiving visit, John received a call from Catherine, begging him to keep their son for his entire academic year.

"I can't control him," she complained. "He's sixteen, now, he needs his father. He's failing in school so can you take him? Brookline High is near you; it's a great place."

John was elated. "No problem. We'll try to get him into Brookline High, and I'm delighted he'll be here with me."

"Thanks, John. I know how much you care about Roger."

Her voice was warm and friendly and it demonstrated to John how a little success could wipe away the negatives like envy. She had always hungered for the spotlight and finally found it at a small college in the country.

His mood was buoyant; he would have his son again, and he hurried out to the terrace where Erika was enjoying a morning coffee in the bright November sun. For that time of year, the day was surprisingly warm. A month ago, a sea of crimson foliage blazed in the distance. Today, the trees stood bare and still.

After sharing the news with her, John smiled and said, "It's the right thing to do, darling." He drew up a chair. "Roger will be much better off with us."

Clutching her throat, she cried out, "I thought he was out of our lives!"

He stared at her in dismay. Would nothing ever change? He had hoped, foolishly perhaps, that she cared for his son. "We've been through all this before, Erika, haven't we?" he said.

Forcing a smile, she said, "I'm sorry, I didn't mean it, John. I don't know what came over me. Of course he can be here with us."

"Thank you, darling." Maybe there was hope after all, he thought to himself. "I know you're a lot happier when we're alone together here," he said, "but this is a matter of some urgency. The boy is doing poorly in school and the situation calls for intervention. With us on his case, I believe he can succeed. Catherine and I are in complete agreement on that point."

"You talked to her?"

"Just now on the phone. She understands how much he needs me."

"Will he be bringing Adriana as well?"

"I suppose so though there was no mention of her in our conversation."

"Poor girl," Erika said with a sigh. "I wish I could help her."

"Don't worry yourself about her. She's a hostile adolescent and sometimes she'll like us but most of the time she won't. You can't let her get you down," he said, reaching for Erika's hand.

Later in his study, John began gathering together some key papers on his desk to prepare for his Harvard speech but his mind kept returning to Adriana. Finally, he reached for the phone and called Roger. Was he bringing Adriana?

"Dad, Adriana's my girlfriend so she'll be with me if that's okay. Mom's not happy about it and I figure Erika's going to be pretty annoyed, too. Women don't much like Adriana." He gave a nervous giggle.

"She's got issues, Roger."

"Yeah, tell me about it. So what am I supposed to do?"

"Bring her along, I guess, but right now we need to talk about Erika."

"Erika?"

"Yes. You should know that Erika is very fond of both you and Adriana but she finds it hard to express her feelings. Her childhood was pretty miserable. She had a violent and abusive father."

"But wasn't her father some kind of mafia tycoon? That's what Mom told me. I mean, she's really rich, isn't she?"

"Roger, money has nothing to do with abuse. Abuse occurs at all levels of society." John was silent for a moment then plunged ahead. "I don't believe I ever told you that she was once my patient."

"No, but I heard like she was insane and went to see you."

"She was never insane, just depressed. But she's much healthier, now. I continue giving her therapy so she can discover her latent creativity."

"'Latent creativity'? Hey, what's that? Sounds cool."

"Sometime I'll explain it to you. In any event, Erika is well and happy and will be fine with Adriana, I'll see to that."

"Dad, you're the greatest!"

When Roger and Adriana arrived, Erika was out at a fund-raising luncheon for the Boston Symphony and John settled the two in adjoining rooms on the second floor of the house.

At dinner, ignoring Erika and Adriana, Roger and John discussed the future of the Boston Celtics. When Erika tried to engage Adriana in conversation, she turned abruptly away.

"Adriana, please, I'm talking to you, and it's hurtful to ignore me like this," Erika said sternly. "What's going on?"

"Sorry, I didn't mean to make you feel bad," Adriana said softly. Biting her lip, she stared down at the floor and said nothing more.

"You're probably exhausted from your trip," Erika said, rising from the table. "Get some sleep. In the morning you'll feel a lot better, I know you will." Giving Adriana's hand a friendly squeeze, she smiled at her and went upstairs to bed.

The soft morning light of autumn flooded through the window above their bed as John drew his fingers through Erika's shimmering blonde hair. He was hungry, and ready for breakfast.

He studied Erika in sleep, her full red mouth slightly opened now, a lazy smile on her lips. She was more beautiful asleep than awake, her skin appearing as smooth as a young girl. Recently, during their therapeutic sessions he had observed small lines around her eyes and between her eyebrows. "You're developing permanent control lines," he admonished her. "That's not a good thing; they compromise your beauty." He had also noticed a certain downward turn to her lips that had not been there before, marring the perfection of her face.

She was breathing more quickly now, her breasts rising and falling, (was she dreaming?) and he twisted a tendril of her hair through his fingers. Brushing it off her neck, he discovered long gray hairs hiding discreetly beneath the golden tresses. His heart tightened. Surely these strands were a trick of the light. Returning to her face, he traced the contour of her cheek with his little finger, sliding down the perfect nose, lightly touching the tip of her ear. She stirred slightly, then opened her eyes. Smiling sleepily, she drew her arms around his neck, arching up beneath him. Bending down, he kissed her on the nape of her neck. "You're beautiful, you know. Come here to me." He drew her against him. "Let thy love in kisses rain deep upon my lips again," he whispered in her ear.

"Oh, John, don't stop loving me, please," she cried, her arms tightening around his neck. "No, don't ever stop!"

"Last night at dinner you were angry, weren't you darling," John murmured later in her ear.

"You boys were ignoring us and that made me unhappy. Also, something was bothering Adriana."

"Yes, I noticed she wasn't communicating with you or anybody else, for that matter. It's not surprising, the girl's hostile. But Roger's a different case. I was merely talking to my son about basketball scores so why should that be a problem?"

"You leave us out in the cold, that's all, especially me, and I don't like it."

"Erika, your neediness is an issue you must face. Up to this point, you've avoided confronting it. You don't seem to understand that Roger's a boy and talking team scores is a guy thing, a bonding mechanism."

"I do understand and I'd never want to get in the way of your bonding with your son. But last night Adriana was very upset and I tried to find out what was wrong but she wouldn't tell me. She needs a friend and I want to be that friend."

"You can't be a so-called friend if you take on the mothering role."

"I think I can. She's so vulnerable. She needs help."

"So we're going to have to worry about Adriana?" He let out an exasperated sigh.

"Don't you care about her, John?"

"Frankly, no. By the way, what did you say to her at the dinner table?"

"I asked her what was wrong."

"And?"

"She didn't answer the question."

"She's never going to open up to you; the girl needs professional help."

"Miracles have happened before."

"But what makes you think you can deal with her problems, darling? You've never had any training and it takes years to develop those skills."

"I can try to be a kind of lay psychologist." Erika gave a short laugh. "It's absurd, I know, but I've always felt empathy for someone who is suffering."

"Empathy's important, so go ahead and play the psychologist but don't be disappointed if it doesn't turn out the way you want." He threw off his bathrobe and quickly dressed.

"The kids are up and waiting for us and it's time for banana pancakes and strawberries," he announced cheerfully. "Ready, darling?" He kissed her and went down to the kitchen. It was the cook's day off and he was ready to work.

In the afternoon as he walked down the stairs to his writing desk, John heard the children's laughter outside by the pool, and the sound of it made him melancholy. It had been a long time since he had laughed like that around Erika. It was odd, though, that despite the tensions between them, the pace of their lovemaking never slackened and John concluded that the act itself assumed a life of its own, separate and complete, not beholden to love or friendship. How else could he explain his continued pleasure in a woman who set his loins on fire but whose neediness kept him in a state of perpetual anxiety and distracted him from his work.

He stepped outside where Roger and Adriana were sitting on the steps playing cards.

"She's winning, Dad," Roger said cheerfully.

"The luck of the cards," John smiled.

Roger shrugged good-naturedly and winked at his father. He had recently confided that he no longer wanted to live with his mother and John was relieved. At long last, he had his son back.

ELEVEN

Determined to find someone to take over Erika's therapy, John came up with the idea of Hilda Payne. Like himself, she had the gift of charm, dazzling people she sought to impress and establishing an immediate rapport with her patients. She was also a hugely popular society therapist for rich women and much of her clientele suffered from depression and low self esteem. Her therapy mostly involved helping them develop positive energy and inner wisdom. Her expertise was not in Di Brioni's creativity theories, but in the latest feminist approaches to psychological wellness. She was just the right therapist for Erika, John decided.

John had first met Hilda Payne at a Boston party where she was his dinner partner. A rotund, perky woman in her late forties, she exuded confidence. "I'm great at what I do, my patients get better, they send out the word, so I do well by doing good!" she laughed, placing her hand over John's. He suspected she might initiate a romantic relationship if he gave her any encouragement, but women therapists had never interested him, especially those past their prime like Hilda Payne. Pretending to reach for his napkin, he gently disengaged his hand and she quickly turned away.

Hilda's first husband was a failed actor who drank and partied until he was arrested one night for drunk driving and ordered into rehab. There he discovered religion, briefly studied theology, and went on to become a popular evangelical pastor whose fiery sermons inspired loyal devotion from his congregation. Unable to conceive despite repeated interventions from fertility experts, Hilda was not about to spend her life as the dutiful wife of a star pastor. Instead, she returned to her hometown, Boston, divorced her husband, and won a scholarship to U. Mass Boston. Always interested in the history of culture, she studied anthropology.

It was a "coup de foudre" when she first laid eyes on her professor, Humphrey Levin, the discoverer of Sundial Uxmal in the

Yucatan, who bore an uncanny resemblance to the young Clint Eastwood. Like herself, he was also divorced, and she immediately set about catching his attentions with her brilliant insights and sexy demeanor. It wasn't long before he was smitten with her and their mutual passion became so intense that even in the company of friends they were unable to keep from fondling each other. Within two months of meeting, Humphrey Levin and Hilda Payne were married.

At the end of the summer, they journeyed to the Yucatan, settling in a small hut in the village of Chan Kom next to the jungle. Hilda mastered the local dialect and under Levin's supervision, set about studying a possible moral component in the gossip of village women. Levin's work centered on deciphering the hieroglyphics on the Sundial, located several miles away in the interior.

Unhappily, less than two years after arriving in Chan Kom, Humphrey Levin was brutally murdered. His decision to move the Sundial to the regional museum some thirty miles away from its pyramidal site in the jungle where he and his team could study it further, turned out to be a fatal error. Set upon by hostile natives wielding machetes, Humphrey Levin was hacked to death. Hilda learned later that his remains were burned and his ashes dispersed in a cave infested with poisonous snakes and scorpions. The natives believed Humphrey Levin to be an evil spirit intent on stealing their most sacred treasure. Subsequently, they returned the Sundial to its original, honored spot.

Humphrey Levin's party of eight Mexican assistants escaped through torrential rains by swimming a river filled with crocodiles and, amazingly, lived to tell the story. A shaken Hilda Payne returned to Cambridge with the resolution she would never revisit that part of the world. It had been a living nightmare and she renounced her work in anthropology and Indian dialects. To deal with the trauma she experienced, she went for psychiatric help and soon after, took up the study of psychology. Marrying again was now out of the question. She would not expose herself to further suffering.

Hilda described to John in excruciating detail how her second husband was murdered, chopped up and burned by hostile natives.

"We had such a passion, our marriage was a continuous acting out of sexual desire. I was devastated by his loss until I discovered psychology," she said. "When I started my training as a therapist, I found my voice. I was thirty-six years old, and I learned that women do not necessarily need men to be happy. In fact, women can experience full sexual satisfaction without them. Does that surprise you?"

"Not at all," John said smoothly. What was she trying to tell him? That she didn't need *him*? Clearly, she was getting back at him since he had shown no romantic interest in her.

How much money was left her by her husband, John could only guess, but he assumed it to be a meager sum. Her house in Brookline was scruffy, typical of her circle of impoverished academics. In the back patio, however, was an impressive Crilo sculpture, probably worth close to six figures. It was a gift from a wealthy patient and reached a full story in height, casting a long shadow across the far side of the house.

TWELVE

One evening before dinner while Erika was enjoying a glass of Montelena Chardonnay with John, she announced that Katie, the maid, would be departing because of her advanced age and the untidy habits of Roger and Adriana. No longer willing to clean up after them, she was ready to retire.

"There won't be a problem replacing her with the generous wages we pay. Anyway, Katie's quite anal," John said.

"Anal?"

"She makes her living cleaning up dirt." He paused, allowing his words to sink in. "I never liked her anyway. Something sneaky about her, can't exactly put my finger on it. And while we're on the subject of the staff, that second maid around here annoys me, too."

"Tilly?"

"Yes, she's always poking around where she doesn't belong." He studied the patterns in the Oriental rug beneath his feet. "Anyway," he said, swirling the wine in his glass, "I want to talk about the kids." He gave Erika a penetrating look. "That business of throwing their dirty laundry around on the floor is unacceptable Of course, we know it's adolescent rebelliousness."

"So what can we do?"

"Get tougher, Erika. Tougher. We're too nice!"

"But aren't we working on their self-esteem?"

"Sure we are, and it's tricky getting the right balance – not too tough and not too weak. We've been overdoing the positive reinforcement."

"Trying to be their mother as well as their friend is probably counterproductive," Erika said.

"Right. Forget the friend stuff, and we'll tighten the rules a bit."

Feeling suddenly faint, Erika fell back against the sofa pillows before taking another sip of wine.

"You're hyperventilating," John observed. "Are you feeling anxious?"

"No, just a little sad. Katie's worked in the family for years."

"These things happen, darling. It's not the end of the world."

"I know."

"There's some good news, Erika.

"Tell me! Is it about Harvard?" Her eyes shone.

"No, it's got to do with my son. A few days ago Roger told me he's very eager to live with us."

"Permanently?" Her voice broke. The news was almost too much to bear and she prayed John would say for only a few more months.

"Oh, Roger will stay the whole year."

"And Adriana?"

"She's part of the package, I'm afraid."

"Poor girl. So unloved."

"Sure, sure." He waved his hand in the air, as though erasing Adriana from their thoughts. "By the way, I have a proposition for you, darling." His demeanor was suddenly cheerful.

"Proposition?" She didn't like his sudden cheerfulness.

"I'd like to invite Hilda Payne to dinner if she can come."

"Do I know her?"

"Not yet. She's an older colleague of mine and highly regarded as an analyst here in Boston. You'll appreciate her empathy and humor."

"Great," she said, feigning interest.

"I think she might be somebody who could help you."

"Help me? You mean, professionally?"

"Yes, at least for the period of time I'm working on my Harvard paper."

"But you're my analyst," she said firmly. "We were going to start up my daily therapy again this summer, remember?"

"Yes, but there's a problem, darling," John said.

"What sort of problem?"

"Confronting those dependency issues of yours. We're not getting to your creativity gene."

"But I *am* confronting my dependency issues so why am I failing?"

"It's not about failing, Erika, and I'm thinking that therapy with someone other than your husband might speed up the whole process. Have you ever considered that our relationship as husband and wife might be holding you back?"

"I never heard you say that before, John. In fact, you've always debunked such a notion. What's come over you?"

"I want to do what's best for you, believe me. Seeing Hilda Payne would merely be a temporary solution, of course."

"And after your presentation? You'd be my therapist again?"

"I would think so."

"What's that supposed to mean?"

"It means I'd be your therapist again."

"That's a deal?"

"Come on, Erika. You're dragging this out."

"Alright, I'll agree to this short-term therapy plan but I'm not happy about it."

"You'll change your mind once you start working with her," he said, giving her a warm smile. Picking up the phone, he dialed Hilda Payne. Erika could hear the ringing on the other end of the line, followed by a message. "I am not available at this time. Please leave your name and telephone number, and I will return your call at the earliest opportunity." It was a deep, heavy voice, like a man's. John spoke slowly and clearly into the phone.

"Hilda, John Starr here. I'd like to discuss a private matter with you and wonder if you can join me and my wife, Erika, tomorrow night for dinner? Seven o'clock? Hope you'll say yes." He left his number and hung up.

"We'll dine with her tomorrow night if she can come. Without the kids, of course. And now, my dear," said John, "it's time to eat."

"I'll be right in. Go ahead."

"Very well. I'll call Roger and Adriana and we'll start without you. Just remember, though, we're a family."

She heard his step, light and quick on the marble floor, then soon after, the sound of laughter emanating from the dining room. What was so amusing? They never laughed like that when she was with them.

Her mind was in turmoil. How long had he planned on dropping her therapy? He was going to get a big surprise when he found out she wasn't as glued to him as he liked to believe! The very fact she agreed to see Hilda Payne spoke for itself.

Maybe she'd been mistaken, thinking him the greatest therapist in America. By now she should have discovered her creativity gene and it hadn't happened. It must be his fault; he wasn't empathetic enough. Early on, she'd been deeply touched by that empathy but lately he seemed to have lost it. Empathy was something very important in the therapeutic process of self-discovery. If back in college she'd chosen psychology instead of French, she would have become a very empathetic psychotherapist. Saving abandoned and wounded animals or saving emotionally damaged people called for the same response: empathy.

When she finally entered the dining room, the laughter quickly died away. John greeted her warmly, then returned to quizzing the kids about the latest teenage music trends. Erika was in no mood to sit around and listen, so after finishing her meal, she left without their noticing.

Up in her room, the full implication of John's decision began to take hold. With their marriage, it had been agreed he would be not only her husband but also her therapist. Now, everything would change.

THIRTEEN

When she came for dinner, Hilda Payne guessed right away that John Starr had never seriously taken on the transference issue with Erika and that in the intimate therapeutic setting he provided, she was ripe for the taking. Why should he point out to her that most patients "fall in love" with their therapists but it isn't really love? Why risk losing such a beautiful woman, an heiress to a vast fortune?

Now he was lord of the manor and the two were the golden couple of Boston society. Would she ever decide to bring up the subject of transference when she took on Erika in therapy? Maybe yes, maybe no. It would all depend on how things played out.

To John's immense relief, Erika liked Hilda Payne. "A wonderful woman. Very impressive."

"Didn't I tell you?"

"She's not you, of course. She's a stranger, and how am I going to talk to a stranger?"

"She's very professional, Erika, she'll get right into the dependency issues."

"How do you know? Are you supervising her?"

"Of course not. Why would you say that?"

"Just a thought."

"You're upset, darling, because I'm releasing you to someone else but I can promise you she'll scrutinize your dependency issues from an abusive childhood and your collusion with that abuse."

"You're saying I encouraged the abuse?"

"Not exactly but if you're willing to take a modicum of responsibility, you'll be greatly empowered."

"Didn't you tell me that being a mother to Roger would empower me?"

"I did. But you've slipped up a bit. A while back when you first got to know him, you made a real effort but I haven't seen you take much of an interest in him recently."

"I'm trying to set some rules around here, like you told me to do. No more dirty laundry on the floor for a start."

"And that's all to the good."

"I'm also trying to develop a relationship with Adriana."

"But Roger's our son. He needs you, too."

Maybe he needs his real mother, thought Erika, not me.

PART V
ONE

In the days before starting therapy with Hilda Payne, Erika slept until noon and blamed their nights of ardor for her chronic fatigue. She refused to host even the most modest of luncheons or dinners and tore up invitations to fundraisers and parties.

"You're taking revenge because I'm dropping your therapy temporarily, right, Erika?" John remarked with a grim smile.

Without looking at him, she said with a toss of her head, "My father instructed me from an early age to get back at the person who wronged me and I've always followed his advice."

Hilda Payne's office was dark and disorganized. On the patio outside, an enormous black sculpture with a large hole in the center stood a short distance from the window, casting the room in shadow. Prints, old photographs and paintings covered the walls; piles of papers, magazines, and books littered the bookcases. A large stuffed chair covered in frayed chintz and a rocking chair faced each other at the center of the room. Between them stood a low glass table with a box of tissues.

"Come, sit down," she said, indicating the stuffed chair. "The rocking chair's mine. Better for my back. We'll be facing each other because I think that's important. I need to observe your facial expressions."

"It's like that with John," Erika said, "so I'm used to facing my analyst."

"Good, your husband and I agree on that point." She laughed. "Therapy with me will be a creative journey. We'll be developing trust and intimacy. That way, important breakthroughs can happen."

Settling back in her rocker, Hilda Payne waited for Erika to speak first.

"John will be in a forum at Boston College next Thursday," she said at last.

"That's great, just great. John's a star in the creativity field."

"Yes."

"He just charms the socks off me!" Hilda Payne flashed a girlish smile. "But, hey, let's not get distracted talking about your husband because I'm focusing on *you*! My job is to help *you*!"

Hilda pointed out her Crilo, the abstract sculpture looming outside the window and asked what Erika thought it was. She was at a loss for words; it was so ugly and sinister she didn't want to tell her and Hilda quickly changed the subject.

"I'll be like a sister and friend to you, not an authority figure," said Hilda in a soothing voice. "You and I will be affirming each other each step of our journey. We'll be celebrating our female selves."

"'Celebrating our female selves'?"

"Absolutely. It's crucial to women's health. I want to tell you right at the beginning that my view is no man, no matter how caring, can validate a woman. She must do it for herself by separating her psyche from his. And that's not so easy if your therapist is also your husband."

"Like John?"

"You got it. Not the best thing."

"But he's a great analyst. I was lucky he agreed to treat me."

"That's what you like to think, but it's a questionable assumption."

"Because he's also my husband?"

"It's a symbiotic relationship, the mutual dependency of a married couple."

"You call marriage a 'mutual dependency'?"

"What else is it?"

"But a man and a woman belong together!"

"Sure, but not in the analytic context. Has John ever dealt with your transference issue?"

For a moment, Erika's mind went blank. Then she remembered that long ago at the start of therapy John had briefly explained the concept of "transference" but she'd forgotten what it meant.

"Never mind," said Hilda Payne, "it's no big deal. Transference is just a theory Freud came up with when he was analyzing a bunch of rich, neurotic women in male chauvinist Vienna."

"It must have been a challenge to be a Viennese woman in those days."

"You better believe it! Look, try to understand what I'm saying. John's a man, a guy, and that's the point here. You're a woman and there's no way in hell any man can really help a woman."

Erika couldn't fully agree. John was able to banish the frightened little girl within her and help her reinvent herself as a confident woman. He had failed with the creativity issue, but she said nothing about this to Hilda Paine.

Hilda Paine explained that a woman possesses a mysterious, primal power deep within her, a female energy source. To connect with it, a woman must honor her body, her soul, and the intuitive and instinctual sides of her nature that are linked to the moon.

Because this female energy source remains inaccessible and incomprehensible to the male psyche, throughout human history men have labeled women as goddesses, witches, virgins or whores.

"It's a power thing to control women," Hilda said.

She asked Erika again to look at the Crilo sculpture outside, now looming dark and menacing in the late afternoon light.

"Tell me what you see. Come on!"

Feeling free and unencumbered for the first time, Erika allowed her imagination to flow. "I see a grinning Cheshire cat in the circle of the sculpture. Its teeth are large and white, and it's speaking in a singsong voice." She giggled. Was she recalling a scene from *Alice in Wonderland?*

"What's it saying?" Hilda bent forward and clutched her hand.

"A kind of gibberish, I think."

"Erika, there are times," Hilda whispered, "when wonderful things happen with my patients at the very beginning of the therapy like today with you. Let's talk about the circle in the sculpture because it connects us to our energy source. Tell me more." She leaned forward. "Remember, I'm your sister and we're making this spiritual journey together. Tell me what you see out there."

"The sun is going down and the sculpture has turned dark at the center and I see a dried-up womb. Perhaps the Cheshire cat I saw before is a dead fetus."

"A dead fetus?"

"I lost a baby long ago. Maybe that's what was in my mind."

"Could be."

"It never got born. The dried-up womb. Is that mine?"

"No, not at all. You are still young and able to conceive." Hilda smiled warmly. "I am going to tell you something that may surprise you. Do you know the fetus is actually *you*?"

"*Me*?"

"Yes! But you are not a dead fetus because you have just been reborn here today in my office! You are *alive* and the power is *yours* and that's wonderful, absolutely wonderful! It's a time to celebrate, Erika! Come, give your sister a big hug!" Rising to her feet, Hilda Payne stretched out her arms. "After the darkness and the pain comes rebirth," she said, embracing Erika.

Driving home, Erika felt an extraordinary lightness of being, something she had never experienced before.

TWO

Preparing for his spring lecture at Harvard, John sat long hours at his office desk with a yellow pad and pencil and all the relevant material he needed. He avoided using his computer. By its very nature of mechanical perfection, John was convinced it hampered the flow of creative ideas.

His speech was set for April, and he was reminded of T.S. Eliot's famous line: "April is the cruelest month." Was spring's wake-up call for self-renewal, love and creativity too painful after the long, cold winter of sleep and forgetting? In Scandinavia, suicides came with spring.

The speech was in trouble; the right words to describe his thoughts were elusive. Was it writer's block? Failure was not an option; his entire future was at stake.

He was setting the bar too high. His creativity juices had dried up, he needed to back off, lay low, relax and enjoy life. Then he might find his rhythm again and the lecture would write itself. A standing ovation and the Chair would follow.

Marsha believed Dr. Starr to be writing his paper. How else to explain the hours he spent alone in his office? His briefcase bulged with notes and she expected he would soon ask her to edit his work on her iMac.

One Wednesday evening, Linda Rawlins, personal secretary to Jane Phillips, TV star interviewer for WGBH TV, left a message for Dr. Starr on the office answering machine. Widely admired in the Cambridge community for her TV interviews of local academic luminaries, Jane Phillips wanted to meet with him to discuss a project.

John was excited at the idea of showcasing his latest insights with the glamorous celebrity, Jane Phillips, and just thinking that Russell Plunkett might be watching her program made him chuckle.

He did not wish to appear too eager, however, a little waiting game would make him all the more desirable to the TV bigwigs, so he instructed Marsha to set up a meeting a week or two later. Things were "too busy at present".

When Marsha checked the calendar, she noted that he had only two afternoon TV and radio appearances scheduled. His patients usually came in the morning. Clearly, Dr. Starr must want this extra time in the day to prepare for his important Harvard lecture.

"Are you actually telling me that Dr. Starr can't see Miss Phillips right away?" her secretary cried out in astonishment when Marsha returned the call.

"That's right."

"My God! I can't believe this! Nobody puts off Jane Phillips!"

"Sorry."

"Okay, okay. You're saying he's too busy?"

"He's very busy."

"Jesus, Jane's got projects up to her eyeballs and she's put him ahead of everybody else."

"I can't help that. Dr. Starr's patient load and his media appearances make it impossible for him to meet with her for two weeks, at least."

"Got it. Now I'm looking at her schedule. It's totally jammed and I mean but totally. That's how it goes with celebrities, you know, everybody wants a piece of them. You've gotta help me here, though 'cause she'll have a hissy fit if she doesn't see him soon. Oh my god, what did I just say?"

"You said…"

"Forget it, sweetheart, you didn't hear a thing. So you say he's busy? Okay, okay. Hmm, we're all the way to the middle of December, here. Hey wait a second! There's an opening on the third. How's that?"

"Fine. Three o'clock?"

"It's a done deal!"

When Jane Phillips appeared at the office, Dr. Starr was there to greet her.

"How nice to meet you, Miss Phillips. I've admired your TV program for a long time now."

Jane Phillips was a tall and glowing presence and Marsha watched him smile in that rakish way he reserved for pretty, sexy women. He never smiled like that at her.

He seated Jane Phillips directly across from his desk in a handsome Early-American Amish chair so he could get a good look at her. She was even more striking in person than on television. He noted her baby-blue eyes and thick black lashes, her lightly painted lips and perfect teeth. (Capped, perhaps? Nobody's teeth could be that even and white without a little dental intervention). Her saucy suede shoes with high square heels showed off a pair of long, shapely legs and her emerald green silk suit accentuated her slim hips and full breasts. He calculated she was somewhere in her mid-thirties though she might be younger.

"Dr. Starr, I am presently developing a creativity project for WGBH TV and I hope you'll help me," she said with an enticing smile.

"Project? You mean you're not here to talk about your roundtable program?"

"Oh, no, I've got something totally different in mind."

He stiffened. So he would not get the TV exposure he had hoped for.

"And what would that be, Miss Phillips?" he said coolly.

"I'm thinking of taking a camera crew to New York and interviewing the most creative and successful young artists we can find. I would like you to conduct the interviews." Her blue eyes sparkled with anticipation.

"You want to film me?"

"Absolutely. It would be a documentary."

"To be aired on TV later?"

"Of course."

"Hmm, sounds interesting. Tell me, how long would it take to film this documentary?"

"Oh, just a couple of days. A week at most."

"My schedule's pretty tight right now. Research, patients, an important lecture coming up in the spring. However, if it's only going to take a few days, I might be able to do it."

"Great."

"Do I detect a hint of a British accent in your speech?" he asked her.

"You're very observant," she replied. "After Wellesley, I worked for the BBC in London."

So she was smart as well as beautiful.

When their meeting was over, Jane suggested an afternoon drink at the Harvest Bar just off Harvard Square. "Be my guest," she said, and he did not object. He announced to Marsha that he wouldn't be back until the next day and the two of them left the office together, engaged in animated conversation.

"Make another appointment for Miss Phillips at the same hour two weeks from now," he called out as they went out the door.

Facing each other at a table for two at the Harvest Bar, they shared a bottle of ale.

"I learned to drink it with my colleagues in London," Jane said, "enough to get nicely high, but never drunk!" They both laughed, feeling at once relaxed and happy.

He was intrigued by the way she twisted her locks of shimmering dark hair around her little finger when she talked and he found himself wondering what she was like in bed. He felt a tightening in his chest. A heart attack? Was he going to have a heart attack in front of this young woman? Mercifully, the sensation passed, though not at once, and he found himself gripping the edge of the table so tightly that the tips of his fingers went white. He ordered another bottle of ale, seeking to draw out their time together. Finally, after draining her second glass, Jane signaled for the bill. John felt a pang of disappointment similar to that of a small boy when his birthday party is over.

After paying with a credit card, Jane stood up and John slowly rose to his feet. Shaking her hand, he found it surprisingly firm. "Thanks, but you mustn't go."

"I wish I could stay," she said softly, gently withdrawing her hand. "I'll call you."

He watched her as she slipped away through the crowd, then suddenly drained of energy, sat back down in his seat.

"Another ale, Sir?"

"No, no," John said, reaching for his briefcase. "I'm leaving."

THREE

Jane was wearing a short, white linen skirt with a matching silk blouse the next time she visited the office. Her shoes were beige espadrilles, and she carried a small beige knit bag over her shoulder. She wore no makeup other than a soft cream-colored lipstick.

She did not speak to Marsha who pretended to be busy at her desk. Standing by the window, Jane looked out at the Charles River sparkling in the distance. Dr. Starr was fifteen minutes late for their meeting; his patient had taken up more time than expected, and she was annoyed.

On seeing her again, John was arrested by her youth and unaffected beauty.

"Tell me, how are you?" He gave her a searching look.

"I'm good," she said, holding his gaze.

"Please sit down. Would you like a coffee? My assistant, Miss Romano, brews up a very tasty cup."

"Thanks, but no," Jane Phillips said briefly. She leaned towards him. "It's all set!"

"What's set?"

"Our documentary on Creativity in the Arts Today is on go! I've got full backing from the network. WGBH loves the idea as I knew they would, exactly because you're not an art historian or an artist yourself. You're a famous creativity expert who has written extensively about artists. You'll give us a unique analysis of what's happening in the arts today."

"True enough."

"It should be a lot of fun," she smiled.

"Of course we'll have to keep it pretty general, not get too abstract in our approach if we are going to appeal to your viewers," he said crisply.

"Naturally."

"When do we get started?"

"Whenever you want."

"How's that?"

"Well, the folks up top usually let me run my own ship. I'm not dumb, you know, I really earned that magna cum laude from Wellesley."

"I wouldn't doubt it," he smiled.

This woman knew her own worth. No doubt she'd learned the hard way in the entertainment business.

"I'm ready any time," he said.

"I'll round up my camera crew and we'll fly down to New York first thing Monday morning. Of course, we'll take care of your expenses. I'll let you know the flight time tomorrow."

When he shook her hand to say goodbye, his spirits soared. This was his chance to break out of the mold, re-energize himself. It was exactly what the doctor ordered and when he returned to writing his lecture, his thoughts and words would flow freshly, like a mountain stream after the rains. Maybe his writing block would mercifully come to an end in a different venue like New York.

John told Erika that night the project had the full backing of the TV station and filming would start the following week.

"Oh, darling," Erika said. "New York is so exciting, not like dull old Boston!"

"Yes, it's full of creative energy. It's the cultural oasis of our country and I'll be meeting our most innovative, young artists. I'll probably include my observations in the Harvard speech."

Erika clapped her hands and ran to embrace him. "I can't wait! We'll have such fun, going to restaurants, walking in Central Park. We'll finally be alone together, darling, and that's the most important thing for me, being with you!"

"Erika, darling, I'm so sorry, it's my fault. I didn't make it clear that this is a professional project of WGBH TV's Jane Phillips, a serious commitment, with interviews that will be shown to millions of TV viewers. It's not a vacation; I've got to be working all the time."

"But I want to be with you and I thought you'd want to be with me, too." Throwing herself down on the sofa, she looked at him through angry tears.

"Your dependence is a heavy burden, Erika," John sighed. "I said I was sorry, didn't I? You know how much I would have loved going to New York with you."

Tilly, the maid, appeared to announce dinner.

"Come along, Erika, don't just sit there being unhappy," John said.

"I'm thinking about what you said, about my dependence being a burden to you."

"Let's not dwell on that now," he said brightly. "The kids are out tonight so we can discuss your issues at dinner."

But Erika did not wish to talk and they ate their meal in silence. Though the veal parmigiana was excellent, she picked at her food. Later in bed, John stroked her face in a moment of sudden tenderness and was surprised by her passionate response.

FOUR

At her next appointment with Hilda Payne, Erika told her she was unable to resist John's sexual advances even when she was upset with him.

"You mean you can't say no?" said Hilda Payne.

"That's right."

"Well, you're not the first woman with that problem," Hilda chuckled, drawing a laugh from Erika. "And since you're both at your sexual peak, that may explain part of it. However," she said, growing serious, "try to explain how it happens."

"When he touches me he wakes me up in the fullest sense, as though I've been dead all along. The other night, I was upset he didn't want me with him in New York but after we made love I felt happy and whole again."

"What's he doing in New York?" Hilda's question came sharp and pointed, like a surgical cut.

"'Strictly business' is what he told me."

"'Strictly business'? And what do you think that means?"

"Who knows? I guess it's another way of saying he won't have time for me. He's interviewing creative young artists for a documentary about the current art scene."

"Sounds interesting. It's nothing to do with you so give him some space," Hilda Payne said flatly

"And that's just what I've done." Erika took a deep breath. Did he actually think she'd *want* to sit in on the interviews? For her, New York was about breathing in the excitement that was so much part of the city. "He's teaming up with Jane Phillips," Erika said.

"*The* Jane Phillips from WGBH TV?"

"Right. It's very exciting."

"A great move on his part. Jane Phillips is quite the star around here. You must be proud of him."

"But..."

"But what?"

"We could have had such fun in New York together! When he comes back, he'll be busy preparing for his lecture at Harvard in the spring so I won't see him much."

"What? John's lecturing at Harvard?"

"Yes, in April. We're both very excited, of course. It's quite an honor."

"Yes, but let's not get too worked up about it," retorted Hilda. "There are others more widely known in the field of creativity than John Starr."

"'More widely known'? What do you mean?"

"Just what I said. Others are better known than John. Like Colin Martindale. Ever heard of him?"

"No."

"Well, he's considered the world's leading expert in the field right now. He's both an author and editor and he's written quite a number of books on the subject. He's a superstar." Almost as an afterthought, she added, "John's published very little, you know."

Her comments stung. Were there actually people better in the field than John? No, it couldn't be true. Hilda always enjoyed tearing him down. She'd already pointed out that Erika's illusions about him were holding her back and that she needed to look at John, warts and all, if she were to reclaim her real self. At this point, however, Erika wasn't sure anymore what 'real self' meant.

It was true he'd published very little. Right now he was suffering from a writing block he blamed on her "dependency issues". If she even tiptoed into his study for a kiss when he was in his "creative thinking mode," he reacted with impatience, insisting that these disruptions unsettled his mind and arrested the delicate flow of new ideas.

But she never meant to bother him! She loved him more than life itself!

"Let me ask you this, Erika," Hilda was saying, "Is it the passionate lover you must have who feeds this addiction/ dependency? Is it the creativity expert who systematically dismantles your confidence and makes you feel stupid and crazy? Tell me, Erika, can you honestly say that John gives you the emotional support you're looking for?"

How tough Hilda was, whacking away at her illusions, exposing the cruel realities of life with John.

"Because John has left you to navigate on your own, you feel abandoned, right?" Erika nodded. "But the other side of the coin is that he has given you a chance to break away and get a life. All your vulnerability and masochistic dependency could disappear tomorrow if you let go of your illusions, Erika. You can do it, I'm sure of it. With my help, you will drop your chains."

After John left for New York, Erika made a visit to the room he had used for her therapy at the far end of the house. She'd never been able to persuade him to bring his practice there, his argument being that the Institute was the appropriate venue, not his home.

She hadn't returned since starting with Hilda Payne. The long drapes were still closed, John's wooden chair stood across from her comfortable, upholstered chair. Her eyes filled with tears.

Their therapeutic sessions brought them together in so many intimate ways and this room belonged to them. Why couldn't he have kept her on? Why had he sent her away? As she moved around the room, something seemed changed. Yes, John's filing cabinet containing financial records and important documents was no longer next to his desk but positioned against the wall near the fireplace. She began opening the heavy drawers of the cabinet, one by one, searching for Catherine's letters. Long ago she had secretly read them all and later confessed to John. His reaction had been unusually mild; he empathized with her curiosity. The presence of a first wife could loom large over the psyche of a second wife, he told her, the desire to read the letters was entirely normal. She remembered him sitting down next to her on the sofa and taking her in his arms. "Never forget," he had whispered in her ear, "you, Erika, are the only woman I have ever loved."

When she reached the last drawer, there were still no letters. Had he thrown them away? She felt a wave of relief; he was finally hers. His nostalgia of a time when he was young and in love with Catherine was over. Shifting through the piles of official papers in the drawer, she came upon a large faded photograph of a young girl. No more than sixteen or seventeen, with a heart shaped face and a radiant smile, she was exquisite. Her tight dress revealed a beautiful, voluptuous figure. Scribbled in a girlish hand across the bottom of the picture were the words: "To John, my gorgeous hunk. Your Doreen." Her heart stopped. Who was this girl? He had never mentioned her.

Later, when Erika called him in New York, she asked him about the photo.

"Who is she, John?"

"Erika, why are you snooping through my drawers?"

"I wasn't snooping. I was simply wondering who the girl was and why you never told me about her."

"She's somebody I knew in high school."

"She signs the picture 'your Doreen.' You call that just 'somebody'?"

"Okay, she was my girlfriend. That was a long time ago."

"Were you in love with her?"

"Erika, this is getting ridiculous. We had a little thing going, that's all. I just told you."

"Did you sleep with her?"

"No, like I said, we played around and then I went off to Andover. That was the end of it."

"So why did you keep the picture?"

"I actually forgot I even had it."

"Really?"

A heavy silence ensued. "Darling," John said finally, "there's something I need to tell you."

"What?"

"The filming is taking longer than we thought." He sounded very far away.

"How much longer?"

"About a week."

"A whole week?" Did her voice betray her disappointment?

"Yes," he was saying. "I'm afraid it'll be a week."

"Are you happy with what's been filmed?"

"Extremely. We've got a very competent team."

"That's good. Jane Phillips is part of your team, isn't she?"

"Sometimes."

"She's beautiful, isn't she?"

"Not really, not like you."

"Every day you're with her, right?"

"Stop this, Erika. Look, I hardly have anything to do with her."

"No?"

"What are you trying to get at?"

"Nothing, darling. Nothing at all." She quickly changed the subject. "Is the Four Seasons as lovely as I remember?"

"Not as lovely without you."

"Oh, John, we were so happy then." Her voice broke. "Will we ever be like that again?"

"Like what again, Erika?"

"Never mind."

"Now be a good girl and work hard with Hilda Payne. Don't let the kids get to you. I'll be back soon, darling."

"John, I love you."

"I love you, too."

"You really mean that?"

"What a silly question. Of course I do, darling. Talk to you later."

FIVE

Meeting the young artists was an exhilarating experience for John; they were happy to talk about themselves and their art and he was eager to draw out the psychological dimensions of their creativity.

A papier maché sculpture stood in the middle of the first studio he visited with Jane Phillips and her camera crew. It was a floral arrangement of gigantic cone-shaped white flowers imbedded with baby pacifiers whose rubber nipples were painted crimson. The cameras zeroed in on the flowers, then on John who was staring closely at the nipples. The artist, Rachael Train, a tall, curvaceous brunette with black eye shadow was wearing a see-through black blouse that revealed high, pointed breasts. Her tight black skirt hung down to the floor.

"Have you named your work, Rachael?" was John's first question.

"Yup. 'Candy Cones.'"

"How so?"

"Candy's sweet."

"I see. Tell me, Rachael, what motivated you to create this work?"

"I play with forms. I can't say I ever have anything specific in mind when I begin a work, but this time I ended up with flowers in the shape of breasts."

"You open yourself up to the imaginative flow, in other words."

"Right."

"Like a child at play."

"You got it."

"Now these flowers, is there a reason they're colored white?"

"My own breasts are white. If they were black, I'd make the flowers black!" She gave him a vampire look.

"I see. And the red nipples on the pacifiers?"

"A sexual invitation; what else? Hell, isn't that the way you guys see them? Breasts are for lovers to play with, to suck, to get it on!"

"In other words, you are saying that by painting the nipples crimson you remove breasts from the symbol of the nurturing mother to the symbol of the seductive lover."

"Hey, Doc, are you ever in the zone!" Inching up to him, she yanked down her blouse and her ample breasts rolled into view.

"So tell me, Doc, am I the sainted mother or the whore?"

"Cut!" shouted Jane to the shocked camera crew. "We're not filming porno, Rachel, so that's it. We're closing down. We're behind schedule, anyway." Turning to John, she said smartly, "Thank you, Dr. Starr, for your incisive comments about this artist's creativity and best of luck to you in the future, Rachael."

After a long day of work, John usually met up with Jane and the film crew for a drink in the Four Seasons bar, and afterwards, dined with her in various dark and intimate restaurants near the hotel. New York was full of such places.

John appreciated Jane's listening skills, finely honed from her years as a professional interviewer. One night, he found himself describing his years in Mexico, the collapse of his first marriage and his struggles with Erika's psychological vulnerabilities.

"She's a victim of an abusive childhood," he explained. "She sees me as her greatest source of strength."

"And you are, I'm sure. She's a lucky woman."

"Thank you."

"Your wife is Boston's premier hostess, and I guess you know invitations to your events are highly coveted. You'll have to invite me one day." She gave him a teasing smile.

"Certainly."

"She inherited great wealth I've heard."

"Yes."

"Life must be really satisfying when you have such a gorgeous wife and so much money."

"Couldn't be better," he said pleasantly.

So she had a taste for money. When they parted company after dinner, he bowed and kissed her hand. Later, alone in the elevator, he could hear the pounding of his heart, alarming him.

Eager for long, intimate conversations, Erika persisted in her early morning phone calls to John but he usually cut her short by telling her the camera crew was waiting for him down in the lobby. But it was the beautiful Jane, alone in the Four Seasons dining room, who waited for him to join her. Despite the chronic stiffness in his shoulders and knees, old injuries, no doubt, from his days as a swimming star, she made him feel young and vigorous.

The breakfasts were superb. Along with blueberry pancakes and a variety of hot (the Irish oatmeal was especially tasty) and cold cereals, the breakfast menu's highlights included freshly baked blueberry and cranberry muffins, feathery scrambled eggs, small, succulent croissants, oat breads hot from the oven, strawberries with whipped cream, freshly squeezed orange juice in crystal goblets and steaming, dark Colombian coffee. Could it get any better? A feast fit for a king, and now with Jane Phillips, he was experiencing once again the richness and happiness of life.

One evening, Jane turned down his offer to join him for dinner. She had been invited to a party.

"I won't stay long," she told him. "Have to get up in the morning, right?"

"So who's giving the party?" He tried to sound casual.

"An old friend. Someone in the business. He's got a great apartment over on Park and he's been very generous to me."

John ate dinner with the movie crew at a nearby French restaurant. He drank several glasses of wine and talked about moviemaking and creativity. It was past midnight when he returned to his room. Stepping out of the elevator, he spied Jane at the end of the hall, unlocking her door.

"It looks like you didn't make it an early night," he said with a laugh. "Hey, I didn't know you're just a couple of doors down."

"So why don't you drop in?"

"Right now?"

"Why not?"

"I'm pretty tired."

"Come on, I'll give you a drink."

"I'd like that," he said. "I'll be there in a minute."

Quickly, he shaved and changed his shirt, replacing his tie with a patterned Ferragamo ascot that complemented his dark blue blazer. He was ready for adventure. Clearly, their mutual attraction had reached a defining moment and he wondered if she would make the first move. If not, he would. For the first time in his life with Erika he would not resist temptation. Fidelity had always been a point of honor for him and Erika was the only woman he had ever loved. Their sexual passion continued unabated but he missed the relatedness, the melding of mind and heart that had once existed between them. Was it her self-absorption, her excessive dependency and vulnerability that left him dissatisfied?

Ever since Arthur Watts proposed the lecture at Harvard, he had been immobilized. His writing block had put everything at risk, his career, in effect, his entire future. Could Jane, this near-stranger waiting for him down the hall, have been sent by God to release his creative powers through the sexual act?

Jane opened her door right away when he knocked.

"Come in and make yourself at home," she said, kissing him lightly on each cheek, European style. "I'm just going to slip into something more comfortable." She disappeared into the bathroom.

Her suite was larger than John's, and the walls were decorated with bright abstract paintings. Settling down on the sofa with a view of the city, John gazed out on the lights flickering in the darkness, but as the minutes went by, he began to wonder what was taking her so long. His watch said twelve forty-five, it was getting late, and he was ready to leave.

At last, Jane reappeared dressed in a white terrycloth robe, her hair loosely hanging, her face without makeup except for her lips which were painted a deep red. Handing him a glass of champagne, she raised her own for a toast.

"To you and me, John, and to our many future projects together. You've gone out of your way to share your brilliant insights with me and I'm truly grateful. Thank you, John." Her baby blue eyes sparkled as she sat down beside him on the sofa.

"We make a good team," John said with an easy smile.

They sipped the champagne slowly, luxuriating in its fine, fruity flavor.

"It's been a lot of fun," John added.

"And the best part of it has been getting to know you." Jane said in a husky voice. "May I play the shrink and tell you why you came to my room tonight?" Her face was close to his.

"Tell me."

"I believe you and I have reached a stage in our relationship when we're ready for a greater intimacy."

This was the moment to leave and he knew it. He simply needed to get up off the sofa and return to his room. But something was holding him back. He could barely move, so he leaned back against the pillows and closed his eyes. She was making all the moves and he made no effort to stop her. She had taken his hand and was slowly drawing it down over her bare breasts and stomach. He became aware that she was wearing nothing under her robe and he opened his eyes.

"Would you like to untie the sash, John? Go ahead, I want you to." She stood up to fully face him and he lazily untied it. The kimono fell open.

Her body was fuller than Erika's, with dark pubic hair, long, shapely legs, a tiny waist, and high, round breasts.

"Now, take *your* clothes off," she commanded as he struggled to stand up. Helping him remove his blazer, she hung it on the back of a chair and watched him undress, her eyes glittering with a special brightness as she admired the still-supple and muscular body of a champion swimmer.

"Wow!" she murmured, dropping to her knees, "you really turn me on!"

"Get up off your knees, Jane. That's not my style," he said coldly, pulling her roughly to her feet.

"It's our special moment," she said, rubbing her soft, naked body against him like a cat. "Ever since we met, I've been wanting this to happen." Leading him into her dimly lit bedroom, she said, "We must make our lovemaking a process of mutual pleasuring so each of us can experience our full sexual potential."

Unlike Erika who was always ready for him at any time of day or night, Jane insisted on long, drawn out caresses to reach her desired state of readiness. Unaccustomed to this endless foreplay and fighting off a headache, John's initial excitement began to wane. Then without warning, Jane suddenly cried out, "Now! Now!" just as he was about to end their erotic play, and he fell on her with a burst of passion and relief.

Afterwards, she declared him to be the best of all the lovers she had known and sprang nimbly off the bed to refill their champagne glasses.

"Don't fall asleep yet, darling," she cried, handing him his glass. "Let me make a toast." She held up her glass, her naked body glowing in the soft light. "To a thousand nights like this one!"

They drank slowly and deeply, then set down their empty glasses on the bedside table.

"You naughty boy, you're going to be waking me up every half hour to make love, I know, and I'll want you again and again!" she whispered in his ear but John did not hear her. He had already fallen into a deep slumber.

He dreamed he was visiting Notre Dame in Paris with Jane, and, after climbing the one thousand steps to the tower, they feasted their eyes on the magnificent city spread out below them. A hideous gargoyle from the cornice of the tower, fangs bared, bulbous eyes ablaze, landed beside him and grabbing hold of him, began squeezing his neck. Screaming, Jane backed away, covering her face with her hands. After wrestling the creature to the ground, John twisted free and raced down the steep stone steps of the tower. His dream abruptly ended because someone was tugging at his arm. It was Jane.

"Make love to me again! Come on, John, I can tell you're ready!"

"Stop it, Jane," he said, pushing her away. "You interrupted my dream and that's not good! It's going to be hard to interpret later."

"But you're supposed to be able to interpret any part of a dream."

"That's not quite true. He moved away from her. "I have to leave now. My notebook's in my room and I've got to jot down the dream while it's fresh in my mind." Climbing off the bed, he dressed quickly, sweating profusely.

"But you can write it here! I've got some notepaper so why do you have to go?" She reminded him of a spoiled child.

"No, that won't work," John said shortly.

"Fuck you!" Jane cried, her face screwed up in anger.

"What do I hear coming out of that luscious mouth, Jane darling? It doesn't become you, my lovely one." He kissed her ear lobe. "We'll meet for breakfast in the morning and eat fresh strawberries and whipped cream."

"I'll want bacon and eggs," she muttered.

When he leaned over her to say goodnight she gripped his shoulders tightly and gave him a long, deep kiss, her tongue twisting around his own, awakening his desire once again. But he had made up his mind. The dream was a warning.

SIX

John continued his nightly trysts with Jane during the filming in New York. But she was wearing him down and he made sure to get back to his own room for at least six hours of uninterrupted sleep before Erika woke him up with her phone call. Early each morning, he practiced meditation and deep breathing, exercises he had long neglected. Why had he broken off this habit shortly after his marriage? Was he too tired after their late night parties, the balls, the dinners? Was maintaining their reputation as Most Glamorous Couple in Boston Society becoming counterproductive for both Erika and himself? Here in the quiet of his hotel room he was able to empty his mind of unimportant matters, free up his creative energies. It was a relief not to have Erika around with her endless demands, interrupting him when he was on the verge of a theoretical breakthrough.

He returned to working on his Harvard speech and miraculously, on the seventh day, the words began to flow. His writer's block and the despair that accompanied it were finally laid to rest.

He did not feel guilty about his affair with Jane because he credited her and his return to the practice of daily meditation with restoring his ability to write again. His relationship with her was something akin to a restorative visit to a health spa. He was not in love with her; he loved Erika. Despite her Wellesley education, he found Jane to be superficial and obsessed with fame and money. She was much too crude for him; her sexual aggressiveness repelled him, but he had to admit she had given him back his sense of confidence and his adventurous spirit.

Once back in Boston, he planned to end the relationship. He would not jeopardize his marriage and risk losing everything.

The last artist on their list was Marcus Gordon, a strapping young man who had recently completed an enormous black and white portrait in oil inspired by a childhood photograph of the infamous serial killer, Ted Bundy, who murdered thirty six young women before he was finally caught and executed in 1989. The painting rested against a wall at the back of his studio, lit by naked bulbs hanging from the ceiling. Black splotches were splattered across Bundy's handsome, boyish face, his hair was neatly combed, and he was dressed in a white shirt and shorts for tennis. His V-neck sweater was slung carelessly around his shoulders, a style favored by society figures in the 1930s. Other than the black splotches, there was nothing in this canvas to suggest the killer of dozens of pretty college women he seduced. He could have been any affluent young man setting out to play a game of tennis.

"A good likeness, but no warning of the murderer here," John began, "except for those blotches on his face. Did you splatter them on the canvas?"

"Yeah."

"Like dried blood. Very radical. Very audacious."

"Yeah."

"However, I see you chose to copy the photograph of Ted Bundy as a young man rather than as a mature adult because you wanted to make a statement about loss."

"Loss?"

"Well, yes, in this case, most likely your own loss of innocence. You are improvising, playing freely with the concept of the young person within us all who exists even within the psyche of a ferocious killer. Am I not correct?"

"Never thought of it that way."

"Tell me, are we looking at the killer who was once young, or the youth who will grow up to be a killer? We're into necrophilia here."

"What's 'necrophilia'?"

"The love of death."

"Look, I'm an artist, a creator, and you can see what you want." Marcus Gordon paused to let his words sink in, sweeping a large hand through his wavy black hair as he grinned at the cameras. John saw immediately he was a conceited fool with no self-awareness.

"We don't work in a vacuum, Marcus," John explained, " and your unconscious is on view here. It is the engine for your interpretation of Ted Bundy."

"Bullshit, Starr! What's this 'unconscious' crap? Hell, I'm more awake than you are!"

"You seem not to understand the creative drives," John said with a heavy sigh.

"Look, people who see my paintings get turned on, okay?" He pointed a finger in John's face. "Hey, Mr. Starr, I've got another painting to show you!"

"I'm 'Dr. Starr'," John corrected him.

Marcus Gordon gave no indication of hearing John and walked ahead of him into a larger room with Jane and the camera crew following excitedly behind. Against a bare, cracked wall stood a huge oil painting of a small, elderly nun holding a tiny, starving child in her arms. Beside her, a homely young girl in a green velvet dress appeared to be singing before a rapt audience of family and friends. On closer inspection it became clear that these two women were one and the same at different stages of life. The soft smooth face of the girl was in sharp juxtaposition to the wrinkled countenance of the aged nun.

"She looks familiar," John murmured.

"You're looking at Mother Teresa, Mr. Starr. Bet you didn't know she was a singer as a kid, did you?"

"Actually, I was aware of that fact," John said. Recently, by chance, he had come across this bit of minutia.

"Okay," said Marcus grudgingly, "so you knew. Anyway, we're looking at the child inside us, get it?"

John suddenly had a thought. Gordon was rejecting the grown-up grandiose person, maybe with the wish to regress even further. "Could it be that you wish to go back to the innocence of childhood?"

"You've gotta be joking, Mr. Starr!" Shaking his head in disbelief, Marcus, laughed loudly, showing a row of perfect white teeth. "'Childhood'? Is this some kind of joke?" To John's disgust, Jane and the crew burst out laughing.

Jane then interceded to conduct her own interview with Marcus and asked him a whole range of questions unrelated to the subject of creativity. She wanted to know his age (thirty five), marital status (single), and his interests (flying small planes, rollerblading, snowboarding, surfboarding, and wild sex). Everyone chuckled appreciatively at his last answer except John.

"What a guy!" cried Jane as their chauffeur-driven car hummed down Fifth Avenue. "So brilliant and sexy! And his insights into creativity were impressive, weren't they, John? I think we'll be hearing a lot more from Marcus for sure!"

John made no reply. There was nothing he could say that she would understand and he wondered how he could have ever thought her intelligent. He had come to realize she was using him just the way she planned to use Marcus. A celebrity hound, that's what Jane was, and she'd met her match in that young man.

If he never saw Jane again he would have few regrets.

It wasn't until their plane began its final descent into Boston's Logan Airport that John told Jane their affair was over. Seated next to one another in the ample, leather seats provided in first class, they had both napped during the flight out of New York and it was the captain's voice announcing their proximity to Boston that roused John, reminding him of what he must do.

"Jane, darling..."

"What's going on?" Her face was full of sleep.

"We can't see each other anymore."

"What the hell are you talking about?" Now fully awake, she gripped the arms of her seat, staring at him in shock.

"I'm talking about us, Jane. You know my situation with Erika is delicate. We're dealing with a person who is extremely vulnerable psychologically."

"You're not making sense, John."

"We have to accept the fact that it's over between us."

"But why?" she cried, flushing angrily. "I'm not asking you to leave Erika!"

"She's not well, Jane. If she found out about us, it would kill her. Just think about it!"

"You really do care about her, don't you," she said slowly. "You'd give up all that wonderful wild sex we have together just for Erika." Her face was full of pain; he would have to soften the message.

"Jane, I owe you a great deal, but it can't go on."

"I can't bear it!" Taking his face in her hands, she gave him a long, wet kiss. "You're so right for me, I can't get enough of you!" Her voice had taken on a new urgency.

"Easy," John said, carefully pushing her away. "The camera crew's going to catch on." Jane wheeled around in her seat to stare into the back of the plane.

"Who cares about them? They can't see us from back there in coach. Besides, they're all fucking each other."

"How do you know?"

"You missed what was going on?" She gave a contemptuous laugh.

"I wasn't watching them, I was watching you."

"John, are you really serious about our not seeing each other anymore?"

"It's too big a risk."

"Haven't I told you a million times you're my hunk?"

"Stop it, Jane," he said sharply.

"But it's true!" Leaning closer to him, she whispered in conspiratorial tones: "I have a video camera over my bed! While we're making love we could watch ourselves!"

"Pretty cool, pretty cool," he murmured, briefly aroused. Peering out the window, he watched the darkening clouds swirling past as the plane lurched downward in a sudden gust of turbulence. "Jane, we really can't meet."

"I won't accept that."

"We haven't a choice darling. I'll call you."

"Tomorrow?"

"Maybe."

"You better not put me off, John, or I'll tell the whole town about us!"

Was she threatening him? He couldn't tell. All he knew was that he'd have to keep her at bay.

Heading towards the exit at Logan airport, John heard Erika's voice. She was running towards him, her face lit up with smiles.

"Darling, there you are! I looked all over for you at the gate, but I couldn't find you. Aren't you surprised to see me? You didn't expect me, did you, because you told me not to bother coming to the airport!" She laughed happily, her nervous fingers searching his face, her warm breath caressing his cheek. Catching a glimpse of Jane behind him, she whispered excitedly in his ear. "I know that woman!"

"What woman?"

"Behind you! It's Jane Phillips, isn't it?"

"Jane Phillips?"

"The TV interviewer! You were working with her, right?"

Grabbing her hand, John said briskly, "Erika, let's get out of here."

Hurrying beside him through the thick crowd, she looked up into his face, her eyes shining. "Oh, John darling, I've missed you so much! It seems like you've been away forever and ever!"

Coming to an abrupt halt, he held her at arm's length. She did not look well. The circles under her eyes attested to sleepless nights, the worry lines around her mouth appeared deeper. Never one to wear makeup, she needed it now for her skin was sallow. Perhaps he was still under the spell of Jane whose beauty seemed so

244

fresh, so young. Erika, for all her loveliness, seemed somehow faded, like a cherished photograph from long ago.

SEVEN

Workmen now flooded the house daily to install an indoor lap pool where John and Roger could swim in cold weather. At the same time, the library was being enlarged to include the complete set of the writings by Carl Jung and Sigmund Freud, recently bound in dark red leather. Their twenty-foot-long-rectangular antique table in the dining room was being replaced with a ninety-two-inch round wooden table so that dinner conversations would flow more easily. Long ago, Dr. Di Brioni had lectured John on the superiority of the round table over the square or rectangular model for creative social discourse.

Tilly, the maid, reported to Erika that she was hearing fits of barking and yapping in the rooms above the pantry.

"Where did you say you heard barking, Tilly?"

"Upstairs, where the kids live, you know, at the end of the hall."

"You're sure it was a dog barking? "

"Oh, yes, Ma'am! No doubt about it!"

"A dog? How incredible! I've got to find him right away!"

Hurrying upstairs, she tried to open Roger's door but it was locked. There was no sound of a dog and she returned downstairs for dinner.

Once seated at the table, John confronted Roger. The idea of a dog in the house had little appeal for him; unlike Erika, he was not an animal lover.

"Did you bring in a dog in here?" he asked his son.

"A dog?"

"Do I have to repeat myself?"

"You're talking about a dog around here?" Roger shrugged his shoulders. "Don't know anything about *that*."

"We've heard barking," John said, studying his son.

Erika cried out. "If you've got a little dog upstairs in your room, I want to meet him!" Her eyes sparkled with excitement.

Roger shook his head. "Haven't a clue," he said airily.

How clever he was, Adriana was thinking. When he lied he was *so* convincing! Probably John Starr lied just like his son because even though Roger resembled his bitch mother, he was *so* like his fucking father! In fact she was sure she'd caught John Starr in deep shit a couple of times, but he was a lot faster on his feet than Roger. He also made people think the mistake was theirs, not his. A shrink trick and she laughed to herself, remembering how she'd always managed to outwit those creeps in therapy. Yep, every single time!

Erika wasn't mad about the dog; in fact she was smiling. So what was going on? Then Adriana remembered Roger had told her Erika once adopted a little dog around the time she went insane and that poor dog was run over by a truck. That's when Erika became John Starr's patient and they fell madly in love.

It was always hard to figure Erika's moods. From one minute to the next, she could go from normal-nice to weird-bitchy. Sometimes, she acted really nice and gave Adriana fancy jewelry and expensive new clothes. On those occasions she imagined herself as Erika's daughter, living in this grand house for the rest of her life, enjoying all its elegance and luxury. Her name would be Adriana Starr and she'd be pictured along with all the other pampered socialites she read about in glossy magazines. To be rich and spoiled with a gorgeous mother like Erika was too awesome! It made her almost giddy!

And so what if the woman was crazy! Everybody was crazy!

Sometimes Adriana felt guilty about putting her off especially when Erika wanted to discuss something dumb like cleaning up their room. Erika was very attached to the maid who cleaned the rooms. It seems she'd been with the family like *forever*! The maid left because Roger didn't pick up his clothes and what a lot of crap that was! That old woman hated cleaning up after them even though it was her job so she complained about them to Erika because she hated their guts! And that's why she left!

Erika made Adriana nervous because she was so intense and the way she behaved around John Starr was totally *pathetic*! Did she think he was some kind of fucking *god*?

Adriana could hear Roger getting all obsequious and queer at the table like he sometimes did with his mother when he thought she was going to get mad. It made Adriana want to scream that he was such a fucking wimp. She hated wimps! Her father was so wimpish she couldn't stand being around him.

EIGHT

When Erika went upstairs to check out Roger's room to see if there was actually a dog she could hear Adriana and Roger talking in loud voices.

"What a fucking drag to have to sit at that crappy table and deal with the King," Adriana was saying. "I mean, it's just *so* annoying! He's *so* boring!"

Standing in the shadow of their open door, Erika stood frozen on the spot. "The "King"? Was the girl talking about John?

"Yeah," Roger said. "They like figured out the dog thing, I guess. Erika's probably on her way up here *as we speak*!"

"Hey, she's not going to do anything."

"Hell, I won't mind if she comes in here. *Jesus!* When she walks into a room, she's some sexy dame. It's awesome!"

"Shut the fuck up, Roger, you're like *so* evil! Yeah, she's sexy, but she looks *sallow* and *old* because the King won't even let her wear makeup! I mean if he's the *king*, she's gotta be the *queen*. So how can she let him tell her what to do? Your father ought to fuck off! I mean, like what's wrong with makeup, for crissake? *Hello*, Roger! You're not even listening to me! Why are you such an asshole?"

"Sorry." He gave her a sheepish grin.

"I noticed the Queen didn't look mad at all about Rufus and I think it's because she totally went insane when her little dog was run over. Remember? She told us so herself."

"Yeah, we don't have to worry about her. It's my dad, you know, he hates animals and like I don't know how the fuck he found out. I mean, like Rufus gets his pill every morning so he's out of commission for the rest of the day. How can he bark if he's asleep?"

"Yeah. It's just *so* weird."

Though Erika barely spoke to Roger anymore, she was taken aback that he still saw her as a sexual object and she didn't know whether to be pleased or annoyed. Adriana's remarks about her being "sallow" and "old" cut deep, reminding her that the years were slipping by; she would be forty-one her next birthday. Would she still be able to have the baby she so desperately wanted? Her heart ached. The passage of time was like the relentless ticking of a clock, barely audible in youth but noisy and distracting with advancing age.

Now she heard sounds of scuffling and laughter, then Roger's voice.

"Hey, girl, come over here and give the *man* a kiss! I want a kiss, baby, in fact, I want a whole lot more!" The door slammed shut then flew open again, and the music of *Black Sabbath* blasted out into the hall, its ear-splitting percussion roiling the quiet of the house.

Erika banged repeatedly on the door and Roger finally appeared, his shirt rumpled and his hair in his eyes. Behind him, Erika caught a glimpse of Adriana running to turn off the music.

A dank aroma of dirty laundry and dog odor greeted Erika as she stepped into the room where large, empty boxes lay on the floor. Moving gingerly past them, she reached the French doors leading out to the balcony and turning around, faced them both.

"I think there's a dog in here," she said slowly, "I can smell him!"

Adriana quickly slid past her through the connecting door to her own room where she sat down at the vanity table and lit up a cigarette.

"Please don't smoke," Erika said. "I'm allergic."

"Sorry, I didn't know."

"Well, now you do." She looked straight at Roger. "Where's the little fellow?"

He laughed softly. "He's under the bed. We rescued him after he was almost run over by a truck."

"You saved him?" Erika said. "That's so great!"

"You're not mad?" he said, rolling his eyes in amazement. "We were afraid you would be, that's why I lied about it. Sorry."

"Saving animals is something I believe in."

"Gee, can we keep him here for a while?"

"Of course! Can I see him?"

"Sure thing. You can come out of there, Rufus!"

Whimpering and scratching his way out from his hiding place under the bed, a small, brown dog of dubious parentage with long spotted ears and large, dark eyes emerged trembling and wagging his tail.

"O, poor little Rufus," she said, taking him in her arms. "How old is he?"

"Maybe a year?" Roger looked at Adriana who nodded.

"Oh, he's only a baby! You should have told me."

"I know," Roger said.

"He's so sweet," Erika said, gently stroking the dog's face while he licked her ear. "I love him. We'll share him, okay, and walk him every day, how about that?"

"Great!"

"And when you go back home, I'll keep him here with me."

"No problem, Erika, no problem." Roger's voice cracked.

"He'll make us all so happy! I'm sure John will love him, too. We'll get some nice doggie beds and he can sleep here with you but I'll take him sometimes, too."

"Sure thing."

"You're a cool chick, Erika," Adriana said, smiling.

When Erika went to her room, she threw open the windows to let in the fresh night air. Peeling off her sweater, she leaned against the sill, inhaling deeply as she looked up at the starry sky. She felt happier than she had been in months. Adriana had actually called her "cool" and she couldn't have expected a greater compliment from this troubled girl.

Peering at herself in the bathroom mirror, she decided that John was doing her no favors when he ordered her to stop wearing makeup and she wondered why she had so eagerly agreed. Tonight, she'd heard the unvarnished truth from Adriana and she wasn't going to look "sallow" anymore.

Thanks to Hilda Payne, she was through with playing the obedient wife and ready to exert her womanly power.

NINE

John's work on creativity was gaining increased attention around Boston, and with a little more exposure, he hoped to be appointed to the governor's commission on mental health. His speech was developing well, Marsha was editing his third draft, and his relationship with Erika was more stress-free than it had been in a long time. He sighed with relief that, finally, Erika's neediness was being addressed by someone else.

As the Harvard seminar drew closer, he tried to spend every free minute reworking his paper. Reluctantly, however, he kept on a few of his more seriously disturbed patients and out of deference to Erika, Robert Giuliani as well.

The man was difficult, no question about it; but he was Erika's beloved uncle, so John took pains not to be confrontational.

In the early sessions, Robert discussed his hope that someday he might be able to return to documentary filmmaking. His physical therapy would most likely continue the rest of his life, but when he was strong enough, he wanted to film the Haitian orphanage he knew and loved.

John encouraged this creative hope, but he told Robert he was avoiding the gut issue: dealing with the psychological and physiological trauma of the plane crash.

"You must touch your feet to the fire if you wish to be free," John said. "We must expose those feelings you have repressed. Once you deal with these issues fully, you will fly, take off, so to speak."

"I think my flying days are over," Robert said dryly.

"You know perfectly well I was using a figure of speech. Shall we look at why you took my remark amiss? Your self-destructive negativity?"

His "self-destructive negativity" was born the day he crashed the fucking plane so why couldn't Starr understand? Everything turned upside down after that.

"Look, we were talking about your filmmaking before the accident and the only way we can succeed in bringing back your creative gifts is to confront your demons," observed Dr. Starr.

"I keep forgetting you're the creativity guru around here," Robert said, closing his eyes, and for the next few minutes, John watched him fall into a light sleep.

John was temporarily stymied. Exploring ways to unlock Robert's creative potential seemed impossible in such an uncooperative patient. Dozing off during the therapy was passive-aggressive, a way to escape unpleasant truths and John looked forward to the day when he could drop him. He reminded himself, however, that fundraising time was coming up at his institute and Robert happened to be the CEO of a hugely successful company. If he played it right, he might succeed in getting Robert to make a generous contribution to the Institute.

Increasingly during their therapy sessions, Robert took issue with Erika's opulent lifestyle.

"She's living just the way my brother, Emilio, would have wanted her to, spending the big bucks, hobnobbing with the fat cats in Boston society. Funny, the way things turn out. Have you any theories as to what's come over Erika? She once lived so simply."

A hostile remark aimed at him, clearly, but John did not take the bait.

"Erika is not our subject right now. Discussing her present life style would be inappropriate," he said coldly.

"Inappropriate"? Robert laughed bitterly to himself. Where was this guy coming from? As her uncle, he had every right to ask questions.

"What's your opinion about a therapist having sex with his patient?"

He'd fired the first shot and the silence was deafening. Minutes ticked by while Robert waited for the answer.

"What are you getting at?" Starr said heavily.

"Can't you guess?"

"I think I can. But I'm not prepared to discuss personal issues with you right now."

"Shall we take it up another day?"

"We'll see."

Starr shifted the subject to Emilio's extravagant spending habits and asked if Robert was ever jealous of his big brother's business success.

"Certainly not. Business was never an interest of mine, though I'm learning a lot running the company, now."

"Erika tells me you've made the company even more profitable."

"We got lucky. Sure, I admired my brother's drive and talent for making money, but I didn't like his associates. A bunch of crooks, if the truth be told. He was also a control freak. All the people around him, his daughter, his wife, everybody would tell you that. To put it plainly, he was one sonofabitch. I didn't ever want to be like him."

"No?"

"Never."

"But today, you've assumed the mantle of your brother."

"Not at all. I'm the CEO, but not for long."

"No?"

"I've got plans."

"Plans?"

"But I'm not going to talk about them right now."

His words had an ominous ring. What was the man up to? Was he giving up the business? Eventually, he would talk. There was nothing quite like the therapeutic hour to elicit crucial information.

TEN

Every time Robert came in to see Dr. Starr, Marsha was ready with his coffee, just the way he liked it, with two teaspoons of sugar and a third of a cup of milk. He always arrived early and today he was there a full thirty-five minutes before his appointment. When they sat alone in the waiting room and the conversation ebbed and flowed so naturally, she felt as though they had known each other all their lives.

In recent weeks, however, she perceived a certain edginess when he was near her as if her presence rankled him in some way. Her heart sank. Perhaps she had been too eager, too quick to sit with him as though she had nothing else to do. But on seeing him, she always hurried to his side. This ashen-faced man in the wheel-chair had captured her heart.

Always a light sleeper, she stayed awake until well into the early morning, worrying that one day he would quit seeing Dr. Starr and be lost to her forever. It had become increasingly obvious that he didn't like Dr. Starr. She couldn't imagine why this was so; Dr. Starr was the kindest man she had ever met.

She avoided her tenant, Jason, who had picked up on her unhappiness and advised her to end the relationship. But there wasn't any relationship; it was all in her mind, a fantasy love. Robert Giuliani probably took coffee with her because he had nothing else to do. The man she loved didn't love her, he barely knew she existed.

Her emotions were in such turmoil she was unable to eat. The chocolate candies in her desk drawer grew hard and stale, her dresses hung loose on her body and she was forced to buy new ones. She suspected a connection between her dramatic weight loss and falling in love.

Dr. Starr asked her if she were attending Weight Watchers. "You're looking great, Marsha! Whatever you're doing, it's working. I'd say you've lost a good thirty pounds. Am I right?"

She was at a loss for words because he had never before mentioned her weight. She flushed with anger. Her obesity had been offensive to Dr. Starr and she hadn't even known it! She had thought him different from the other men she'd known, non-judgmental, sensitive and caring. Maybe she should order in a huge hot fudge sundae and eat it right in front of him here in the office just to spite him.

She would not forget this moment.

As the weeks sped by, Dr. Starr kept after her to finish editing his latest draft of the Harvard speech, but Marsha was reluctant to alter his rambling style so popular on talk shows. Asking him to tighten up the prose and clarify his theories for a scholarly lecture would only make him angry; he did not take kindly to criticism. Once she saw him dressing down an assistant researcher at the institute who challenged his theories, reducing the young woman to tears.

Marsha would correct only the paper's grammar. Making a big fuss over style was a no-winner. After all, Dr. Starr could mesmerize any kind of audience if he simply turned on the charm and Marsha expected him to do just that with the Harvard people.

Robert Giuliani registered surprise on the day she hastily gave him his coffee then hurried right away to her desk. To her astonishment, he wheeled himself over to her tiny cubicle and asked her to come out.

"I have to see you, Marsha. Why are you back here?"

"I thought…"

"What?"

"I thought maybe you wanted to be alone."

"Be alone? Look you're the reason I'm here! You should know that by now."

Marsha was not sure she had heard him correctly.

"Know what by now?" she finally asked, drawing near him.

"That he's not the one I want to see. It's you, Marsha."

"Me?" Her voice trembled.

"He's not helping me much."

"Oh, but he's the best there is!"

"I'm convinced whatever progress I've made here is because of you. When I'm with you, when we talk, I feel better. I'm actually happy, Marsha. You have healing powers." He stretched out his arm and took her hand.

Her heart turned somersaults. "I can't believe what I've just heard," she said, tears of happiness welling up in her eyes.

"I've upset you. I'm terribly sorry. I shouldn't have said anything, I guess. Please forgive me." He dropped her hand. "It was quite presumptuous of me to think that someone like you could actually…" He stopped short, then pressed on, "…want to be with me."

"Want to be with you?" Could he hear the singing of her heart?

"It's a lot to ask, I know. You've been especially good to me. We've had great talks."

"Oh, yes."

"I mean that," he said with a brilliant smile. Then a shadow crossed his face. "I'm not like other people, you know. I'll never be right."

"I know," Marsha said, taking his hand again.

"It's hard," he said. "Every day's a struggle just to get up out of bed but it's easier now that I can come and see you."

"I'm so glad!"

"We're alike, you and I, fellow souls, I think. Do you feel that way?"

"Yes, yes." Her spirits soared.

"But we must keep this to ourselves because somehow I don't think Starr would understand."

"No, he wouldn't. Not at all."

"I don't want him involved. Trust me, I have my reasons." He paused for a moment. Then his words came in a rush. "Are you free tonight for dinner? You have my address, of course, but here it is again: Sixteen sixty Memorial Drive, Apartment 42. Seven o'clock?"

"I'll be there," whispered Marsha, quickly pulling away her hand as John opened the office door to greet Robert.

After work, Marsha made her daily visit to the Home to see her mother who no longer knew her but seemed quite content. She was resting in her wheelchair with her eyes closed and she was smiling. Perhaps she was back playing bridge with her friends and winning.

Marsha could scarcely concentrate on what the nurse was telling her though she heard the words "a little spell but we're very pleased; she'll live to be a hundred." Her heart was light, her mother was doing well and Robert loved her. The burden of uncertainty that had weighed upon her had been lifted and tonight would be a new beginning for them both.

The brightness of the day was lingering now; her mother's room was bathed in an afternoon glow. Soon the buds on the large oak tree outside her window would open into soft, green leaves and the room would flicker with light and shade.

Later that evening, Marsha and Robert made love. For years, medical experts had held the view that his spinal injuries were so severe normal sex would never again be an option. But the ravages of his body held no particular interest for Marsha. She loved him as he was, heart and soul, and her soft, tender kisses and nimble fingers awakened parts of his body he had long believed dead. The sexual act came like a storm, overwhelming them both, ending forever his self-imposed exile of loneliness and grief.

"You've given me back my life!" he said in a hoarse whisper. "You did it!" He kissed her once again before falling back, exhausted, on the pillows. "It's been so long. It's a miracle."

She looked down at him, her eyes shining. "It's not a miracle, my darling. It's the power of love."

"You're a gift from God," he said, opening his arms.

ELEVEN

When Erika spotted two enormous tractors parked in the corner of the lawn, her first thought was they arrived in the dead of night by some sinister design. She would speak to John. Then with a shudder, she remembered. He had long argued that his daily meditation would be more successful if performed near a body of natural water in the Zen tradition and this was the day construction crews would be ripping up the lawn to accommodate his Japanese viewing pool. Despite her misgivings, she had gone along with him. Her opinions counted for so little these days it was pointless arguing.

Aware that Arthur had put his reputation on the line by inviting in someone who had published minimally in the field, John now spent nearly all his waking hours at his institute working on his presentation and much to Erika's annoyance, he often did not return home for dinner. It rankled him that she showed so little understanding of the challenge he was facing. Despite the best efforts of Hilda Payne, her neediness and dependency issues remained an unresolved problem. Maybe it was in his best interest to finally agree to have the baby she wanted so much. Her focus would then be on the baby and not on him.

The night before his lecture he would inform her she was psychologically strong enough to be a mother and the time was ripe. He would not tell her why he had changed his mind, that he saw it as the only way to gain his freedom.

Full of energy and high spirits, he was certain that his Harvard speech would inspire the faculty to support him for the creativity chair.

Spring that year had been slow in coming to New England, but the day of John's lecture at Harvard was warm and full of brilliant sunshine. Erika felt happier than she could remember because during the night John had taken her in his arms and they made love with reckless abandon. There would be a baby, she was sure, and on awakening, she heard the first robin of the season singing in the chestnut tree outside the window. He must be singing to her; a good omen.

Just beyond the bedroom windows, tulip buds had opened up overnight, a symphony of brilliant reds, oranges and yellows. A luncheon was planned in John's honor at the Faculty Club just after the speech so Erika studied her wardrobe carefully, finally selecting a lavender silk suit and matching lavender suede pumps. Her Fulani scarf would add a touch of pink and blue to set off the lavender. John expected her to look especially beautiful because she would be meeting the most stellar members of the psychology department, the School of Education, and the Divinity School.

In the fifth floor seminar room at William James Hall, Erika sat near the back to get a better view of the crowd of luminaries. One of the last arrivals was Professor Plunkett, just now sitting down two rows ahead of her with a group of colleagues from the psychology department. She was relieved to see him there. He was so busy, so hugely important, that urgent business might have kept him away. Now he would see for himself John's originality and brilliance and reward him with the Creativity Chair.

Plunkett was turning around in his seat. Was he searching for her? She leaned forward, waving, eager for his greeting, but he seemed not to see her.

She caught a glimpse of Uncle Robert in his wheelchair talking animatedly to a woman beside him at the end of the row. Much to her surprise, it turned out to be Marsha. Months had passed since Erika had last seen her and she was remarkably changed. Her face was delicate and fine, lovely, really, and her hair was swept up in a twist revealing a swan-like neck. Gone were the rolls of fat, the loose-fitting Indian blouses and long, wide skirt. Her form-fitting floral print dress revealed a dramatically altered, slimmed-down body. What had happened to produce such a transformation?

She was upset that Uncle Robert wasn't sitting with her. John must have known he was attending the lecture but forgot to tell her. How handsome he looked, though pale as a ghost and all bent over in his wheelchair. She remembered sadly the spell he once cast over women and how they flocked around him. Right now, though, his face was bright with happiness; he was smiling his radiant smile. It had been years since she'd seen him like this so his therapy with John must be working in wondrous ways. Her husband was the greatest analyst in America, a true healer.

Arthur Watts introduced John to warm applause and he began his speech exuding an air of confidence and erudition as he cited the theories on creativity of Jung and Freud, Di Brioni, and others. Marsha had set up his power point to show several masterpieces by Van Gogh and Picasso as examples of creative genius. Tall and erect, he was an impressive figure with his graying hair, piercing blue eyes, and craggy features. In his quiet, understated way, he was there to shake up this audience of smug, pedantic professors with his radical new take on creativity. A thrill ran through Erika. How bold and fearless he was to stand in front of this venerated group of establishment figures and how proud she was to be his wife! He was hers, hers alone. And soon she would be the mother of his child!

Her mind wandered off imagining how John would design the nursery, interview baby sitters, and devote himself to tapping into the unique creativity of their infant child. Then a worrisome thought crossed her mind. Was it already too late to become pregnant? In recent days she had noticed small changes in her body; a fertility expert might have to be called in and she'd heard that whole business was horribly painful. She didn't want that, oh, no! So many of her friends went through terrible ordeals to become pregnant only to fail and failure wasn't an option. Then there were the hormone-induced multiple births she read about in supermarket rags, along with hospital pictures of triplets and quadruplets each weighing barely a pound. Looking at these bewildered, bird-like newborns made her heartsick and she yearned for a baby boy who would spring all plump and smiling from her womb. And she would name him Baby John.

A ripple of light applause alerted her that John's speech was over. She'd missed most of it, her thoughts had run away with her and she was upset with herself. How could she have let that happen? The greatest moment of John's career? She'd been so excited, so ecstatic about the baby that somehow, she wasn't sure exactly how, she'd slipped away from this packed lecture hall to a quiet place where it was only the three of them; John, herself, and the baby.

Surely he had overwhelmed them with his brilliance and originality. Wasn't he always the star no matter where he appeared? On TV, he dominated the screen so thoroughly that nothing else existed. He was her sun god, and she, his moon goddess. That's what he always told her and that's what she believed deep in her heart.

The clapping died out almost as soon as it began and the room was rapidly emptying out. Why were people hurrying off? Would there be no question-and answer-period?

TWELVE

Someone behind her was talking loudly about "a lot of rubbish" and a chorus of voices chimed in. John stood very still on the podium, his face expressionless. Beside him, a grim Arthur Watts eyed the steady exodus.

"It looks like everybody's in a big rush," Arthur said loudly. "They're going to miss all the fun!"

Professor Plunkett had risen from his chair and was moving hastily towards the exit door, followed by several of his colleagues. His face was glum and when he saw Erika, he gave her a wintry smile and hurried on. She was momentarily shaken; he seemed to barely know her. How dare he! Hadn't she always tried to please him at dinner parties, seat him next to her, endure his fat, sweaty hands on her arm, listen to his obsequious mutterings of sexual desire? How she hated the sight of him! She'd put up with him for John's sake, of course; she would do anything for this man she loved.

In the near empty hall, Arthur was doggedly taking questions for John. A young man in blue jeans and torn sweater raised his hand.

"Yes, Sir?"

"Dr. Starr, some of our most creative geniuses created havoc in their personal lives. Van Gogh and Picasso are perfect examples and you never mentioned that fact."

"A creative genius can't be judged by the usual standards for human behavior because he's a committed being in ways unlike anyone else. That's why great artists are so often attacked for their morals or their ideas. But I'd also like to add that especially among expressive artists like Van Gogh, there seems to be a propensity for depression and mania. For these people, their creative work is the one thing that keeps them sane."

Arthur Watts cut off further communication with the young man by abruptly turning to a bald-headed personage in the front row who had raised his hand. It was Wilbur Grunniger, the famous art critic presently teaching at Wellesley and author of a best-selling book on Winslow Homer, *The Gulf Stream*.

"Yes, Professor Grunniger?"

"Doctor Starr, I want to thank you for recognizing genius as authentic and not merely a 'socially-constructed category' as academic art critics like Professor Keith Moxley are now claiming. Van Gogh is a perfect example of the so-called 'mad' genius who knew exactly what he wanted to express in his art. As you probably know, there is a trend among academic critics to deliberately ignore the artist's vision so they can put forward their own. It's a way of impressing their fellow intellectuals with their brilliance. But what they say is often total nonsense that has nothing to do with the painting. A very alarming trend in art scholarship, Dr. Starr, and we need your insights into creativity to set the record straight. You are ahead of your time, Sir."

"Thank you, Professor Grunniger," John said, his face lighting up. "I deeply appreciate your comments."

Dr. Tolakovsky, a visiting psychology professor from Princeton, raised his hand. At present he was at work on studies of the interaction between genetics and the environment and had determined in a celebrated paper that boys were genetically more aggressive than girls.

"Dr. Starr," he said in heavily accented English. "Your use of the word 'creativity' seems to be limited mainly to the arts, and the cases you present are all artists of one sort or another. Where are your studies of creativity in the new fields of technology and the environment?"

"You're quite right," John answered, "I've only included artists today, but genius is genius. Di Brioni and my own most recent studies include great scientists as well, and we've observed that like artists and writers, they experience a direct relationship between the content of their dreams and their creations."

A white-haired man in a black suit and clerical collar rose from his seat close to the front of the room.

"Father Phil, how nice you're here," John said at once. "It's been a while. Haven't seen you since my seminar two years ago."

"It's good to hear you speak, Dr. Starr, I'm always inspired by your insights. I hope we can get you back to Boston College for another seminar this year."

"I'd welcome that opportunity, Father."

Nodding enthusiastically, the genial priest regained his seat.

A man in a rumpled brown suit and long dark hair was the next person to speak. He was the sociology professor, Professor Lawrence Butler, widely known in intellectual circles for his stinging critical essays debunking the self-esteem movement. Erika could tell from the expression on his face that he was displeased for some reason but she wasn't prepared for his aggressive comments.

"I'm not satisfied with your answer about technology, Dr. Starr. Hasn't our colleague, Howard Gardner, already shown us that there are many kinds of creativity? Your views sound simplistic, one-sided. How can you base all your theories on Jung and your so-called expert, Dr. Di Brioni? Everybody knows that except for the idea of introversion-extroversion, Jung is extremely subjective, and nobody listens to Di Brioni. There's no science in all this, just your opinions."

"Most work we call science and that includes psychology, Professor Butler, is either description or filling in the formulas. Think of Darwin's descriptions. I didn't want to repeat what you already know from Professor Gardner," continued John smoothly, "but like him, my goal is to raise our awareness of those aspects of creativity that remain inaccessible to the conscious mind. And I would argue that Dr. Di Brioni is one of our most respected experts in this field."

A visiting faculty member, Professor Marianne Carlsson from Stockholm University, spoke up. "Why do you ignore the research on what influences scientific creativity such as Anne Roe's work on childhood factors?"

John smiled. "All real creativity in the sciences and social sciences is like poetry or painting. Einstein's $E=mc^2$ is like a haiku. It has spirit, soul."

"Is this how you define 'creativity' then?" asked Professor Carlsson. "The inclusion of the spirit? The soul? What does that mean?"

"It means that there is a transformational aspect to all creativity. It's acting out of freedom to relate to the potential within oneself and without. It's leaving the world a little bit different than before," John said.

A silence fell over the group until a short, heavyset man in a dark blue suit stood up. It was the social psychologist, Fred Shapiro.

"I would like to address this question to Professor Watts because I think I'm hearing about dreams and the soul. Sir, is this deeply flawed analysis of creativity in agreement with your own?"

"Well, Professor Shapiro, I hadn't really thought about it, but I'm convinced the analysis offered here today explains much of my own creative experience."

"If that's true, then you believe in the tooth fairy!" said Professor Shapiro with a dismissive wave of the hand, and noisily pushing back his chair, left the room.

THIRTEEN

Erika remained seated until the hall was completely emptied out and then waited by the podium for John.

"Thanks a lot," Arthur Watts said firmly, stepping forward to grip John's hand. "You made a good case for your argument but you had a tough crowd out there, no doubt about it."

"Surprisingly resistant, with the exception of Wilbur Grunniger."

"Yes, thank god for him, though he's pretty much discounted these days by art critics in academia. John, let's face it. You and I just don't fit into the new Harvard. But here's a little perspective. Over a century ago, the reactionaries refused to allow Ralph Waldo Emerson to give a speech here. America's greatest thinker of the times!"

"That happened?"

"It did because he'd made the shocking decision to switch religions. Just think of that! He became a Transcendentalist after being a Unitarian. People here at Harvard couldn't handle it."

"Too mired in their shallow, rigid way of thinking."

"Then there was our hero, William James, who was always considered an outsider, never accepted by Harvard. It's pretty ironic when we see that both Emerson and James later had halls named after them."

"Maybe I'll get a hall named after me someday," John said with a sardonic smile.

"Never can tell." Arthur leaned down to pick up his briefcase. "With this debacle today and the stuff going on in the department, I'm tempted to make the big move."

"You're still thinking of going somewhere else?"

"I've gotten a lot of interest from North Carolina."

"Arthur, you can't leave! What about the creativity chair? Don't let me down now!"

"John, are you blind or something? Despite everything we've done, there's not a goddamn chance of getting you in here now. Didn't you notice that Plunkett took off without saying a fucking word?"

"Yeah."

"I've got a meeting now, but we'll talk later. How about a drink at the club later this month?" Shaking his head, he patted John affectionately on the back, nodded amiably to Erika and went on his way.

When John and Erika reached the exit, he headed directly for the car and she reminded him of the luncheon in his honor at the Faculty Club.

"My mistake," he said hastily, "I should have told you. The luncheon was last week."

"Last week? That's impossible! Why didn't you tell me? I'm all dressed up!"

"It totally slipped my mind."

"I can't believe this! What happened?"

'What happened'?"

"At the luncheon!"

"Oh, yes, yes, the luncheon. Well, if you must know, it was very boring, you didn't miss a thing." Brushing past her, he strode off towards the car.

Angry and disappointed, Erika stood motionless. He'd forgotten to tell her about the luncheon and he wasn't even sorry. She started walking slowly down the street away from him. He had brushed her aside as though she didn't even exist and she felt numb.

"Erika! Wait!" He hurried back to her. "I'm sorry about all this. I really am."

"I don't know what to think, really I don't. How could you forget to let me know?"

"I've said I'm sorry, but this is a bad time, right now. A very bad time. Try to think about me for once."

"But I think about you too much, John, isn't that what you constantly tell me?"

"Okay, okay. Look, it's a beautiful day and we can go down by the river. Everything's going to be fine." Holding her tightly by the elbow, he directed her through the winding Cambridge streets, past Winthrop House and across Memorial Drive. He found a quiet spot near the banks of the Charles away from the crowds of students enjoying the sun and threw himself down on the ground. Spreading out her Fulani scarf on the damp grass so as not to ruin her lavender silk suit, Erika removed her jacket and sat down beside him.

The Harvard crews were out in their long, graceful sculls, floating along the glittering surface of the river, but she hardly noticed them. She was watching John who lay on his back with his eyes tightly shut, his face to the sky. For the first time, she understood the depth of his despair.

It had been a public humiliation. His speech was a disaster and worse yet, Plunkett had ignored him, actually turned his back on him when he left the hall. A sickening feeling took hold of her as she realized the implications of this day. There would be no Harvard professorship for John, no creativity chair. All his dreams of glory had gone up in smoke.

Attacks from the floor focused on flaws in methodology, a lack of hard evidence to back up his theories. It was odd how passive he'd been with his aggressors. Wasn't John the expert, the guru of creativity? Professor Wilbur Grunniger seemed to think so. But there were chinks in his armor she had refused to see; he wasn't entirely what he claimed to be. Hilda Payne never hesitated to point out that there were others in the creativity field far better than John and she hadn't believed her. Now, she wasn't so sure.

She was disappointed that he hadn't reacted more forcefully to his critics. A few choice words and he could have cut them to shreds. Her father would have annihilated them and remembering his pugnacious ways, she was filled with an overwhelming sense of loss.

Driving home, John said little, playing his favorite tape, Dietrich Fischer-Dieskau singing Mozart's *Die Zauberflöte*. When they arrived at the house, he made no immediate effort to get out of the car.

"Some people were threatened by what I had to say today, Erika," he said with a shrug. "The Harvard professors couldn't handle it, I'm a threat to their intellectual capital." He gave a bitter laugh. "Wilbur Grunniger had it right. That's the way it is when you're ahead of your time. Like William James in his day, I'm an outsider. It's to be expected." Opening his door, he got out of the car and strode on ahead of her into the house.

FOURTEEN

Tonight was Marsha's thirty-eighth birthday but she didn't expect Robert to remember, she'd only mentioned it in passing. Right now her life was so full of happiness it didn't matter any more that in two more years she'd hit the big four O. Would she still be working for Dr. Starr? She had her doubts. Ever since that time he mentioned her weight loss she hadn't felt the same about him but she still respected his ability to heal the psychologically afflicted.

Robert's handsome, six-room modern apartment, always sparsely furnished and filled with Haitian paintings, was transformed for Marsha's surprise birthday party. He had directed his staff to decorate every room with festoons of pink roses. In the dining room, thirty-eight red and yellow balloons floated on the ceiling. A mariachi band waited in the foyer, ready to start up when Marsha stepped through the door. At the sound of the bell, Robert wheeled himself across the marble floor to open the door himself and the musicians struck up with the first chords of *Las Mañanitas*.

"Welcome, sweet Marsha. Happy birthday!" Robert said with a bright smile.

Marsha sank down on the floor and wrapped her arms around Robert's frail shoulders.

"I can't believe this," she said. "You remembered. Oh, my dearest Robert, it's so beautiful!"

"Could I forget the birthday of the most important person in my life? Come my love, dinner's ready. Eduardo's cooked up a Mexican surprise."

Speeding ahead in his wheelchair, Robert led Marsha into the dining room where rows of white candles by the windows bathed it in a soft, warm glow. Mirrored placemats picked up the light, reflecting the purple and blue Orrefors wine glasses. Seating Marsha beside him, Robert called for Eduardo, the chef, to serve the *pollo poblano con mole*, white rice and *frijoles*. Fresh corn tortillas hot off the grill were placed on the table in a straw basket covered with a linen napkin to keep them warm.

During dinner, the mariachi band played *El Barco de Oro* and Mexican love songs outside in the hall, far enough away so Robert and Marsha could talk.

"You've thought of everything," Marsha said.

"It's been a lot of fun. That's what you've done for me, Marsha, given me a merry heart."

"Oh, Robert."

"Let's drink to our future," Robert said, holding up his glass of Montepulciano.

"Don't wake me up, ever," Marsha smiled as they touched glasses.

"There's something I need to tell you though, darling," Robert said, setting down his glass and turning to look at her, his expression serious. "I hope you won't be upset."

"What is it?" Her heart skipped a beat.

"I'm going to quit therapy with Starr. Not right away, because I don't want to hurt Erika, but soon."

"Oh?" Relief swept over her.

"Marsha, you're the one who restored me to life, not Starr. He hasn't done a thing for me so why should I keep seeing him? It's a terrible bore and he's usually dead wrong when he thinks he's on to something. After his lecture the other day, I got the impression that the professors didn't think much of what he had to say, either."

"No, that's not true. There was one person, a Professor Grunniger, who really liked his lecture. Remember him? He recog-

276

nized that Dr. Starr is on to something. Anyway, you may not agree with his theories about creativity but at least give him credit for helping suffering people."

"How do you know?"

"They stop at my desk to tell me!"

"Well, he hasn't helped me."

"Maybe not, but most of his patients get better."

"You're full of illusions, Marsha."

"You're judging him when you don't have all the facts!" she said heatedly.

"Sorry, I didn't realize you were such a loyal employee."

"That's a put-down, Robert."

"Okay, I take it back."

"I've actually seen people change, get better, be happy again."

"But he says the obvious and thinks he's making big discoveries, Marsha. I'd like to label him the Great Pretender."

"The 'Great Pretender'?" How could Robert claim that Dr. Starr was anyone but himself?

"He's not what he seems, my darling."

"Please, let's not talk about Dr. Starr anymore," she said. "He's a flawed person but there's nothing I can do about it, can I?"

"No, and I was insensitive in bringing up the subject of Starr so please forgive me."

"Of course I forgive you." And she couldn't have loved him more than at that moment.

"Darling, let's stay focused on what we're celebrating; your birthday and mine as well!" he said brightly.

"Your birthday? Why didn't you tell me?" Her eyes opened wide with surprise.

"Well actually, it's not really my birthday, it's just that when I met you that's when I started to live." Laughing softly, Robert leaned close to her face and kissed her on the lips.

"You mean, when we both started to live," Marsha said softly, and with a tremulous smile, drew her arms around his neck.

Later, lingering over in the flickering candlelight after the band had left, Robert talked animatedly about the future.

"I want to change my life, Marsha. Making a whole lot of money gets boring after a while. Maybe it's because being CEO of the family company has nothing to do with making the world a better place." His face brightened. "I've got ideas that have nothing to do with the business."

"Tell me."

"Well, I've learned how tough it is to be handicapped and because of my relationship with the Haitian orphanage, I'd like to do something for the kids there with disabilities."

"Like what?"

"I've thought of looking for a good rehabilitation center in Miami – that's only a short flight from Haiti – and it would have first class surgical facilities. I could bring some of the handicapped kids over for treatment."

"A great idea. Maybe we could include some Mexican orphans as well."

"Why not? I speak French, you know Spanish. We could do this project together."

"I'd have to stop working for Dr. Starr."

"That's long overdue. There's nothing in it for you."

"I need to make a living, Robert, I can't just throw every-thing over."

"Baby, I'm going to take care of you from now on," Robert said. "Don't you know that? Our life is just beginning!"

Taking her face in his hands, he kissed her again, this time with a fierce passion.

John kept his patient load light and to his relief, Erika wanted to continue her therapy with Hilda Payne. He was not completely surprised; women patients idolized Hilda. Obviously, all along, Erika had needed a mother figure to address her issues. A male, such as himself, was too threatening.

Despite the Harvard debacle, John was approaching his creativity research with renewed energy, having concluded that the Harvard academics were a bunch of obsessives who needed to revise their reductionist approach if they were to accept his own. He was especially proud to be in the august company of William James and Ralph Waldo Emerson.

One jarring note in John's otherwise pleasant workplace was Marsha's changed demeanor. Increasingly argumentative, she was not her usual cheerful self. John remembered her telling him a while back about a young man, a third grade teacher, who rented a room in her apartment. A loser, no doubt, choosing a career dominated by women. Marsha would always make poor choices in men because she lacked self-esteem. Her Indian lover down in Mexico who died was a perfect example. This schoolteacher, another.

He made a special effort to be pleasant around her but he was concerned about her growing friendship with Giuliani. She seemed to be under an illusion that the man in the wheelchair was a nice man but John knew better.

Lately, he had taken to dropping in on Cambridge bookstores at odd hours and revisiting galleries he had long neglected. When the weather was pleasant, he drove out alone to Walden Pond for spiritual renewal, which he believed to be key in becoming more innovative with his creativity studies. Erika accepted his need to be alone and he attributed this new attitude to her work with Hilda Payne.

He avoided Jane Phillips with excuses of pressing work and family obligations. She sent him daily e-mails accusing him of being cruel and uncaring. Did he feel nothing for her? Had he forgotten their passionate nights together?

He did not answer any of her messages.

In desperation, she took to calling him on his private line at the office, her voice soft and inviting, begging him to meet her. He became adept at shifting the conversation to their documentary not yet aired. What was holding it up? He wanted specifics. Her answers were vague and he suspected someone at the studio might be sabotaging efforts to show the film.

One afternoon, John picked up a copy of *One Hundred Years of Solitude* at Grolier's bookstore and on leaving the shop, ran squarely into Arthur Watts.

"Arthur! Where have you been all this time?"

"Busy, John, really busy. Good things are happening though," Arthur said jubilantly.

"What's going on?"

"I'll be taking that job down at Chapel Hill. They've offered me the chairmanship of the psychology department."

"Congratulations! But you're leaving! That's a disaster for me!"

"John, I'm really sorry. And it looks like Elaine Locke's been hired to fill my spot in the department, though for some reason, Plunkett's keeping mum about it."

"Elaine? How do you know he wants her for that position?"

"I've got my spies. Seems like the feminists want to spill the beans about his affairs with graduate students and he can't hold on to his chairmanship if they bring out all the dirt. I guess I'm doing him a big favor by leaving. This way he can hire a woman in my place and shut them up."

"Pretty ironic. He'll hire Elaine, the girl he used to fuck."

"Life's full of ironies, John. The older I get, the more I'm aware of that fact."

"Your departure is going to be tough on me, Arthur."

"I've got to get out of here, I'm fed up. The very fact Plunkett's chosen a numbers person with no imagination, whose research is totally mediocre, reinforces my views of what's happening around here. He's filled the department with mechanics, there's not a single creative thinker in the bunch, except Steven Pinker who's interested in the brain but not much in people. The Creativity Chair is still up for grabs, John, and I figure Plunkett must be considering you since there's been no announcement. Frankly, why you'd want anything to do with any of these jerks is a mystery to me."

"I've often wondered myself, Arthur," John said.

Hadn't he been badly burned already? Why was he so eager to be at Harvard? Its nasty politics bored him, the machinations, the petty rivalries were beneath him. He didn't belong among these people. It was evident now that Plunkett was one of the worst, and inviting the man to his parties had been a no-winner. The guy had enjoyed his best wines, his gourmet dinners, and lusted after his wife. Neither Erika nor her fortune could ever be his, of course, and Plunkett knew it. That was probably the reason he hadn't contacted him yet, why he'd walked out just after John finished his lecture. He was actually glad Plunkett hadn't stayed on to see him humiliated. A bad scene.

The Chair remained unclaimed. Plunkett hadn't yet chosen his candidate, and the Chair shimmered in the light of his imagination like a throne of gold.

"John," Arthur was saying, "How about getting in touch with Elaine? She's back here in Cambridge, I hear."

"Elaine? You think she can help?"

"Didn't you once tell me she had the hots for you?"

"Arthur, that was a long time ago. We were kids. Still," John said, a hopeful note creeping into his voice, "I see what you're getting at. She might be a little lonely. Who knows?"

"You've got nothing to lose, nothing at all," said Arthur. "I've got to run, now. We'll talk."

Settling back in his leather seat, John pressed his foot down on the gas and the Ferrari took off like lightning. As the soft spring wind caressed his face, his spirits lifted. It was a lovely day and Arthur's suggestion to get in touch with Elaine Locke appealed to him. He wondered how she looked after all these years. As sexy as ever?

Professor Plunkett had rushed out of the lecture hall right after John's speech because he wanted to avoid not only John, but Erika as well. He had no wish to speak to her that day or any other. He now recognized that her beauty cast a spell over him, he became putty in her hands and his critical faculties all but ceased functioning. Her soft smile, her dulcet tones, never failed to stir his lovesick heart. At her dinner parties he had hovered close to her, watching the rise and fall of her beautiful breasts, pressing her creamy, bare arm while she talked endlessly about her husband's special gifts, pleading his case. Profoundly bored with the subject of John Starr, he pretended interest since his fervent hope was that she might return his ardor. But she kept him permanently on edge and like a young man, he suffered the pangs of unrequited love. If she had offered him the slightest encouragement, he might have been induced to take the fateful step of selecting John Starr for the endowed Creativity Chair. The professorship this man so desperately craved might have actually been his.

The Starr lecture was a disaster, of course, and in the cold light of day without Erika's voice in his ear, Plunkett saw him for the charming lightweight he was, a second-rate thinker and a sloppy researcher. For months, Arthur Watts had been promoting Starr for the Chair and to accommodate him, Plunkett had kept an open mind. Twenty years ago the graduate student, John Starr, had failed to impress him. Years later, nothing had changed.

Plunkett now determined that Elaine Locke would be perfect for the Chair but he would have to wait until the ad hoc committee met which was sometime during the summer. He didn't expect any problems, Elaine had a stellar reputation among the academics, he'd already checked her out. She might not be a great intellectual light, but her work on intelligence and gender could be loosely construed as creative and it was measurable and rigorously controlled. Recently he had come across a review she had written of new brain research at Cal Tech making a direct connection to certain areas of the frontal lobes to creativity. Good for her! She wasn't bothering with all that soft stuff he was hearing from John Starr and Arthur Watts that had been discounted ages ago.

An added point, but not insignificant, was how sexy Elaine looked when she showed up a couple of weeks ago at his office. After twenty years the woman still turned him on despite her shapeless plaid suit and thick, brown, Earth shoes. He could imagine the voluptuous body underneath the wretched clothes. The breasts might not be quite so firm, the hips and thighs a trifle heavier, but so what? This icon of the feminists, this pretty, cheerful woman, was dynamite in bed!

As he crossed Harvard Yard in the bright sunshine, Plunkett walked with a new spring in his step. Things were looking up. The selection of Elaine for the Creativity Chair was going to make most of the department members happy. She fit so naturally into the group, and he would finally get the feminists off his back. Yes, it would be a smart decision.

"Hey, Dad, can I use the Ferrari tonight?" Roger called out from the hall.

"Come in here, Roger and we'll discuss it."

Roger and Adriana entered the room with Rufus skipping along beside them. They had just returned from walking him around the neighborhood. Heading straight to Erika, Rufus jumped up on her lap.

"Oh, Rufus, darling!" she cried, "My sweet baby!"

Wagging his tail, he licked her face and everyone laughed. Dressed in black, Roger and Adriana were off to a party.

"It's a weeknight. What about your homework?" John said.

"No sweat, Dad. Finals are five days away. The Rippers, well, like, we've talked about them, remember, Dad? So they're here in Boston tonight and my friend gave me two tickets to the concert. We need some space after hitting the books so hard." He winked at his father to elicit a smile. "Come on, Dad. Can I use the Ferrari?"

"I don't know," John said, frowning slightly. "You'll be out late, I suppose. Maybe you should take the Lexus."

"Whatever. Then can I use the Ferrari some other time?"

"We'll see," John said. "Here are the keys. Now, run along. Tell me about the show."

"Sure thing, Dad."

"Have fun!" Erika called out as they were leaving. Then the front doors slammed shut and minutes later, the Lexus purred softly as it moved down the driveway.

.

"They'll have a great time," Erika said, settling down close to John on the couch. Rufus came running across the room and jumped up on her lap.

"Down, Rufus! Down!" John snapped, slapping the little dog on his ears. Squealing and barking, Rufus tumbled to the floor and ran out of the room.

"Why did you do that?" Erika cried.

"Damn dog! He's a nuisance and he's stupid!"

"He's not stupid!"

"Okay, so he's not stupid. He's Einstein reincarnated!" John laughed heartily at his joke, but Erika looked grim. For a moment, neither spoke.

"She doesn't hate me anymore," Erika suddenly said.

"Who are we talking about now, Erika?"

"Can't you guess?

"You mean Adriana?"

"Who else?"

"Darling, she doesn't hate you and never has. Why should she? I've told you all along the problem was yours and you're learning to handle them. You're much more relaxed and friendly and she's responding positively to that. All to the good."

"I have to give Rufus some credit."

"Rufus?"

"That's right. My little dog changed everything. I made the right move allowing him to stay here with all of us so now we're on the same page."

"Well, he's probably helped, though I think your work with Hilda Payne has made most of the difference. It's interesting to see how a dog, not young people, brings out your maternal feelings."

"I've been very maternal towards Adriana recently. Haven't you noticed?"

"No."

"No? Well, when we have the baby you'll finally see how maternal I can be because Rufus is a wonderful teacher." She giggled. "Darling, was there any follow-up to your Harvard lecture?"

"My lecture?"

"Yes."

"Well, Arthur thanked me, if that's what you mean. He said he was very impressed with my presentation. That's about it. Why are you bringing this up now?"

"I was just wondering. Plunkett never contacted you, did he?"

"No, but he had nothing to do with my lecture. Anyway, he's a pompous old fool. It's pretty obvious I'm a threat to him and the rest of the department for that matter. We've discussed this before, Erika. You shouldn't concern yourself with matters you know nothing about."

"I'm not a fool, John, I know a lot of things, believe it or not. Obviously, my efforts failed with Plunkett and your speech didn't help. I'm aware how much the Chair means to you, though Hilda thinks you'd be more independent not being locked into a professorship."

"Hilda Payne? What's she got to do with this?"

"Forget what I said. So where do we go from here?"

John made no reply.

"You don't want to talk about it with me, do you?" Her expression hardened. "Hilda's pointed out to me how much you devalue my opinions and deliberately keep me in the dark."

"Hilda Payne seems to be talking a lot of nonsense these days. I've always believed her to be an experienced therapist who would never collude with your distortions but maybe I've been mistaken."

"I'm not distorting. I'm telling you the truth." She stood up. "And now I'm going to bed. Good night, darling."

Later when he joined her in bed, she gently pushed him away when he began to caress her. "Don't," she whispered, "I'm in the middle of a wonderful dream!"

In June the weather grew warm and summer loomed long and hot. Roger and Adriana set off for Vermont. Later in August, they planned to return to Boston for a two-week European tour with John and Erika. It had been decided that a bit of old world culture would be a good thing for them both and Erika was willing to underwrite the trip.

John was shocked how little the kids knew about history. Ancient or modern, it made no difference; ignorance ruled. Only the present had any reality for them; what came before held little interest. Their knowledge of Middle Eastern, African, and Asian cultures was limited to music. Besides some dates, the few historical facts they picked up along the way were not acquired in history class, but came from videos or old movies on TV starring movie stars now dead.

Ben Hur and *El Cid*, starring Charlton Heston, and *Alexander the Great*, with Richard Burton were both shown at school and proved far more exciting to Adriana and Roger than their history teacher. Adriana was hugely moved by the romantic story of *Cleopatra*, where Antony, played by this same Richard Burton, fell in love with the amazing star, Elizabeth Taylor, who played Cleopatra. A small confusion was created in Adriana's mind because Richard

Burton played both Alexander the Great and Mark Antony so she couldn't help mixing up their identities and their feats of bravery. Was Alexander the Great Roman? No, that must have been Mark Antony. In any case, these two men were *so* handsome and powerful! Adriana thought that maybe the gorgeous Cleopatra should have married Alexander the Great and then she wouldn't have died of snakebite.

SEVENTEEN

"I'm dropping the therapy," Robert confided to Marsha one night as they lay in each other's arms, surfeited from making love. "It's not my mind, it's my body I need back, Marsha. I want to be like other people, melt into the crowd. This wheelchair business is the pits." He heaved a deep sigh.

"I know; it's hard."

"Why can't I walk again?"

"Doctors can be wrong, you know."

"That's for sure, just look at my love life! If I hadn't met you, I'd be a bitter old man by now."

"Maybe you should see some other doctors."

"Doctors, doctors. They've set me up for a lifetime of pain and pills and a wheelchair. Thank god for you, precious girl, thank god. Anyway, let's talk about something else, like the fact you're still working for Starr when I've already told you I'd take care of you." He drew her closer. "It's time to reinvent yourself as Starr likes to say."

"Why should I?"

"You know how much I love you and if you hang around with Starr we can't be together all the time. We should be figuring out how to help those disabled orphans in Haiti."

"I know."

Robert looked deep into her eyes. "Will you marry me, darling Marsha?"

"Marry you?"

"Maybe I shouldn't have asked." His face turned dark. "I'm a huge burden, I know."

"Oh, Robert, don't say that! Would you feel better if I said 'no'?"

"Let's end this conversation."

"Good, because you know perfectly well I want to be with you for the rest of my life. So of course I'll be your wife!"

"You've said exactly what I wanted to hear!" Smiling joyfully, he kissed her again and again. Then he turned serious. "There's a matter that concerns me, dearest. It's about Matt. You know he's good with me. He takes care of things. It'll be the three of us a lot of the time. You won't mind?" His anxiety was palpable.

"Haven't I made myself clear? No, I won't mind because I love you, Robert, with all my heart and soul."

"The wonder of it! I still can't believe I found you." He hugged her tightly.

"I'll quit my job," Marsha said firmly. "Tomorrow!"

"Bravo! I'd almost given up. It looks like Starr's in for a little surprise." He gave a short laugh.

"He thinks I'll hang around forever. But the truth is he doesn't need me anymore. Anybody can do my work. It was fun in the old days when I helped him with his papers but for a long time he hasn't published anything." Her daily routine had become a relentless parade of empty hours at her desk dealing with the minutiae of office work and endless telephone calls. "I've become an appointments secretary," she said wistfully.

"He doesn't respect your gifts like I do," Robert declared triumphantly. "So it's all settled; you're going to leave him first chance you get. Hey, why are we talking about Starr? Come closer, darling. There are more important things to do, wouldn't you agree?"

The following Monday, Marsha decided to submit her resignation and ask Dr. Starr to find a replacement. He would want to know why she was leaving and she would tell him her life was at a turning point but she wouldn't say anything more.

When his final patient of the day departed, Dr. Starr sauntered over to her cubicle.

"Marsha," he said pleasantly. "Come in later tomorrow. I won't be seeing anyone early in the morning."

"Dr. Starr, I have something to tell you." She stood up.

"Oh?" His eyes flashed a brilliant blue.

"I'll be leaving at the end of the month."

"Leaving? How can you? You're part of the operation here!" His face registered a quizzical look. "Things going wrong with your love life?" He chuckled unpleasantly.

Marsha ignored his remark. "I'll be making some changes, that's all."

"What kinds of changes, Marsha?"

"I can't talk about that right now. I'm just giving you notice."

"Well, maybe it's a good thing; you seem like you're ready for something different. I have to tell you that lately I've been quite concerned with what I consider unprofessional behavior on your part."

"Like what?" She stared at him blankly, then remembered when Robert was waiting in his wheelchair to see Dr. Starr she momentarily caressed his face. Had he noticed?

"I observed you stroking the face of one of my patients. I said nothing to you at the time, but planned to bring it up later. Actually, I was shocked."

"'Shocked?'" She was surprised to hear him use that word because psychotherapists were never supposed to be shocked.

"It looks like you're dealing with some issues of rivalry here, Marsha. You want to be loved and admired like me and you believe that fondling a helpless cripple will do the trick."

She cried out. "You don't understand! You don't know anything about it!"

"Oh, I think I do, and that's why you're so angry. I've caught you out, my dear. Now let's talk about that teacher who lives in your apartment because I think he's the reason for this recent hostility of yours. If he makes you unhappy, leave the relationship, that's my advice. As a psychoanalyst, I don't like to tell people what to do, but in your case, I'm making an exception. Remember, life is short and frankly, you're not getting any younger."

His words cut deep and she struggled to maintain her composure.

"Confronting reality can be tough," he said gently.

"I have to run along now," Marsha said quickly. "Someone's waiting for me and it's been a long day."

"Tell your teacher friend what I just said. You'll feel better if you do."

Marsha rushed past him, avoiding his gaze. How could he believe she had feelings of rivalry towards him or that her boarder, Jason Marcus, was her lover? He was so off base that she almost laughed. What a conceited ass and what a pity the month had just begun before she could leave the job and she would have to sit in her cubicle with such a rage in her heart!

One evening in the library, John announced that Roger and Adriana would not be returning for the European tour.

"He's playing guitar in some kind of rock band and she'll be in Argentina with her mother for most of August."

"Oh, well, it's too hot in Europe that time of year, anyway," Erika said. "There's hardly any air conditioning anywhere though most Europeans accept the idea of global warming. It's bizarre." She seemed lost in thought. "I'm sorry about the kids, though," she said abruptly and hugged Rufus, who was sitting on her lap.

"I'm not sure you really mean that but it doesn't matter."

"Of course I mean it. We got along beautifully after Rufus came to live with us. Adriana and I actually became quite close. I made a big effort with her and it paid off. The two of us finally bonded and I think Roger bonded with me as well."

"What makes you think so?"

"You might remember we read a lot of books on adolescent psychology together so I'm not a complete neophyte anymore. Adriana has changed for the better thanks to my intervention."

"Frankly, I have seen very little change in Adriana. You are not a professional therapist, Erika, much as you might want to believe it. You forget that I'm a trained analyst and you are not."

"I could have been," she said wistfully.

"What?"

"You don't remember, do you?"

"Erika, you're not making any sense."

"I told you long ago that when I was a girl I wanted to study psychology."

"Studying psychology and actually becoming a therapist are two different things, my dear."

"I know."

"Besides, you wouldn't be an effective therapist."

"Why not?"

"Confronting conflict in a patient isn't for softies."

"You think I'm a 'softie'?"

"In many ways, yes. Your dependency issues keep you from developing the necessary toughness."

Forcing a smile, she changed the subject. "Tell me, are the kids going to visit us at all?"

"They'll come for the occasional holiday."

"Like Thanksgiving and Christmas?"

"I don't know yet," John shrugged.

"Well, maybe it's for the best," she said brightly.

"What do you mean 'it's for the best'?" His voice had an ominous ring.

"It's not like Roger's a little boy and maybe he needs more autonomy."

Abruptly, John rose from his chair and strode past her out the door.

"I have work to do," he said curtly. "I'll be in my study."

Erika headed upstairs with Rufus still in her arms. She'd stood up to John and felt the better for it. The tables were turning.

After preparing for bed, she settled Rufus down on his doggie pillow, then slipped between the satin sheets. Almost immediately, she fell into a deep sleep and dreamed that she was swollen from pregnancy. When she awoke the next day, she quickly touched her belly with her fingers. It was flat and smooth.

Up and dressed, John leaned over her and kissed her tenderly. "Darling, let me look at you. My God, you're so gorgeous in that white satin nightgown! Didn't I pick it out for you? Sexy, that's what I said at the time and I was right."

Erika gave a short laugh. "Aren't you always right?"

"Absolutely," he said with a chuckle. Turning serious, he said, "Darling, if I was hurtful to you last night, forgive me. It's the pressure of my work, you see. I thought about what you said, how you and the kids have really bonded and how much you've helped Adriana, and I'm very proud of you; you've surpassed my expectations. He kissed her again. "Now, let's have a hot cup of coffee together. I know Cook's making some delicious blueberry muffins!"

"What time do you see Hilda today?" he asked over breakfast.

"The usual."

"Four o'clock?"

"Yes, and today she's giving me another forty-five minutes so that I'll be a little late getting home. That's a whole hour and a half of therapy." Erika was especially eager to see Hilda Payne.

"Excellent, excellent. She's doing a good job with you." Draining his coffee cup, he smiled as he picked up the newspaper.

As he rose from the table to leave he said, "I might be back early; my patient load is pretty light today."

"You work too hard."

"We'll take that European trip, anyway, just the two of us."

"Unless we discover I'm pregnant, darling! Those first three months I'll have to stay put."

"Of course, my love. Enjoy the day."

After planting a kiss on her forehead, he walked away, whistling. He was dressed in his beige Armani gabardine suit with a Gucci ascot rich in russet hues to complement it and she wondered if he planned to meet someone important.

NINETEEN

John had set up a date to meet Elaine Locke for a coffee at Mug'n Muffin in Harvard Square before he went to the office. He had wasted no time in calling her when he heard she was in town. His chances of landing the Creativity Chair were actually much improved now that Arthur was gone and she had taken his place. As Plunkett's old girlfriend and an icon of the feminists, she could be a powerful advocate for him, better than Erika or poor old Arthur.

It had been a mistake never to have responded to the postcards she sent him long ago. How many had there been, eight or nine? Oh well, he was a simple, callow youth in those days. On the phone, her voice was warm and familiar. No grudges there. Anyway, he would make it up to her, whatever it took.

It was a lovely bright day, so he sat down at a table outdoors to wait for her. For a while he read the *Boston Globe*, then glanced at his watch. Five past ten. She was twenty minutes late; they had agreed to meet at nine forty-five. Where was she? He'd left his cell phone in the car so he couldn't call her; maybe she was inside the restaurant. After a fruitless search, he returned to his table outside.

"Are you Dr. Starr?" It was the restaurant manager.

"Yes?"

"Phone call for you. At the end of the hall."

"Thanks." He hurried inside.

"Is that you, John?" Elaine's voice sounded very close by.

"Yes. I've been waiting for you. What's happened?"

"Oh, it's awful. I can't get out of this silly meeting. Thought I could. I'm so sorry."

"Me, too."

"Can we meet towards the end of the week?"

"Of course. When?" He wanted a definite date; he wasn't going to let her get away.

"I'll call you. And please forgive me. I know how busy you are." He'd forgotten she was so polite.

"No problem. But I want to see you. We've got a lot to talk about."

"Absolutely." Her throaty voice stirred up old memories of a friendship that could have been something more. "I'll get back to you, John," she said softly. "Can't wait."

Momentarily disappointed, he hung up and walked out of the dark restaurant into the bright morning light. But she held out the promise of meeting him later in the week and his heart beat faster. She would get him the Chair, he was sure of it now. She would do that for him.

PART VI

ONE

"Why do you suppose John insists I never bonded with the kids?" Erika asked Hilda Payne.

"He enjoys keeping you off balance. It's a control device."

It was coming out in the therapy how he controlled her with his mind games. Like a master puppeteer, he had been able to manipulate her thoughts without her even knowing.

"It's his special charm," Hilda said with a dry laugh. "When he puts that charm to work he can convince everybody of anything. Except me, that is, because I don't trust charming men. I'm not like you, Erika."

"You think I'm naïve?"

"Maybe a little, though it's not the worst thing in the world. However, it can set you up for victimhood."

Victimhood? How could she be a victim when in the heat of lovemaking he always told her she was his inspiration and his muse? There was no way she could explain to Hilda the intensity of their mutual passion.

Abruptly changing the subject, Erika said, "I'm trying to get pregnant."

"What? Pregnant? This is what you really want?"

"Absolutely. It's what we've both looked forward to for a long time, now."

Hilda gave a loud whistle. "John, too?"

"Yes."

"Hmm. You seem upset and yet you say you're happy. What's going on?"

"It's just that…" Erika fidgeted in her chair.

"Go on."

"I'm not pregnant yet. We're trying, but…" Tears welled up in her eyes.

"You think it's your fault, don't you?"

"Maybe."

"But you've been on the Pill for a long time, right? Your body has to adjust," Hilda insisted.

"You think that's the problem? Oh, I hope you're right."

"I know I am, honey!" Hilda's smile lit up her face and Erika felt as though a great burden had been lifted from her shoulders. Yes, the Pill was to blame.

"It's only a matter of time before you'll be holding a baby in your arms," Hilda said.

"And you're the one who has helped me believe in myself, made me stronger in every way," Erika said. "I'm so grateful."

Hilda nodded. "And the test of your newfound strength will be if you can still love this flawed man to the same degree as before since I've made you aware of his weaknesses."

"I love him today as much as I loved him when I married him. I'll always love him, Hilda."

Hilda's expression grew more serious. "Tell me, were there ever other women during the marriage?"

"'Other women'? What do you mean by 'other women'?" A chill passed through her and she threw a sweater over her shoulders. What an absurd question Hilda was asking and hurtful, too.

Impugning John. Was there no limit to the lengths this woman would go?

"It happens sometimes," Hilda Payne was saying casually. "Men are not the most loyal of creatures. They're predators."

"If John ever cheated on me, it would be the end."

"End of what? Of the marriage?"

"No, of me. I think I would die."

"Come, come, " Hilda Payne chuckled. "No man's worth dying for, not even John, believe me."

"I think I've had enough for today," Erika said heavily.

"But you were going to stay at least another thirty or forty minutes. I left my schedule open for you. We can stop now but next time we meet you'll have to face the truth."

"What truth?"

"John's intention to diminish your womanly power. At heart, he's a mother's boy, Erika. He's weak."

"No, he's not weak. I'm the one who's weak!"

"You're wrong. He's done what weak men do. He's tried to crush your spirit, spend your money, shame you, make you feel guilty, but it's not going to work anymore."

"No," Erika said without conviction."

"Be proactive. He's had his way up until now. It's your turn. You'll be taking the initiative, not him."

Erika gazed absently out the window at the pink roses blooming in the patio. John and Hilda had a way with flowers. A green thumb was it called?

"Pretty, aren't they?" Hilda said.

"Lovely. I guess you could say he's like you, he's got a green thumb. Nothing grows for me."

"Come, come," scolded Hilda Payne. "It's time for you to start learning how to acquire that green thumb. It's not very complicated, my dear. Simply love your plant. Put out positive vibes and your plant will grow for you. Buy a flowering plant on your way home, something exotic, something John has never seen before. You'll be on your own, the choice will be yours, and he will be very impressed. Then everything will come together and you'll create a healthy, balanced relationship with this very flawed man you love so much."

"He'll love me more, won't he?"

"Sure thing."

TWO

Eager to practice yoga beside his newly installed Japanese reflecting pool, John arrived home from the Institute slightly after four-thirty. Erika would not be back before six since Hilda Payne had promised her an extra therapeutic hour.

Being alone was the most important part of practicing yoga. As one of his favorite authors, Kahlil Gibran, described it, John would become a 'seeker of silences' by emptying his mind of all the debris of the day.

Right now, it was warm and sunny and he immediately went to the bamboo bathhouse by the pool to change into a loin-cloth and a white, silk robe. Settling himself down on a blue rubber mat beside the water, he faced east and systematically executed his stretching and relaxation exercises, placing special emphasis on deep breathing. He had recently reread *The Sadhana*, by Swami Sivnanda, which revealed that breath-control through meditation led to longevity. "A healthy man takes fourteen or sixteen breaths in a minute…A snake breathes twice or thrice in a minute. It lives for five hundred or one thousand years."

A slight breeze stirred the still waters of the pool, and John began to experience the spiritual high that was becoming a daily necessity.

"Dr. Starr! A lady to see you, Sir!"

Startled by the interruption, John opened his eyes to the unwelcome sight of Tilly, the maid, calling to him from across the reflecting pool.

"What is it, Tilly? Can't you see I'm not to be disturbed?"

"Sorry, Dr. Starr, but the lady said…"

"What lady?"

"Don't know, I'm sure."

"Didn't she give you her name?"

"She did, Sir."

"Well?"

"Oh my goodness, my mind's gone blank!"

"Tilly, go back and find out who it is! I've left orders not to be disturbed when I'm in the middle of my exercises! You should know that!"

"Yes, Sir, it's just that she said it was important, Sir."

"Important?"

"Yes, Sir. She's very well spoken, the lady. I think I've seen her on TV," Tilly said excitedly.

John knew instantly it was Jane. How dare she come to his home without warning! She was getting back at him, yes, that was it. He had turned down her latest effort to talk about their documentary in person because it was obviously a ruse.

He would get dressed at once and show her the door. Thank god, Erika wasn't around, but there wasn't a minute to lose. She'd be home soon.

"One of those decorators, most likely. Probably wants a house tour," he said offhandedly. "Tell her I'll be right along."

"Yes, Sir. Sorry to have disturbed you, Sir, it was just that..."

"Never mind, Tilly. And by the way, why don't you take the rest of the evening off?"

"You don't need me, Sir?"

"No."

"Thank you, Sir." Smiling, she hurried away.

That woman was a snoop, always hovering around, gossiping with that anal Katie. It occurred to him that Katie had given notice a couple of months ago and Erika had kept her on but hadn't bothered to tell him. Oh, well, he'd take care of the matter one of these days. Right now all he knew was he didn't want Tilly around when he got rid of Jane because she'd be hiding behind a door listening to their every word.

On her way home, Erika decided stop off at Everett's Flower Center to buy a plant for the back patio, something unusual, so that John would be surprised and impressed by her initiative. In a far corner of the nursery, hidden behind broken pots and rusty shovels, she discovered a small, exquisite, bell-shaped plant in a brightly painted clay pot. Its delicate blossoms were a rich shade of dark purple.

"What's the flower over there?" she asked the gardener. "It's so unusual."

"That's Monkshood, Ma'am," he said, "a common plant, I guess you'd say. Poisonous, though, real poisonous. Can kill you. It's them roots, Ma'am, they got the poison in 'em, and if the fluid comes out and gets into a little scratch on your skin, well, you're a goner, dead as a doornail, just like that! We don't sell the Monkshood, of course, don't want no trouble. Heaven knows how it even got in here."

"Oh, please, I'd like to buy it!"

"You want it?" He gave her a quizzical look. "That little poisonous weed?"

"Oh, yes, it's so lovely! So exotic! My husband will love it." Erika gave him a brilliant smile.

"Okay, okay. For you I'll make an exception, but don't forget your gardening gloves when you go planting it. No sense in taking chances."

"It's not going in the ground," she said firmly. "I'll keep it in that pretty, little pot. You know, as a houseplant." She picked it up. "It's not heavy at all."

"No, no, it don't weigh much. Light as a feather it is."

It was only five-fifteen when Erika arrived home and she was tempted to go for a swim, but after she parked the car down by the pool house, a chilly breeze blew up and she headed to the house holding the potted plant in her arms. She passed by the heavy construction equipment still littering the property, an unpleasant reminder that the formal gardens were still dug up, waiting interminably for John and his landscape architects to make up their minds on a permanent design.

Behind the stone wall, peach-colored roses grew lush and full. Just ahead, thickets of pink and white impatiens dotted the hillside, a splash of late-summer brilliance beneath the dark green foliage of the trees. John had promised that every season the gardens would be a celebration of nature's beauty and he'd made it happen.

Looking down at the small plant she was holding, she observed how its thick, velvety flowers glowed in the dim afternoon light. The Monkshood belonged in their bedroom by the window where the bright morning sun would turn its rich purple tones into the softest shades of lavender. Its exotic beauty would impress John. He would want to search out its history because his mind was always questioning and seeking answers.

It disturbed her sometimes that Hilda Payne took such pleasure in exposing the chinks in his armor. If he ever found out her low opinion of him he would be furious but she would never let on. She didn't want to lose Hilda Payne; she was her anchor now, the only voice of reality in her life.

On entering the house through the kitchen, Rufus rushed up to greet her and when she set her plant down on the table, she noticed an open bottle of Meursault and beside it, two empty wine glasses. Who was here? A white chiffon scarf was draped over the back of a chair and the fragrance of Arpège hung heavy in the air. Where was John?

Tilly appeared at the far kitchen door. Dressed in street clothes, she was flushed and out of breath.

"Oh, Mrs. Starr," she said in a rush, "the Doctor told me I could go home early but I missed the bus so I guess I'll stay for the night. Cook'll be happy to see me, I'm sure." She shot a glance at the Monkshood plant. "That's a pretty flower you have there."

"Yes, I'm going to put it in our bedroom."

"Nice."

"By the way, my Uncle Robert will be dropping by for a drink soon and maybe he'll stay for dinner. He has some important news." Erika smiled. "I wonder what he's going to tell us."

"Such a brave, good man," Tilly said.

"Yes, a rare soul." Picking up her plant, she passed by the scarf hanging on the chair.

"Who's here?"

"My goodness, maybe it's the lady's."

"What lady?"

"The decorator lady who's taking a tour of the house."

THREE

Sounds of voices emanating from the living room suggested to Erika that John must be showing off the Prendergast paintings. This time, though, the French doors of the living room were closed. Was a private conversation going on? Opening the doors a crack, Erika heard John speaking in an angry, harsh voice she hardly recognized.

"So the network's not going to show our interviews? And you told me you had those people in the palm of your hand? That was a lie! You lied to me, you bitch!"

"Stop, John! It wasn't my fault!"

"You could have told me on the phone. I've been asking about the deal for weeks! But no, you had to come over here."

"You can't stay away from me, I know you can't!"

"Wrong again! What we had together in New York is history!"

"John, I had to come!" The woman's voice was low and urgent. "You've been playing games with me and nobody does that to Jane Phillips!"

Jane Phillips, the TV star? The woman he worked with on the documentary? Erika felt suddenly faint. Her heart lurched.

"You are ready for me right now, lover boy, I can tell! So just drop your pants and come make love to me like you did in New York!" Jane giggled

"You've got to be crazy! Erika's coming home any minute!"

"So?" The woman gave a husky laugh. "I want you! You're my special hunk!"

Holding her potted plant against her like a shield, Erika shoved open the doors. Naked from the waist down, Jane Phillips was sprawled on the sofa, writhing up and down, her legs spread wide.

"Oh, my God! Get out! Get out! Now! Go! Go!" screamed Erika, smashing her potted plant down on the marble floor. Shards of broken pottery and clumps of uprooted Monkshood scattered across the room.

"Erika, let me explain, it's not what you think!" John cried, hoisting up his pants and quickly buckling his belt.

"I can't bear it! It's too horrible!" Erika sobbed, sinking down against the wall. "She's your whore, John! Your whore!"

"I'm telling you, what you think you saw didn't happen!" he repeated, rushing to her side.

"Stay away from me! I hate you!"

"Erika, stop! You love me! You know you love me! That's how it is with us. Nothing can change that. I'm your husband and your doctor. Come now, my darling, come to me." Bending over her, he held out his arms.

"You're making me crazy," gasped Erika. "Stay away from me!"

"You're upset but I'm asking you to get up." He knelt down beside her.

"Oh, John, John, what have you done?" she whimpered.

"My precious, everything can be explained. Come now, take my hand."

"Don't touch me!" Trembling violently, she curled up in a fetal position and began rocking back and forth.

"I won't let you do this to yourself! You are not to have a seizure!" He slapped her hard across the face with the back of his hand and she slumped down against the wall. A large, red welt formed on her left cheek.

Breathing hard, John stood up and stepping backward, crushed a clump of Monkshood roots under the heel of his shoe. Slowly, its deadly liquid oozed its way over the shards of broken pottery, spreading an oily film across the glittering surface of the marble floor. John took another step backward, slipped and fell down heavily, his left hand breaking the fall. A riveting pain shot through his palm where the sharp, sticky shards pierced his skin.

"I'm bleeding like a stuck pig," he said furiously, wiping his wounds with a handkerchief as he struggled to his feet.

"Poor John," a voice said in mocking tones. It was Jane Phillips, buttoning up her dress. "A big, strong man like you. Hell, you beat up on your wife and then worry about a couple of scratches." She came up to him and bent over his bleeding hand, studying the wounds with exaggerated interest and gave a derisive laugh. "John Starr, the great guru of creativity, can't handle a little blood!"

John made no reply, his face contorted in pain as he bound up his bleeding hand with his handkerchief.

Dimly aware of an eerie silence settling over the room, Erika opened her eyes and saw her husband nursing an injured hand that was bleeding profusely. What had happened?

"Call me a cab," Jane said in a harsh voice.

"Don't worry, I'm taking you home," John said, his voice hoarse and despairing, "but you never should have come, Jane! You want to destroy me!"

"Destroy you? Hey, get real! We had a good thing going and you wanted me as much as I wanted you! If the little wife hadn't come in, we'd have had a great fuck!"

"Shut up!"

"You kept putting me off, you wouldn't see me!" Her voice was rising. "Sonofabitch!"

"Watch your language! Show some respect! This is my wife on the floor."

"Respect? You gotta be kidding! You don't even know the meaning of that word!"

John ignored her, bending down close to Erika. "Darling, don't listen to this woman! Listen to me!"

"Lies, all lies," Erika whispered. "Everything you say is a lie. You never told me about *her*." She closed her eyes as a feeling of suffocation swept over her. Everything true and good had been wiped out of her life forever.

"You don't understand, darling, you've drawn conclusions about this women and myself which aren't true. I don't love her, Erika. I've never loved her or anybody but you, you must understand. She is nothing to me, nothing! I love only you. This woman is a vampire! She wants to bleed me dry!"

"What the hell are you telling her, John? So now I'm a 'vampire'?"

"Shut up, Jane. Erika, she wants to ruin me!"

"I don't understand," Erika stammered.

"You must! You must and you can!"

"You're so full of crap!" shouted Jane.

"Jane, can't you see I'm trying to calm her down? She's in bad shape."

"Asshole!"

"Stop it, Jane, don't talk like that in front of my wife."

"I can talk any way I want in front of your fucking wife! Is she the Queen of England or something? Come off it! And what's this you're saying that I'm nothing to you, nothing at all? What the fuck are you up to?" Jane's face was white with fury. "Get me the hell out of here! Now!"

"Jane, don't worry, we're leaving," he said angrily. He knelt down next to Erika. "Everything's going to be fine, you'll see."

"John," she whispered, "so much blood! So much! Oh, why are you bleeding? Why?"

"I slipped on that broken pottery, that's all. I think Katie put down too much wax on the floor, but it's just a scratch, really, so don't worry."

Erika struggled to speak. "The poison! It was the poison!" But her voice failed her and John leaned closer. "Poison? What are you talking about, my darling?"

Jane came over to observe Erika's swollen face. "This battered woman can't be the gorgeous Mrs. Starr! You hit her really hard, John. She doesn't look good, her face is all black and blue."

"She'll be fine."

"How do you know? You're not even a real doctor!"

"Shut up."

Quickly, John rose to his feet and escorted Jane out of the room. Was that Tilly lurking in the darkened dining room? His eyes must be playing tricks on him; he had sent her home on the bus hours ago. Opening the great oak door with his right hand, he slammed it shut behind them and hurried Jane to the car.

Once inside the black, shiny Lexus, she slid over to the far corner of the front seat and opened the window wide.

"We're not children here, Jane," John said. "I may have been a little violent tonight, but hell, it wasn't a pretty situation. Erika was having the beginnings of a seizure and I had to stop that from getting worse. You can understand now why you and I can't be together."

"That's not the reason and we both know it! You think you can manipulate me the way you do to your wife?"

"You're being irrational."

"You're running around with somebody else, aren't you, John? What's she got, good connections at Harvard? I'll bet that's what you're up to! Going after the Chair! You'd do anything to get it, wouldn't you?"

How could the woman know about Elaine and his plans for the future? She was a wily one, this Jane, he'd give her credit for that.

A thin rain was falling steadily and the car clock showed seven o'clock, later than he thought. He remembered suddenly that Robert was dropping by the house with some news he wanted to share. By the time he returned, Robert might be gone. Oh, well, the man was high maintenance and John only kept him on to please Erika.

"I left my Ferragamo scarf in your kitchen," Jane was saying, "but never mind, it's the least of my worries." Her voice was raspy. "You know, I hope you burn in hell, John Starr. There's only one person in the world you can love if you love at all and it's not me or your trophy wife. It's you, fucker! You! You think you can dump people and get away with it just 'cause you're a hunk and a shrink and you turn on the charm! Well, it's not going to work with me!"

Her rantings didn't touch him. Soon he'd be rid of her for good.

When he reached Jane's apartment building, he braked hard and the car skidded to a halt. Despite her seat belt, she lurched forward against the glove compartment.

"You did that on purpose, didn't you, fucker!" she said, kicking at the door as she pushed it open. "John Starr, you're a loser and a wife beater too! By this time tomorrow the whole world will know it, too!" Her voice rose loud and clear in the damp air. A passerby paused to stare at her as she rushed past him and through the revolving doors of her building.

Starting up the car, he leaned back in his leather seat and sighed with relief. Thank God that was over. The woman was out of his life. People like her were the worst. She'd tricked him with all that Wellesley "cum laude" stuff; she'd probably made the whole thing up. And that crap about his not being able to love anyone but himself. What was she, some kind of expert on the subject? No, she was a schemer with delusions of grandeur, out to entrap him because he was rich and famous. Erika was right about Jane. She was a whore.

His spirits picked up. Her threat to badmouth him all over town would backfire. She couldn't hurt him; he was too big. His work was going to turn things upside down all over the world.

Now it was back to Erika; he had some work to do on that score. He'd made a bad error in judgment getting involved with Jane but Erika had to forgive him because in her heart she knew that they were fated to be together.

FOUR

After she heard the front door slam, Erika rose slowly to her feet; she had remained curled up against the wall for what seemed hours. Limping out into the hall, she started up the stairs, one step at a time, holding tightly to the banister. At the landing, she caught a glimpse of herself in the large, antique mirror. Her right cheek and eye were black and blue and grossly swollen. Heading to the bathroom, she leaned over the sink and ran cold water over her face.

Nothing mattered anymore. Nothing, except getting away from John. He would be coming back soon so she needed to gather her things, some fresh clothes, and throw them into a bag. Uncle Robert was going to stop by to tell her some good news but she couldn't remember what else he had told her. Oh, yes, he'd be by at seven. It was almost seven now. She'd better hurry.

Then she remembered John's badly injured hand, the blood pouring out of his wound after he slipped and fell down on the marble floor and she prayed that the plant's poisonous fluids never entered his bloodstream. She had tried to warn him but he didn't hear her because he was in such pain, but so was she! Her beloved John had betrayed her with another woman and she wanted to die.

Once downstairs, she called Tilly who hurried to her side.

"What happened, Ma'am?" Tilly asked, her expression one of deep concern. "Did you have some kind of accident? I thought I heard some commotion in the living room." She pretended ignorance at what had gone on though she'd listened from the dining room and heard everything. A disgraceful business.

"I slipped on the marble floor, that's all, Tilly. Silly me. Dr. Starr slipped, too. There was a lot of blood. You'll have to clean it all up, I'm afraid."

"Right away, Ma'am, right away. Are you sure you're alright?"

"I'm okay, but my face hurts."

"I'll get some ice packs, they'll help, Ma'am."

"Thank you." The clock in the foyer struck seven. "My uncle's due any minute. I'll be leaving with him."

"Leaving? You won't be staying for dinner? Should you be going out?" Tilly said, returning with the ice packs.

"Don't worry, Tilly. When I'm with my uncle, I always feel better."

The minutes ticked by. Erika didn't know how long she could sit there pretending to be calm. Jumping up in her lap, Rufus licked her face with his rough, warm tongue and she felt an excruciating pain. Poor, darling Rufus, trying to make her feel better!

"Just one for dinner, then?"

"Dr. Starr."

"Yes, Ma'am."

At the first sighting of her Uncle Robert's silver BMW, she quickly grabbed her coat and overnight bag.

"Tell Dr. Starr I'm not sure when I'll be back."

"Yes, Ma'am," Tilly said, opening the heavy front door. "Take care, now."

Once in the back seat next to Uncle Robert, Erika broke down in tears.

"Hey, what's going on? What happened to your face?" Shocked at her appearance, he quickly put his arms around her.

"Take me away! Hurry!" Her body shook with sobs.

"Matt, drive on. We'll go back to my apartment."

"Right."

Fog was descending upon the city, blotting out the tallest buildings, shrouding the trees by the Charles River as Robert's sleek new BMW sped across the B.U. Bridge and down Memorial Drive to his apartment. Her mind a blank, Erika sat without speaking and Robert asked her no more questions. When they arrived at his place, he showed her to her room, then went away to make a brief phone call. Erika could tell he was talking to a woman because he called her "my darling" and she wondered who it might be.

She had no appetite for the gourmet food served by Robert's chef, and soon went to bed, pressing an ice bag against her swollen face. Later, Robert knocked on the door of her room and with great delicacy and persistence, persuaded her to sketch out what had happened that afternoon. Their conversation continued well into the night

Despite his disapproval of divorce, Robert concluded that it was the only way out for Erika. One thing was certain: Starr wouldn't get a penny.

FIVE

When John arrived home, Erika was gone. The living room, which was covered with broken crockery, had been completely restored to its pristine state. The marble floor shone like a mirror and not a single object was out of place. Someone had cleaned up the mess, but who? It must have been one of the servants. Walking slowly back down the hall, he saw Tilly waiting for him by the dining room door.

"I thought I gave you the rest of the day off," he said sharply.

"I missed the bus so I came back, Doctor Starr."

"And Mrs. Starr?"

"The Mrs. was picked up by Mr. Giuliani. I'm not sure what time she said she'd be home. She took a bad fall in the living room, you see, and her face was very swollen so I fixed her up with some ice."

"That was good of you, Tilly."

"Thank you, Doctor Starr. She stared down at the bloody handkerchief wrapped around his hand. "Looks like you hurt yourself real bad too, Dr. Starr. Better take care of that hand right away. I'm afraid Katie shined up the floor too much today and I'll have to get after her about that. A newly polished marble floor can be very dangerous!" She paused, her expression grim. "With all that broken pottery, I had to be extra careful so I wore my thickest rubber gloves. There was sticky oil all over the floor, never seen it before, and some blood, too. Her eyes narrowed. "I didn't like the sight of *that*, I can tell you! Anyway, everything looks just like it did before. You'd never know there'd been any kind of trouble."

"Good work, Tilly."

"Thank you, Sir." She beamed with satisfaction. "Oh, and I forgot to tell you, Dr. Starr. The plant the Mrs. dropped by mistake in the living room was meant for you."

"For me?"

"Yes, yes! It was very unusual, you see, real exotic wildflowers with dark purple blossoms. Like velvet, they were, and she meant to give it to you as a surprise. Such a shame it got all smashed up along with the pot. She wanted it for your bedroom."

"The bedroom?" John said absently.

"Dr. Starr, are you feeling alright?" Tilly could plainly see the doctor was not himself. He was unusually pale and unsteady on his feet. Carrying on with that other woman had taken its toll and the white handkerchief wrapped around his hand had turned a dark crimson. What had he done to himself? How had he bloodied his hand like that? Beating up on his wife? Yes, that was it. That woman had called the doctor a wife-beater!

"What made you ask that, Tilly?" he was saying. "I'm fine, never felt better. Tonight it's 'Eat, drink, and be merry for tomorrow we die!' A great saying, don't you think, Tilly? Now how about my meal? I'm famished!"

He slumped down in his dining room chair and Tilly hurried out to the kitchen.

He'd talk to Erika in the morning about this meddlesome woman. He wanted her out of the house, the sooner, the better. Mostly likely she'd heard the whole terrible business, probably even listened at the door. She seemed unusually cheerful, like she'd swallowed a canary. God knows what vicious gossip she'd spread around the neighborhood.

Right now he needed to get himself centered. All that violence and negativity had affected him, he felt washed out, lethargic.

He drank a couple of glasses of wine with dinner and then ordered Tilly to bring in the bottle of apricot brandy with dessert.

"To settle the stomach. I'm feeling slightly under the weather." His speech was slurred and his face was gray.

"There's not much brandy left, Dr. Starr, the bottle's nearly empty. Are you sure you want to drink anymore, Sir? You're not looking so good."

"I don't need advice from you, Tilly! Do me a favor and get the bottle!" he shouted.

Tilly blanched, then disappeared without a word. The doctor had never raised his voice like that before. Always the perfect gentleman. But after what she'd heard and seen today, it was clear he was a very different man from the one she thought she knew.

The bottle of brandy turned out to be nearly a third full, and after finishing it off, John started up to his room. His legs were so weak he could only manage the stairs by hanging on to the banister and pulling himself up with his right arm. Must be a touch of the flu. One of his patients had coughed in his face earlier in the day and he's forgotten to wash his hands after the session. Freud had been wrong, scaring off generations from hand-washing, claiming it was obsessional, a neurotic habit. Now medical science had proved that germs...what was it now? Oh, yes, germs could be eradicated by soap and water, hand-washing, the key to good health. Not fifteen times a day, of course, but at least six times or was it seven? He couldn't remember. What was happening to his memory?

He'd talk to Erika in the morning. He'd hit her a little hard, he had to admit, but she was having a seizure. He'd had no other option than to smack her like her father must have smacked her. Maybe Emilio hadn't been so abusive after all; maybe he was simply trying to get her attention, calm her down. Anyway, he'd tell her how sorry he was and ask her to forgive him.

After closing the bedroom door, he sank down on the bed and stared absently up at the ceiling. Reading, his usual activity before settling down to sleep or making love, was not an option this night. An overwhelming ennui had settled over him like a damp, thick fog. A hot bath, the healing powers of the womb, that's what he needed. But getting off the bed? It seemed insurmountable. Would it be his legs first? By swinging them over the side of the bed, would the rest of his body follow? Up and onward, he would try it, absolutely.

There, he was standing on his feet, trembling like a leaf and the room wasn't even cold. What was going on? Had he eaten something bad? Something poisonous? But what? His mind went blank. All he knew was that he must get himself to the bathroom, reach the tub, fill it with hot water. He had never felt such cold. There, he'd switched on the overhead light. The face in the mirror looking back at him wasn't his own. A stranger's perhaps, someone he didn't know. And that burning sensation in his hand. Yes, he could make out small gashes in his palm where it hurt, burning, searing the flesh, an intense pain. Removing his clothes was a major effort. Now he was down on his hands and knees. Naked as the day he was born. Hanging on to the rim of the tub, hoisting himself up and over, splashing heavily down into the water. It was gushing out now, lovely and hot. The tub was filling up, must turn down the flow. There, done. But that dripping sound. It was the hot water, never fixed the screw on the handle. Tick, tock, tick, tock. Drip, drop, drip, drop. He covered his ears with his wet hands and stretching out the full length of the tub, he felt the negatives in his life fading away.

But now, what was this? Roaches creeping up his neck. A sensation of impending doom. Was he going to die? He was still young, he had another twenty or thirty years, didn't he? Things were looking up. The Creativity Chair, Elaine, beautiful, wonderful Elaine in his corner right where he wanted her. She'd make it happen. Sure, she would.

But he couldn't lift his arms, couldn't even breathe! He was on a roller coaster, spiraling up and down, over and under, and he couldn't get enough air!

He drifted deeper into the water. The light went out, the bathroom plunged into darkness. Resting his head against the back of the tub, he dozed off until the sound of an opening door jolted him awake. Standing in a pool of light was a woman. He knew the shape, the feel of her, the face. It was his mother and she was telling him something very important.

"Johnny baby, you're a genius, unrecognized in your time and it's been that way with geniuses throughout human history. It's time to leave it all behind, Harvard, those women. Get away. Be an artist! Be the painter you always wanted to be!"

"But Mom, the Harvard deal! How can I leave when it's about to happen?"

"You must, my darling boy."

"And Erika?"

"She won't help you now."

"I love her, Mom."

"Forget her, darling boy. Hurry, there's not much time."

"How much?"

"Only a little."

SIX

He was soaring like an eagle into a starry sky with the moonbeams guiding his way, steering him on to a small studio on a beach in Santa Cruz, California.

I'll live here and be the artist I was meant to be, he said to himself. And I'll call myself "Jack"; it suits me. It's casual, boyish, and stylish, too.

On days when the Monterrey coastline was hidden by a long grey curtain of clouds stretching across the horizon, he imagined China lay just beyond. The modest one-bedroom studio was built on stilts so he had to climb up its steep, rickety steps to enter the front door. His only heating was an old fashioned wood- burning stove which he used on cold, foggy days, fueled by bits and pieces of driftwood collected on the beach. He had no cell phone, no TV or radio to distract him from his work and right away he finished six large, abstract oil paintings for the local art show.

His work was getting a lot of attention and one afternoon, an important art dealer knocked loudly at his door. Known locally as Billy, this dealer was famous for making talented artists into a household word.

John had spent thirty minutes meditating before this important meeting and greeted his visitor in his usual paint-spattered blue jeans and torn blue cashmere sweater (a gift from Erika long ago).

He was tall, this famous dealer, and old, with white hair reaching his shoulders. Dressed in khaki pants and a blue striped shirt, he carried a yachting cap in his hand. He looked familiar and John was sure they'd met before. But where?

"How you doing? I'm Billy," the man smiled. "I've heard great things about you, Jack. Nice to meet you." John led him into the small living room and offered him a chilled glass of California wine.

"Thanks, but no. I don't drink anymore. Hey, I like what I'm seeing around here." He radiated excitement, moving from painting to painting, peering closely at each one.

"Your opinion means a lot to me," John said.

"This is terrific, you've got the right stuff, young man. Hell, where have you been all these years? I'd like to introduce you to a collector I know. She's always looking for people like you, the ones with the creative spark. She'll try to bargain you down, of course."

"Thanks, but I'm sure I can handle the situation. I've had plenty of experience dealing with women," John said with a small smile.

Offering the old man the antique rocking chair, John sat down on the rough wooden bench next to a line of acrylic paint jars.

"You're not native to this area, are you, Jack? Somehow I feel like we've run into each other before," Billy said.

"Me, too, I was trying to figure it out. Maybe I knew you in an earlier life, like back East."

"And where's that?"

"I grew up in Washington."

"The capital of the world," said Billy with an easy laugh. "I lived there once."

"Nice, isn't it? Anyway, I went up to Harvard and I've pretty much stayed around Boston doing research most of my adult life. I don't miss it, though. My life's been turned around out here in the West and for the better."

"What kind of research did you do?"

"Creativity studies. And now I'm actually living the creative experience!"

"You sure are!"

"I ran an institute in Cambridge where we studied artists and scientists to understand how creativity works. Now I've become like one of the people we interviewed and it's a great feeling."

"You ran an institute in Cambridge?" the old man said, looking quizzically at John. "I've heard of a John Starr who was doing something like that. But your name's Jack, not John."

"No, I'm actually called John. I renamed myself Jack now that I'm an artist."

"Am I talking to John Starr, the creativity guru?"

"You are, indeed," said John with a wide smile.

"You are THE John Starr?"

"One and the same!"

Billy repeated John's full name several times. "So you gave it all up to become an artist," he said at last.

"I did."

"How about that." His hands on his knees, the old man sat silently staring at the floor. When he finally raised his head, his eyes were brimming with tears.

"You don't know who I am, do you, Jack. You were just a little boy, so why should you?"

"I think I do know you," John said trying to keep his voice steady. "I've got a feeling that I'm right."

"Who am I?"

"You're my father," he said very quietly. The words, shockingly simple and true, came out with no effort. Though aged and wrinkled, the face of the man before him was the very same one he has seen in the dozens of photographs his mother saved of his father. Growing up, he studied them over and over, memorizing each one, struggling to understand why this smiling, elegantly dressed man never came back to them.

"I didn't want it that way," the old man was saying. "I got scared, and in those days, I wasn't ready to settle down. Your mother tricked me into marrying her, pretending she was going to have a baby when it wasn't true. I stuck it out, later we had you, but she was used to a lot of money and I couldn't give her the life she wanted. Her father had cut her off, and we drank a lot, you see, and she was always bragging about her Southern roots, her debutante days. Anyway, I went off to fight in Vietnam and brought back a Vietnamese girl but she left me after a couple of years because of my drinking. It's a terrible thing I did, running out on you and your mother and I've never forgiven myself. But I was always thinking about you, son, following your career starting back in your Harvard days. I kept track of your writings and whatever was printed about you in magazines. That's my boy, I'd say to myself. I thought about getting in touch with you, but I never did. I'm a louse, that's what I am, a louse." His face was wet with tears and he pushed the rocking chair back and forth. "I wouldn't blame you if you sent me away and never spoke to me again," his father muttered bitterly.

John stood up and glanced out at the sea where the clouds floated across the bright blue sky. His memories of those years of deprivation, his mother's sorrow, the loneliness and bitterness of his childhood, had been miraculously driven away and love and forgiveness flooded his heart.

"I would never send you away," John said.

"I'll do my best for you, Jack!" his father shouted, "I'll market your work, bring you money and fame!"

"Let's not worry about that right now, dad. We've got a lot to talk about. How about some supper? I was just about to make some soup."

"It's okay?"

John smiled. "Absolutely."

"Thanks, I'd like that a whole lot," his father said finally.

John went into the tiny kitchen to start up the meal. The sky was darkening; there would be a late afternoon rain. His father called out to him from the other room but it was his mother's voice he heard instead.

"It's time to go back now, Johnny."

"Back where?"

"Back to where you were, remember?"

"I did what you told me. I'm an artist now."

"Yes, and it's wonderful, isn't it?"

"I'm so happy, Mom. I found Dad."

"Yes, it was meant to be."

"I found him, Mom, and I don't want to leave him."

"You must."

"Why?"

"Come with me."

He seemed to be floating alongside his mother and she was holding his hand like she did when he was a boy, drawing him down a tunnel of light. When he looked at her, she was smiling that sweet smile he'd waited half a lifetime to see again.

SEVEN

John Starr had not shown up at the office and it was already eleven in the morning. Concerned as to his whereabouts, Marsha phoned Robert who recounted the events of the night before.

"It was pretty bad, Marsha. Starr struck her so hard she's got a huge purple bruise on the side of her face. She never had a clue he was in a relationship with Jane Phillips, that TV star we watch all the time. You can imagine the shock. Besides being a phony, the guy's a cad as well, and I'll be pressing charges against him for assault and battery."

"This is unbelievable!" Marsha cried. "What will Erika do now?"

"She doesn't ever want to see him again. I told her she could stay at my place and she's still asleep."

"This whole thing's a nightmare. It makes no sense! He loved her. I can't understand how this happened. There was never a hint that anything was wrong."

"Obviously, he's been leading a double life."

"It sounds like it," Marsha breathed. "I still can't believe it."

Her boss, the great Dr. Starr, renowned psychoanalyst, national guru of creativity, had beaten up his wife and cheated on her as well.

"I'm sorry to be the bearer of bad news," Robert said with genuine regret.

"The perfect couple. All ruined." From her desk in her little cubicle, she stared sadly out at the empty office. "I've been waiting for him for hours and he still hasn't come in. What could he be doing?"

"Who knows?"

"Nobody's seen him and he hasn't called, Robert. I canceled his patients when he didn't show up here today. A family emergency, that's what I said. I hope it was the right thing to do. It's very bizarre, his acting this way. When he's late, he always lets me know."

"Oh, he'll show up. Don't worry about old Starr. He's got all those patients whose lives revolve around him so he'll put in an appearance. They're going to have to find another shrink, though."

"Why?"

"I'll be calling the authorities. Face it, sweetheart. The guy seduces his patient, marries her, then betrays her with another woman. He's a scoundrel, pure and simple. You didn't know our boy was also a bit of a gold digger, did you? I mean, the guy's been squandering Erika's money."

"He once told me *The Great Gatsby* was his favorite book."

"Gatsby? That figures. But Gatsby didn't get his money from marrying a rich woman. He made it all himself. Anyway, we're closing down the accounts. Starr will get nothing."

"Nothing?"

"Not a penny. He'll have to depend on his own resources from now on."

"Maybe Erika will feel sorry for him and give him money."

"Don't count on it. Erika has no wish to see him again. She's like that, you know. Once she's done with people, they're dead meat."

"He's not going to let that happen, he'll try to win her back."

"He'll fail; count on it. And he'll lose his license to practice psychotherapy."

"Oh, Robert! I don't know what to think!"

"Don't go all soft and mushy on me, Marsha."

"Well, he's helped a lot of people though you don't want to believe me. But you're right about Erika. What he did to her was very wrong."

"Worse than wrong."

"I saw Jane Phillips a couple of times at the office. She was bad news, I could tell right away, and I wanted to warn him but I never did." Marsha sighed deeply.

"Don't waste your pity on Starr, darling."

"You know, he didn't believe marrying his patient was a problem. He once said he wasn't actually analyzing Erika, just helping her discover her creative self."

"That's crazy, Marsha! He's not trustworthy!"

"But you agreed to have therapy with him, didn't you?"

"I did it to please Erika. You know that."

"Yes," Marsha said. "And if you hadn't..."

"We never would have met and that would have been a disaster," Robert said. "Actually, I shouldn't be so hard on Starr, should I, darling? He did us a big favor."

"Without his even knowing," she murmured and they both laughed.

"Sweetheart, I've got something important to tell you," Robert said, suddenly somber.

"What is it, darling?"

"I think you'll agree that because of Erika's situation, we'll have to delay our marriage."

Marsha closed her eyes.

"But only a little while, until she's on her feet," Robert quickly added. "Do you remember meeting Judge Borenstein with me? He's a good man and a justice of the peace as well. He could marry us when the time is right."

"Are you doing this for me because I'm a Jewish nonbeliever? You're a Catholic, a religious man, you'll want a priest."

"Well, there is just one thing."

"What's that?"

"After our honeymoon we can fly to Haiti. I'd like you to see the orphanage and meet Father Richard. He could bless our marriage. How would you feel about that?"

"Great," Marsha said.

It couldn't happen too soon. She was ready to go. At the end of the month her job with Dr. Starr would thankfully be over and she and Robert could leave Boston for Miami to start a new life. She would not abandon her mother. Most holidays, she planned to fly up to visit her at the Home though each time they were together now her mother appeared more remote, deep in her world of dreams.

For months, she and Robert had been discussing their project of a rehabilitation center in Miami for severely disabled Mexican and Haitian orphans. Robert decided to remain on his company's board but to step down as CEO and he and Marsha would live in Miami.

Now with Erika's crisis, would their dream still come true? Erika might want to hold on to Robert and never let go.

Several days passed without any sign of Dr. Starr and the door to the master bedroom remained closed. Erika was in seclusion at her uncle's apartment and the house was eerily silent. The staff was increasingly edgy. Rufus hid under the living room sofa and it was only after holding out a slab of red meat that Tilly was finally able to grab him. She took him home and settled him into her large, cheerful family where he acted as though he had never lived anywhere else.

The third day, Mary, the second maid, discovered puddles of water on a downstairs bathroom floor. A slow, steady drip oozed through the ceiling from the master bath above. Alarmed, she alerted the head butler, Ben.

"Water's coming down from upstairs, Ben, and there's nobody up there!" Her eyes were wide with fright.

"You mean the master bath?"

"Seems like it. How could that be? And it's all over the bathroom floor downstairs here!"

"I'd better take a look.

After noting the problem, Ben went immediately to the master bedroom and knocked on the locked door. There was no response and since there was no other way of entering the bathroom, he broke down the door.

The bed was unmade and Dr. Starr was nowhere to be seen. Calling out his name, Ben carefully searched the room, then entered the bathroom. Immediately, he saw the problem: someone had never fully shut off the tap so water was dripping over the rim of the tub onto the floor.

Drawing closer, he recoiled in horror, for floating in the water was the naked body of John Starr.

EIGHT

All the experts agreed there had been no foul play. John Starr choked on his own vomit due to his state of inebriation and subsequently drowned in the bathtub. According to Tilly, he consumed so much alcohol at dinner that fateful night he was barely able to stand up. Goodness knows, she'd tried her best to stop him when she noticed how sick and pale he looked but he paid no attention. She knew all the signs; her husband did himself in with the drink as well. Too young he was, only forty at the time, a terrible waste. Of course, Dr. Starr wasn't a drunkard like her husband; usually, he only drank a glass or two of wine at dinnertime with Mrs. Starr, certainly no more. But on the night in question, he appeared especially worried about something and kept repeating, "Eat, drink, and be merry for tomorrow we die!" and it seemed to Tilly a very strange thing that he would talk like that on the very day he met his death. She was careful not to mention to the police or anybody else the awful things that went on in the house that afternoon. Certain matters were nobody's business.

Erika did not visit the body at Warton's Funeral Parlor. On hearing the tragic news, she overdosed on sleeping pills and was discovered unconscious in her bed the next morning by Robert. Rushed by ambulance to the psychiatric ward of the Massachusetts General Hospital, she was treated and was later transferred to McLean, the psychiatric hospital for the rich, where she was to be closely watched and carefully medicated.

A grief-stricken Roger, accompanied by his mother and Adriana, journeyed to Boston to pick up his father's ashes. Following the instructions in his will, John's body had been cremated and placed in a handsome, bronze urn. Together, the family flew to

Nantucket where Roger hired a small motorboat. Then they sailed far out from the shore where Roger tossed his father's ashes into the ocean, all the while reciting the Lord's Prayer above the roar of the wind and waves.

Discussing the tragedy in later days, it seemed inconceivable to them that John, who usually drank very little and kept himself remarkably fit, should come to such an untimely end. What really happened? Word was out that John was depressed the day of his death and Catherine recalled his mood swings during their marriage. Most likely they would never get satisfactory answers any time soon since Erika would be confined indefinitely to McLean.

John's lawyers notified Roger he would inherit all the money his father had accrued over the years as well as his possessions. He and his mother would be well provided for, though Erika's millions remained hers alone.

Despite Robert's intense dislike of John Starr, Marsha mourned his loss. A romantic, he would have been horrified by the sordid nature of his death. Until those last few months when he was clearly not himself, he treated her as a trusted and valued colleague. They had shared the heady days when he was a celebrity around town, eagerly sought after by people who mattered. He and his beautiful Erika were the power couple of Boston society; everyone wanted invitations to their brilliant parties.

What went wrong? What broke the spell? Was it the Harvard debacle? The loss of the Chair? He was never quite the same after that. He seemed diminished in some way, oddly vulnerable.

His life was all too brief and now that he was gone. There was an emptiness in her heart and nothing would ever be the same.

After Erika's suicide attempt, Robert ordered the staff dismissed and the house permanently closed. The gardens were left untended, and the estate was put up for sale. Robert and Marsha visited Erika at McLean a number of times, but she seemed listless and uncommunicative in their presence. Experts were treating Erika with a range of new antidepressant drugs but she showed no improvement. She recalled little of what happened between her and John that last day and when Marsha tried to speak to her, she turned away.

PART VII
ONE

And what did Erika remember? Only that her husband, the man she had trusted so utterly had betrayed her. He was someone she did not know. When he hit her in the face, she saw the back of her father's hand and she couldn't stop screaming.

She had believed that she and John were different from other people. He was her sun and she was his moon. That's what he repeated to her so many times that she believed him. But he was wrong. He was like everybody else, an ordinary man who played her for a fool and now without him she was left in darkness, invisible even to herself.

One day she told the young psychiatrist at Mclean that she needed to see Hilda Payne. "If I don't, I will die."

"We'll look for her at once," he said but later reported that a Hilda Paine was registered in the directory of psychotherapists but not a Hilda Payne; Her telephone was unlisted.

"It would make it easier for us if you try to remember her phone number," he said.

"I can't remember anything."

Later that day, resting in her chair, she dreamed of her father and Hilda Payne. Wearing a brown mink hat, Hilda was playing the piano while her father was singing an Italian aria at the top of his voice. Neither of them noticed her. She called out to them but they did not hear her.

Suddenly, she remembered Hilda's telephone number and woke up.

When Hilda appeared at last, Erika wept like a child and Hilda wrapped her arms around her.

"I've missed you, Erika," she said in her deep, soothing voice. "I was told you'd gone away on a trip and wouldn't be back for a very long time. You won't stay here in this place, I promise you that! You'll come and live with me. I've been in touch with your Uncle Robert." Hilda hugged her again, and it was only then Erika noticed that Hilda was wearing a brown mink hat.

She went to live in a small, furnished bedroom overlooking the patio with the Crilo sculpture at the rear of Hilda's home, caught up in the feelings of hopelessness she had experienced so long ago after Frank's drowning. This time, however, Hilda was at her side, working for a recovery that seemed increasingly uncertain.

One day, frustrated by their lack of progress, Hilda said grimly, "You're hiding something from me, Erika. What is it?"

"What makes you say that?" Erika asked, carefully averting her gaze.

"We're not getting anywhere. You're hiding something and I want to know what it is."

"Why do you want to know?"

"Because we must have transparency if you are to overcome your depression."

Her eyes suddenly brimming with tears, Erika looked directly at Hilda. "I'm remembering things, bad things," she said.

"We've been over John's betrayal many times, Erika."

"It's not about his betrayal. Something else happened that day, something so terrible I've never spoken of it."

"Are you ready to tell me now?"

"I think so. It's all my fault, you see." Her voice shook.

"What's your fault?"

"That John died!"

"Are you saying you are responsible for John's death?"

"I killed him!" Erika burst out.

"You didn't kill John, Erika; he drank himself to death because he betrayed you with another woman!" Hilda exclaimed.

"No, no! It's different! I killed him but it was an accident! When I saw John and that woman together, I smashed the plant down on the floor!"

"What plant?"

"Don't you remember? You told me that day to buy an exotic plant to impress John and I did," Erika stammered between sobs. "The gardener told me at the store that the plant carried a deadly poison inside its roots and if it ever escaped and seeped into an open wound, well, it could kill a person in hours. That's what happened to John! I just know it! When he slipped on the floor, he reached out to save himself from the fall and injured his hand on some shards of broken pottery. They must have been covered by that sticky poison. He was poisoned, don't you understand?"

"Poisoned?"

"When I saw him with that woman, I smashed the flower pot on the floor and the roots scattered everywhere, along with all the broken bits and pieces of the flower pot." Rocking back and forth on her chair, Erika struggled to contain her emotions.

"How did the poisons seep out of the roots?"

"John stepped backwards and crushed the roots with the heel of his shoe. He had no idea what he had done, of course. I tried to warn him about the poison but earlier he'd hit me in the face and I couldn't speak well. But I saw everything that happened."

"Where were you, exactly?"

"On the floor, against the wall."

"Incredible," breathed Hilda Payne. "This is all true?"

"Yes! The poison went directly into his wound. I know it did. There was so much blood."

"You could see the blood?"

"Yes, yes! When he stood up, he tied up his bloody hand in his handkerchief but I could see he was in pain, that he was badly injured."

"You saw all that? You weren't knocked out?"

"No, I was never unconscious."

"Why didn't you tell me this before?"

"I was afraid."

"Why?"

"I killed him."

"It was an accident, Erika. You didn't poison him on purpose!"

"But it was my fault he died…" She stared past Hilda Payne at the Crilo sculpture. "I've been having so many scary dreams, recently. So many."

"Lets hear the latest one. Can you tell me?" said Hilda Payne.

TWO

"I was gathering a whole bouquet of exquisite purple flowers in a medieval garden below a castle on a hill. An old woman sitting under a tree shouted at me not to pick the flowers called Monkshood because the roots contained a poisonous fluid that could kill, and Prince John, who lived in the castle would be very angry if he found out. He used the poisonous roots to make a lethal brew for captured enemy soldiers.

I paid no attention to what she said and gathered dozens of Monkshood blossoms until I couldn't hold any more. I found myself wandering down the hill to the lake to meet Prince John. The old woman had told me that every day he was there waiting for his beloved Princess Erika to return. She had been taken from him years earlier by an evil fairy.

When I saw the knight in silver armor standing by the lake, I knew it was John and I hid my flowers under a rock and ran over to him. He pushed me away saying he didn't know me. When I told him I was his wife he said he had no wife and turned away to stare into the dark waters. I asked him if he was studying his reflection and he said yes, he was looking for the self that was truly his, the self he'd been searching for all his life. When I awoke, my pillow was wet with tears."

"He didn't even know me!" cried Erika, "and he's never coming back to me."

"Yes, he's gone forever, Erika."

"Not forever! When I die, we'll be together again. I loved him so much and believed in him. All that time together I thought he loved me, too. But he didn't, Hilda, not really."

"Of course he loved you, but in his own way. Success on the grand scale, having lots of money, those things came first. If there were someone around who could get him what he wanted, he'd make that connection. You came in a distant second, I'm afraid."

"Yes, you're right. He was always wanting more. More money, more fame, the Chair at Harvard."

"In your dream he was studying his reflection, wasn't he?"

"Yes."

"Since dreams are telling us what we truly feel, it looks like you felt John was so obsessed with himself that he could never love anyone and I think we should leave it there, Erika. It's time to move on," said Hilda Payne.

"Move on? How can I?"

"You can and you will, with my help."

THREE

Matt was thinking that he'd never seen Giuliani so happy. Nobody could have guessed the pain the guy was in earlier that day when he ordered Matt to dope him up with painkillers because it was his wedding day. Marsha didn't object. She wanted him free from pain, if only for a little while. The judge performed the ceremony in the living room with a crowd of friends and associates and the powerful scent of lilies and roses hung in the air. Giuliani sat in his wheelchair holding hands with Marsha and when the judge pronounced them man and wife, there wasn't a dry eye in the place.

Giuliani sure looked good in the dark suit and red tie. They all had one heck of a time choosing his tie. Marsha won out. It seems when she first met Giuliani, he was wearing that same red tie. Marsha wore a white silk suit and matching shoes and she was prettier than Matt had ever seen her. He liked the diamond brooch on her lapel. Giuliani's gift to his bride.

His niece, Erika, wasn't able to make it but the flowers she sent were enough to fill up a hotel lobby. He'd heard about the doctor husband of hers. Died of the drink. Such a good-looking pair, those two, the perfect couple, you might say, but he'd noticed in life that shocking things often happened to the so-called "perfect couples".

Poor Erika. Movie-star gorgeous and nice, too. Real nice. Too bad she'd gone nuts after the husband died. Right now she was in London with her shrink, the funny fat lady, Dr. Payne.

At the reception there was plenty of caviar, champagne and chocolate mousse, and the guests hung around, talking, kissing the bride, congratulating Giuliani. Then he gave Matt the signal. The hand high in the air meant it was time to bring the limo around.

The party was over and they were off to the airport. Giuliani's jet was all set to go. Down to Miami and the condo to start a new life.

The skies over Miami were growing dark the day the children were due to arrive from Haiti. Warnings of heavy rains were flashing across the TV screen. Normally, news of this sort did not worry Robert and Marsha but now it was different. Would the furies of nature deny them this special day they had worked so hard to make happen? The first two orphans were expected just after eleven thirty that morning so they set off for the airport early.

"The plane's been delayed an hour and a half, Sir," Matt told Robert after studying the arrivals board. "We've a bit of a wait here. They're not due in until one o'clock."

"There's a storm down there as well?"

"Looks like it, Sir," Matt said, parking Robert's wheelchair next to an armchair in the Executive Lounge.

"Ma'am, here's a seat."

"Thanks, Matt."

"Well, I'm off for a bite to eat," Matt said. "I'll pick up the morning papers for you."

"Thanks," Robert said.

Marsha sat down next to her husband. "Oh, I hate waiting like this!"

"Me, too, but it's out of our hands." Robert drew her into his arms and a couple nearby stared at them. Had they never seen a man in a wheelchair embracing his wife? Marsha kissed him on the lips.

"Hey, that's nice," he laughed. "Do it again." Smiling, she kissed him once more.

"Those poor kids," Marsha said. "Stuck for two hours in the Port au Prince airport."

"Let's hope their attendants play some games with them, get their minds off the weather," Robert said.

The children expected were only seven and nine years old, a little boy and girl. Marsha had seen their picture and the image stayed with her. They were sitting awkwardly on straight-backed wooden chairs, their crutches resting against the wall behind them. Their smiling faces revealed their pride at being chosen to come to Miami for specialized medical treatment not available in their own country.

"Dr. Pritchard and his surgical staff are meeting us at ten o'clock tomorrow morning," Marsha said. "We mustn't be late, he's been so generous with his time."

"For such a world famous orthopedic surgeon to take on the kids, well, it's really great."

After lunch, Matt checked the arrival time, returning right away. "The plane's landed," he announced.

Robert glanced at his watch. Exactly one fifteen. A quarter of an hour early. Not a minute to lose.

"Matt, let's get going. We can't be late!"

With Marsha hurrying by his side, Matt expertly directed the wheelchair through the busy crowds who parted to let them through. In minutes they would be the arrival area, ready to greet the children.

The next morning Robert and Marsha met Dr. Rowland Pritchard for the first time. Tall and gray haired with twinkling blue eyes, he was wearing a white coat with a row of pens across his breast pocket. He exuded warmth and confidence.

"We'll get the kids on their feet, you'll see," he said, smiling cheerfully. "I've examined them and they'll be able to lead normal lives. There's a lot of rehabilitation involved after the operation, of course, but they're going to be okay."

"It's a miracle," Robert said. "You're giving them a future!" His eyes shone with a special brightness.

"How about yourself?" Dr. Pritchard asked. "I was told about your accident. Ever considered surgery in your own case?"

"The doctors in Boston never brought up that possibility," Robert said bitterly. "Just rehabilitation, nothing else, and you know what that means. Pain. Jesus! And what pain!"

"Would you be interested in another opinion?"

"Sure." His heart was beating so fast he feared he might faint. Marsha pressed his hand.

"I have some extra time now. I could give you a preliminary exam."

"Exam? My god, I don't know, I didn't come prepared for this."

"There's no hurry, we can look at you another day. Just remember that my interest is always seeing if I can get the patient out of his wheelchair and walking on his own," Dr. Pritchard said.

"Marsha!" Robert pulled her face down close to his. "Tell me what to do! I've waited so long and now I'm scared as hell! Tell me! I can't think!"

"Let him examine you now. Why wait? Make it happen!"

Robert turned away and looked directly at Dr. Pritchard.

"Sure," he announced in a strong voice. "I'll have my exam today, Dr. Pritchard."

"Come on, Marsha, let's go," he whispered fiercely, wheeling himself after Dr. Pritchard who was leading them down the hospital corridor towards his examining room. No one before had ever given him reason to believe things could change. Could he hope for a miracle?

FOUR

"I think you're up for a trip, Erika; you're ready and I know I am," Hilda said. Rachel Martin, a British colleague had recently suggested in an email to Hilda that there might be a job opening for her at the prestigious Institute for Transcendent Psychology (ITP) in London. "You'd be the perfect person to start up a women's studies program there, Hilda. I read your latest article in *The Feminist Mystique* and clearly, ITP could use you. I've heard they don't have any women's studies."

What a grand opportunity and Erika's money could make it happen! Hilda was no longer getting new patients; her income had plummeted since the death of John Starr who had steered neurotic women her way when he didn't want to treat them.

Erika was enthusiastic about a trip. "I'm much stronger now thanks to you, Hilda, and optimistic, too, because I see myself making real changes."

"Such as what?"

"Helping people cope with loss."

"Like the less fortunate? How much are you thinking of giving?"

"Oh, no, I'm not talking about money! It's about discovering ways I can personally help people."

"You think you can help people?" Hilda laughed scornfully. "I'd say that's a serious conversation we need to have, my dear. But first, let's get you out of,this town for a while. Too many unhappy memories keep resurfacing here."

"What about Uncle Robert's wedding? We've already accepted."

"Tell your uncle you're not yet ready for a celebration. Send flowers. Besides, seeing your uncle in a wheelchair is not what you need right now."

So two weeks before Robert's marriage, Hilda Payne and Erika flew off to London first class on British Air and settled in at Claridge's for a couple of weeks. Their itinerary included the new plays, art exhibitions, and shopping for Wedgwood china. Hilda Payne had never owned a proper set of dinnerware for her gatherings of Boston notables and Erika wanted to buy it for her as a way of expressing her appreciation for all she had done. When Hilda discovered a shop with Limoges dinnerware, she beamed.

"Much better than Wedgwood dinnerware and I want three sets of Limoges!" she declared triumphantly.

Erika whispered in her ear. "I can buy them cheaper when we're in Paris, Hilda."

"No, Erika," she said firmly, "resisting immediate gratification is not going to work for me right now. I'm ordering the Limoges so it will be waiting for me when I get back to Boston."

Erika was stunned. What had come over Hilda Payne? She had suddenly grown greedy. Hadn't she always mocked the rampant materialism of her nouveau riche patients?

There had been a similar pattern with John. When she met him, he was living simply. After their marriage, she could never satisfy his cravings and along with his growing avarice there was a steady decline in his empathy towards her. Early in their relationship he had tried to alleviate her suffering; later on, he showed little interest in her unhappiness. Did her money make those closest to her greedy? Was she responsible in some way?

A side trip had been set up to visit ITP (the Institute for Transcendent Psychology) where Hilda's British colleague had arranged for Hilda and Erika to meet with its director, Dr. Norman Brown, personally trained in psychoanalysis, transcendental meditation, and Reiki by the globally renowned guru of healing, Dr. Ronald Wasserstein. Not only was Dr. Brown an expert in the latest psychotherapeutic techniques, but he was also considered particularly adept at raising much-needed funds for ITP. Poor John, Erika thought sadly, always struggling to raise money for his institute. Now, she wished she'd helped him more.

"It's puzzling, but there's no women's studies program at ITP," Hilda said. "Norman Brown must be living in the last century! Women's issues, that's where it's at now. So, Erika, you should offer a sizable contribution to ITP."

"Why?"

"Because Dr. Brown will be more inclined to choose me to head up a women's studies program here."

"That's like buying him off!"

"Erika, my dear," said Hilda forcefully. "That's not 'buying him off'; it's paving the way. " She looked squarely at Erika. "I've done a lot for you, haven't I?"

"And I deeply appreciate it," Erika said with emotion.

"So now it's time to do something for me. With your beauty and money, he'll come around right away."

"But what about your patients back in Boston, Hilda? They need you, don't they?"

"I've got excellent colleagues seeing them."

"But they'll be upset if you stay over here in England, won't they?"

"Perhaps a little, and that makes me sad. But if I get the directorship for women's studies, we won't be here in England for more than a year or two and of course you and I will continue the therapy. We'll keep working on those dependency issues of yours."

"Right."

"London is such a sophisticated city! There's so much going on, so much to see."

"It's a great city!" said Erika with enthusiasm.

"And I've got plans," Hilda said with a bright smile.

"Plans? What sort of plans?"

"Oh, like our living in a gorgeous house in Holland Park. It's the most elegant part of London."

At this point, Erika wasn't sure she wanted to live in an elegant neighborhood. Hanging out with the rich had never appeal-ed to her.

"And if you can swing this thing for me, we'll be all set. But first you have to sell it to Dr. Brown," Hilda was saying.

"Sell what?"

"You aren't listening, are you, my dear? I'm talking about selling my candidacy and I hope you will make an offer to ITP so Dr. Brown chooses me for the women's studies program."

"I don't know if I can get him to agree to your starting the program."

"Just turn on the charm and with your beauty and charm. It'll all work out."

"It's not the kind of thing I like to do," said Erika.

"I know, but you'll be helping me," said Hilda Payne, "and I will deeply appreciate it."

Later, when Erika walked into his office with Hilda, Dr. Brown was momentarily taken off guard. No one had warned him to expect such a beautiful woman. He'd been told only that she was the heiress to a very large fortune. Leaping up from his desk, he seized her hand.

"Delighted to meet you, Mrs. Starr," he said in a smartly clipped British voice. Turning to Hilda, he summarily greeted her and then suggested she tour ITP with one of his colleagues so he and Erika could be alone. Hilda readily agreed, figuring Erika could succeed with her plan better without her.

Of medium height and in his late forties, Dr. Brown cut an imposing figure. Trim and casually attired in a black cashmere sweater, open-necked striped shirt, and dark flannel trousers, his head was closely shaven and his carefully trimmed moustache and goatee were flecked with grey. His face was square and even-featured and his light grey eyes crinkled up at the corners when he smiled. Recently divorced from his wife of twenty years, he was feeling especially happy because he no longer was having to deal with a narcissistic woman and could focus on his intellectual needs and spiritual quest. He blamed the breakup of the marriage on her stubborn refusal to recognize the value of his work, her lack of intellectual curiosity and her need for constant amusement. Their mutual boredom led to extramarital affairs and when Norman asked for a divorce, his wife agreed at once, eager to marry her latest lover, an aging American playboy.

His colleagues expressed genuine regret at this turn of events because Mrs. Brown was lively and pretty; but, as seasoned psychotherapists, they were aware that one could never judge the quality of a relationship from the outside. So often a couple that appeared content was actually miserable.

When Erika questioned him about the institute, Norman Brown gave her a short, impassioned speech.

"We're moving in a different direction here at ITP, into an exciting, new world. It's all about the ART of healing. Naturally, we offer the standard courses in psychoanalytic technique, all the clinical programs on psychotherapy practice, but we're NEW WAVE! We're into spiritual health and healing that goes beyond the old psychoanalytic techniques. A member of the royal family was recently successfully treated here for clinical depression through Reiki healing and it took only a week. Just imagine that! In the old days, he would have been lying on the couch for years."

"Yes," sighed Erika. "Conventional therapy takes a long time."

"Quite so," said Dr. Brown, rising to his feet. "Now, Mrs. Starr, would you like me to take you on a tour of the institute?"

"Thank you, yes," she murmured, excited and pleased when he offered her his arm.

Dr. Brown introduced her to both the staff and they met with students. He noted that this was the training ground for the most talented future therapists from the U.K. and also from other parts of the world. "Hello there, Betty!" Dr. Brown called out to a perky young woman in a white jacket and low heels. "Mrs. Starr, meet Dr. Netter. She's our expert in life coaching, meditation and breathing techniques. She lives an exemplary life, an example to us all. Imagine: she gets up at sunrise and retires at sundown! She also follows a strict vegan diet." His eyes sparkled with admiration.

"I have to conserve my psychic energy to be able to heal on a daily basis," Dr. Netter declared.

"*Rather!* You've got more psychic energy than the rest of us put together!" Dr. Brown gave a burst of loud laughter.

"You're a psychologist?" asked Erika, thinking how attractive and intelligent she seemed.

"Yes, but the therapy I practice includes nutrition, vitamins, herbs, supplements, yoga, Tai Chi, Reiki energy healing and love. When my patients are sick, my colleagues and I wrap them in purple blankets of love."

"Let's not forget the guided imagery and our policy of allowing patients to choose the natural healing system that works best for them because we know that each human being is unique." added Dr. Brown.

"Yes, that is so," said Dr. Netter quietly. "And now I must go. My patients are waiting for me."

"Of course," Erika said, taking her small hand in her own and feeling the warmth of her psychic power.

"We are very supportive here of our staff," said Dr. Brown. "Wonderful, idealistic and caring young people. We're lucky."

"It's very impressive," said Erika, as they continued strolling through the institute. "I was just thinking about what you said, that all of us are unique. My husband and I always felt we were different from everyone else but I guess that means we were different from each other as well."

"Each person is different, like every blade of grass," pronounced Dr. Brown in his deep, sonorous voice that so perfectly conveyed experience and knowledge.

After the tour, Dr. Brown invited Erika back to his office where she found herself describing her breakdown after John Starr's untimely death. His loss had cast a dark cloud over her life and when she recounted her years of therapy with her husband, Dr.

Brown asked if John had ever discussed the transference issue with her.

"Maybe in passing, but he never analyzed it. I'm sure my husband wasn't going to let a dubious theory of Freud's get in the way of our happiness."

"Hardly a 'dubious theory,' Mrs. Starr. Transference is very much a reality and taken seriously by all of us in the therapy field. Did your present therapist, Hilda Payne, address the issue with you?"

"No, not at all."

Dr. Brown slowly shook his head. "It does seem, in recent years, that the transference issue has taken a back seat in the training of psychotherapists. A great pity, I believe, because the patient becomes excessively dependant on the therapist and I have to tell you, Mrs. Starr, that you have been ill served by both your husband and Mrs. Payne. I am particularly puzzled that Dr. Starr, a renowned psychotherapist from what you've told me, avoided the transference issue."

"We were deeply in love."

"It's somewhat unlikely this so-called passion was a sustainable love, my dear Mrs. Starr. You were merely transferring your closest emotional ties of childhood onto your analyst. That's what we mean by transference. It's a normal development in therapy that everyone goes through and should always be analyzed."

Shaken by what she had just heard, Erika asked herself if she might have misread her own heart. No, it was impossible. She and John had been swept up in a grand passion and nothing could have stopped them, not even analyzing the transference. Her love for him was so deep it wasn't an illusion or stage of therapy. No, the two of them were different, unlike ordinary people. Stages in the therapy and rules of behavior did not apply to them, though at this moment, a seed of doubt crept into her mind.

Surely John would have analyzed the transference if he had thought it important and his teacher and training analyst, Di Brioni, most likely brushed it aside as well. When John began to focus on her excessive dependency, he never connected it to the transference. Instead he talked about trees in a wood, together but separate, urging her to be like one of those trees. But, no matter how hard she tried, she could not separate herself from him.

"As your therapist, your husband was doing you no favors by not analyzing the transference," Dr. Brown said dryly. "You were his patient, after all. If you had understood what was going on, most likely you would not have married him."

"No, that's not true! I would have married him!" she said defiantly,

"I won't argue with you on that point, Mrs. Starr, but I want to call your attention to the fact that romance between patient and therapist is considered unethical by the psychiatric community."

"I'm aware of that. We fell deeply in love. It's as simple as that. We were meant to be together; he was my sun and I was his moon."

"That's how he rationalized it for you, I suppose," said Dr. Brown with a sympathetic smile, "so we'll speak no more about it."

After their talk, they discussed the Institute for Transcendent Psychology and its philosophy of treating patients in a holistic way. "John would have been very impressed with your humanistic and holistic approach to psychology," Erika said. "Surely you have heard of my husband, John Starr. He was very well known in America."

"Known for what?"

"His work on creativity."

"Sorry, no, he's not known here in England."

"Well, perhaps he was only famous in the States. Anyway, he believed that the field of psychology was treating people more and more like machines by focusing solely on the brain to understand human emotions and motivation."

"Entirely true. It's an approach that undermines the search for creativity and meaning," Dr. Brown intoned. "Psychological understanding comes in a holistic way. Here at ITP, we encourage our students not only to learn techniques from ancient spiritual and medical practices but to go back to reading the Great Books as well. All the brain scans and simplistic experiments do little to expand the understanding we gain from writers like Shakespeare, Dante, Cervantes and Tolstoy. And I would add, Freud, as well."

"Would you? He's not out of date?"

"Many of his theories have stood the test of time," Dr. Brown said.

"Would it be possible for me to sit in on some courses here?" Her request surprised even herself.

He studied her carefully. "Why would you want to do that?"

"I've always been interested in psychology. As a girl, I considered a career in the field and now I'm thinking that maybe it's not too late to take it up in a serious way."

"It's never too late." Her luminous beauty dazzled him, her bright spirit touched his heart.

"I'd like to study the art of healing, become a holistic psychologist so I can help women who have suffered. Is it hubris on my part to believe it's possible?"

"Not at all."

"I've been a patient for too long, I want to reverse the role."

"Splendid. And what is your academic background?"

After she told him, he nodded and said, "Naturally, there's some course work to do first."

"I would make up whatever basic studies I need right here in London. Is there a chance the institute would accept my application afterwards for training in psychotherapy?"

"I'll speak to the Dean," said Dr. Brown, his spirits soaring. "But I think there is a very good chance, Mrs. Starr."

He couldn't imagine turning her down; he was besotted with her. Her desire to learn, to develop herself, to help others, was extraordinary in such a rich and beautiful woman. She might have so easily been tempted to fritter away her days like so many women with money. He was confident of his quick evaluation of her excellent potential and he would support her in every way he could.

The journey would not be easy, he told her, but he would give her all the help she needed. ITP was unique in the richness and diversity of its offerings for the psychology profession.

When their meeting was finally over, he tucked her hand under his arm and personally escorted her to the limo where Hilda Payne eagerly awaited.

FIVE

During the time Erika was with Dr. Brown, Hilda had been given her own tour of ITP and though she regretted not hearing what went on in their meeting, she wasn't about to complain. After all, Erika was proposing her for the feminist studies directorship. There was always the possibility, of course, that Dr. Brown might not readily consider her for the directorship since she was unknown in England and had only published in the magazine, *The Feminine Mystique*, not in academic journals. She put that thought aside. She had instructed Erika exactly how to respond if Dr. Brown showed any hesitation in taking her on as head of feminist studies: no contributions to ITP. Not a single penny. They would get nothing from Erika unless she was hired.

Recalling their first meeting earlier in the day and how Dr. Brown appeared overwhelmed by Erika's dazzling beauty, there seemed no way she could fail in her mission. She assumed he was already informed of her great wealth so he wouldn't want to turn down her offer of a donation.

As the limo pulled slowly away from ITP, a smiling Hilda settled back against the leather cushions of the limo and closed her eyes while Erika marveled at the beauty of the rolling English countryside during their long drive back to the hotel.

For Hilda, the prospect of being on the staff at ITP, rubbing shoulders with its renowned scholars and therapists filled her with happiness. The institute offered a wider range of programs than she had anticipated; clearly Dr. Brown was a new wave adherent, but she liked the emphasis on life coaching and meditation. Reiki healing was not anything she knew much about but she could learn. There were no programs on women's issues but that was an opportunity for her. Once she was hired, she'd fill that gap.

Living in London was going to be more exciting than she could ever imagine: the theatre several times a week, dinners in elegant restaurants with interesting new friends, a gorgeous house in Holland Park and no more worries about paying bills.

With Erika's encouragement, Hilda got out every morning to enjoy London's rich historical and cultural heritage. "I won't be going with you because I've seen it all before, several times, actually," Erika explained. "When I was a student in France I'd visit friends here and we'd take a tour of all the palaces and museums."

"So what are you going to do when I'm touring?"

"Well, Dr. Brown has invited me to a number of presentations at ITP this week."

"Really? Do you plan to attend? It might be interesting for you. Have you raised the issue of my appointment yet?"

"No, Hilda, not yet. I'm waiting for the right moment to bring it up. I have to get to know him better."

Hilda placed her arm around her shoulder. "I've been pushing you too hard, haven't I?"

"A little."

"I understand. There's no hurry, anyway, Erika. " Hilda searched her face. "Should I worry about you?"

"No," Erika said cheerfully, though she wasn't so sure. The night before, she had awakened from a disturbing dream that she couldn't forget.

She was a child strolling through the family garden with her mother when suddenly she turned into Alice in Wonderland and her mother became the Red Queen. Hurling insults at her and chasing after her, the Red Queen stopped beneath a tree hung with paper hearts. Alice watched from behind a flowerpot as the Red Queen tore off the hearts and tossed them up in the air where they hung in the sky like broken birds.

Alice was able to rescue the paper hearts because in seconds she had grown ten feet tall while the Red Queen had shrunk to the size of a teaspoon. Alice recoiled in horror when she peered down at the Red Queen and recognized the face of Hilda Payne.

Once Hilda was off on a tour, Erika ordered the limo to take her over to the Institute for Transcendent Psychology where she went to presentations and later met with Dr. Brown to discuss her future.

"You are uniquely suited for a career in the helping profession of psychology, Erika," he announced one day. "Everything points to it. You are intuitive, intellectually disciplined, and empathetic."

"You've made me so happy and I won't disappoint you," she said. "I'll do everything I can to live up to your expectations."

"Once you have completed your academic requirements, I have no doubt that you will succeed here magnificently and as I told you, I will be fully supportive."

Erika was filled with hope; her life had finally taken on meaning. There was only one task that remained: promoting Hilda Payne for the directorship of a women's studies program at ITP.

"There's something I need to discuss with you, Dr. Brown," she said.

"And what might that be?"

"My therapist, Hilda Payne, would like you to consider her for the directorship of a women's studies program here. She's an expert in that area and noticed your offerings don't include it. I would be willing to endow the program."

Dr. Brown fidgeted impatiently in his chair. "My dear Erika, this is not a matter of money. Our programs are based on what we have learned is most valuable for our patients. Women's studies are *over*. They're so *yesterday*! Back fifteen years ago, it was cutting edge, but now? No, my dear, we've moved on to the spiritual and emotional health of *people* and that includes *men* as well as *women*." He leaned forward, a puzzled expression on his face. "Your therapist, Mrs. Payne, did I not meet her the first day you were here?" His frown suggested he was struggling to remember her.

"Yes, she was with me."

Clearing his throat, he said, "Has she ever written anything important in the field of women's studies?"

"I'm not quite sure," Erika stammered. "I do know she writes occasional articles for a magazine called *The Feminist Mystique.*"

"Never heard of it. In any case, she lacks a reputation over here. I am *so* sorry. Also, from what you've told me, she never analyzed the transference with you, so she must have kept you quite dependent on her."

"Yes, and I couldn't understand why I felt I needed her so much until you explained the transference theory. Now I know."

"Quite so."

"I must try to be on my own."

"I fully agree."

"You have opened my eyes, Dr. Brown," Erika said slowly. "I see that I must try to make a break with Hilda Payne if I am to lead a creative life."

"That is true." Dr. Brown gave her a penetrating look. "Mrs. Starr, let me change the subject for a minute. I have a rather delicate matter to discuss with you."

"Yes?" Was that her heart beating like a wild thing?

"I believe we have a strong mutual attraction, would you not agree?"

"Yes." Oh, how right he was!

"As soon as I met you," said Norman Brown, "I knew you were ready to travel the path I have been working to forge. I will be a caring guide and exacting mentor, and you, in turn, will inspire me with your insights and desire to learn."

"I've been searching a long time for an honest man whose most important values are encouraging others, nurturing growth, loving and being loved. I'm a little afraid, though. Could this feeling I'm experiencing when I'm with you- could it be the transference?" Erika asked breathlessly.

"That is something we can carefully analyze," responded Norman Brown. "But Freud did say there is a bit of transference in all loving relationships."

SIX

Up until their last evening in London together, Erika had avoided telling Hilda there was no interest at the Institute for Transcendent Psychology for her to start up a women's studies program.

Over a late dinner, Erika gave Hilda the bad news.

"I can't believe this!" cried Hilda in disbelief. "Did you tell Dr. Brown you'd make a large contribution to ITP if I were given the women's studies directorship?"

"I did, but he made it clear he doesn't want women's studies. He told me it's 'so yesterday'."

"Well, you've failed me, plain and simple, dear girl. He would have agreed to it if you'd played your hand right. Believe me, I've met his type before. I should have known you needed me with you."

"Well, things are about to change," Erika said.

"Change? How?"

"I won't be needing you anymore, Hilda," Erika said.

Hilda stared at her in astonishment.

"You saved me and brought me back to health and I'll always be deeply grateful, Hilda. You gave me the strength to speak to you as I am doing now. It's time for me to be on my own, to manage my life. I don't want to be a patient anymore."

"What do you mean?"

"By never analyzing the transference issue, Hilda, you kept me a patient, dependent and unable to make my own decisions."

"Am I hearing Dr. Brown here?" Hilda asked.

"Probably; we've had some very edifying conversations."

"You're talking about an old theory of Freud's that's been discounted, Erika. He's a dead white male who hated women and nobody bothers with his misogynist nattering anymore."

"As I understand it, Hilda, analyzing the transference is central to a good analysis."

"That's not necessarily true."

"No?"

"Erika, we've been working on your dependence issues for months! And what about John? He never got around to the so-called 'transference', did he? I asked you early on if he'd worked on the transference and it was pretty obvious from your response that he never even got close."

"He was in love with me. If he'd analyzed the transference I might have walked out of his life and he would have lost me forever. He didn't want to take that chance."

Hilda screwed up her face in disgust. "Honey, he saw a gold mine and a beautiful woman all rolled into one when he first laid eyes on you and that's the unvarnished truth."

"You don't want to believe he was in love with me, do you, Hilda?"

"That's not what we're talking about here. You want to listen to Dr. Brown or me? I'm telling you, the so-called transference doesn't exist! It's fantasyland! And you believe *him* just because he's so classy and good looking?"

"But the transference issue explains why I've struggled so hard with my dependency and always failed!"

Hilda flushed. "Those are Dr. Brown's words coming straight out of your mouth, my dear, and it makes me very sad. You don't love me, anymore, Erika. If you cared about me, you'd have convinced Dr. Brown to give me a directorship for women's studies. Did you even ask him? I'll bet you just sat there looking cute and never said a word!"

"I told you. I asked him and he said no. And there's one other thing I have to tell you."

"And what's that?"

"I'm staying here."

"You're doing *what?*"

"Staying in London. I won't be coming with you to Paris."

"Why not?"

"I'll be starting the courses I need to qualify for a doctorate in psychology. I'm going to be a therapist and I've been accepted at ITP for my training.

"*You? You* want to be a therapist?" Her huge breasts jiggling up and down, Hilda Payne laughed so hard tears streamed down her face.

"You've got to be kidding," she said finally, drying her eyes with the back of her hand. "What is this, Erika, some kind of joke?"

"No, I'm completely serious. When I was young, I wanted to be a psychologist. We talked about it in my therapy but you don't remember. It will be in helping others that I'll find my creativity gene because all those painting lessons John insisted I take never amounted to anything. That's not where my talent lies."

"But the rigorous study you'll have to do; it may be too much for you."

"Why do you say that? I'm strong again and I've always been a good student. You're laughing, Hilda. What's so funny?"

"It's just that you *can't* be a therapist!" Hilda cried. "You're the *patient, not* the *doctor!*"

"Norman is fully supportive."

"Of course, and all this has happened behind my back," mumbled Hilda Payne.

"I knew you wouldn't approve so I didn't tell you." Erika fought to maintain her calm. "I'll complete all my studies and later get my degree at ITP; the graduate training is the very best in the world. Once I'm a professional, I'll treat women who've been abused psychologically like myself."

"My child, you have delusions of grandeur!"

"Hilda. I get your point. So let's imagine ourselves as two trees next to each other in a wood. We shouldn't take up the other's space because then we wouldn't be able to get enough nourishment from the soil or warmth from the sun. It's simple. I need my space and you're blocking my light, Hilda. My new life is here in London."

"You're definitely going to skip Paris?"

"I have many wonderful memories of it and now it's your turn. You've got a first-class ticket to Paris tomorrow morning. Then you'll go to Rome the week after that, and back to America. All expenses are paid-transportation, hotels, theater tickets, tours-I've taken care of everything. You must respect my decision. Please try to understand."

Back at the hotel, Hilda settled down on the living room sofa in their suite with a scotch and soda to soothe her nerves, and her loud mutterings were fully audible to Erika who was feigning sleep in the next room.

"What a con artist, that Norman Brown! He's gotten hold of my poor little Erika who never could resist a handsome man. He wants her money and she has no idea. She's an innocent in the clutches of a con artist! He'll do anything to get her money, even to taking her on as a graduate student. I can't believe this is happening!

Oh, what am I to do? She doesn't love me anymore and I feel so bad!"

A long silence followed this tirade interrupted by muffled sobs. Then Hilda said in a loud voice, "In the morning, she'll see how wrong she was. Yes, everything will turn out all right because she can't get along without me!"

On awakening early the next morning, Erika could hear the sound of Hilda snoring in the adjoining room. For so long now she had listened to Hilda praising womanly power, and wondered how she could mock her aspirations to become a therapist. Why did she resent her newfound happiness with Norman? What would her father have said if he were still alive? Like Hilda Payne, he was a cynic, and since money was his obsession, he'd probably tell her that both Hilda and Norman were after her money and that Norman couldn't be trusted either. If the man hurt her someday, it would be her own fault.

Hilda did not wake up until late the next morning. Her three glasses of red wine at dinner and a scotch and soda afterwards induced a heavy sleep and when she opened her eyes, there was a note on the table from Erika.

> *Hilda, Dear,*
>
> *In a way I'm sorry not to be going with you to Paris, but as I told you last night, my life has taken on a whole new direction. With Norman's help, I am sloughing off the old me and reinventing myself like John hoped I could. Learning about transference has made so many things clear to me, especially the dependence aspect. I've forgiven you for not analyzing it and as I told you before, you should take full*

credit for helping me recover from the trauma of John's death. It's too bad you won't see how Norman is a wise, caring man. He brings me great joy.

You may laugh at my hopes of becoming a therapist, but I think I'll turn out pretty well. I will have actually lived what I expect to hear from many of the women I want to help and I'll make sure to analyze the transference.

I'll let you know where I'll be living in London once I get things sorted out. You are always welcome.

Love, Erika

THE END

ACKNOWLEDGMENTS

I'm grateful to Leona Schecter, who gave me advice on early drafts of this novel, and to Nora Harriet Hathaway, who offered helpful suggestions. I'd also like to thank Maria Stroffolino for her help in preparing this manuscript.

I very much appreciate all that Silver Birch Press has done to publish *The Therapist*.

Most of all, I have benefited from the loving guidance of my husband, Michael Maccoby. He has shared his experience as a psychoanalyst, a member of the Harvard faculty, and a successful author.